THE SPIRIT OF THE AUTUMN WIND

DORAE SHAE

 FriesenPress

Suite 300 - 990 Fort St
Victoria, BC, V8V 3K2
Canada

www.friesenpress.com

Copyright © 2019 by Dorae Shae
First Edition — 2019

All rights reserved.

No part of this publication may be reproduced in any form, or by any means, electronic or mechanical, including photocopying, recording, or any information browsing, storage, or retrieval system, without permission in writing from FriesenPress.

ISBN
978-1-5255-3314-3 (Hardcover)
978-1-5255-3315-0 (Paperback)
978-1-5255-3316-7 (eBook)

1. FICTION

Distributed to the trade by The Ingram Book Company

CHAPTER ONE

Regan Quinn watched as the small fishing boat disappeared into the black swells of the Mediterranean Sea. Standing in the shadows, he let the darkness surround and shield him from the sickening guilt that had settled into the pit of his stomach. He took a deep breath. There was comfort in knowing his precious son and trusted friend were safe on board the *Autumn Wind*. He stood quiet, deaf to the activity around him, looking out into the night and reliving his meeting with Niko and the last few hours.

"My old friend." Regan wrapped Niko's solid frame in his long arms. Taller than Niko, he was always the one to embrace first.

Niko relaxed. Regan had always been his keeper, had always defended him from the bullies. While they saw only his vulnerability and his handicap, Regan saw a friend. Niko grasped his friend's shoulder. "Aren't you a splendid sight in that captain's uniform? You look like an admiral or some such thing."

Regan laughed. It was good to see his boyhood friend's face again. He and Niko had grown up together in Saviours of the Sea, a Greek orphanage, and became like brothers. They left together at sixteen and found jobs on the ships. Regan was born to sail. He was strong and smart, and he rose quickly to the position of captain. Niko's handicap stood in his way, as it always had. His right foot was twisted and turned slightly outward, causing him to walk with a rhythmic dragging gate. He could not participate in physical activities, even as a child, so was usually assigned to assist in the kitchen at the orphanage. He had a culinary gift, became an excellent cook, and found his way to a career in the galleys of the ships. Their sea careers kept the two old friends apart, and rare was the occasion that the two could meet for a drink. But they had finally come together in Tangiers, Regan on board the *Seaward Angel* and Niko on the *Autumn Wind*.

"How's that leg?" There was concern in Regan's voice; his friend looked tired.

"Eh, same old thing. Stiff on the chilly days at sea, but nothing a good shot of rum won't help."

They laughed. "Well, I have some good news," Regan said excitedly.

He put his arm around his friend's shoulders and pulled the door to the bar open.

The fatigued interior of the Sea Gull Bar smelled of sweat, liquor, and cigar smoke. The men took a table at the back, allowing for a full view of the other patrons gathered in the dimly lit establishment. Regan removed his long captain's overcoat, exposing the full elegance of his dark uniform. Seating himself, he surveyed the crowd, concluding they were mostly dock workers and crewmen off the ships; there were three in port, so the bar was crowded. He felt out of place. The other uniformed sailors drank at the lounge in the International Hotel, but Niko had decided on the Sea Gull. Regan knew he chose it because it was close to the dock and Niko felt more at home among the crewmen. Any uneasiness Regan felt was insignificant compared to the pleasure of seeing his old friend again, and he smiled as Niko slid in quickly across from him with his back to the crowd. From the time he was a child, Niko had borne the brunt of ridicule and bullying; he was self-conscious about his handicap, and didn't remove his coat until he was seated.

A slender young woman arrived at the table. She was no longer in her twenties, but still attractive, with a bit of brightly coloured lipstick accenting her tawny skin and dark eyes. She shared her rehearsed smile with them as she lay the menus on the table, then quickly rushed off. Both Niko and Regan were thirty-six and single, and were not oblivious to the opposite sex. Moroccan women were beautiful, but only those discarded from society because they were barren or adulterous would be found working in a bar like the Sea Gull.

Regan had married at twenty to Cala Christos. He was running a cargo ship out of Greece and she was working at the embassy as an interpreter when they met. When Cala and Regan's son was born, Cala wanted him to carry on the family's Spanish surname, which she used, not the Moroccan family name that her parents were known by, and so he was named Christos Quinn. Cala died in an automobile accident when Christos was two. After a devastating year with Regan trying to work and care for a small child, Cala's parents, Shima and Abasi Bakari, stepped in to take care of their only grandchild. Christos had lived with them since.

"Gentlemen, what can I bring you two handsome sailors?" The young woman waiting the tables had returned, and took a moment to assess her customers while setting down a complimentary snack plate of stuffed msemen.

"Rum, my friend?" Niko asked in an assuming tone.

Regan nodded. It was what they always drank.

"Rum it is. Thank you, miss."

She smiled at Niko as she walked away. Although he knew nothing about her, he knew she was considered damaged goods, just as he was, and for her, like him, even the smallest gesture of kindness had meaning.

"I think she likes you," Regan said.

"Maybe you?"

They laughed. Neither felt a sailor's life should include a woman, but that didn't stop them from giving the idea consideration.

Niko did not see marriage as a possibility. He accepted his life alone as a reality, the same way he accepted his twisted foot. The closest he had come to sharing Regan's happiness as a husband

and father was the day he stood in front of the priest and held tiny Christos in his arms to accept his role as the boy's godfather. That day Regan had given him a gold pocket watch. On the back was engraved the phrase: To the Friendship of Men. It was a gift Niko cherished, and it was always on his person; in his pocket and anchored securely to his belt.

Niko had been left on the steps of the orphanage as a newborn on Christmas Eve. The nuns named him Nikolas Mararious, which translated to "blessed"—obviously, a sentiment not shared by his parents, as they did not feel blessed enough to want or to keep a handicapped child. Regan was given up to the same orphanage by a teenage mother who had been abandoned by a wayward sailor. He used the name on his birth certificate but had no idea if the name belonged to his mother or the sailor or if it was a creation of the orphanage nuns.

Growing up together in the orphanage had bonded the two men together in a friendship without compromise.

"So, what is this good news?" Niko asked his friend across the table.

There was eagerness in Regan's voice. "Know how we always said we wanted to own a marina on the sea, with a fine restaurant?"

Niko nodded and listened attentively.

"I bought one!" Regan blurted out, hardly able to contain himself. "In Ireland, on the south shore of Sona Bay."

Niko nodded. He knew Sona Bay. It was a deep harbour and a busy shipping transportation centre, but when the *Autumn Wind* unloaded cargo in Ireland, the captain would not use the harbour. He would anchor the ship in international waters and use the shuttles for supplies, so Niko had only been on shore there for a few hours on three separate occasions.

"The marina is in a place called Suaimhneas Cove, named for peace, tranquility, and comfort." Regan smiled at the idea of all three being a part of their future. "It's only two miles from Sona

Bay harbour, where Seaward has set up their head office for their new Mediterranean division. I was looking around for a place to live when I found this property. I got a bit of a bargain, as it was being sold by the bank to settle proceedings, and they were anxious to get rid of it." Regan was pleased with himself, and continued, "The property is the old Dolan shipyard. It was partly converted to a marina resort before it went into foreclosure. Suaimhneas Cove is the old townsite and the place is crawling with tourists. Sailboats and yachts come in to the marina and there is a waiting list for the slips." Niko was listening carefully. This had always been just a dream, so he remained silent, trying to envision what his friend was saying as reality.

"The restaurant, Niko…" Regan grasped a proud mental vision before he continued. "It's closed now, but it overlooks the sea and the marina and has big windows in every direction. There's seating for seventy-five and there's an Irish pub too, called Irish Luck."

Regan chuckled, having given some thought to the ambiguous meaning of the name, and Niko laughed impulsively. He was caught up in the dream, and Regan's mention of the Restaurant had him clinging to his friend's every word as he continued to pour out the details.

"Most of the people that work at the harbour live in Suaimhneas and use the boardwalk in front of the pub to come and go from work. They never pass by without stopping for a pint of ale. The place is busy. The old shipyard building and drydock are still there and are part of the property, so there is lots of room to expand the marina or lease or sell some of the property we don't need. There's a large house with two suites and some extra rooms, and a smaller home for the caretaker. A member of the Dolan family and an old sailor, Mike McGaffy, are looking after the property until we are able to take possession." Regan was beaming with pride as he pulled some photos from his pocket.

"We?" Niko hesitated. His friend did not know that he had been unemployed and had depleted most of his savings. He did not have enough money to buy into this business, but he did not want to tell Regan why.

"Yes, we. I put the deed in both our names," Regan said casually.

Niko was concerned. "Regan, I haven't much money saved. I have not been able to stay on the big ships where the pay is better. I can't keep up the pace of a big galley where there's no room for a guy with a gimpy leg." His eyes drifted away from his friend, hiding his shame as he finished his thought. "The small ships like the *Autumn Wind*, they don't pay much."

His apologetic tone moved Regan, who reached across the table and laid his hand on his friend's arm. "Niko, you are Christos's godfather. We are like brothers, and now we are business partners. I have no doubt that you will make a success of the restaurant and together we will make a success of this business; enough of ships' galleys and working for someone else. We own a marina and a restaurant!"

The pride that drove his friend's eagerness brought a smile to Niko's face just as the young woman arrived with their rum. The men clinked their glasses to the idea and downed the cool drinks.

Regan reached inside his uniform jacket and secured an envelope. "This is a copy of the deed. Here's the key to the safety deposit box at the Bank of Ireland on Main Street in Sona Bay. The original is in there with other ownership documents." Regan pushed it across the table with the photographs.

Nikos face kept no secrets; he was impressed. He stared down at the photos of a sprawling development along the waterfront, with an elegantly designed restaurant. "What a fine property."

There was a pub located along a boardwalk that skirted the front of the establishment, and the adjoining businesses were all decorated with rustic streetlights and nautical handrails. He looked up, his eyes damp with tears that he fought to hold back. They touched glasses, and what was said between them in silence was understood between the two men.

As the friends shuffled the glossy photos between them and talked more about plans for the property, they could feel the tangible reality of the dream they had harboured since boyhood. Niko suffered with his handicapped leg, Christos was almost done school, and his grandparents were growing older. Regan saw this venture as a fantastic opportunity to give all the people that mattered to him a better life in Ireland. As they discussed plans for their future, Regan was pleased to see how excited Niko was.

Niko looked at his old friend. "The *Autumn Wind* is heading up the Atlantic coast back to Ireland, and she will dock in a month, in late summer. It will be my last voyage." He looked down at the photos and took a swallow from his rum glass.

Niko hesitated, carefully selecting his words before adding, "The ship, she is not well run now. She's a fine vessel, but she's now privately owned by Liam O'Hare, and he does not take care of her. She's a tramp ship that operates without proper permits. It's time for a change for me, and I look forward to the restaurant and marina." Niko put the key, deed, and photos in his shirt pocket.

Regan smiled at his friend and nodded. "Me too. Christos has almost grown up without a father. With Seaward's new head office in Sona Bay, it has plans to develop some shorter routes into the Mediterranean for the growing tourist trade. I would have more time to spend with Christos and it's time we all had a real home." He raised his glass to Niko's. "To old friends."

Niko responded, "To new beginnings."

They spoke in unison as their glasses touched and their eyes met. "To the friendship of men."

They sat a while longer, lingering over another rum and a plate of seafood and catching up on the last months of their lives. Regan's life was full of pleasant adventures and Niko listened with envy. He did not speak of fine adventures or of the activities on board the

Autumn Wind. He wanted to tell his friend about the disgusting and cruel behaviour of Captain Liam O'Hare, and the deplorable way he treated the crew, and about the people he smuggled on the ship for outrageous sums of money. To tell him how just yesterday, after a disagreement over the maintenance of the engines, O'Hare had tied his first mate, Gavin Connor, to the mooring post. Gavin would have died at the hand of O'Hare, if Niko had not freed him in the night to swim to the safety of the fisherman at the lighthouse at dawn, before the ship reached the channel near Tangiers.

Niko would be the one to die if O'Hare ever found out what he had done. He had been thinking all day of not returning to the ship, of just hiding out and never going back. He did not speak of what went on aboard the ship; no one did, because the crew was made up of desperate men who were safer on the *Autumn Wind* than anywhere else. O'Hare guaranteed the return of the crew by holding their identification cards. No man could travel or get another job without one, Niko included. So, he said nothing.

Niko was consumed with the idea of the restaurant and marina, and while he listened to his friend talk of his adventures at sea, he was mentally sorting through his options. *He could get a false ID card. There was a man in the market that could make one; he had made one for Christos. But could he get into Ireland with forged identification? If it was discovered the card was false, he would be jailed and shamed. He would not survive in jail, and he could not let Regan down like that.*

Or he could go back on board and confront O'Hare, threaten him with a kitchen knife to get his card, then dive into the sea and hope to make it ashore, just as he had instructed Gavin Connor to do. But Niko could not swim, so he would perish, and so would the men that worked on deck and in the engine room of the Autumn Wind. *O'Hare would sail without a proper galley crew and the men would die at sea. O'Hare was ruthless—it was the galley that kept the men alive, and as evil as some of them were, Niko did not want to spend the rest of his life ridden with the guilt of having caused the death of his fellow seamen.*

These past three hours with his friend had been his happiest in a long while. Niko checked his watch. "The *Autumn Wind* is not in the harbour, she is anchored out at sea. I have to catch one of the fishing vessels before eleven tonight; we sail at midnight."

Regan was very aware of the reputation of the *Autumn Wind* and other tramp ships that ran cargo without proper port authority. There were only a few of the coal-fuelled cargo ships left now. They had been replaced by bigger, faster, diesel-fuelled-engine vessels. Most of the smaller coal-fuelled cargo ships had been removed from service, or sold to private entrepreneurs like Liam O'Hare, who ran small cargo operations up and down the coast. They were poorly financed businesses that usually loaded and offloaded their cargo at sea because they lacked proper harbour permits. Rumours of poor working conditions and illegal activities on board the tramp ships circulated quietly among the sailors.

The men rose to go, and Regan hesitated to ask his friend the question he had been avoiding, as he did not want to make him uncomfortable. "Niko, are you safe on the *Autumn Wind*? You could just go to Ireland now. I could get you on the *Seaward Angel*."

Niko took a moment to respond. Taking help from his friend had become difficult as he grew into his manhood. "The galley is safe. O'Hare needs the men fed. I do not go on deck or involve myself with his business. I just feed the crew. This will be my last voyage." Niko's determined tone reassured Regan and he said no more.

The last big cargo ship Niko had worked on was the *Mediterranean Lady*. The galley was basic, and every resource provided had to be skillfully used to accommodate the large crew. The dormitory-style accommodations had offered little or no privacy, and with crew changes at all hours, it had been a difficult environment for Niko. He'd had three young cooks to teach, along with the demands of the galley, but he'd never complained. At the end of the war, he'd quietly kept his humiliation to himself when his three trainees were offered positions in the ship's galley and he was not.

Mediterranean Lines had bought up some of the small cargo ships used during the war, and needed a galley master for the *Autumn Wind*. As part of Niko's job interview, the captain had given him a tour of the ship.

Her design was unusual for a ship built during the war years. Most were large, bulky cargo haulers with minimum creature comforts. Niko loved the *Autumn Wind* the moment he boarded. She was small and classy, with a shallow hull that accommodated only the engine room, the crew's quarters, an infirmary, and the galley. The captain and the first mate had quarters on deck and at the opposite end of the ship. Two big loading cranes loomed up at each end, and one large wide stack was positioned behind the bridge. Niko was surprised to see three large engines instead of the one that was usually found in a slow cargo freighter with a single stack.

The galley was impressive. It was spacious and well equipped with stoves, ovens, refrigerators, and coolers, all designed around a large central chopping block. An elegant oak table, still beautiful despite the scars and scratches on the surface, was positioned along one wall, with six oak chairs on one side and a matching bench on the other. On the wall at the end of the galley, and in full view of the table, hung the most realistic map of the world Niko had ever seen. It was trimmed in oak and positioned below a compass set in a brass plaque engraved with "Dolan Shipyards." Niko imagined many a dream had been conceived in its realistic presence. He was later to discover that it rolled up like a blind, revealing equally realistic versions of the seas and oceans of the world.

Located just off the galley were four cabins, including one that could accommodate a couple, and there was a private bathroom and laundry for the galley staff. A small stairway led to an upper deck area that was privately enclosed from the main deck.

Niko was impressed with the galley and fascinated by the ship. The pay was less than he had been receiving, but the management showed respect, giving him equal opportunity despite his leg.

The Spirit of the Autumn Wind

He accepted the job, and it was the beginning of three enjoyable years. The ship was well run and well cared for, and the crew was happy and stable. They accepted him without judgment as a fellow seaman and respected him as the galley master. He was happy on the *Autumn Wind*.

After Mediterranean Lines lost their business to the bank, Niko placed his resumé on file with the port authority but was unable to secure new employment, and his savings dwindled. He was forced to live in the alley behind the Sea Gull Bar with the street vagrants for almost six months.

Niko had never told Regan about those desperate months with the soup kitchen as his only means of survival. He lived in filth and feared for his life, hiding with the other vagrants from the ongoing activities of the drug trade that infiltrated the Moroccan dock and festered in the alley behind the Sea Gull Bar. Like the other homeless men, he would hide in the shadows, dreading the appearance of Ivory, the son of the elusive and feared drug lord known as Nigeria. Ivory would frequent this alley near the dock to negotiate with the underworld of the shipping industry, so he could move drugs around the Mediterranean, up the coast to Ireland and on to America. Niko heard what the men said and saw the lack of interest the police showed when a man was shot or beaten to death in the alley. The ambulance would take the nameless deceased away and new desperate men would arrive.

Niko volunteered to help at the soup kitchen on Wednesdays, and as compensation, he could use the shower to clean up and shave. He would put on the clean shirt, pants, and jacket that he kept folded in his sack, clean his shoes, and walk to the port authority to see if anyone had responded to his resumé. Months passed with nothing; he would return to the alley, crawl back into his dirty street clothes, cover himself with his djellaba, and cling to the block wall, silently reciting to perfection every prayer the nuns at the orphanage had taught him. His small savings were almost depleted, and he saw only more hopeless days ahead.

The Wednesday the letter from Captain Liam O'Hare appeared in his mailbox, he was ecstatic. Liam O'Hare had bought the *Autumn Wind* at a public auction and offered him his old job as galley master back. Finally, an opportunity to get back on his feet, to get back to work; back to the sea. He arrived at the *Autumn Wind* five minutes early that Friday morning, enthusiastically looking forward to the future.

Liam O'Hare was a certified ship's captain, and presented himself as a knowledgeable, professional businessman who was eager to get his new shipping business underway. He was the captain of a cargo ship during the war and had been stationed in Greece, where he had learned the language. Niko had learned to speak Greek from the cook at the orphanage and the men could converse in both English and Greek. Two fellow sailors from Mediterranean Lines, First Mate Gavin Connor, and a deckhand, Sleeman, had already signed on.

If Niko suspected there was a cruel and dangerous man behind the cleanshaven face and captain's uniform, he chose to ignore it, but he was soon to discover that Liam O'Hare was a very different man than what he appeared.

On his first voyage under O'Hare's command, Niko ran the galley entirely by himself, and getting three meals a day out to twenty men was exhausting. The budget O'Hare set out was inadequate, and Niko used what little personal money he had left to make up the difference, so the men would not be hungry. He approached O'Hare, requesting a galley assistant and a bigger budget. O'Hare delegated Sleeman to assist with the meal service and told him additional help would come from passengers paying to travel discreetly on board the ship in the galley cabins. They would pay $5,000 each, with some of the money going to supplement the galley budget. These passengers were being provided with confidential passage and concealment by posing as galley assistants and were expected to perform light galley duties as a part of the arrangement. Niko objected to being ordered to take part in what amounted to passenger smuggling.

O'Hare's terse response was, "You signed on for three years, and you will complete the contract as agreed. That is an order!"

A sailor never disobeyed the captain's orders. Realizing his position was already compromised, Niko reluctantly agreed, but on the condition that no less than three-quarters of the passenger fees be delegated to the galley. If he had no choice but to break the law, it would be on the condition that the men be properly fed. Mediterranean Lines had run the *Autumn Wind* with a crew of twenty-five, and O'Hare had only twenty men, including Niko and one man in the laundry. The crew was being pushed to the working limit. Men that were overworked and underfed were vulnerable to sickness and accidents, and Niko would not run a galley without the resources to feed the crew properly.

O'Hare resented the defiance of Niko Mararious but was smart enough to realize that Niko was recognized by the crews that worked on the ships as one of the best cooks a galley could have. Deckhands could get work on any cargo ship, lots better than the *Autumn Wind*, but they would choose the ship with the best galley master, and Niko had that reputation. O'Hare knew the contraband he was hauling was worth a lot more than the visible cargo on the deck, so a few groceries for the obedience and silence of this galley master was a small price to pay.

But he would not be outsmarted by this cook. His chief mate, Axel Morgan, was the crewman that had initiated the lucrative illegal cargo opportunity, and the only other one on board who was aware of the contraband. He would be put in charge of finding and bringing the passengers to the ship to be supervised by the galley master. If Niko turned on him, O'Hare would deny any knowledge of the passenger smuggling, and Axel Morgan would have no choice but to defend him, leaving Niko Mararious to take the blame.

Niko was embarrassed that his desperation had led him to make a mistake that had taken away his independence and made him vulnerable to this bully who was now making him an accomplice to illegal activity. Open threats to the crew, including Niko, were not taken lightly. On the first voyage under O'Hare's command, one defiant crew member had been shot and thrown to the sea by the captain. The incident instilled the degree of fear required to guarantee the obedience and silence of the remaining crew. The silver pistol that hung at O'Hare's side served as a constant reminder. He pushed the ship hard and gave the men very little shore time.

Niko had only himself to blame for the situation he was in. He was ashamed, and Regan would never know about these degrading months of his life. If he told Regan about O'Hare, his friend would get involved to help him, just as he always had. Niko would not put Regan in danger. This would be his last voyage. Somehow, he would get his identification card back and leave the *Autumn Wind* without putting any man's life in danger, and then he would start a new life in Ireland.

CHAPTER TWO

"Cool breeze tonight," Niko commented as he stepped to the now-darkened street just ahead of Regan, and instinctively pulled the collar of his seaman's coat around his neck.

"Weather radar said there was a storm disturbance off the Atlantic. Should have passed through by the time you sail at midnight." Regan secured the centre button on his long captain's coat as he spoke.

Niko adjusted his body and turned his lame leg toward the direction of his thoughts. "Let's go this way, through the alley. It's shorter and I can get a cab back to the dock at the International."

Regan turned without hesitation, and they headed down the dark alley. The narrow backstreet was like a cobblestoned lifeline between the chaos and lights of the Tangiers street and the mystical torchlit entrance of the International Hotel, visible at the opposite end. The passageway was shadowy and reeked of stale exhaust and human sweat. A single street lamp and a flickering crock fire exposed the vagrants that huddled in the darkness against the buildings, settling in for the night and waiting for the soup kitchen at the mission in the centre of the alley to open in the morning.

Regan and Niko walked in silence, aware of the defensive glances of these hopeless street men. Niko thought of Gavin Connor. *Had he made it ashore, was he alive?* Just yesterday Niko had unleashed the man's hands from the mooring post and gave him a life preserver.

His distraught instructions to Gavin were precise, and were partly acquired from the time he spent with the vagrants in the alley, and partly from his personal knowledge. "Swim toward the lighthouse. About a half-mile from shore, there is a shelf; the water will become shallow. Look for a fishing boat. It will have one running light on the hull. There is an old fisherman who is there every morning looking for his son who fell overboard a few years ago. They say he is crazy. The ships always see him and pay him no mind. Get his attention. They say he takes ashore every sailor he finds adrift. Find your way to the mission in the alley behind the Sea Gull Bar; there is a soup kitchen there and a bin where you can get dry clothes. Go to the market bakery and ask for Abasi Bakari. There is a man in Tangiers that makes false ID cards and he will tell you how to find him. But be discreet. My friend Regan Quinn is captain of the *Seaward Angel* and the Bakaris are his family and take care of his son. I don't want to cause any of them trouble. It is against the law, but if you don't get caught with a false card you can get out of Morocco and back to England. At least you have a chance. If you remain on this ship it will mean certain death."

Just before dawn Gavin slipped overboard, and disappeared into the dark sea. Niko prayed he had not sent his friend to his death.

Niko pushed his memory of yesterday's events out of his mind and focused on his familiarity of the alley. They slowed their pace, to avoid some rubbish piled in their pathway, and moved into the darkness of the adjacent building, unexpectantly encountering two men in an obvious exchange of drugs and money. The dim streetlight exposed the African features of the man that faced them, and the obscured shadow of another man clad in dark clothes with his back to them.

Alarmed by the intruders, the African man, who stood the height of Niko, thrust his arm forward and secured Niko firmly by the neck, then pressed a gun to his temple.

"Let him go! Let him go!" Regan shouted, then pleaded, "Just let us pass! We just want to pass by!"

The man reacted wildly and pointed the weapon directly up at Regan's face.

"You see! You die!" He spit the words out furiously.

Regan's first instinct was to defend himself. He was taller than his aggressor, and impulsively grabbed at the gun and pushed it against the African man's body, lunging forward and forcing the man to the ground beneath him. Niko fell awkwardly to the street an arm's length away from the two men as his attacker lost the strangling hold he had around his neck.

The gun discharged. The man below Regan fell limp as a single gunshot echoed through the narrow alley, and a pool of blood began to seep from beneath the motionless body. In the same heartbeat, the man standing in the shadows disappeared into the darkness. Regan forced himself from the ground and away from the smell of the warm human blood that penetrated his nostrils, his trembling hand still gripping the pistol. His mind froze, his soul quivered, and there was only the thundering of his heart, surrounded by the deathly silence of the night.

Niko pushed himself to his knees, just as two vagrants appeared in the alley and one of them shouted, "That's Nigeria's son you just killed! Called Ivory, thiefin' murderer, good riddins to the bastard!"

The other vagrant yelled out a warning. "You better run, mister! Nigeria is pure evil, he'll hunt you, kill you, your family, and your friends! You're a dead man!" the vagrant declared with a tone of finality.

"It was an accident!" Regan pleaded. "An accident! He attacked my friend! He was going to shoot me!"

"Better run, mister!" The vagrant repeated his warning, ignoring Regan's desperate words.

A garbage can clattered to the street along the building beside them, and a man scurried off into the night.

"Wait! Wait! Please wait! Did you see? It was an accident! Did you see?" Regan's frantic shout echoed into the darkness, and the man did not stop.

Regan looked down at the pistol in his trembling hand. He released his grip and the gun fell to the side of the dead man lying in the street. Niko was crouched on his knees, his eyes frozen on the limp body that lay before him. Regan placed his shaking hand on his friend's shoulder, knelt beside him, and pulled the billfold from the dead man's jacket. Regan helped Niko and they stood up and read the ID card. Abdul Nakarasa, twenty-five years old, born in Nigeria.

"Regan." Niko's voice was barely audible and riddled with concern. "I have heard of this man. They call him Ivory, and he is the son of the drug lord, Nigeria, like the vagrant said. He sells drugs and they say he is a ruthless murderer. That vagrant is right—he will kill you, Christos, all of us! We need to run! Get away from here, figure out what to do. I'll take the gun and throw it into the sea when I sail."

Niko grasped the gun off the filth of the worn cobblestones beneath them, the barrel still warm to his touch as he shoved it into his coat pocket. "Let's run! Get out of the alley!" Niko tugged at Regan's arm for support and they rushed into the darkness.

The men ran as fast as Niko's leg would allow, finding security in a dark doorway two streets over.

"You okay?" Regan asked as Niko nodded and slid down against the building, exhausted. Regan sat beside him, shivering with the cold sweat of sheer panic. They were in the shadows, hidden. Regan was shaking, overcome by what had just happened; he had killed a man, taken a life.

He turned to Niko. "We need to go to the police."

Niko was emphatic. "No! Nigeria is brutal; he has friends he pays to give him information, drug-dealer friends everywhere, including the police. You will be killed for sure. You will not get a fair trial in Morocco. Everyone is afraid of him."

Niko was in control. He was skilled at adapting to problems and making quick decisions; it was what made him an outstanding galley master. Regan wondered how he knew so much about Nigeria, but listened helplessly as his friend continued.

"We need to get out of here before we go to the police. We need to find that man who knocked the garbage can over, the man by the building; he must have seen what happened."

Regan began to focus. "The other man that was standing there with his back to us...he would know what happened, too."

Niko shook his head. "He is probably afraid Nigeria will accuse him of the shooting. He ran away. He won't step up."

Regan knew Niko was right. "I have to find the man in the alley."

Niko looked at his friend, nodding acknowledgement of the plan. "First, you need to get Christos and his grandparents to safety. Those vagrants in the alley, they will tell Nigeria what they saw in exchange for money. He has connections at the ports, and he will find you and find your family. They will say you killed his son and he will kill yours."

Nikos words pierced Regan's heart like a sword. He was right.

"Regan." Niko spoke calmly to his friend. "The *Autumn Wind* sails at midnight. I could take Christos with me to Ireland, so it won't look like you are fleeing with your son, and everything will seem normal. Christos will travel with me as galley help. O'Hare takes illegal passengers on the ship. He hides them in the galley as kitchen staff. Once we sail, they won't be able to find him. He will be safe at sea and you will be safe; your ship has security. We will meet in Ireland and go to the police there. We will tell them what happened and that it was self-defence and that there was a witness; at least you'll have a chance of a fair trial. Can you get $6,000 in American money tonight? O'Hare charges $5,000 to take illegal passengers on board the ship. If you offer $6,000, he will take Christos and not ask questions. He cannot resist the money."

Regan was stunned by what Niko had just said, but nodded, incapable of reason. "Yes, I give Abasi money. He will have that much."

"Then get the money, put Christos's Moroccan ID card with the money for the captain, and put his real card in an envelope for Christos to give to me. Bring good whisky and cigars and bring your son to the dock. I will have a fishing boat waiting to take us to the ship. When we board the *Autumn Wind*, I will tell O'Hare he is the illegitimate son of a dock vendor. He will not offend the dock vendors. He buys their loyalty and needs their help and silence when he uses the ports illegally. He will not ask questions if he is generously paid. What about Abasi and Shima?"

Regan was still processing the details of the plan but responded without hesitation. "They can go to the country. Shima has a brother that lives in the mountains. They will be safe there among the farmers."

Regan stood up and helped his friend to his feet. "Here. Take my captain's coat."

He removed his coat and pulled his captain's cap from the large inside pocket. "The coat will cover your leg and you can wear the cap; uniformed sailors are seldom stopped or questioned. You should be able to catch a cab a block from the International. Give me your coat."

Niko handed his dark seaman's overcoat to his friend and showed him the toque in the inside pocket as he removed the pistol and put it in the pocket of Regan's captain's overcoat. Niko knew that, clothed in the toque and seaman's coat, Regan would look like every other crewman out drinking in the streets that night.

Regan's words were self-controlled. "I will walk to the International and phone Abasi, so he can have Christos ready. The uniformed sailors all drink there and with three ships in port tonight, it will be busy. If I'm seen there in uniform, it will seem I had been there all evening."

It was as though they were boys again, speedily devising a plan to avoid punishment for misbehaving at the orphanage. Perhaps, had it not been for the intense seriousness of the situation, they might have found it amusing. The men embraced and parted without speaking.

Heart pounding, Regan took a deep breath to compose himself, folded Niko's coat neatly over his arm, and walked calmly toward the International Hotel. The place was busy with sailors enjoying the liquor and women who frequented the establishment when the ships came in. He entered the lobby and used the phone furthest from the door, ensuring his privacy. His call to Abasi was disciplined and urgent. He explained what had happened, what would happen, and what he needed to do. Regan could feel Abasi's distress at the other end of the line, but he assured him Christos, the money, and the ID cards would be ready in a half-hour.

"Captain Quinn."

Regan turned, his heart hammering.

"Captain Quinn, how are you?" Crewman Peters, one of his ship's crew, was waving happily from the lobby as he left with a young brightly dressed woman on his arm.

Regan pushed a smile to his lips. "Fine, Crewman Peters. Enjoy your leave." He responded as casually as he could and waved back in acknowledgement, thinking it was a lucky encounter. Someone he knew had seen him—someone could say he was at the International.

Regan was burning up with fear, but he put on Niko's overcoat and crossed the street. Staying in the shadows, he joined a boisterous group of sailors gathered on the street corner, waiting for the cabs that were stopping in the streets. He summoned a driver, and entered a cab with instructions to go to the market. The driver was hurried, anxious to get to his next customer, and annoyed with the police cars rushing through the streets; he paid little attention to his passenger. Regan watched the commotion outside. There were some fights among drunken and disorderly sailors and brewing arguments with displeased merchants. The streets were noisy with cars honking, and bustling with human activity, and there were police cars in the street near the Sea Gull Bar. He looked away as though disinterested, relieved that the police were too busy to pay attention to the cabs coming and going from the dock.

He asked the cab driver to stop at the liquor vendor near the dock. He paid for the service, and the driver rushed off into the night, barely acknowledging his fare. Regan was pleased that the vendor that usually ran this liquor market stall was not there, and quickly secured some good whisky and cigars from the stranger in charge. He summoned a different cab to drive him to the other end of the market. Regan slipped the driver a generous sum and asked him to wait while he picked up a friend and then drive them to the dock. This was not an unusual request, and the driver nodded and appeared to pay no attention to which direction Regan went, immediately becoming distracted by the activity of the night market and chatting with a fellow cab driver also waiting for his dock fare to return.

CHAPTER THREE

Abasi hung up the phone, then spoke quietly to Shima before they told Christos his father was coming, and he would be going on a trip to Ireland.

"Why? I am not finished school."

Abasi pulled Christos to him. "Something happened that has put your father and perhaps all of us in danger, and your father is concerned you may not be safe here. This matter will be cleared up in Ireland. Your father will explain."

"What happened, Grampa? What? Why are we in danger?"

"Trust your father and do as you are told; he will keep you safe. You have been with us since you were three years old, you have used our name, so you would be accepted and could live here in Morocco without prejudice. We cared for you and kept you safe, but now perhaps it is our name that will put you in danger, so you must go with your father and do as he asks. We love you, Christos, and we must do this to keep you safe. Go now, pack only what you need, and your father will be here soon."

The boy returned to his room and placed his two favourite books at the bottom of the bag: the one about the sea and ships and the one on Trinity College in Ireland that his father had brought on his last visit. He was almost done school, and his father wanted him to go to college in Ireland. He was sixteen years old now. He admired and loved his father, but he was afraid to leave his home and his grandparents. He loved them, and how would they manage in the bakery without his help? They were older now; his grandmother struggled with the stairs and his grandfather depended on him to help with the bread and the ovens. He was already homesick, and he wanted to cry like a child.

When the quiet knock came on the door and his father pulled him into his arms, there was no tea and milk as usual; only hurried greetings and goodbyes filled with tears. Regan hugged Shima and Abasi. "Go now, quickly, to your brothers in the country, as we discussed; do not stay the night here. It may not be safe. If you travel by night, it will be easier for you to stay out of sight. I will contact you when it is safe."

Abasi responded with an obedient nod. Christos knew that at night the streets were crammed with trucks and wagons bringing produce and meats for the morning market and they could pass by without being noticed. But why did they have to hide?

"Christos, come now, we need to hurry." His father seemed tense and impatient.

Abasi squeezed a thick sweater and coat into Christos's duffel bag. "These are warm clothes, Christos. You will need them on the ship."

Shima passed Regan two envelopes, and Regan put one in his pocket the other into Christos's jacket. "You will be travelling to Ireland on a ship called the *Autumn Wind*, with Niko. It has been a while since you last saw your godfather, but he cares a great deal about you, and he will see you safely to Ireland, where I will be waiting for you."

There was an unfamiliar anxiousness in his father's voice. "Why? Papa, why do I have to leave now? I am not finished school. Why do I have to go to Ireland now? Why can't I go with you on your ship? Why do Grampa and Gramma have to hide?"

"Christos." His father's tone became firm and commanding. "You will be safe on the *Autumn Wind* with Niko. It is the safest way for you to travel. It is anchored at sea near Tangiers. Niko will take you to the ship. It sails at midnight. Please do as Niko tells you, and I will explain everything to you when we are safely in Ireland. It is better that you not know details now. You will help Niko in the galley while you are at sea. The voyage will take a month, so do as he asks, and give him this envelope."

His father showed him the one he had pushed into Christos's coat. "But only when you are alone, once the captain has returned to his quarters."

Christos remained silent, and he felt anxious. He wanted to cry as his father pulled him affectionately into his arms, but he did not.

"I love you, son. Everything will be fine."

"I love you, Papa." Christos pushed out of his father's arms and hugged his grandparents. He did not want to leave them or leave his home, and he wanted to tell his father he was afraid, but instead he followed him in silence as they hurried to the cab waiting in the alley.

The unknown that lay ahead was all Christos could think about on the short ride to the dock. Niko was waiting by a fishing boat moored to the pier.

His father hugged him one last time. "I love you, son. Obey Niko. I will be waiting for you in Ireland."

His father handed Niko an envelope and a bag with liquor, then pulled Niko to him as they grasped hands and their hearts spoke a silent farewell.

"Come, Christos. You have grown since I last saw you," Niko said gently as he offered his arm to assist the boy on to the fishing boat that was bobbing in the water, and made room next to him on the side bench. The boat was crammed with cargo going to the ship, and Christos pushed in beside him, clinging tightly to his duffel bag. They travelled in silence, the cold spray of saltwater splashing against his face as the small boat pounded over the waves, rushing through the night to the *Autumn Wind* waiting there in the darkness. The fishing boat crept up to her side, and she seemed huge, looming there in the blackness of the sea. The captain was waiting on deck and shouted something to the navigator of the fishing vessel. Crewmen rushed to bring the supplies on board as Niko hurried Christos up the ladder. The captain was dressed in black and his figure was almost indistinguishable from the night. He smelled of liquor. Christos's heart pounded, and he felt chilled. Niko spoke in Greek to the captain, whose obvious annoyance diminished when Niko pulled the envelope from his pocket and opened it slightly, exposing cash and Christos's identification card, which the captain removed from the envelope.

"Christos Bakari." The captain spoke the name quietly while glancing briefly at Christos, then placed it back in the envelope and nodded once as he pushed it into his jacket pocket and took the bag with the liquor and cigars Niko offered. Christos stood in silence, his attention focused on the silver sidearm the captain made no effort to hide.

The ship was surrounded by night mist, and Christos could see men in coveralls securing the cargo and moving about like ghosts in the darkness, their shouts and commands fading into the eerie sounds of the restless sea. Two large cranes, fore and aft, ascended into the night sky, and the ship seemed mystical and frightening to Christos. The captain motioned him and Niko toward the galley. Niko pushed open a large metal door, exposing a long wide hallway that was haunted by shadows stretching off the dim lights. The lingering smell of fresh sea air wrestled with the stale odour of human existence. The vessel creaked as she shifted in the water, and Christos clung to the brass railing mounted on the deep cherry walls as he followed Niko along the worn hardwood planking, then down a stairwell, where they came to a wide wooden door with a brass name plate labelled "Galley." Niko pushed it open.

The galley was warm and brightly lit.

"Please sit, Christos. I will get you some hot tea." Niko pulled out a wooden chair at the oak table along the wall. Christos sat, surveying the galley while Niko poured hot water into a metal teapot and returned to the table with it and two cups and a small black notebook. Christos was cold, his hands were shaking, and he could hardly hold the warm tea that Niko had placed on the table in front of him.

Niko's voice was strong but gentle. Christos knew Niko Mararious was his godfather. His father had told him he and Niko had grown up together in an orphanage, and he often referred to him as his best friend or being like a brother. He had met Niko when the older man visited a few times at Abasi's when his father was there, but it had been a long time since his last visit, and he was like a stranger now.

He was not a big man, standing just under six feet, but trim and muscular. His arms and shoulders were strong from the extensive lifting of supplies in the ship's galley, but his hands remarkably nimble and refined. Aside from his one leg that dragged to the side, he seemed fit. His dark curly hair was forced into a short seamen's cut. He was a good-looking man with black eyes and a slender nose that balanced into his strong jaw. His skin was tawny, and Christos's father had told him Niko was from Greece.

They were alone, and as instructed by his father, Christos took the envelope from his pocket and gave it to Niko. Niko looked at him carefully, as if assessing him and deciding what his fate would be, then he smiled, exposing his clean white teeth. His smile was genuine and caring, and a tiny feeling of comfort crept into Christos's soul.

Niko took a large gulp of tea from the mug in front of him. "Drink some tea, Christos, it will warm you."

Christos took a sip. It was dark and strong, like Moroccan coffee. Niko smiled again, pushing a jug of milk toward him.

Christos added it to the tea, using both hands so Niko wouldn't see how badly he was shaking.

"We will be at sea a month, so best you get used to my tea." Niko seemed amused, and Christo acknowledged with a slight nod, but did not speak.

Niko observed the envelope on the table, and in what was obviously his sailor's logbook, wrote the date and name of the port and then, "Christos Bakari; Tangiers, Morocco," and his birthdate, then wrote something in Greek off to the side. Christos could see other names in the book, but not all had a place of birth or date. There was money in the envelope and another ID card. Christos sat quietly, quivering inside and holding back his tears. He would not cry.

Niko put the logbook to the side and looked up. He spoke, his tone serious but gentle. "You will sleep in the cabin where I show you, obey me in the galley, never go anywhere on the ship beyond the small open deck." He pointed toward the door off to the side of the galley. "Mind your business, don't ask questions of anyone in the galley, and never get in the path of Captain O'Hare; do not speak to him if he comes to the galley. Do you understand?" Niko was emphatic, especially about the captain.

Christos nodded.

Niko rose, and Christos followed him to a cabin not far from the galley. Niko pushed the door open. "It is small, but the bed is comfortable, and there's a closet there for your things." Niko motioned with his hand. "We share the bathroom in between the cabins. Try and get some sleep. You are trained in the bakery, so tomorrow you will help with the bread for the crew. The bread needs to be in the ovens by four in the morn."

"Yes Niko," he responded obediently. Christos was not sure what to do next, and sought some direction from Niko, but there was none. "Good night, Niko."

Niko was obviously as uncomfortable as he was, but he smiled and pulled Christos clumsily into his strong arms, his awkward hug relieving the fear that had almost overcome them both.

"Good night, Christos. Everything will be fine. Get some rest."

Christos surveyed his cabin. It seemed familiar, like the pictures from the books his father had given him. As he unpacked his clothes, the cool night sea air drifted into his cabin and he was grateful for the warm coat Abasi had added to his bag. The small bathroom offered a shower, a sink, and a storage cabinet with a mirror. He splashed chilly water on his face to wash away the salt of the sea and returned to his cabin, crawled into the single bed, and pulled the blankets around him.

He missed his home with Shima and Abasi, and he missed his warm bed. They had sent him away to keep him safe. Safe from what? He did not feel safe, and he did not understand anything that happened in the last few hours. He was homesick; he just wanted to go home. He thought of his father—what was it he was better off not knowing now, that could be explained in Ireland? He would not see his father for a month. He would be alone on the *Autumn Wind*, at sea, with Niko. His father trusted Niko to take care of him and Christos trusted his father. Perhaps Niko would tell him more in the days ahead.

His thoughts were interrupted by the sound of the three high-powered engines rumbling to life. Tar-laden smoke penetrated the air. The ship thrust forward, becoming one with the sea. He looked at his watch, and it was midnight. The *Autumn Wind* had just sailed.

CHAPTER FOUR

Someone was close to him, behind him; Regan spun, to see the figure of a man moving quickly from the shadows, scurrying through the dim haze of a streetlight. He was heavyset, agile, and cloaked in the dark of the night.

This time Regan had spent watching the fishing boat take his son and Niko away had left him vulnerable. Cold shivers of fear ran up his spine, startling him back to the reality of the situation.

He pulled the collar of the overcoat up around his neck and tugged Niko's toque tighter down around his head, which somehow made him feel less visible. Staying in the shadows, he began making his way back to the alley where all this had started. He purchased four small bottles of cheap rum from a corner street vendor and pushed them into the large pockets of Niko's overcoat, then followed the streets back to the corner near the Sea Gull Bar. He took a big swallow of rum to steady his nerves, and stood in the shadows watching and listening. The police were gone, and the alley where he had killed a man just a few hours before was quiet. He took another drink, then worked his way toward the clothing bin for the homeless. Regan found a loose dark-coloured djellaba and pulled the garment around him, covering his clothes to the ground. He let the baggy hood fall around his head, hiding as much of his face as possible.

It was late, and the vagrants were sleeping in their secured spots. He wanted to look like the other street vagrants, blend in and see if someone might say something about what had happened in the alley, or if someone might know the man that had fled in the darkness. He kept his distance, knowing these men would see him as an intruder and a threat to their humble existence. Regan found a spot close to three men sharing a fire built in a crock tub. He leaned against the wall. The djellaba-clad figures were visible in the flicker of the fire. He waited anxiously to see if they would approach him, threaten him, or accept him. They huddled around the flames, repositioning themselves slightly, improving their view of the newcomer, then resumed warming their hands and chatting quietly among themselves. Regan pulled the open bottle of rum from his pocket and took a drink, knowing they would observe his actions. The three exchanged glances, and one of the men motioned for Regan to come to the fire. He moved cautiously toward them, immediately passing the rum to the stranger that had summoned him. The man passed the rum to his two friends and then back to Regan.

"Another seaweed," one of them said.

A question or an assumption? Regan did not respond to the man's comment, and a genuine smile appeared through the man's growth of beard and the long grey curly hair that camouflaged a tweed sailor's cap beneath the hood of his djellaba. The man slid to the right as he spoke, making room for Regan on an old cushioned seat.

"Seaweed?" Regan questioned.

He passed the rum to the man again, hoping to keep him talking.

"Yeah! A seaweed. Had one in here this morning, fresh off the sea, smelling like seaweed. The crazy fisherman plucks them out of the sea when they jump ship out there by the lighthouse. His kid drowned out there years ago, and he trolls around looking for him; crazy old fool. All he finds are these seaweeds. Jumped ship, did yah?"

The man answered his own question. Regan shrugged, relieved he did not have to respond.

"Damn near dead, that seaweed was, off one of those tramp ships," the man continued, and Regan listened quietly, not wanting to disturb the flow of information. "A snob, not much of a talker. English accent. Got himself some dry clothes and soup and hid down there in the alley, by the big stone building, all day by himself…'til that murder tonight, and then he ran like a scared alley cat."

"Murder?" Regan didn't have to work at sounding interested, he needed to know.

The small bottle of rum was empty, so Regan pulled the second one from his coat pocket; he wanted to keep this man talking. As the rum passed between them, the other men relaxed and joined in, detailing how a couple of sailors, one in a long uniform coat, got into a fracas with Ivory, Nigeria's son, and shot him. "They were probably buying drugs. Too bad they didn't get Nigeria too! That thievin' bastard."

"Who's Nigeria?" Regan asked, as he shifted his position and looked down, struggling to fake ignorance when he already knew the answer.

"Drug dealer, thievin' bastard, mysterious son of a bitch too; never seen him, just that son of his that calls himself Ivory. Deals drugs in the alley, scares the shit out of the people that run the soup kitchen with that pistol he packs. Big piece with an ivory handle, right out of Africa, they say, and uses some special bullets that kills a man instantly. Those sailors done us a favour gettin' rid of him, but they should have known better then to buy drugs from that murderer."

The bearded man's comments started another round of stories from the vagrants outlining the brutality of this hated man and his unique pistol. Regan's heart raced with anxiety—these vagrants thought he had deliberately shot Ivory and was buying drugs. Regan let the rum loosen their tongues and build their trust.

"Think the seaweed saw what happened? The murder, I mean?" Regan asked, hoping he wasn't overstepping the boundaries of this precarious relationship.

"I bet he did," the bearded man said. "I stayed in that spot myself when I jumped ship; it's warm there from the afternoon sun on the stone building, and it's close to the soup kitchen too, so you can get first in line. You can see good too, with that streetlamp, so nobody can sneak up on you, either. It's a good spot, and we leave it for the seaweeds. They are in a bad way—worse than us, I mean."

The man took a swallow from the rum bottle, then continued. "Good thing Ivory didn't see him before those sailors came along; he'd a bin a dead man for sure."

Regan sat quietly sorting out the information. *Seaweed, sleeping by the stone building…off the tramp ships…a day ago…Englishman with an accent… Who was in port? He could find the names of the legally docked ships in the harbour, and the tramp ships anchored out at sea, but how would he ever find this man who had run into the night? If he jumped ship, he would not want to be found.*

The vagrants began to drift off to secure spots to sleep for the night, and Regan slid back against the building. The sleeping body of the bearded man in the sea cap lay in a heap by the fire, and Regan felt a twinge of shame for thinking this frail old street bum being there might somehow keep him safe from the unknowns of the night street.

Feelings of disgust and guilt consumed him, and he fought back tears and looked up at the night sky splattered with stars, distant, far away like Christos and Niko, far away like Abasi and Shima, far away like his life from yesterday. Christos and Niko would be on board the *Autumn Wind*. Christos would be confused and maybe angry; he was just a boy. But he was strong and well brought up. He would do as he was told, help Niko, and Niko would keep him safe. Shima and Abasi would just be getting to the country. Regan knew they would be safe among the mountain farmers. Shima had grown up there and the country folk looked out for their own.

He stared into the fire, watching it fade to a glowing ember, and glanced at his watch. Midnight. The *Autumn Wind* would have just sailed.

CHAPTER FIVE

It was midnight. Niko listened as one by one the three high-powered engines rumbled to life and the smell of smoke began to drift across the deck. The engines harmonized into a familiar rhythm and the clang of the anchor settling on board released the ship to the grasp of the ocean. Niko quickly rechecked the temperature on the thermostat in the galley cooler to ensure that the supplies brought on board by the fishing boats earlier that day were properly refrigerated. Then he checked the dining area, just off the galley, to confirm it was cleaned and ready for the morning breakfast service.

Niko could not feel the steady forceful thrust of the ship pushing through the water. He could still see the lights of the harbour clearly through the port window; they should already be behind them. He rushed through the galley to the small upper deck to better assess the location. His heart dropped into the pit of his stomach—the ship was not heading into the Atlantic toward Ireland, but instead into the Mediterranean Sea.

The door of the galley slammed open. Niko hurried down the narrow steps from the deck and was surprised to find Captain Liam O'Hare's bulky figure looming in the doorway. The captain had left the ship early that morning. Each night at ten, Niko was to deliver to the captain's cabin a fried-egg sandwich and a pot of hot tea, which he did without fail except on the days when O'Hare left the ship. When Captain O'Hare came back on board from a day at the docks he was always well-fed and smelling of rum. He was seldom seen once the ship sailed.

Niko despised the man, who smelled of days-old sweat, rum, and cigars; a direct contrast to Niko's spotless appearance. The nuns at the Saviours of the Sea Orphanage always used cleanliness and godliness in the same sentence, so the concept was second nature to Niko. He was always bathed, clean-shaven, and well-groomed. His cook's mocks were gleaming white, and no matter how poor the working conditions, a meal never left his galley with less than the perfection he demanded of himself.

O'Hare scratched at his unkept beard, digging through the mass of thick red curls for some unknown source of discomfort. His greasy hair was chopped off bluntly just below his ears and curled around a grimy captain's cap that looked permanently attached to his skull. He raised his right hand, which habitually rested on the pistol hanging at his side, and trolled along his unshaven face, his dirty fingernails coming to rest just below his crimson booze-infused nose. His voice rumbled from his large chest on waves of disgusting breath.

"Ship's rounding the Mediterranean Sea, next stop will be Egypt, and we'll anchor at sea. We'll go into port in Turkey for water and coal. I'll let you know after that, so keep the supply list up to date. Get that kid settled down?"

Niko nodded. "Yes, he is fine."

"Hope he's some help. Axel didn't bring any passengers on board here. Maybe in Egypt. I can't spare any of the deck crew but Sleeman."

"I'll manage." Niko responded with the answer he knew the captain expected to hear. He understood the conversation they were having was in fact his orders. If they were anchored at sea, whatever Niko needed for the galley had to come in by fishing boats, which meant Niko could go ashore and shop at the markets on the dock for galley supplies. If they went into a harbour, he could get other meats and larger quantities of flour, rice, olive oil for cooking, and other staples, but he had to let the captain know what was required in advance. The *Autumn Wind* did not have the proper permits or authorization to use the harbours, so her cargo was loaded and unloaded at sea or through the smaller, less-regulated ports. When she needed coal and water, O'Hare would sneak her into the larger harbours, usually under cover of darkness. O'Hare would have the supplies arranged and waiting on the dock, so the ship could get back out to sea quickly, with as little attention as possible.

A demeaning smirk spread across O'Hare's red lips, exposing his stained teeth. "Well, that is it then."

He turned his back and left. The Captain's tone was always condescending toward Niko, but tonight it seemed more so than usual, prompting Niko to wonder if somehow the man had found out he had freed Gavin Connor. Niko slammed the deadbolt into the doorjamb of the galley door.

O'Hare assumed Niko's tolerance to the activities on board the ship was because his handicap prevented him from getting a better job. Since their first confrontation, Niko had made no comment on the passengers being smuggled through the galley, and handled the situation remarkably well. O'Hare wasn't sure what the breaking point of his galley master was, but he wanted to keep him, so for the most part he stayed out of the galley.

The men spoke only when necessity demanded. Niko despised the way O'Hare treated the crew. True, some were less-than-stellar human beings, but human beings just the same, and as long as their hearts beat, they deserved to be treated as such. O'Hare stomped about the ship with the persona of the grim reaper in his unkept black uniform with his pistol swinging at his side. He never missed a chance to degrade a man in front of his fellow sailors or make an example of one, as he had with Gavin Connor. He was not only a bully but a dangerous man. Niko hated bullies.

The episode with Gavin Connor had been the last straw. Niko had disembarked that morning with thoughts of not returning to the ship, and of just disappearing, thoughts that had resurfaced with

Regan's news of the marina. Had it not been for what had happened in the alley, Niko might not be standing there right now. Maybe he would have found the courage to just disappear and not get back on board.

Niko slapped the bread dough against the chopping block, exerting a bit more vengeance than usual. Every night before bed he would prepare the dough and set it on the upper tray of the stove, so the yeast could rise. In the morning he would break it into bun-sized portions, so the men could enjoy fresh-baked buns with their breakfast. The visit from O'Hare a few minutes earlier had taken Niko to the peak of frustration. With everything that had happened the last few hours, the last thing he needed to hear was that he would be at sea a month longer than planned. He would have to get word to Regan.

There were rumours that in addition to the passenger smuggling, Liam O'Hare was suspected of transporting contraband goods on the ship. On more than one occasion the coast guard had boarded and searched the ship thoroughly. The fact that they had never been able to find anything was making an arrogant ass out of O'Hare. Niko felt certain this voyage along the coast had little to do with delivering the visible cargo on the deck, but more to do with the invisible cargo somewhere else on this ship. Niko had chosen to ignore the whole disgusting business just to keep a job, but with one last punch to the blob of bread dough that lay before him he announced decisively, "My last trip on the *Autumn Wind*! My last!" The defenceless mass of dough spread itself out on the tray, which Niko set on the top shelf of the stove and lightly covered with a linen.

Niko reached into a small cabinet alongside the cooler where he kept his personal stash of rum and poured himself a drink. Every evening before retiring, he would pour himself a half-glass, while reviewing the accuracy of the galley inventory and the menu plans for the next day. Tonight, he left the paperwork unattended and secured Regan's coat from the same cabinet as the rum. He had discreetly brought the coat on board in a seaman's bag and stored it beside the liquor. He took the pistol from the pocket then spread a cloth on the table and carefully laid the gun down on it. His leg was aching from the run down the alley. He filled his rum glass to the top.

Niko had little use for guns. During the war years, every sailor received some basic weapons training, but he knew nothing about the pistol that lay before him. It was unusual; the grip was polished white ivory and the barrel was engraved with gold designs. He spun the chamber and saw five odd-looking bullets. One was missing, and Niko knew where that one was. He had told Regan he would throw the gun into the sea, but maybe he would keep it, hide it. Just before they docked in Ireland, he would go to O'Hare's cabin and use it to demand his ID card. He had Christos to look out for too, and the sudden change in the route to include the Mediterranean coast had him concerned. Everything that had happened tonight put them in danger. He wiped the handle and barrel clean, left the safety off, and put it in a small hidden drawer under the galley knives. The drawer looked like a solid panel, but a firm push in the lower right corner opened a long flat compartment. Niko had discovered it by accident, but now used it to store some emergency cash and his sailor's logbook, where he had been keeping a record of all the people O'Hare had smuggled through his galley. After Christos went to bed he had added the envelope Regan had sent with cash and Christos's real ID card. The gun fit nicely in the front of the drawer. All Niko threw into the sea that night, was Regan's coat and cap.

CHAPTER SIX

A street truck clanged, then squeaked to a stop, startling Regan awake. The morning air was cool, but he could feel the rays of sun filtering through the dust that hung in the alley; it would be hot by noon.

The truck had stopped in front of the mission. Four men, identically clothed in loose grey-striped djellaba, busily set up the food truck and began passing out plates to the vagrants who were already gathering. Regan pushed his aching bones upright and, with his head lowered, moved toward the group, where a line was already forming. There were mumbles of discontent among them about the seniority of the alley community, which eventually resolved into an orderly line. Not wanting to draw any attention to himself, Regan took a place at the end. As he inched toward the smell of warm bread and coffee, he noticed a man huddled against the stone building where the man who had run into the night had been concealed. The others paid no attention to him and there was no talk among the vagrants about what had happened in the street the night before. This death that had occurred only a few feet away just hours ago held less significance to these desperate men than the warm meal that awaited them.

Others began to form the line behind Regan, and he accepted the chipped clay plate with a portion of warm meal mixed with milk, a sweet bun, and hot coffee. He secured a second cup of coffee from the extras set off to the side and moved slowly toward the man huddled on the ground in the shadows by the stone building. Regan seated himself on the ground beside him, and the man raised his lowered head and looked at his intruder. Regan watched his face and his movements before cautiously handing him the plate of food. The man extended a shaking hand as he accepted the plate, then pulled away slightly, as if expecting some retaliation. He smelled of seaweed.

"Take it. I got food yesterday and there will be soup at noon. You need to have something to eat," Regan assured the man, who hurriedly consumed the food.

Regan pulled another small bottle of rum from his jacket, put some in his coffee, and gestured the same to the man. "A sailor's drink?" Regan wanted to know if the man came off the ships. The stranger nodded as he placed the empty plate on the ground beside him and raised his cup slightly to Regan's.

"Thank you, you are a kind soul. Rum has saved many a sailor on a chilly night at sea." The stranger's voice reflected his gratitude and Regan was pleased he wanted to talk.

"These are tough times. You a sailor?" Regan questioned the man gently.

"Yeah, worked in the engine room shovelling that shittin' coal till I couldn't take it anymore. You?"

"Work on the tugboats in the harbour," Regan responded evasively. "Which ship?" he quizzed, wanting to know where this man had come from.

"The *Destiny*," the man said, and Regan knew it was a tramp ship.

"Docked in the harbour then, is she?" he asked.

"Don't know!" The sailor could not hide his anger. "Jumped overboard yesterday, don't know if she anchored at sea or just kept going. Figured I was dead either way, so just jumped out there where they say the crazy fisherman is; didn't think I would make it."

"Crazy fisherman?" Regan prodded carefully. The men by the fire had spoken of the crazy fisherman.

"Out there." The sailor waved his arm in no defining direction, then added, "by the lighthouse. Heard lots of stories about him, thought it was just a bunch of bullshit, but when you get desperate you just don't care." The man hesitated, and Regan waited as the stranger gathered his thoughts. "He's real, all right, probably crazy, too, but he plucked me out of the sea, damned near dead I was, gave me some rum and blankets to get dry, and took me ashore. Told me to follow the goat path along the shore up against the cliffs into Tangiers. I walked a few hours, then a goat herder let me ride in his wagon and dropped me off here. I thank God I made it."

Regan added more rum to the man's almost-empty cup. "What will you do now?" Regan's concern was genuine.

"Try and get back home to France. Don't have my ID card, they take them away when you work on those tramp ships, so you have to keep coming back, but even bein' thrown in jail as an illegal would be better then another hour on the *Destiny*. Name's Gordon La'Vrie, by the way." He extended his dirty, calloused hand.

Regan accepted. "John Smith." It was a safe name and it rolled off Regan's tongue without hesitation.

"What about you?" the stranger asked.

"Just trying to find some work. It's been harder since the war." Regan motioned to the vagrants scattered about the alley, implying it was hard for all of them, too. "A few bucks a month. I get by." Regan was lying, but it seemed a small sin compared to the one he had committed just a few feet away the night before. "Well, good luck to you." Regan rose and extended a hand to the man, helping him to his feet.

"You too. Thank you for your kindness."

Regan nodded, turned his back, and walked away. He didn't want to get caught by a lie and couldn't risk staying in the alley any longer.

Regan's djellaba hung over his overcoat and he could feel the heat of the sun. He had only a few hours today. It was time he had planned to spend with Christos. He would have to be on board the

Seaward by four, and she would sail at midnight. The lighthouse and the crazy fisherman weren't much information, but it was possible the first man, the man who had witnessed the shooting, might have ended up in this alley the same way Gordon La'Vrie had. The vagrants referred to him as an Englishman. There were three tramp ships in the waters that ran cargo from Tangiers to the ports of the Mediterranean and up the Atlantic to Ireland: the *Destiny*, *Seabreeze*, and the *Autumn Wind*. The tramp ships that ran in the shipping lanes were required to communicate with other vessels and port authorities and identify themselves and their whereabouts even if they were anchored out at sea. As captain of the *Seaward*, he would have access to this information and could find out which tramp ships were near Tangiers the last few days.

The tramp ships were always a source of secretive discussion among the sailors. The truth of the tales was unproven, but captivating enough for many rum-fuelled discussions, twisted from rumours and sparse details provided by survivors brave enough to talk about their misadventures. Maybe someone on board the *Seaward* had heard of a man overboard around Tangiers, a sailor jumping ship, or a conflict on board one of the ships—anything that might have led to this Englishman being in Tangiers that night, and which tramp ship he might have come from.

The road to the lighthouse was winding, and it would take at least three hours by vehicle. A small fishing boat could be there in less than an hour. He wanted to talk to the fisherman at the lighthouse; crazy or not, maybe he could help Regan find the Englishman or at least identify the ship he came off of. There were lots of small fishing boats docked after the morning catch. Regan noticed a fisherman busily fixing his net in a small boat near the end of the pier. Before he approached, he removed his djellaba and stuffed it inside his coat, then removed Niko's coat and exposed his uniform. He pulled some money out of his wallet and passed it to the man. "Could you give me a ride out to the lighthouse?"

The Spirit of the Autumn Wind

The man nodded and motioned Regan on board, no doubt curious why this uniformed sailor would want to go to the lighthouse.

"Old fisherman out there is a friend of my mother's and I said I would call in on him." Another lie—his life was becoming a collection of deceit and lies. The fisherman seemed satisfied with the explanation, and immediately started his engine and manoeuvred his small boat away from the pier. He headed out to sea. Regan took the seat next to him. The man was a bit older than Regan, and eager to break the routine of the boat trip with a bit of chat.

"He's crazy, that old fisherman. Came back after the war a little crazy. Bin goin' out there every morning lookin' for his son. No one around here really remembers the kid drowning. Plumb crazy, he is."

The man seemed knowledgeable about what was going on up and down the coast and respectful enough of Regan's uniform to provide information. *Maybe he's heard of a sailor overboard?* "Any of those tramp ships out here lately?" he asked.

"*Autumn Wind* in the channel a day ago." Regan was puzzled. *He must be wrong*, he thought. But the certainty with which the fisherman identified the vessel had brought the beat of Regan's heart to an anxious pace.

"You sure?" he asked, trying to hide his alarm. "Thought I saw her heading up the Atlantic Coast."

"It was her, alright, can always tell that ship," the man responded confidently. "Those two big loading cranes, and that big wide stack. Old coal burner, but she looks different than the others. Her hull is shallow, so she's the only tramp ship that can go through the channel. It was her, alright. *Destiny* came in the next day. Those small freighters come into the channel to load cargo because they don't have port authority and they can see the coast guard coming from two directions."

Regan listened with interest as the man continued.

"Fishing boats meet the ships with cargo, coffee, rum...and drugs too, I hear." He hesitated and shot Regan a cautious glance, realizing he might have said too much, then justified his remark. "Hard times for a fisherman now. A man's gotta feed his kids."

Regan nodded indifferently, approving his defence of his fellow fishermen's actions, and the man continued.

"Tramps load their cargo in the channel, then anchor out at sea by Tangiers to pick up provisions, then head up the Atlantic or round the Mediterranean. Don't waste no time, either. Coast guard is really watchin' for those drug runners, especially that one guy out of Africa packin' some kind of African pistol with special bullets, spos'ta kill a man dead in a flash."

The man pulled the fishing boat up to a small wooden pier that extended into the water. "Over there in that shack right above the shoreline." He motioned toward the only building in sight that was located on a rocky knoll just below the lighthouse.

Regan stepped out of the boat onto the weathered pier. "I won't be long," he said. "Just have to say hello, tell my mother I called in on the old guy."

The man waved him off carelessly. As Regan began the walk up the rocky path to the shack the fisherman called out from his boat, "Take your time, got a net to mend, I can wait."

Regan approached the shack. The door was propped open with an empty rum bottle and he could see an old man sitting at a table, fiddling with a mass of tangled fishing line. He knocked on the door as he peered in, and the man looked up and observed the uniformed sailor standing there. "Could I come in?" Regan asked respectfully.

"Aye, Admiral!" The old man jumped to his feet, producing a salute, his stature barely distinguishable beneath the bulky sea slicker that hung off his shoulders.

Regan stood crouched in the doorway of the dingy wooden shack, a bit taken back but quick to respond. "At ease, sailor. May I come in?" he asked again.

The old man pushed the snarled net aside and motioned for Regan to enter. "Sit, sir."

The Spirit of the Autumn Wind

"Thank you." Regan seated himself on a worn wooden chair opposite the fisherman, taking stock of a collection of dusty photos of wartime navy ships that hung on the walls before directing his attention to the old fisherman.

Gnarly red hair fell out from under the man's filthy navy sea cap, blending into a muddled beard that descended into his neckline. His bent posture implied age. He looked directly at Regan, his dark eyes were clear and focused. *Unusual for an older person,* Regan thought, as the man put on a pair of thick eyeglasses that lay on the table in front of him, then rested his dirty hands on a glass, caressing the rim. Regan pulled the last bottle of rum from his jacket and poured some into the glass affixed to the old man's hands. The fisherman reached across the table and pushed a glass in front of Regan, and he poured some for himself. Then the old man raised his glass slightly toward Regan and took a generous swallow of the liquor.

"You live out here alone?" Regan asked.

"Just me and my boy." He pulled a chain from around his neck and opened a locket with the picture of a young boy and a woman. "My wife died when the boy was five. Had to look after him myself. Took him out fishing with me every morning, getting a catch for the market to make a living. A little stormy one morning and I got pushed off the shelf into the deep water. I was fighting to get the vessel back in the shallow water before I lost her, and the boy fell overboard. I should have been watching him. I dived for hours looking for him. Seems like yesterday. Came back here after the war. It was a long time ago, now, I think."

His broken thoughts softened into silence. He refocused when Regan said, "Your son is at rest in the sea, but he is alive in your heart."

The fisherman nodded, then asked, "You got kids?"

"No," Regan responded.

"What ship you on?" The man's question was direct.

Regan pulled a *Seaward* business card from his pocket and handed it to the old fisherman.

"Captain Regan Quinn, *Seaward Angel*," the fisherman read out loud in a respectful tone, then pushed the card into his shirt pocket.

"Tony Phillips, that's my name," he said, raising his glass to Regan's, and the men downed their drinks. "What was it that brought you out here?" Tony asked.

"The lighthouse. You can see the beacon from miles out at sea. I was just curious. I had a few free hours on shore. You must be able to see the entire channel from this section of the coastline?" Regan added, hoping he might disprove what the owner of the fishing boat had said about the *Autumn Wind*.

Tony took a swallow from his glass and leaned back in his chair. "Yeah, it's a narrow strait with a shallow shelf that extends a couple of miles out. The big ships can't navigate it. A few have tried over the years and there were some bad accidents, so they put up this lighthouse at the channel mouth to warn the big vessels. The tramp ships come part way in to meet the fishing boats that shuttle cargo for them. The *Autumn Wind* is the only one that can navigate the entire channel. That ship has a shallow hull, apparently, she was a supply ship that ran up and down the Atlantic during the war. Maybe you heard of her?"

"No," Regan shook his head, making an effort to look sincere.

"Bin hearin' rumours that she's running drugs now," Tony said, and shrugged like it was insignificant.

Regan wanted to know more. "I've heard stories that the working conditions on some of the tramps are pretty bad." he said, hoping the old fisherman might mention the *Autumn Wind* again.

"Not rumours," Tony said emphatically. "I picked up a sailor adrift a day ago, said he was off the *Autumn Wind*. Jumped overboard. First mate, an Englishman. He was half dead when I plucked him from the sea. Said the captain lashed him to the mooring post, meant to kill him—some kinda disagreement over the engines—but the cook helped him get away."

Regan was shocked by what Tony had just said and in his haste to hide his emotions he was oblivious to the fact that this man had just led him into a conversation that was designed to gauge that very reaction. Regan could feel the pace of his heart quicken. His thoughts were consumed with concern for Niko and Christos. *Why had Niko not mentioned helping the sailor who jumped ship? Was Niko safe on board like he'd said? Is Christos safe?*

"What happen to the man?" he asked, and, trying to find his focus, took a drink of rum before looking up and facing the old fisherman.

"Got him dried up, put some rum into him, and sent him up the goat trail along the water's edge. Places to take shelter and hide. Not the first time I plucked one of those sailors off the tramp ships out of the sea. There was another one a day later, a Frenchman, said he jumped off the *Destiny*. I sent him up the goat path too. About a days' walk and they're in Tangiers. Sometimes the goat herders pick them up and drop them off at the soup kitchen. It's a shame the way they treat those sailors," he said, then went silent and gazed down at his glass, his mind seemingly lost to another time.

Regan wanted to know more about the Englishman and tell Tony his friend was Niko, the cook on the *Autumn Wind*, to see what else he knew, but he couldn't take the chance. *Tony could be involved in the drug smuggling. Niko said Nigeria had friends and the fisherman that brought him out to the lighthouse talked about the fishing boats shuttling drugs. He wasn't convinced the man was crazy, maybe just lonely and a drunk. What he just said about the Englishman and the Autumn Wind was detailed, and he mentioned the Destiny.*

If it had not been for his encounter with Gordon La'Vrie that morning and what the vagrants had said about the snobby Englishman the night before, Regan would have assumed the fisherman was just crazy, like everyone said. Maybe by coming out to the lighthouse, he had revealed who he was and put himself in danger.

Regan's heart was pounding. *He had to get back to the Seaward, it was the only place he was safe. He couldn't trust anyone.*

He glanced at his watch. "It's time I was getting back. Thanks for the information on the lighthouse." He left the rum on the table, stood up, and extended his hand. The fisherman looked at him as if assessing his credibility, then acknowledged the gesture. His handshake was strong and clutching, not frail, as one would expect from a man of senior years.

Regan said goodbye, then re-boarded the waiting fishing boat.

Tony Phillips stood in the door and watched the fishing boat disappear into the curves of the coast. He poured the rest of the rum into his glass. Tony Phillips wasn't crazy. He had never had a wife that died or a son that drowned.

In fact, Tony Phillips wasn't Tony Phillips at all.

"So, how was the visit?" The owner of the fishing vessel, obviously eager to secure some tidbits of information to share with his fellow fisherman, began chatting as Regan re-boarded.

"Plumb crazy, like you said," was Regan's response.

"Probably the war. Lots of guys came back like that after the war," the fisherman said, and pushed on the throttle, forcing the fishing boat to accelerate into a rhythmic bounce over the waves. He let the subject of the crazy man in the lighthouse drop and started a discussion with himself about the plight of the fishing industry since the war. Regan implied interest, but what the crazy fisherman had said had him worried, and his thoughts were consumed with concern for Niko and Christos. *What is going on, on board the Autumn Wind?*

Regan disembarked, thanking the fisherman. As soon as he was out of sight, he put on his djellaba and walked toward the busy street, blending in with the bustle of the afternoon. He would need to clean up before he went back to the *Seaward*. He could go back to the market; Abasi's bakery would be closed and he could clean up there. The vendor's shops were joined by a narrow walkway that allowed the merchants to move freely between shops without accessing the street, so he could enter the bakery without being seen. He walked briskly, moving through the crowded street, making sure his djellaba concealed his head and face.

There was a commotion in the street near Abasi's bakery shop. Amid the rushing people, vendors were hurriedly picking up pots, racks, and broken pottery that had been scattered about. It was Abasi's shop, thrown to ruin in the street. Regan stood to the side, and a shop owner rushed past him, waving his arms and shouting "*Hurry up!*" in Arabic.

"What happened?" Regan asked in clumsy Arabic.

The man raised his voice emphatically, continuing to wave his arms, and spoke in English. "Nigeria's man came through here last night and tore Bakari's shop apart looking for a sea captain he said killed Nigeria's son Ivory! The Bakaris were not here, they still have not returned. The man went up and down the shops, threatening us and the cab drivers, breaking things, scaring away my customers. The Bakaris are old people, Abasi is a baker. We are just merchants. There is no sailor here. He was crazy, that man, all those drug men are crazy!" The man raised his arms hopelessly and continued mumbling in disgust while pushing Abasi's things to the front of his now-closed bakery and straightening his own market display.

Regan moved away. His heart pounded, blood rushed from his head, he felt dizzy; he pushed himself into the small alley, grasped the side of the building, and heaved into the street. The smell and heat of Tangiers was nauseating. He slid down the stone building, sat on the filthy ground, buried his head in his hands, and cried. What had he done? How had this vicious man found Abasi and Shima's bakery so fast?

I must have been followed when he picked up Christos, he thought. Niko said Nigeria had drug friends, people he paid, even the police. Someone knew who he was, knew that Niko and Christos were on the *Autumn Wind*, knew that Abasi and Shima were in the country. He had put them all in danger. He had to find a way to warn them. He struggled to think.

He dragged himself up off the filth of the alley and looked up and down the market street. There was an old farmer who came to the market most days with goods supplied by the farmers in the mountain country. His wagon was painted with colourful designs and was pulled by a small horse. Regan could send a message to Abasi with the farmer, tell him that his bakery had been destroyed. Abasi would understand the meaning of the message and know to stay hidden; that they were in danger. Regan spotted the farmer in the distance and pushed through the crowded street of the noisy marketplace.

"Please, sir! Wait!" he called out, and waved to stop the farmer as he prepared to leave. "Please, sir. You know Abasi and Shima from the bakery?"

Regan had seen the man pick up bread at the bakery to take to the orphans in the country, but he had no idea if the man knew him. The man nodded.

"Please tell them what happened to the bakery."

"Yes! Yes! Terrible thing, that!" the farmer acknowledged. His expression revealing his curiosity. Abasi and Shima had just returned to the mountains, and now their bakery had been vandalized. "Yes! Yes!" He waved Regan away as he commanded the horse forward. "Yes! Yes! I will tell."

"Thank you." Regan stepped back as the wagon creaked forward.

The mountain farmer might have been curious, but his only interest in Tangiers was the profitably of the market, and Regan was comfortable his curiosity would not go beyond the delivery of the message. The country farmers wanted to live quietly in peace, so he wouldn't invite trouble.

Regan walked out into the street, checked his wallet to make sure he had money, and walked three blocks toward an older hotel just minutes from where the *Seaward* was docked. He removed his djellaba, leaving it among the garbage strewn along the alley. He entered the hotel appearing as a seaman in Nikos's crewman's coat and toque and secured a room from the elderly Moroccan desk attendant, who was crouched behind the barred window.

He showered, cleaned his uniform as best he could, and folded Niko's coat neatly over his arm as he would his captain's overcoat. He waited until the desk attendant disappeared, then left the hotel in his uniform. He obtained a shave in a small shop next to the hotel and a shoeshine from a street vendor, then threw Nikos crewman's coat into a garbage pile on the edge of the street; it was evidence that he did not want in his possession.

It was almost one o'clock and the waterfront street was bustling with noon day activity. He was minus his captain's cap and overcoat, so he did not stand out among the many uniformed sailors that were gathered on the boardwalk, but still, he felt conspicuous and his heart throbbed as he walked briskly toward the *Seaward Angel*.

CHAPTER SEVEN

"Hi Loren, Jimmy here."

Loren held the phone to her ear and repositioned herself in her deck chair. The warm Italian sea breeze drifted around her long, tanned legs and tossed her soft black hair off her shoulders and around her face.

"Enjoying the vacation?" Jimmy's voice refused to relinquish its Irish accent, and it was one of the things Loren loved about him.

She could visualize his permanently fixed half-smile that conveyed the idea that he knew something you did not, and he usually did; he was a brilliant detective. The curly hair that he kept trimmed close to his head had started to grey, intensifying his sea-blue eyes. He was a good-looking man, physically fit and six-foot-four, and looked younger than his fifty-six years. He had spent some time in the military before joining the Garda. They were years of his life he seldom spoke of but were the influence for his intense devotion to his career. He was a decorated detective and the only two things he cared about more than his job were Molly and Loren.

"Yes, what's not to enjoy? The weather is beautiful on the coast this time of year," she said.

"Well, good to hear your voice, girl." He always called her girl, a playful endearment that rolled off his tongue with the same love that filled his Irish heart.

"How is Mama?" Loren asked.

"Feisty as ever; she sends her love," Jimmy responded cheerfully.

They worked together, and although she had always called him "papa" as a child, now, at thirty-two and as a member of Jimmy Flynn's investigation unit, she called him Jimmy. He oversaw a special Garda unit that had international jurisdiction and handled drug- and contraband-smuggling cases. His team consisted of five male undercover Garda detectives and two female civilian special investigators, of which Loren Lombardi was one.

As a young Garda detective, Jimmy had been the investigator in an Italian Mafia case tied to the high-ranking Lombardi family. Loren had survived the Mafia-instigated car accident that killed her parents, leaving her alone and headed to an orphanage, so Flynn took her home to Ireland. He and Molly were unable to have children of their own. They welcomed the little orphaned girl into their home and hearts and raised her as Loren Flynn, but her legal name was still Lombardi.

When she was sixteen, her family doctor determined she would never be able to have children. As a girl, infertility seemed of little concern, but as her young female friends began to marry and have children, she realized her life would be different, and made the decision to remain single and pursue a career. Jimmy and Molly made sure she got the best secondary education possible, and when she located a college in Naples that allowed women to enroll in their journalism program, they supported her decision to return to Italy to study.

When she turned twenty-one, she inherited what remained of the once-extensive Lombardi estate, which now consisted of only a small cottage and a private harbour on a tract of land along the coast of Italy. Her parents had put the assets in her name as part of a trust fund when she was born, and as she was a minor and still alive when they were killed, the property and trust fund were spared when the courts dispersed the Lombardi possessions. The cottage became her home.

When she completed her studies, she worked as a researcher for the crime editor of a large Italian newspaper. As a child, she had been fascinated by her Papa's stories of mystery and crime-solving, and it was that captivation that made her a keen investigator. Her editor was relentless about exposing the underworld of the Italian Mafia, and over the next few years Loren spent hours investigating the mob bosses and connecting the dots that tied the infamous Mafia families and their illegal activities together. She learned to speak fluently in Italian and would often go undercover to get information. On three occasions, she had sent names and details to Jimmy Flynn that had aided in intercepting smuggling operations.

She spent her spare time researching the history of the notorious Lombardi family. Jimmy and Molly were concerned when she began investigating her family's past. It had all been put to rest years ago, and Jimmy wanted it to stay that way. Loren eventually documented her family's story in a book she called *By the Sea*. Jimmy and Molly were against the publishing of the book, concerned that it might stir up some old hostilities against the Lombardi family, but Loren was determined to put her past to rest in her own way.

Once the book was published, she seemed at peace with what she could not change. A lot of what Jimmy Flynn knew about investigating had rubbed off on Loren, and as much as he was concerned about the book, he was impressed by the perspicacious investigation that had gone into documenting the events. He was proud of her. She had become an authority on the workings of the Mafia and their underground activities. She was a beautiful young woman with exceptional investigative skills, the combination of which Jimmy could use, so he asked her to join his unit as a special civilian investigator. There was one other civilian woman investigator on Jimmy's team, whose extensive knowledge of the IRA was invaluable. The Garda was a male-dominated force. There were those who took objection to Jimmy's use of the female civilian investigators and wanted the jobs to be given to qualified male Garda officers. That men viewed women as insignificant was the reason his female undercover investigators were effective. Men would talk business and disclose secrets in front of women because they considered them to slow-witted to understand, but Jimmy Flynn knew differently. During his time in the military he had witnessed first-hand the strength and intelligence of the women that contributed to the war effort. His response to his superiors was simply, "No, there are no men in the Garda that have their qualifications," and he wasn't just referring to the knowledge they were able to bring to his investigations but the fact that they were female. He let the success of his unit do the rest of the talking.

Loren had been with Jimmy's unit for eight years, and Jimmy Flynn was now a top-ranking officer in charge of an elite undercover criminal-investigation unit. He handpicked the officers for this unit, each with a unique set of skills and the ability to work undercover as a team to piece together the evidence needed to find and convict some of the most wanted criminals in the underworld. Everyone on his team spoke more than one language, and his civilian female investigators received the same training as their male Garda counterparts, including combat and weapons training. They were not allowed to arrest a suspect, so whenever they were on an assignment Jimmy placed a male Garda undercover investigator with them to carry out the official police duties when required. Their cases were difficult and often involved lengthy investigations with ties to other countries. The male Garda investigators with Jimmy's unit recognized the value of their female associates and accepted them as equal.

Jimmy's team would work in vacation time when their schedules permitted, and Loren would return to her cottage on the sea every year for hers. It was not unusual to be called back if there was a new development in a case, and Loren's suspicion that was the reason for Jimmy's call was right.

This case had started almost a year ago with some shootings in Ireland that were tied to activists with the IRA. The weapons used were military issue and were supposed to have been destroyed after the war. Further investigation suggested the weapons were being smuggled in on a tramp ship called the *Autumn Wind*, which made regular voyages between Tangiers and Ireland. Jimmy sent some of his undercover team to Tangiers, where they had linked an African man named Nigeria and his son Ivory to the weapons and drug smuggling.

The problem was, Nigeria made sure he never set foot on Moroccan soil—or any soil, for that matter. He ran his end of the operation out of a private yacht. Jimmy's team had only seen Nigeria from a distance, always in a uniquely painted yacht and anchored out-of-port. To avoid getting caught, he stayed in international waters and never went ashore anywhere. His son, Ivory, ran the operation off the dock in Tangiers, but at the same time the *Autumn Wind* would arrive back in Tangiers on her return trip from Ireland, Nigeria's yacht would show up, and the same man would meet with Ivory in the alley to do the dealing. He was a big seaman with a tattoo of an axe on the right side of his neck. He always wore a toque and black seaman's coat with the collar pulled up. The team suspected he was the crewman in charge of cargo who worked directly with Liam O'Hare, the captain of the *Autumn Wind*.

"There was a shooting behind the Sea Gull Bar in Tangiers last night. Seems it was Ivory that got shot, and with his own gun." Jimmy's words were a balance of elation and confusion.

"Wow, that changes things," Loren said excitedly.

She knew Ivory wielded a pistol with a white, ivory handle. The undercover investigators had seen him shoot one of the vagrants. That death had established that the unique, handmade bullet that came from that gun could be matched to three other shootings. The police had brought Ivory in for questioning, but he was released due to lack of evidence.

The undercover officer had also witnessed the police taking payoffs from Ivory in the alley and knew whatever evidence did exist would never be found. Jimmy didn't want the undercover officer that had witnessed the shooting to be exposed. He knew if Ivory and Nigeria were ever to be brought to justice it would have to be done without involving the local police. Ivory didn't disappear like his father. He stayed in Tangiers. There were continual reports of him harassing the vendors in the market by the dock and selling drugs in the alley behind the Sea Gull, so Jimmy decided to gather more evidence and wait for another opportunity to get Ivory.

"That's for sure," Jimmy responded. "Our undercover man in the alley didn't see the actual shooting but saw a couple of sailors running from the scene. One of the alley vagrants is saying it was them that did the shooting. My UC recognized the one sailor; the guy with the lame leg, that cook on the *Autumn Wind*. The other one was in a long captain's coat. A new player, and we don't know who this guy is, but only the captain of a passenger ship has a uniform like that. The only one in the harbour this weekend was the *Seaward Angel*, and the captain is a man called Regan Quinn.

"When they ran off after the shooting, our UC followed them. They split up, so he stayed with the captain, who went down to the market and picked up a young boy at an apartment above a market stall. Then he met the cripple on the dock and sent the two of them off in a fishing boat that shuttles out to the cargo ships. The only cargo vessel out there last night was the *Autumn Wind*. She sailed at midnight and is headed into the Mediterranean. Looks like her first stop will be Egypt. That lame sailor lived in the alley, and now he's smuggling passengers and working on the *Autumn Wind*. He's got to be involved in dealing drugs with Ivory. Probably this captain is part of the scheme too."

"It would sure seem like it," Loren said positively.

Jimmy continued, "Our UC stayed with this captain—and get this! He went back to the alley, disguised himself, and slept with the vagrants."

"Smart guy," Loren injected with a touch of sarcasm, adding, "Go back to the scene of the crime—last place anyone is going to look for you."

Jimmy's tone reflected his concern at the crafty manoeuvre as he carried on with the details of the investigation. "I'll say! This morning the captain took a boat out to the lighthouse, so he must have some interest in the drug activity in that channel. The UC that was following him let the investigator I have there watching the channel know he was headed his way, so our man was prepared when he got there. The captain pretended he was a tourist, but I'm not buying that. Apparently, he didn't hide that he was the captain of the *Seaward Angel*, even left a business card.

"Our man out there is sharp in his undercover role, and manoeuvred him into a conversation. Quinn said he had never heard of the Autumn Wind, but got anxious when our guy started talking about the Englishman who jumped ship, and when he mentioned the cook. He wanted to know what happened to the Englishman. Not sure why, unless he has evidence that can tie the captain and the cook to these illegal activities. My UC says the Englishman said the cook helped him get off the ship, so maybe he wasn't supposed to make it ashore.

"Then the captain went back to the market store where he'd picked up the kid. Maybe he had some drugs stored there, because the place was trashed last night, the street vendors are saying by a big guy who said he was Nigeria's man. He came into the market, threatening them and wrecking their stores, looking for the bakers that ran the place, and the captain. Then Quinn goes to a hotel, cleans up, and boards the *Seaward Angel*. It's one o'clock now and he's back on the ship; it sails at midnight."

"Nigeria's man sure got there fast. He must have known where to look." Loren said, as she pieced the incident together.

"Yeah, I was thinking the same thing. Nigeria could be using that bakery as a drug transfer point for the captain when he is in port, and that would explain why the passenger was picked up there as well." The puzzled tone in Jimmy's voice remained as he finished his thoughts. "We've been investigating that small tramp ship for running drugs and guns, but now I'm wondering if maybe that big passenger ship might be tied in somehow. These two sailors must be involved with Nigeria, dealing in contraband and moving it on the *Seaward Angel* and the *Autumn Wind*."

Loren confirmed Jimmy's notion. "Probably, and it looks like they got into a disagreement with Ivory and shot him."

"This captain is a new angle, but maybe we can use this?" Jimmy was focused on how the events changed the case. "Even if these two are Nigeria's best drug runners, he's going to come after them for killing his son," he said with certainty. "We could use these two to flush out Nigeria, get him off that damn yacht so we can arrest him. Maybe with a little luck we can get Nigeria and these two sailors too. We already have a solid case for passenger smuggling against that cook on the *Autumn Wind*. It's the lesser of two evils right now, but if we can get to the bottom of this contraband smuggling we can shut this passenger monkey business down, too."

Over the past few months the *Autumn Wind* had anchored in international waters near Ireland three times. Jimmy's team was doing surveillance each time. It was while doing this surveillance that Loren had noticed that as many as four galley staff would leave the ship, but usually only one would return, a man in his mid-thirties with a lame leg.

After realizing this, some of the team followed the galley staff when they disembarked. They quickly disappeared, but Loren had managed to find a doctor and his wife who admitted they were not galley crew but paid passengers on the cargo ship and were trying to get to the United States. They had a small baby, which they said was born on the ship. They said they had paid $5,000 for each of them, and for the unborn child too, to be able to travel on the ship discreetly. They were Jewish and had both lost their entire family during the war. They had broken no laws and just wanted to travel without being questioned or discriminated against. They had heard of the *Autumn Wind* through a dock vendor in Egypt, and he had made the arrangements through a crewman off the ship who took them to the galley master. The doctor said they travelled disguised as galley crew and were not mistreated. They spoke highly of the lame cook and said he took diligent care of the crew and treated them with respect.

She had found another man, a German soldier, who also said he heard the ship would take passengers through a dock vendor, but in Tangiers. The vendor connected him to a crewman who collected the $5,000 fee, then took him to the galley master. He also was confined to the galley and did not have access to any other areas of the ship, and said he was treated well by the lame cook, whom he referred to as Niko.

Jimmy recognized Loren's investigation gave him enough evidence to charge the *Autumn Wind* for smuggling passengers for money, but wanted to hold off with any charges until they could figure out how the ship was smuggling in the weapons. The passenger-smuggling case was solid and would bring a big fine and put the crewman and the cook in jail, but it would not get the ship off the ocean and stop the gun smuggling.

Loren was listening, making mental notes of everything Jimmy said and waiting to hear what his next step in the investigation would be. The fact that Jimmy's team had pieced the smuggling operation together but had not been able to get Ivory into jail or catch Nigeria on land was frustrating, and Jimmy was more determined than ever to shut down this smuggling operation, put everyone involved in jail, and get the *Autumn Wind* off the ocean.

"I want to put you on board the *Seaward Angel* to watch this Captain Quinn. I arranged for a private plane to fly you into Tangiers. Can you be ready by two-thirty? It's a short flight."

Loren looked at her watch. "Sure, I can."

She was used to Jimmy's investigations and knew if the schedule was tight, he was on to something that he thought was important to the case.

"You should be there by four and the *Seaward Angel* isn't scheduled to leave until midnight. This morning I embedded a Garda officer with the ship's security crew. He works undercover with the coast guard and will be discreetly checking the ship for contraband. His name is Emanuel Garcia. He will meet you at the boarding ramp and have your boarding pass. He is the only one on board that knows you are there to conduct an undercover investigation. Until we find out what this captain is up to and who else is involved, we need to keep things confidential. I've pulled the personal details on Regan Quinn and included the information with your boarding pass. Get close to him and find out what you can. Quinn is about your age, good-looking guy, too, so pack some nice clothes. The *Seaward Angel* is supposed to be a pretty luxurious vessel, and it will take about a month to get back to Ireland. Maybe you can have a little fun while you're working on this case, to kind of make up for ruining your vacation, girl." Jimmy's tone had changed from serious to playful.

Loren knew exactly what Jimmy was saying. It was not the first time he had used her feminine attributes to get close to a suspect. She chuckled. "Well, I was thinking of taking a trip on one of those new passenger ships anyway." She knew to always listen to everything Jimmy had to say before asking questions. "What about the other sailor, the cook that got on the *Autumn Wind*?"

"Well, he's not going anywhere. He will eventually end up in Ireland, but I'm trying to find out more about the *Autumn Wind*. I contacted the navy. All they will admit is that she was specially built for the war effort, but everything about her is classified. A strange bit of business, and I can't help but wonder what they were doing with that vessel. No one is talking and won't break protocol even though the war is over. Mac Flanagan...you remember Flanagan, don't you, girl? With the Egyptian Police Service?"

"Yes," she said.

"He's aware of our investigation into the weapons smuggling and my inquiries about the construction and role of the *Autumn Wind* during the war, and gave me a call early this morning. He's got a young man there on probation for a bar brawl, an Irish lad named Sean Dolan. Seems he's got a quick temper and an even quicker right hook. Apparently, he and a friend were in the bar, just having a quiet drink, when a drunk sailor started swinging a knife, threatening people and busting up the bar. So, Dolan decked him. The guy got up, then fell over, hit his head, and died. Everyone in the place is defending Dolan, but it's his second offence for fighting. The lawyers are saying he caused the death and he's looking at some serious time in jail.

"Flanagan says Dolan is a ship-design engineer working for Phoenix Ship Lines. Apparently, Sean Dolan designed the *Autumn Wind* when his family owned Dolan Ship Lines. Mac says this Dolan's not a bad guy, just a bit of a scrapper. The sailor who died was bad news, dealing drugs, assault, weapons charges; Flanagan figures Dolan did society a favour, and would like to help him out.

"Mac thinks if Dolan built the ship he can give me the information the navy won't and maybe help us to figure out where they're hiding the contraband on the vessel. Mac likes the guy, says he's smart and well-respected when it comes to building ships, and he figures he'll co-operate in exchange for getting the charges dropped. If we are ever going to shut this weapon-smuggling ring down, we need to catch O'Hare in possession of the guns. Then we can pressure him and use the evidence we have to get to Nigeria. The UCs are saying there's a rumour in the alley that O'Hare's looking for a new first mate, so I am going to see if I can work that angle and get a couple of UCs on board when the ship stops in Egypt. Maybe with some help from this guy, Dolan, we can figure out where they're hiding the contraband on that ship. I have a private plane waiting and I'm heading down to Egypt."

Jimmy always called his undercover agents UCs. Early in his career he'd lost an officer when a man under surveillance overheard a name and made a connection to the undercover officer in the operation. After that, Jimmy never used the names of his officers. It was the same reason his agents didn't know how Jimmy had placed them in the investigation until they encountered each other when the plan came together.

"Loren, girl, you are getting the best assignment; these new passenger ships are all the rage these days. You're still on vacation, so you get the best assignment."

"Yeah, and I'm better-looking than the guys."

Jimmy laughed, acknowledging they both knew that was exactly why she was assigned to investigate Regan Quinn.

Jimmy's tone went from playful to serious. "One more thing. That pistol Ivory packed, with the white ivory handle, it was not found with the body and that captain could have it. That weapon is deadly, so be extra careful and stay alert. I'll contact you through Garcia once you're on board. Be careful. Love you, girl."

"I love you too, Papa, and give my love to Mama."

"I will, girl." Jimmy hung up the phone.

Loren pushed her deck chair to the edge of the veranda and closed the shutters. Her wardrobe at the cottage consisted of mostly warm-weather clothes, so she chose a pair of navy cotton slacks and a white blouse to wear on the plane and packed her light summer dresses and accessories for the trip. She showered and dressed and called a cab, then hurried next door to leave the cottage key with the neighbour who took care of the property when she wasn't there. She arrived at the airport to find her private plane waiting.

Loren settled in for the flight and used the time to outline the details of the recent events in the case. Every time she worked on a case, she kept a journal and wrote down times, places, dates, and any detail that might hold some relevance as the case progressed. Jimmy was amazing; he could keep things sorted out in his head and rattle off a summary of events from memory. Loren found writing things down helped to sort through the details and identify areas where the information didn't add up. And there were details in this case that seemed out of place and didn't make sense.

Why would a man who had just committed a murder and was in danger of being murdered risk going to the market to pick up a passenger? Why was this passenger left at the bakery instead of being brought to the ship by the first mate like the others? The cook was using the dock vendors to find passengers and could pick up one at any port en route for extra money. Even if the captain and the cook were getting well-paid to smuggle these passengers, why risk your life over one? The captain of a passenger ship was well-paid. Why risk being caught by Nigeria by hiding in the alley and going to the channel? Why didn't he just go right back to his ship?

Loren underlined her last thought and tucked her notebook in her handbag as the plane began its descent.

CHAPTER EIGHT

It was one o'clock when Regan walked up the gangplank and boarded the *Seaward Angel*. He straightened his posture and focused his mind, then checked his watch again.

"Good leave, sir?" the deck attendant asked.

"Yes. We loaded and on schedule?" Regan responded with a smile, maintaining the routine of casual chatter that went on as the ship's crew boarded and prepared to leave port.

"Seems so, sir." That his opinion mattered was reflected in the enthusiasm of the young man's voice as he grinned and nodded respectfully to the captain of the ship.

Regan went to his cabin and changed into his bathrobe. He called down to the galley and asked that a steward bring a sandwich and tea to his cabin, which he consumed with the same survival instincts that had driven him through the last hours of his life, then fell exhausted onto his bed.

He woke at four to the jangle of his alarm clock, then showered and put on a clean uniform. There were always four crisp clean uniforms in his closet. Each included a cap and overcoat, for which he was silently grateful. He made sure his hair was neatly in place, his nails and teeth were clean, and his shave impeccable. Any lack of personal hygiene was not tolerated growing up in the orphanage, and Regan had learned the lesson well.

Making sure his shirt and tie were properly aligned, he gazed into the mirror at his face. He was not looking at the face of the man he had been a day ago; now he was looking at a murderer and a fugitive. He just wanted to end this and go to the police, but he could not. Nigeria had found the bakery, and he would find the *Autumn Wind* and Niko and Christos. He would take an eye for an eye, equal the score.

Regan had to get word to Niko and Christos, tell them to get off the ship at the next port and find a safer way to Ireland. No one could board the *Seaward Angel* without an authorization pass, so he would be safe if he stayed on board. Niko's plan made sense; they would go to the police in Ireland and tell them what had happened. Regan took a moment to compose his thoughts, to become Regan Quinn, captain of the *Seaward Angel,* and left his cabin.

As he walked to the bridge, he encountered Crewman Peters. Peters shot him a quick smile, and Regan's responsive nod of approval acknowledged their encounter at the International Hotel. Co-captain on the bridge, Tim Johnson, was beginning the preparations to sail when Regan arrived.

"Good afternoon, sir," Tim acknowledged him as he entered the bridge. "How was the leave?"

"Good," he responded with what should have been the truth. "And you?"

"Good, too. My wife wanted a silk scarf, so I went down to the market and ended up with three." Tim chuckled at his own impulsiveness.

Regan laughed. "Those market merchants are pretty good salesmen."

"I'll say." Tim's chuckle turned into a laugh, which Regan shared, both having experienced the persuasive persistence of the street-market merchants.

He liked Tim; they had sailed together in the past and had both joined Seaward Lines at the same time. They worked well together, and their mutual respect made them a good team. The round trip between Ireland and Tangiers took two months and was a regular voyage for the *Seaward Angel*. The ship would stay for two days in Tangiers before starting the leg back to Ireland, and that was the reason Regan had applied for the position of captain of the passenger vessel. Six times a year he was able to spend time with his son and the Bakaris.

Tim turned toward his friend. "Lots of activity on shore…three big ships in port."

Regan nodded and listened as Tim recounted the details of a street fight and the excitement of witnessing a merchant chasing a thief down the market row. "Heard there was a murder too."

"Really? Who got murdered?" Regan responded, acting disinterested.

"One of the crew said it was Ivory, the son of that drug dealer they call Nigeria." Tim hesitated. "He was supposed to be a real nasty piece of work."

"Catch the guy?" Regan focused on sounding casual.

"Don't know. Supposed to have been a couple of sailors. Who knows?" Tim shrugged it off, then added, "Could have been anybody with all that ruckus going on."

Regan let the conversation die, silently relieved that no connection had been made to him. He observed the charts for the shipping channel, paying special attention to the location of any confirmed tramp ships.

"These ghost ships still out there?" he asked Tim.

Between themselves they referred to the tramp ships as ghost ships, as they were never sure exactly where they were, and they would sometimes just appear like a ghost anchored out to sea, creating a constant worry to the navigators of the *Seaward Angel*.

Tim responded in an official manner. "The *Destiny* and the *Autumn Wind* were near Tangiers when we docked. The *Autumn Wind* was scheduled to leave the shipping lane yesterday at midnight and was supposed to be headed up the Atlantic toward Ireland; expect we will encounter her again, but she should be ahead of us now. The *Destiny* sailed this morning into the Mediterranean Sea. The *Seabreeze* is in the Mediterranean too, so they should be out of our hair for a while."

Regan settled into the captain's chair and forced his mind to concentrate on his duties, checking all the port authorizations for accuracy and reviewing all the weather and information required for a safe voyage. Passengers were to be finished boarding by six, leaving time for the crew to have supper. He always took his supper at seven. His reserved table allowed for a view of the sea and harbour, giving him time to observe the weather and activity in port while he ate, with plenty of time left for the final procedure checks before the ship sailed at midnight.

At the same time Captain Regan Quinn was making his way to the bridge, Loren Lombardi was arriving at the dock where the *Seaward Angel* was anchored. Emanuel Garcia was waiting with her boarding pass and the package from Jimmy. He was a handsome man of medium stature, about Jimmy's age. His skin was tawny-coloured, and his straight hair was combed back, emphasizing the greying along his temples. The word "Security" was embroidered in dark navy on the front of his beige uniform, just above his name tag. He introduced himself, and a kind smile accompanied his gentle manners as he extended his hand. "You are from Italy, Miss?"

"Yes," she responded, thinking, *Jimmy has obviously provided this man with some details.*

"My family is from Spain," he offered in return. "Come, Miss Lombardi, I will show you to your cabin." He escorted her up the long hallway, carrying the larger of her two suitcases, then unlocked the door and handed her two cabin keys. "There are always two, Miss. The cabin door locks automatically when it closes, so be sure to keep one with you."

Loren nodded.

"Emanuel Garcia." He pointed to his name pin. "Remember my name. If you need anything, you ask for Emanuel," he said emphatically.

"Yes. Thank you, Emanuel."

Then, as he turned to leave, he added, "The bridge staff eats in the dining room, and they serve supper from six to eight. Have a pleasant voyage, Miss." Garcia was a skilled undercover agent. He had tactfully left her a clue that revealed their connection, but had kept his identity concealed even in her presence. Loren could see why Jimmy had involved him in the case.

"Thank you." Loren shut the door.

The cabin was small but pleasant. She opened a door that led to the balcony and looked down at the crew busily loading supplies on the ship for the departure later that night. She had never been on a passenger ship before and was intrigued with all the activity surrounding the vessel. The bathroom and closet were spacious, and she was impressed with how convenient everything was. She unpacked her clothes and laid out her lilac sundress to wear to the dining room for supper. Loren glanced at her watch. It was four-thirty; there was time to look around before the meal. She placed the envelope Jimmy had provided in her hand bag, along with the cabin keys, then followed the hallway and circular central staircase down to the main deck.

Passengers were milling about, strolling on the deck and lounging in the open passenger area. The doors to the dining room were open. It was a glamorous room, with decorated tables surrounded by windows that offered a view of the ocean in every direction. The galley staff was rushing about, and nicely dressed stewards were tending to a few guests enjoying afternoon tea and sweets. A table in a private alcove was marked "Reserved, Captain Quinn," and two others were reserved for bridge staff. Now she knew where he would be seated in the dining room. She would be dressed for supper by six, find a place to wait discreetly until he came for his evening meal, then go into the dining room, so she could get a look at the man. She noted a couple of tables with good lines of vision to his reserved one.

The elegant clock on the wall in the dining room showed five. She found a seat in the lounge, ordered a glass of wine, and opened the envelope Jimmy had left with Garcia. She skimmed over the details. Captain Regan Quinn, thirty-six years old, raised at Saviours of the Sea, an orphanage in Greece. Left at sixteen years of age. Two years of dock labour, two years as a junior seaman, five years as a first mate. Eleven years as a captain, and the last five with Seaward Lines as captain of the *Seaward Angel*. He was certified as a notary public, which was a standard requirement for the captains of large sea vessels, but also an indication of integrity. He had been married at twenty in Greece to Cala Christos, an interpreter for the Greek embassy, then widowed at twenty-two when she died in an automobile accident. No children or family. No criminal record. There was a small photo attached, which appeared to have come from his identification card file. There was nothing outstanding or sinister about Captain Regan Quinn; in fact, he seemed like a pretty ordinary guy. She made a mental picture of him, then returned the envelope to her bag. As she sipped her wine, she watched the passengers milling about in eager anticipation of the departure. The ship was beautiful. She was looking forward to her assignment.

For the past three hours, Regan had focused on his duties in preparation to sail. The ship would leave the Strait of Gibraltar, making stops in Portugal, Spain, France, and Great Britain, allowing port time for passenger sightseeing tours and the replenishing of ship supplies. The *Seaward Angel* would arrive back in Ireland in a month, the same time as the *Autumn Wind*. Tim had gone for supper at six o'clock, leaving Regan alone to reassess the charts and review any updated information concerning the whereabouts of the tramp ships.

Tramp ships didn't have a set schedule through the ports. Regan's sailing schedule and ports of call were pre-set, so it was Niko who would initiate contact through Seaward's office to arrange a meeting or phone call whenever he could. He knew Niko would phone at his first opportunity. Regan would have to be vigilant about the details of the whereabouts of the *Autumn Wind* if he had any hope of getting a message to Niko and Christos.

When Tim returned from his supper break, he reported that most of the passengers were boarded. Regan checked his watch, then headed down to the dining room. On evenings when they were leaving port, he would always have a poached egg on toast and a cup of tea. As a young sailor, his first days at sea were plagued with sea sickness, and an old cook had solved the problem with the egg and tea. Although the sea had not bothered him for years, he still chose the simple meal before the rigours of getting his passenger vessel out to sea.

At precisely seven o'clock, Captain Regan Quinn appeared. Loren sat quietly near the dining room entrance, pretending to be reading, and he passed by without noticing her. She immediately rose, followed him into the dining room, and brushed by him as he prepared to seat himself for supper. The soft fabric of her dress touched his hand.

"Excuse me, miss." He smiled cordially as he stepped back and touched his captain's cap.

She turned slightly and looked at him. "Yes, of course."

He studied her face for a moment. Her voice was gentle but confident, revealing the tiniest bit of an Italian accent, and a small smile settled on her lips. Dark hair fell in soft curls about her face and rested on her shoulders. Long lashes partly concealed her eyes, which seemed coal-black against her light olive skin. She pushed away a loose curl and stood gazing at him for a moment, then turned and moved away.

He is a gentleman, and far more handsome than in the photo, Loren thought as she tore her eyes away and gathered her composure,

Regan watched the woman as she walked away. The lilac dress she wore revealed her narrow waist, and the flared skirt hung delicately just below her knees, emphasizing her long legs. Her open-toed high heel shoes were a slightly darker shade of lilac and matched perfectly with her hand bag. He did not take his eyes off her until she had seated herself at a table for two with a view of the ocean, and his table.

As she took her seat she glanced back briefly at him with a polite smile, then took a book from her bag and opened it while surveying the view from her window.

Regan seated himself at his reserved table and removed his cap.

"Good evening, Captain," the cook quickly acknowledged him as he settled in. "The usual, sir?"

"You bet," Regan responded respectfully.

The cook was accustomed to Regan's routine when leaving port. He was eager to please and would add a bit of fruit and deliver the meal personally to Regan's table.

Loren glanced up briefly from her book; the captain had removed his cap and set it to the side of the table, revealing his neatly trimmed black, wavy hair. She wanted to look at him again but did not want to stare. She pretended to read, but her thoughts were on Captain Regan Quinn. He was a handsome man, probably six-foot-four or five, and his face was strong but gentle. His coal-black eyes were focused and inquisitive. His nose sloped perfectly off the bridge of his forehead into his strong jawline and soft, flawlessly formed lips, which had offered a relaxed smile when he had asked to be excused. He looked fit, and she visualized his strong, masculine legs and arms beneath his elegantly tailored uniform. Had it not been for his lighter skin, she would have guessed him to be Italian, but Quinn? That sounded like an English—or maybe even an Irish—surname. She felt slightly aroused by her thoughts, which were interrupted by the steward who came to her table to offer the choices for the meal.

She saw the captain watching her, and it was what she wanted, what she was there for...but what was he thinking?

Regan usually used the privacy of the captain's table to assess the port conditions and do a mental review of his duties before they sailed. But tonight, his eyes and thoughts were not on the harbour, but on the beautiful woman who sat in his line of vision.

These modern women; he'd seen them before. Since the war, they had liberated themselves from childbearing and housecleaning and joined the workforce. They were travelling and flaunting their independence. He would see them smoking and drinking with the men in the ship's lounge, their skirts hiked up above their knees and their modern loose hairstyles defying what was considered proper. For some who had lost husbands to the war by death or to adultery it was a necessity, but for most it was an illusion of life. He had seen enough of them to know which of them were faking freedom, but were still just needy dependents looking for a man to take care of them. He had worked too hard and too long to get caught up in their fantasies. They were just entertainment that sailed in and out of his life like the next port of call.

This woman intrigued him, though. She seemed to be naturally what the others aspired to be. Her clothes were fashionable, not gaudy and loud, and her dark hair was styled to rest on her shoulders. She was elegant and confident, her independence a lifestyle—a choice. A choice Regan Quinn understood, because it was the same choice he had made.

Loren watched the cook deliver a meal to the captain. He was having a poached egg on toast. *What a strange meal for the captain of the ship, when there are so many fine choices on the menu,* she thought.

"Thank you, Paulo. I know it will taste as good as it looks."

"Thank you, sir."

Regan's friendship with Niko had made him extensively aware of how hard the ship's cook worked, and he never missed a chance to show appreciation and acknowledge the cook by name. It had been hours since Regan's last proper meal, but he was as nourished by the comfort of the ocean and the security of the *Seaward Angel* as he was by the food in front of him.

He glanced over at the woman, to find her watching him. She quickly looked away and then down at the book as if she had lost interest.

But she had not. Her interest had to appear casual. She was there to find out what this man was up to, and she would not disappoint Jimmy or the rest of his undercover investigation team. She would plan another encounter.

Regan had married young, and over the last years had never felt the need to remarry; he had Christos to raise and a desire to succeed in his career. He was a good-looking man, and had no problem satisfying his male urges when in port. The arrival of a ship loaded with uniformed sailors anywhere always brought out a selection of young women looking for a good time, and Regan had his share. Marriage had no appeal, since he was married to the sea, but still, this young woman was interesting. Perhaps there would be another encounter, and he would talk to her then.

At midnight, Regan Quinn sailed the *Seaward Angel* into the dark Atlantic waters, silently grateful that he had made it out of Tangiers alive, and deeply concerned about the safety of his son and his friend.

The fading harbour lights blended into the embrace of the ocean and stars dotted the night sky. He felt safe on the *Seaward Angel*; the ocean was his home. A sense of comfort came over him.

Loren Lombardi sat on her moonlit balcony watching the stars drop into the dark ocean. The sound of the ship gently pushing through the water mingled with a warm night breeze. She felt safe, and a quiet peacefulness filled her heart.

It was midnight, and the *Seaward Angel* had just sailed.

CHAPTER NINE

Christos woke to the drizzle of the bathroom shower next to his cabin. It was 3:30 a.m.

The clang of pans in the kitchen signalled the vacancy of the bathroom. He let the warm spray of the shower drain over his maturing male body. Abasi did not discuss matters of sexuality, but his father had talked to him about the importance of being a gentleman and the responsibilities of being a man. He was curious but felt no immediate pressure to change his interest into action.

He hurried to get dressed. Niko said the bread had to be in the ovens by four, so he headed toward the galley, but his stomach was churning and he felt an overwhelming urge to vomit and fell to his knees over the toilet bowl.

His second attempt to make it to the galley landed him on the wooden chair by the oak table, but his stomach was keeping time with the wave-induced motion of the ship. Niko placed a steaming cup of herb tea in front of him and a comforting arm on his shoulder. Christos inhaled the soothing vapour.

"When your father was a young sailor, he suffered with sea sickness too. It will come and go, but in time it will pass. A poached egg on toast with some herb tea worked for your dad."

Niko placed a perfectly formed poached egg on toast on the table in front of him. Christos's concern about heaving was equally balanced by the fact that he was hungry.

"Thank you, Niko."

"Eat, Christos, it will help."

Christos ate. Niko busily prepared the bread pans while assessing the favourable results of the egg and tea. "You are like your father," he commented with satisfaction. Niko pointed to the now-swollen blob of bread dough. "Think you can turn that into some sailor's buns?" he asked, while ripping off a chunk to demonstrate the process.

Christos nodded and got started. He knew how to make buns and was glad to be asked to help with something. Niko pointed to some spices on the upper tray of the stove. "And a cinnamon roll for us after the men are fed?"

Christos smiled. He was anxious to show off the skills he had acquired in Abasi's bakery. Niko worked non-stop for the next two hours, at which time he looked at his watch, opened the galley door, and called to a crewman busying himself in the eating area. "Sleeman!"

The sailor arrived at the galley door. He observed Christos with a curious glance, which Niko ignored. Sleeman began helping Niko carry the trays of cooked ham, eggs, potatoes, warm buns, and coffee to the serving trolley set up beside the galley door.

"I could help," Christos offered.

"You are to stay in the galley. Do not go among the men. You can start cleaning up the kitchen."

Christos nodded, remembering Niko's instructions from the night before. His youthful curiosity outweighed his obedience, and as soon as Niko and Sleeman were busy serving the meal, he cracked the galley door open enough to observe what was going on.

The eating area resembled a large dining room. Fifteen men were gathered, including the captain, and formed a line that passed in orderly fashion along the serving trolley. They filled their plates and took places at the tables. Some more men came in through a door at the back. Their faces and hands were dirty, their clothes laden with black dust. They sat together at one table and some others, who appeared to be deckhands, also sat together. The captain sat by himself at a separate table set for two. A man with his hair pulled into a ponytail and his right pant leg rolled up, exposing a wooden stub, entered, pushing a large laundry table. He ate with the men at the crew table.

The men talked quietly among themselves. Niko and Sleeman went from table to table, refilling the coffee cups and delivering a rice pudding that Niko had sprinkled with cinnamon and tucked into the oven to warm just minutes before he began serving the men.

As the men began leaving, the man with the wooden leg positioned himself by the laundry table and handed each of them a pair of clean coveralls. Christos quietly shut the door and began washing the bread pans. Less than an hour later, Niko and Sleeman returned to the galley pushing a trolley filled with dirty dishes. Sleeman filled the big sink next to where Christos was standing and began washing the mountain of dishes.

"Christos, this is Sleeman. He helps with the meals and dishes."

Christos looked over at the man, who showed no interest and continued with the task at hand.

"This is Christos. He will be in the galley this trip."

Sleeman nodded.

Niko began drying and replacing the dishes on the trolley. Within a half-hour, the galley was back in order. "Thank you, Sleeman and Christos. Now, coffee and rolls for the cooks." Niko motioned them to the table.

Christos took a seat across from Sleeman. Niko poured coffee and passed the cinnamon rolls that Christos had made earlier, then seated himself at the end of the table.

"Headed around the Mediterranean, I hear," Sleeman commented to Niko.

Niko responded less than enthusiastically. "Yeah, at least another month at sea."

"Hear anything about Gavin?" Sleeman asked.

Niko shook his head, adding, "I was expecting there would be a new first mate when we sailed."

"I haven't heard anything on the deck," Sleeman responded between bites.

Sleeman, Gavin, and Niko had been crew together on board the *Autumn Wind* when she was owned by Mediterranean Lines. Sleeman suspected Niko had had a hand in helping Gavin off the ship, but they both pretended to know nothing of the affair and never spoke of the incident. O'Hare could never know. It would cost Niko his life and probably Sleeman's too. Except for these few minutes they spent together after breakfast, they kept the friendship between them private.

"Better get back, lots to do on deck today—short-handed as usual," Sleeman said. "Very good cinnamon roll!"

Niko put his hand on Christos's shoulder. "Got a fine young baker this time," he said proudly, and Sleeman finally smiled.

Christos was glad to see Sleeman's show of friendship, as it appeared the man would be helping in the galley, and obviously he and Niko were friends. Sleeman rose and left the galley.

"Niko, you said we were headed around the Mediterranean, and would be at least another month at sea. Father said we would be in Ireland in a month."

"That's right, Christos, but the captain changed the route at the last minute."

"So, we won't be in Ireland in a month?"

Niko could sense the concern in Christos's voice. "No, I am afraid not. It usually takes a couple of months to make the trip from Morocco to Ireland when we circle the Mediterranean, so we will have to make the best of it. I will let your father know."

Christos was quiet, and he looked down and poked at his cinnamon roll. Niko watched him and began setting out the cooking pots. He wasn't sure what to say, so remained silent to see if the boy would respond with acceptance or anger. Finally, Christos looked up.

When he did, Niko recognized that same determination to succeed in Christos's eyes that he had seen in his boyhood friend; that will to survive no matter what life threw at him.

Christos began collecting the dishes as he got up from the table and moved to the sink. He was mature and as independent and strong as his father had been at that age, and he had come to terms with what he had just been told.

Niko motioned toward the cooler. "Come, help me with this big sack of potatoes."

Christos responded, quickly lifting the big sack to table height. Niko passed him a knife and, following Niko's lead, he dug into the task of peeling and cutting vegetables for the dinner soup, all the while questioning Niko about the ship.

"Sleeman, he is your friend, Niko?"

"Yes, we have worked together on this ship for almost five years."

"How many people work on the ship?"

"Twenty, usually. The captain and first mate, they are responsible for sailing the ship and overseeing the operation of the vessel. I feed the crew, and there's a laundry attendant and one or two deckhands to help us. Sleeman helps in the galley and laundry as well as cleaning on deck. The other fifteen crewmen look after loading and unloading cargo and keeping the engines stoked with coal."

"What kind of cargo does the ship carry, Niko?'

"Dry goods, mostly: coffee, spices, carpets, clothing, goods that trade between the Mediterranean ports and those along the Atlantic Coast. The ship will load and unload different cargo at different ports and sometimes at sea during the voyage."

Niko weighed the answer to each question carefully, recognizing the boy's need to better understand his surroundings. What Christos really wanted to ask was why he was on the ship, and what had happened with his father, but he did not.

Niko scurried about all day preparing and serving the meals, which played out with the same routine as breakfast. Just after the dinner meal, a fishing boat had come alongside the *Autumn Wind* and fresh fish were brought aboard, which had to be prepared and stored in the cooler. At ten in the evening, Niko delivered a sandwich and tea to the captain, with a list itemizing the galley inventory, explaining to Christos this was an evening task that must not be overlooked. When he returned, he made tea for them to have before bedtime. Christos was quickly beginning to realize how hard Niko worked.

It was his first day at sea, and he was exhausted. He crawled into bed feeling alone and abandoned; he missed his home. He looked at his watch.

It was midnight. His father would have just sailed.

CHAPTER TEN

Jimmy's plane landed in Egypt early that evening. Mac Flanagan was waiting at the airport to pick him up. Mac's welcoming handshake was strong and accompanied by a grin. "Good to see you, Jimmy."

He and Jimmy had both joined the police academy after their military careers, and had worked together in Ireland for a few years. After the death of his wife, Mac took a job with the Egyptian Police Force. It was supposed to have been a temporary position, but five years later he was still there. He and Jimmy had remained friends over the years and were genuinely glad to see each other.

"I see you're still a sharp dresser," Mac teased.

Jimmy liked to be comfortable and his work wardrobe consisted of fashionable linen slacks, a variety of open-neck jersey knit shirts, and an expensive sports jacket that went with everything. Jimmy Flynn would only appear in a suit and tie when professional protocol demanded it. When they worked together, Mac, who always came to work in a three-piece suit and tie, would rib Jimmy about his casual appearance.

Jimmy laughed. "It's good to see you too." The touch of playful sarcasm that seeped into his voice brought Mac to open laughter.

Mac pointed to a dull-grey Ford sedan. "Got a rental car for you. Had a few police units available, but I know you like to keep a low profile, so I got you this little gem. Put a room in your name at the Ocean View too. It's a charming hotel, you'll like it."

"Thank you, Mac."

Mac gave Jimmy a hardy pat on the back. "Let's grab an early supper, my friend. There's a good place a couple of blocks away. You can catch me up on your life and I'll fill you in on Sean Dolan."

The men talked about their careers and lives over supper. Jimmy ordered a brandy, and they moved out of the restaurant to the lounge area. "So, what can you tell me about this Sean Dolan?" Jimmy asked.

Mac leaned back in his chair. "Well, as I mentioned, he's got himself in a tight spot. He was in trouble about four months ago for layin' that right hook of his on his girlfriend's father. The guy's got a quick temper and a solid right hook that's just as quick. Seems he'd been seeing a young Egyptian woman named Sadeh Tahan behind her father's back. Got her pregnant, and when he asked her father for her hand in marriage, the old man held a gun to his daughter's stomach and threatened to kill both her and Dolan. So, Sean decks the old man, and takes off with the girl.

"Apparently, the girl's hand in marriage was promised to some young Egyptian guy as payment for a business deal the old man did years ago. Kamal Tahan, he's old-school, wealthy, and well-connected, with influential friends. Said his daughter disgraced the family name, disowned her, and laid charges against Sean. He said if he ever lays eyes on either of them again it will be their last breath. It was just a domestic problem. Women aren't treated with much respect in this society, so we get a lot of these types of situations. These old traditions are slow to die in this part of the world."

Jimmy was listening carefully to his old friend, and motioned for the waiter to bring a second round of brandy.

"Sadeh Tahan and Sean Dolan, well, they just wanted to get married and live happily ever after. They didn't break any laws, just tradition. Dolan's a ship-design engineer with Phoenix Ship Lines. He said he has six months left to finish out his work contract, then he and Sadeh are going back to Ireland to live. They are not looking to make trouble.

"We gave Dolan a little probation, just to pacify the old man, so Sean reports in to me regularly. He's been staying under the radar and living in a little flat close to the shipyard, but he got himself in a bind with this bar brawl. I handled the case the last time, when we chatted about his going back to Ireland. He said his family owned Dolan Ship Yards when he was growing up. He mentioned the *Autumn Wind* and talked about building the ship with his father when he was nineteen. Said it was a top-secret project commissioned by the navy for the war effort, and his father had to sign an agreement that forbid him from ever discussing the construction or intended use of the ship.

"The contract was with his dad, the Dolan Ship Yard is closed, and the war is over. His wife is pregnant, and he says he wants their baby born on Irish soil, so if he has to choose between jail time in Tangiers and a life back in Ireland, he'll tell us what he knows."

Jimmy downed the rest of his brandy, and Mac set out the plan. "So, let's go pay Mr. Sean Dolan a visit." The men rose.

The smells and sounds of the Egyptian night filled the air as Mac weaved through the evening traffic. The streets turned and twisted into a dark narrow alley with small, older, stone walk-up apartments.

"Not much of a place for an engineer," Jimmy commented. "Thought these guys made good money."

"Well, the couple has been staying hidden from her father until Sean's work contract is up. They don't trust him not to come after them, and neither do I. One of my single officers lives just across the hallway in the same apartment building. He keeps an eye on things. When Sean reports in to me he brings Sadeh with him, and that is probably all that's keeping the old man from coming after them. I heard old Tahan threaten them, and he knows he'll be dealing with me, if anything happens to these two."

Jimmy followed Mac up a narrow staircase and stood behind him. Mac knocked on the shabby wooden door and identified himself. The door swung open, revealing a well-built, curly-haired young man with an attractive, petite Egyptian woman at his side.

"Come to take me away, have you now?" Sean teased Mac.

He was immediately likeable, and Jimmy sensed that the men, despite their odd relationship, liked one another.

"Sean, Sadeh, this is Detective Jimmy Flynn with the Garda, out of Sona Bay in Ireland. May we come in? He has a few questions for you and if you can help him out, I'll see what I can do about getting these charges against you dropped."

Jimmy pulled his Garda badge from his inside jacket pocket and placed it in Sean's line of vision.

Sean paid little attention to the badge, but instead looked Jimmy directly in the eyes. "Yes, please, come in." Sean extended his hand, and Jimmy accepted the young man's strong grip.

Sadeh was a beautiful young woman, with black eyes, olive skin, and delicate features. The black wavy hair that fell loosely around her shoulders and her short, white, cotton sundress defied the required appearance for a woman of her heritage. She appeared to be slightly younger than Sean, and Jimmy, knowing what he did about the tradition of arranged marriage, guessed her age to be early twenties.

Jimmy's trained eye surveyed the small apartment. There was very little furniture and no pictures, but there were books…lots of books. The small kitchen was clearly visible, and the table was covered with structural plans and papers. The door to the bedroom, located off the living room, was open, exposing a neatly made bed. A fan in a tiny window struggled to move the sultry air.

Sean motioned for the men to come in as he buttoned his cotton shirt to partly cover his exposed, muscular physique. As the men seated themselves, Sadeh closed the shutters on the window, locking out the noise of the street, and brought a pitcher of ice water. She filled the glasses she set on the polished stone coffee table in front of the men. Sean took her hand and gently guided her down beside him on the small crescent sofa where he was seated. She might have grown up in a home where women were possessions with no say, but she lived in a home with Sean Dolan, and it was clear she was not a possession, but his beloved soulmate, with a say in whatever decision this man was about to make.

Jimmy took a glass of icy water off the table and looked across at the couple. "Sean, I understand you were involved in the construction and design of the *Autumn Wind* in Ireland a few years ago."

Sean offered a slight nod but said nothing.

Jimmy continued. "I head up a team of undercover investigators that are working on a smuggling case, and for the past year we have been investigating the activity of that ship. She is privately owned now by a man named Liam O'Hare." Jimmy paused, getting the feeling this was something Sean already knew.

Sean's Irish-green eyes went to Mac and back to Jimmy, obviously aware of what Jimmy was there for, but curious about where the conversation was headed. He leaned back on the sofa and put his arm around Sadeh's shoulders, pulling her to him as if to protect her from what was to come next.

"We suspect that ship is smuggling military weapons that were supposed to have been destroyed after the war, and drugs, as well. We are sure the contraband is being picked up in Tangiers and brought into Ireland on the *Autumn Wind*, but every time the coast guard checks her cargo, they can't find anything illegal."

A tiny smile of self-satisfaction crossed Sean's lips; he said nothing, but Jimmy knew he was on to something.

Mac liked to get straight to the point. "Sean, if you could help Jimmy out here, maybe give him some idea where they could be hiding contraband on the ship, I will go to the judge and get the murder charges for that bar brawl dropped."

Sean was silent. He looked at Mac, then focused on Jimmy. He knew that what Mac was offering him was his only way out, but he needed something more.

"Jimmy, I'm sure Mac has told you I'm looking at some jail time."

"Yes." Jimmy nodded. He wasn't sure exactly what was on Sean's mind.

"And that scares the hell out of me, but what scares me more is Sadeh's father. I know he means to kill us both, and I can't protect her if I am in jail. I know the *Autumn Wind* can carry some passengers in the galley; I designed her that way."

Jimmy's adrenalin was pumping—finally, a break. He listened.

"I want you to get Sadeh and me onto that ship without her father finding out. In his world he needs to avenge the disgrace of his family name, and he has no intention of ever letting us leave Egypt alive. He thinks he has two months before my job with Phoenix is finished. If you can get us out of here now on the *Autumn Wind* without him knowing, I can do what you are asking."

"Can you, Sean? Find where the guns are hidden?" Jimmy had to be sure. He could see why Mac liked Sean, but he had too much time invested in the case to be careless.

Sean removed his arm from around Sadeh's shoulders and reached for a pad and pencil on the table next to where he was seated. He lay the pad on the coffee table and pulled himself to the edge of the sofa, and in the next three minutes sketched the ship from memory. Then he looked up at Jimmy. "Here, off the galley there's a room. If you did not know about it, you would never find it." He plunged his pencil at the pad. "It was designed as a communications room. The oversized cranes were built to unload cargo in a hurry, but also to hide the transmitting equipment built into them. The crew in the galley were all communication officers." He pointed again to the pad. "And here, there's a hallway that hooks the communication room to a secret hold hidden above the engine room. It can be accessed from the galley through a concealed door, but it can only be opened from above using a switch hidden on the bridge, which controls a sliding floor concealed under the deck, located under the loading crane on the bow. They're hiding the guns in that secret hold. I travelled with the ship a few times to do some small fixes after she sailed out of Ireland. The navy would load some empty boxes marked as military supplies, boots, provisions, whatever, then load weapons or secret material in the same number of identically marked boxes in the hidden cargo bay. They would exchange the boxes while unloading so anyone keeping track of the cargo wouldn't know the difference.

"That's how these smugglers are getting these guns off the ship without getting caught. The navy made everyone that had anything to do with that ship, including the crew, sign a confidentiality agreement, but she's been sold at auction twice since the end of the war. I'll bet you a bottle of good Irish whisky this O'Hare worked on the ship during the war. Who knows, he may have even been a good sailor at the time." Sean looked at Jimmy, then added, "There's a lot of people out there who are not who they were before the war."

His tone implied he was including himself. Jimmy nodded, and Sean continued. "She was built to do good, and she did. Her primary function was communication. The galley was designed to keep the navy communication specialists comfortable and hidden. That's why the only area on the ship that has a deadbolt is the galley. The *Autumn Wind*, she was ahead of her time when she was built. She had a shallow hull so she could go into small harbours, and her three engines were synchronized to run through one large smoke stack. She was built to travel and unload fast, but she looked like a small, slow cargo freighter."

Sean paused and looked Jimmy in the face, as if re-assessing his credibility before giving him more information, then continued. "She also has a fourth engine that runs off the generator. It is hidden, and can only be accessed through the galley. It runs quietly and has enough power to move the ship. It was installed so the ship could get close to enemy lines without the noise of the engines. Only the military personnel on the ship that travelled in the galley were aware it existed. There are a lot of things built into that ship that are not shown on the registered design plans."

Sean hesitated, and, observing Jimmy's intense interest, decided to add his personal knowledge of the vessel's activities. "When she proved how efficiently she could move around the smaller harbours and channels, the military started using her to move sensitive weapons equipment, as well as some high-profile military VIPs, war strategists, de-coders, people like that. There were a lot of lives saved because of that ship. We never built her to do harm and sure as hell not to run guns and drugs. What I want, Jimmy, is for you to get Sadeh and me on there as galley crew. I can access the communications room from the galley and verify what is in the secret hold. When the ship gets to Ireland, get your people and the coast guard on there the moment she drops anchor, and you'll have this O'Hare red-handed. I don't want the navy coming after my father, Seamus Dolan, for any of this. Just get us out of here and I will take responsibility for breaching the confidentiality agreement with the navy. Sadeh's father is wealthy and has powerful friends and no matter how we try to get out of Egypt, he will find us. We have a baby on the way." Sean's tone was firm and non-negotiable.

Jimmy nodded. "There's a cook in the galley who we think is involved in the smuggling scheme with O'Hare. We already have evidence that he's smuggling passengers in the galley for money but have been holding off arresting him on that charge until we can get to the bottom of the gun smuggling."

"How many passengers in the galley now?" Sean asked.

"Just one—a boy about sixteen they picked up in Tangiers. We've successfully rounded up three of the smuggled passengers and they all say the cook, they call him Niko, treats the passengers and the crew well, so I think you and your wife will be safe in the galley. I can get you on the ship, but will you be able to get into the communications room with the cook right there? If he's involved in the drugs and gun smuggling, we can't trust him."

Sean pulled a Celtic cross from around his neck. "The navy is in possession of all the original keys for that vessel, but this is a unique key made for that ship. There are only two of them. They were specially made by the locksmith who keyed the ship, at my father's request, as a personal keepsake. My father has one, I have the other. The communications room access door is camouflaged in the wall behind a large map of the world that hangs in the galley under a compass built into a Dolan Shipyard plaque. The plaque has a keyhole, and this key opens the hidden door."

Jimmy knew he had the right man. He could get the information he needed. He took a moment to figure out the next move, then laid out the plan. "The ship left Tangiers last night at midnight and is heading around the Mediterranean, then on to Ireland, according to the manifests. The voyage will take about two months. The first scheduled stop is here, in Egypt, so I will arrange to get you and your wife on board here undercover as passengers. It will take about two weeks for the ship to get to Greece; hopefully that will be enough time for you to search. The Greek coast guard does a routine inspection of all ships in their waters. I will come on board with the coast guard, and the name on my tag will say Doyle. The coast guard does a walk-through of the galley on inspection. Don't let on you know me. I will request your name. If you have found the contraband, answer, 'Sean Dolan,' and if you need more time, answer, 'Sean Seamus Dolan.' And Sadeh, when I ask you for your name, answer 'Sadeh Dolan' if you are okay, but if you need help or are concerned for your safety in any way, then answer with your full name. What is your middle name?"

"Alexandra," Sadeh responded with a smile. "My mother's name."

"Then answer 'Sadeh Alexandra Dolan,' and I will know you need assistance. I will request you board the coast guard vessel. The captain won't want any trouble with the Greek authorities, so he will comply. The next coast guard check after Greece will be Italy, if you need more time. Think you can do that, Sean?"

Jimmy was dead serious. He was not only adding two more people to this already complicated investigation, but he could be putting them in danger.

"We are not investigators, but I think we can handle that." Sean looked at Sadeh and squeezed her hand; she smiled and nodded.

"When is your baby due, Sadeh?" Jimmy asked.

"In four months."

"Will you be okay? The ship will be at sea about seven weeks after you board."

"We'll be fine." She smiled. Obviously, they had discussed this situation after Mac spoke to Sean earlier in the day.

Jimmy said to Mac, "Think you can get Sean out of his work contract?"

"Yes, I know a few people in management at Phoenix, I'll handle it."

Jimmy stood up and extended his hand to Sean. "Okay, Sean and Sadeh. I need to make some arrangements. O'Hare charges $5,000 per person and will charge for the unborn child, too. I'll get the money lined up."

"I have the money, Jimmy," Sean eagerly offered.

"I'm sure you do, but I have a budget for this sort of thing. And Sean, if you can help me shut this smuggling down, it's worth every penny. Keep your money for the baby and to get started in Ireland. You and Sadeh make any arrangements you need to, but don't do anything that will alert her father. The ship will anchor at sea near Egypt in four days, and you will have to catch it before it sails at midnight. I will make contact through Mac when I have things set up."

Sean nodded. "Thank you." It was obvious to Jimmy he was grateful as the men shook hands and parted.

The Spirit of the Autumn Wind

Sean Dolan reminded Jimmy of himself as a young man. He, too, had grown up on the docks, and had learned to fight in the alleys and streets of Ireland. A bar brawl over Molly McQuire, his high-school sweetheart, had landed him in trouble, facing a choice of two years military service or two years in jail. Molly promised that she would wait for him, and he came back a changed man. He joined the Garda, and married Molly McQuire without the blessing of her parents. The friends you make in the streets of Ireland are friends you have forever. They were equal to the connections Kamal Tahan had in Egypt. Jimmy Flynn knew exactly why Sean Dolan wanted to get back to Ireland.

Jimmy and Mac walked briskly back to the car. "Nice young man, I can see why you like him."

Mac nodded, then said, "and he is smart enough to pull this off. There are a lot of people that belong in jail, but he's not one of them. They just need to get out of Egypt, so they can make a fresh start."

"Mac, there are risks, but this is the break I needed." Jimmy wanted to lay out the plan so Mac would know he did not intend to take any chances with the lives of this young couple. "There is talk around the dock in Tangiers that O'Hare is looking for a new first mate and a deckhand. I have a couple of UCs I can work into that. Sean won't know who they are, but they will keep an eye on the situation. If it looks like there is any trouble, we'll figure a way for the coast guard to get them off. I don't want anything to happen to them."

Mac dropped Jimmy and the car off at the hotel and took a cab home. Before Jimmy settled in for the night, he was on the phone contacting his undercover investigators in Tangiers and arranging a private flight for them to Egypt. The next morning, the team straggled into the hotel. Jimmy had room service deliver breakfast and coffee, and for the next two hours the team reviewed the recent developments of the case and devised the plan that would take the investigation to the next step.

CHAPTER ELEVEN

A routine began to form over the next three days at sea, each day starting with the negotiation between Christos's stomach and the poached egg. Christos was finding ways to help Niko, so they could both get a few minutes of fresh air and sunshine on the upper deck before supper. The first day at sea, after Niko had told him they would not be going directly to Ireland, he had showed him a map of the Mediterranean Sea and pointed out the ports along the way where they were likely to stop. The map hung on the galley wall, a roll-down blind beneath a map of the world that hung under the big copper plaque engraved with "Dolan Shipyard."

Each day he would look through Niko's binoculars and record the names of passing ships on the map, along with the date and time he saw them. Niko was impressed with the boy's knowledge of navigation and was glad to see him taking an interest in the voyage. After Christos's daily update of the map of the Mediterranean, he would pull the map of the world down over it, protecting it from the eyes of those who entered the galley. He told Niko it was a present for his father when they got to Ireland. Christos was beginning to understand the respect his father had for his friend. He was a gentle, tolerant man, and Christos wanted to please him.

"It is a bit dull for you here on the ship, Christos, and we will be at sea for a long while yet. We will be near Egypt tomorrow and the captain says we will anchor at sea. I go onshore to buy galley supplies from the dock merchants. There is a store near the end of the dock, and they have some books and magazines. I will try and get down there to get some things for you to read. You like to read, I see."

Christos nodded. "I could go with you to help with the supplies."

"Son." Niko placed a gentle hand on Christos's shoulder. "I would like to take you. You are a tremendous help to me, but the captain will not let you leave the ship. You do understand this is a cargo ship, and she is not supposed to carry passengers. You are travelling with me against the rules because of what happened with your father. We do not want harm to come to you. You are safe because no one knows you're here."

"What happened with my father? Could you please tell me? I don't understand what could be so bad that I can't know."

"Your father felt it better you not know, but…" Niko hesitated, as if giving the idea consideration. "Tonight, write your father a letter. I will mail it tomorrow from the dock store."

The oven bell rang, signalling the meat was ready to take out, and the bustle about the kitchen began in earnest. Christos let his question die, but he would ask again. He wanted to know.

The ship anchored at sea early the next afternoon. It had been four days since they had left Tangiers. The Egyptian coastline appeared like a mirage in the haze of the early-afternoon sun. Christos leaned into the rail of the small upper deck, his eyes glued to Niko's binoculars, gazing across the blue of the sea at the distant harbour.

Niko touched his shoulder to get his attention. "Stay in the galley and keep the door locked with the deadbolt. I will be back by four. You can prepare the potatoes for supper while I am away."

"Yes, Niko," Christos acknowledged with a nod.

After Niko left the galley, he locked the deadbolt as instructed. He watched from the small deck until Niko had disappeared into the calm waters on one of the three small lifeboats the ship carried on deck, and then he began to peel and cut the potatoes, glad for the task to help pass the time. His mind was on the letter he had written to his father, telling him he was fine and that his godfather was taking good care of him. He wrote about the trip along the coast of the Mediterranean, the map he was making, and about the ships he saw. He told his father he loved him and couldn't wait to get to Ireland, and he wrote about how much he missed Abasi and Shima and school.

Niko had also written Regan a letter, assuring his friend that his son was safe and complimenting him on what a fine young man he had raised, but his letter was ridden with concern. Had Regan found the witness in the alley? Was Nigeria looking for them? What was going to happen to Regan when he went to the police in Ireland if he had not found the witness? And finally, he told him about the last-minute change in the route of the *Autumn Wind* and the delay in getting to Ireland. Niko put Christos's letter in an envelope with his and addressed it to Captain Regan Quinn, care of Seaward Lines in Sona Bay, Ireland.

Once on the dock, Niko rushed to gather and pay for the galley supplies that needed to be taken out to the ship by the local fisherman. The Egyptian harbour was busy, and Niko was able to get the supplies gathered quickly. While they were being delivered to the dock, he had enough time to go to the store to purchase some books for Christos and mail the letter to Ireland. He was back by three-thirty to supervise the loading of supplies onto the fishing boat hired to take them to the ship.

As the boat cast off, he observed O'Hare talking to two men on the dock and another who appeared to be the navigator of one of the fishing boats that shuttled supplies out to the ship. One man was a slender Caucasian with reddish hair and the other a dark-skinned man with African features. A shiver ran up Niko's spine. He had never seen Nigeria, the feared figurehead of the Tangiers drug trade.

Niko pushed his concerns from his mind as the fishing boat laden with supplies pulled up to the ship. Sleeman met the boat as it arrived and helped get the supplies to the galley. Christos had been watching the arrival from the upper deck and immediately navigated the narrow stairs down to the galley to help. Niko was pleased to see the supper vegetables ready and waiting.

"Did you mail the letter to my father?" Christos asked anxiously.

"Yes."

"When do you think he will get it?"

"Never sure, Christos. There is regular mail service from Egypt to Ireland by air, but probably ten days."

Christos's reaction to the lengthy time was obvious; he had hoped it would be quicker.

Niko sensed his disappointment. "Sometimes it's a bit faster. I write to your father often, and he always gets his mail." Niko's comment brought satisfaction to the boy's face. "The box with the green top…that one is for you." Niko motioned to a cluster of boxes sitting by the cupboard to be unpacked after the meal.

"Books, Niko. Thank you. Lots of books. I can't wait to look."

"After supper, there will be time. I wasn't sure what to buy, so I hope I found some you will like."

"Thank you, Niko."

Christos wrapped Niko in his arms with the spirit of a boy and the strength of a man. Niko responded affectionately. Tears welled in his eyes and he turned quickly so Christos wouldn't notice. "Now, let's get this supper underway. Books later."

Niko hurried into the routine of getting the meal out, and Christos followed along with what were becoming familiar daily tasks.

With the meal complete and the galley cleaned, Christos was busy inspecting the box of books while Niko itemized the inventory before his nightly visit to the captain's quarters at ten. Night had fallen around the ship, and she sat anchored with just her running lights visible. Niko had seen this before—they were waiting for something, or someone.

About 8 p.m., a fishing boat pulled up to the ship. There was a bang on the galley door. Niko opened it to O'Hare.

"Got a couple of passengers for the galley."

Niko looked at Christos and spoke quietly. "Put the kettle on for tea. I will be back in a few minutes. Lock the deadbolt."

Christos rose, acknowledging Niko's request with a nod, and remained silent. He strained to see the captain, whose frame was partly obscured by the door.

Niko remembered the two men he had seen on the dock. The African! His heart pounded. He knew the procedure, and followed O'Hare without discussion to the deck where the people would board. Axel, the first mate, was the crewman that was handpicked by O'Hare to work directly with him for loading and unloading cargo, and he was also the one who brought the passengers to the ship. He boarded first with the African and the red-haired man, spoke with the captain, and then directed them toward the captain's quarters. Relief surged through Niko's body—it was not the African! He was a new crewman, not a passenger.

There were still two people in the boat, a man and a woman. Niko stood back, waiting to be signalled forward to assist with the new passengers, while Axel handled the exchange of money and whisky with O'Hare. O'Hare nodded and motioned to the navigator of the fishing boat to send them aboard. Niko was beckoned forward by the captain as the couple appeared on deck.

The couple was silent. The man looked directly at O'Hare and then at the silver pistol that hung at his side. They were young, perhaps in their mid-twenties. The woman shivered slightly as she adjusted to the cool breeze that swirled about the deck. She wore a loose-fitting coat with a hood that rested over her head, partly concealing her face and hair. The man pulled her close while securing her coat to better protect her from the elements. She was petite, reaching just to the shoulders of the tall, lean man. He wore a dark, hip-length overcoat, and wisps of damp curls poked out along the edges of the sailor's toque pulled over his head.

O'Hare motioned toward Niko, who stood to the Captain's right. "This is the galley master, Niko Mararious," he said, without looking at Niko. "You will be under his supervision while on the ship. There are passenger quarters off the galley. You are confined to the galley and are not to appear on the deck or anywhere on this ship. You will assist in the galley and travel as galley crew. You agreed to these terms when you made the arrangements with the chief mate of this vessel. Do you understand?"

"Yes, sir," the young man responded in a strong, confident tone.

Niko took a step toward the couple. "Come, please, let's get you in where it is warmer." He led the way to the galley as the man followed the woman.

Christos pulled back the deadbolt to Niko's familiar knock at the galley door, and Niko pushed the door open to a surge of warmth and light. He recognized the smell of scones. Christos had taken to making a small pan to have before bedtime. He would wait until after Niko made his nightly visit to the captain and then they would have tea and scones. Niko teased him about always being hungry, but fully understood that as much as he appeared a man, he was still a growing boy.

Christos was surprised at the arrival of the couple. Niko had not said there would be other passengers coming to the galley. The new man quickly took an assessment of his surroundings and smiled slightly. The couple showed no surprise at seeing Christos.

"This young man is Christos Bakari, and he is travelling to Ireland," Niko said.

Accompanied by a spontaneous smile, the man extended his hand to Christos and then to Niko. "I'm Sean Dolan, this is my wife, Sadeh. We are pleased to meet you both. Thank you for your kindness, Mr. Mararious."

"Please call me Niko." The men dropped hands.

Sean pulled the toque off his head, exposing a disorderly mass of curly auburn hair. He removed his jacket and assisted his wife with hers, revealing the protruding stomach of an obviously pregnant woman.

A few months previous a couple had travelled through the galley. The man was a doctor, and following a week of rough seas, the woman had given birth, two weeks earlier than expected. The doctor was in control of the delivery but had called upon Niko to help position the woman's body and assist with the childbirth. As a bachelor, Niko found the intimacy of the whole blessed event a bit overwhelming, and silently hoped they would be in Ireland long before this baby was due.

Sean quickly put Niko's silent concern to rest. "Not due for another four months." Then he added, with a gentle smile that he shared with his wife, "I want my son born on Irish soil."

"Might be your daughter born on Irish soil." The woman's playful comment confirmed this was a discussion they had before.

"Well, congratulations, as long as your son or daughter is not born on board the *Autumn Wind*," Niko added, smiling at the two of them.

They laughed casually. They were a nice couple and Niko liked them.

"Your wife is a bit chilled," he said. "I will show you to your cabin. Then, please join us for a cup of tea, so I can make you aware of the captain's rules for being on board."

Sean was already headed toward the cabins. Most people that came into the galley were confused by the configuration and Niko thought it unusual that Sean was not. He immediately headed toward the only cabin that would accommodate a couple, again raising Niko's interest in the man's familiar knowledge with this ship. He left them to settle in and returned to the kitchen to help Christos with the tea and scones.

"I didn't know there would be more passengers," Christo quizzed Niko.

"Well, there shouldn't be any more. The captain makes these arrangements, and he doesn't discuss this with me. We'll make the best of it, won't we? Some company for you."

Niko placed his arm on the boy's shoulder's and pulled him closer, an assurance of comfort that brought a smile to the boy's face.

"Yeah, they seem nice. It will be fine."

Niko had just set the tea on the table when Sean and Sadeh returned. Sean helped his wife settle in and slid in deliberately close beside her, allowing their bodies to touch. Niko poured the tea and Christos passed the scones with honey. Niko repeated to them what they had been told when they boarded. They responded respectfully, acknowledging the confinement of the galley.

"I will give you each a white galley smock to wear and some light duties to do around the galley. The coast guard boards the ship unannounced from time to time, and as you are on board this ship illegally, it must appear you are galley crew."

Both Sean and Sadeh acknowledged what was expected of them.

Niko visually assessed them, just as he had Christos the night he came on board. "These are tight working quarters, and we respect one another's privacy. Why you are here is no one's business. We just all need to get along and enjoy the voyage."

"Aye, aye," Sean said, accompanied by a charismatic smile as he raised his cup of steaming tea. "To a safe, happy voyage, then. And these are truly fine scones, too."

The teacups clicked, and chatter continued about the schedule of the bathroom, meals, and the routine of the galley. With the tea and instructions complete, Sean and Sadeh excused themselves and went to their cabin to unpack. Christos waited until the bathroom was free and followed. Niko made his nightly visit to the captain's quarters. The captain informed him there would be two more crew to feed: the red-headed man named Kevin Sloan was the new first mate, and the other one, called Mojo, was a deaf-mute who would be added to the cleaning and deck crew.

The captain said nothing about the new passengers, and Niko was glad. He left the inventory list and said goodnight in response to the captain's disgusting grunt as he reached for his whisky. As Niko shuffled up the dimly lit hallway back to the galley, he was thinking about Ireland, being off this ship, and being done with O'Hare. He was almost at the galley when he encountered the new first mate, Sloan.

"Evening, sir." Niko nodded to the man, who responded with a similar acknowledgement, accompanied by a lengthy stare. Niko saw Mojo in the shadows. What was he doing with a mop and pail on deck this time of the night?

Niko was uneasy. He double-checked the security of the deadbolt, then peeked at the bread dough to ensure it was rising properly. He showered and went to bed. For a few hours the galley would be quiet, lit only by the beams of the moon above the night sea.

Christos woke to the sound of Niko in the kitchen, and, knowing the bathroom was now empty, was quick to take his turn. Morning bathroom use would start with Niko then Christos, Sean next and Sadeh last. The opposite was to apply in the evenings.

Christos looked in the mirror at what was becoming a young man's facial hair. His father had teased him and told him that when he was old enough for his first shave, he would be a man. Maybe Niko would consider him enough of a man to tell him what had happened in Tangiers, and he would ask again soon.

Niko was accustomed to dealing with strangers in his galley and, as with all the others, assigned the preparation of vegetables, mixing, stirring, and cleaning to these newcomers. In this case, the pregnancy of Sadeh was given special consideration. Although she was willing to do whatever was asked of her, Niko made sure her duties were few and delegated her a rest period after dinner. Her breakfast was served with juice and milk and the evening snack now included some fruit. Niko knew nothing about the needs of a pregnant woman, but from memory followed along with what the doctor had done for his pregnant wife. Sadeh suffered with an upset stomach most mornings, which she soothed with some Egyptian herb tea she had brought on board with her. Niko's poached egg and toast offered her the same relief it had for Christos. Sean, although he had no issues with the sea, had just taken a liking to Niko's perfectly formed egg and would start the preparations for the simple galley breakfast, leaving Niko free to work on the main crew meal.

Sean was quick to note Niko's consideration toward Sadeh and enthusiastically took on extra duties in response to Niko's thoughtfulness. The first morning he was quick to offer his assistance in serving the meal in the dining room and, as with Christos, was reminded he and his wife were to always remain in the galley. Sean was overcome with the same curiosity as Christos had been, and with a gesture of silence, Christos cracked open the galley door so Sean could observe the activity in the dining area.

As much as Sean was curious about the procedure in the dining room, he was equally curious about the two men that had boarded with them. Sloan sat at the captain's table for two and Mojo at the table with the crew. Sean was relieved; they were exactly where they were supposed to be. Sadeh's father was a powerful man, and Sean had worried he might have found out about their escape and that these men were somehow connected to him.

The boyish antics of the two met with disapproval from Sadeh, who swatted them both with a dishtowel and shook a finger of displeasure at them. Sean's impulsive response was to twirl his wife around the galley, followed by a kiss on her cheek. Christos was amused. He quietly closed the cracked-open galley door, and the trio began the kitchen clean-up.

A new dimension of communication came to the galley with the uncontrollable musical spirit of Sean Dolan, who would spontaneously break into a hum, a whistle, or a song at any moment. Clearly this was a subconscious way of coping, to which Sadeh was accustomed, and although unusual, it was refreshing in the busy galley.

Over the next few days at sea, the new passengers settled into the galley routine as the ship pushed forward, accompanied by a warm breeze and calm waters. With the rigours of another evening meal complete, Niko joined the others, who were gathering on the private upper deck to watch the sunset. Sean arrived with the leather case he had brought on board the night of his arrival and exposed a small wooden harp. Its obviously used condition could not hide what was a beautifully handcrafted musical instrument. Small carvings were etched into the dark, hard cherrywood.

With a natural love for the instrument, Sean held it to his heart and let his fingers caress the taut strings, producing a tangled, heavenly sound. Christos, who had never heard such soothing music, listened in silence. Moroccan music was emotionless and delivered with harsh pounding rhythm. Sean let the notes settle into his soul, then, with his clear, pitch-perfect voice, sang in a language totally foreign to Christos; it was beautiful and enchanting. Sadeh sat with her hand resting on their unborn child. She gazed out across the blue water, her expression peaceful, a gentle smile revealing her inner happiness as she listened with her heart.

Christos was mesmerized by the sounds and intrigued by this newcomer, whose self-confidence allowed him to proudly display the sensitive side of his manhood. He openly showed his affection for his wife and bared his soul through song. Christos had not seen this exposure of vulnerability in a man before. Abasi and Shima's relationship was disciplined by years of tradition; it was formal. He did not remember his mother, and his father, although gentle and affectionate, was always in control and he did not show his emotions openly.

Niko watched the young couple. He envied Sean his strong, perfectly formed human frame, his happiness, his marriage, his confidence. Niko was a private, quiet man who reserved his compassion for those few who earned it. He had never known love and had never opened his heart to anyone.

Niko broke the silence as Sean set the instrument down. "That is beautiful, Sean."

"What language is it?" Christos asked.

"Gaelic. I sing in the old Irish dialect. My father taught me to sing and play like his father taught him. This harp belonged to my great-grandfather. Here, see these carvings?" Sean centred the harp between them, pointing to the top engraving.

"This one with the land, that was the life of my great-grandfather, a farmer, and this is my grandfather, a fisherman. He lived in a small Irish fishing village called Devlin. This one with the merchant steamship is the life of a sailor like my father. This one with the large cargo ship and the harbour is my life in the shipyard." Sean looked over at Sadeh and affectionately touched her swollen stomach. "Our daughter, she will play this harp and have the voice of an angel, and her life will be carved under mine."

His comment brought a smile to Sadeh's face, acknowledging he had finally conceded the idea that their child might be a girl. She reached across and mussed his curly auburn hair, adding, "and her eyes will be Irish-green."

It was the first time Sean had made mention of his life. The words rolled off his lips with no significant concern, but to Niko, it was finally a clue as to who the man was. He worked in a shipyard, which explained his knowledge of the sea and ships, but not his suspicious familiarity with this ship. What was he doing in Egypt? He would have had to pay O'Hare's outrageous fare to travel on the ship. He must have been employed and had the money. There were small passenger ships that could take them to Ireland that were better suited to travel for a pregnant woman. Niko would not break the cardinal rule of privacy, but something seemed out of place. Why were they fleeing secretly, and why on the *Autumn Wind*?

The sun was falling into the sea, mixing swirls of orange and red into the deep blue of the evening water. They sat without talking, listening to the soft evening breeze harmonizing with the gentle strums of Sean's harp.

CHAPTER TWELVE

The tranquility of the evening transformed into a tempest. The ship banged into the waves and rolled relentlessly from side to side. Christos, who had almost completely gained control over his seasickness, was suddenly unable to control anything and spent most of the day heaving over the railing on the upper deck, leaving the bathroom available for Sadeh, who was equally sick. Both were confined to bed, leaving Sean and Niko to handle the galley.

"The captain's sure pushing this old girl." Sean was referring to the ship and the speed at which they were travelling, despite the stormy conditions.

"Yeah, the man shows no mercy," was Niko's response.

Sean had been looking for an opportunity to pull Niko into a conversation about the ship when Christos wasn't present. He was hoping he would disclose some details about the activities on the vessel.

"What's on for cargo?" Sean asked, without looking up from the mountain of vegetables he was preparing.

"Mostly dry goods, coffee, spices, carpets from Morocco, and silk garments from the Middle East. Usually some pottery from Egypt. Just goods they trade between the Mediterranean ports."

"She's got a lot of horsepower, this ship; she's sure pulling hard for light cargo like that," Sean commented as he glanced at Niko, who was absorbed in what he was doing.

The Spirit of the Autumn Wind

Niko finally looked up from the leg of lamb he was stuffing for the next day's evening meal. "You know your ships," he said.

Sean nodded, thinking, *He knows why it is pulling hard. He knows there are weapons being transported on the ship, but he is damn good at covering it. So, let's see if I can rattle him.*

"Yeah! See that Dolan up there on the wall?" Sean pointed with his paring knife to the engraved plaque. "Dolan Shipyard. My grandfather, Danny Dolan, started that shipyard, then my father Seamus ran it. He is gifted and can design a ship in his sleep. I worked there as a kid, and helped my father build this ship. She was a special order for the war effort. We built her with a lighter streamlined hull, so she could be manoeuvred in and out of the smaller harbours, where the big cargo ships couldn't go. The enemy was always after the big ships carrying the armaments and troops and didn't pay much attention to a small cargo ship, so she could sneak around with military supplies, without attracting much attention."

Sean stopped short of telling Niko what the real purpose of the ship was. He expected Niko to comment or say something about what they were doing with the ship now, but instead he found Niko captivated by his every word, listening with the fascination of a child hearing a fairytale for the first time.

He finished his thoughts. "She sailed out of Ireland on the first day of autumn, 1944, and served a couple of years before the war ended. By then the big diesel-powered engines were taking over. She is one of the last coal-fired ships built. Sad to see her end up like this, a tramp ship."

Niko smiled. He was intrigued. "I never knew that about the *Autumn Wind*. I have only known her as a cargo ship that the navy sold because she was obsolete. I've always found her design fascinating, but I never knew about her past."

Niko focused again on the leg of lamb, leaving Sean to ponder if he didn't know the history of the vessel or he was just pretending he didn't. Sean kept the conversation going. "The captain, does he always run those engines like that? All three at the same time?" Sean asked.

Niko looked up and nodded, while his hands methodically continued with his task.

Sean shook his head in disgust. "Crazy ignorant fool. And he calls himself a captain. Those engines are powerful and usually only two are required to maintain the speed of the ship, sometimes only one, even when the ship is fully loaded with cargo. The third engine will automatically cut in and out to add power when it's required, but it does not have to run constantly. An automated control cuts them in and out to accommodate the horsepower needed to maintain the ship's speed. The captain has an override control on the bridge, and during the war, if the ship had to travel quickly to get out of a danger zone or to safety, he could override the system and run the third engine to maximize the speed of the vessel, but when you leave them in override, it undermines the synchronization system. It's hard on them. Smell the tar in the coal smoke?"

Niko nodded.

"They need to be serviced. Italy is the best place. Will he stop there?"

Niko put his knife down. "I have made three trips around the Mediterranean coast under O'Hare's command, and he has never stopped in Italy to service. He bought this ship two years ago. Mediterranean Lines owned it for three years before that, and they made regular voyages around the coast and did stop on each trip in Italy for service, but not since O'Hare bought her."

"I hope they make it to Ireland," was Sean's abrupt response as he stabbed another potato. Niko's answers had given him no clues about the activity on the ship so, he decided to try the direct approach to see if he could catch him in a lie. "That O'Hare is a piece of work. Suppose he always packs that pistol too. I hear he runs illegal contraband on this ship."

Niko shrugged and looked down, thinking, *Who is this guy? He heard the rumours and still he brings his pregnant wife on this vessel?*

"Coast guard officers have been on here a bunch of times and never found a thing, including this passenger-smuggling operation he's been running through this galley."

Sean stopped what he was doing. "Been a lot of us? Passengers, I mean? Smuggled through your galley?"

Niko saw no harm in the question. "Twelve now with you three." Sean obviously understood the conditions of the voyage that he had agreed to with O'Hare and he wanted to keep Sean talking.

"Doesn't it bother you, Niko, what O'Hare asks you to do? It is against the law."

"Yes, but I figure he's going to do it anyway, and if I have control of the galley, at least I know the passengers are safe and the crew gets fed properly. The money from the passengers goes to buy the galley groceries, or most of it anyway. He keeps some to buy whisky and favours at the docks. The rest goes into the stomachs of the crew, I make sure of that. This ship is running with a small crew and he works the men hard, so at least if their bellies are full, they have a chance to fight off illness and injury. Without the money from the passengers that wouldn't be possible, and I can't live with that."

"So, all you get out of this smuggling is a clear conscience?"

Niko looked at Sean, acknowledging with a nod. "Yeah, I guess that's about it."

Sean silently evaluated what Niko had just said. *Flynn was certain Niko was involved in the smuggling of passengers and contraband. But he had spent a lot of time with Niko in the confines of the galley since he had boarded, and he was having a tough time fitting the man to the crime.*

"You seem like a really nice person, Niko. Why do you put up with him? Why do you stay on this ship? You're a good cook. There's got to be better-run ships that would love to have you."

Niko didn't look up from his work. "Not so much, Sean. The ships keep getting bigger and so do the galleys. The galley is a busy place, and I've got this bad leg. There are lots of young guys looking for work that can keep up better than me. After Mediterranean Lines lost the ship, I couldn't get work for six months. I had used most of my savings. When O'Hare bought her and asked me to come back, I needed the work."

Sean was listening with interest and evaluating again. *So, he needs money...he is lying, he must be getting something out of the smuggling.*

Niko finished his thought. "O'Hare is cheap, but I have been able to save a bit of money, and I have a job when I get to Ireland, so this will be my last voyage on the *Autumn Wind*."

So, if he's saving money, it must be coming from the smuggling. "Another ship then?"

"No, a restaurant," Niko replied proudly.

Sean gave him a hardy pat on the back and a smile. "Well, you are too good for this."

Sean's show of confidence brought a smile to Niko's face. The idea that Sean cared about his life had brought some warmth to his heart, and he kept talking even if he was on the verge of breaking the cardinal rule of privacy in the galley.

"Sean, what about you when we get to Ireland?" Niko asked, wanting to keep the conversation going. "Back to work at your father's shipyard?"

"Hell, no! It's not even there now. When the diesel engines started coming in, we couldn't keep up with the changes, so my father signed an agreement with Phoenix Shipyards out of Egypt. They were going to retool the yard, bring in state-of-the-art equipment, and build a Dolan line of ships on the family property, with my dad as a full partner. The whole industry started to change fast after the war. More people were travelling on passenger ships and the cargo ships were getting bigger and bigger. It seemed like the only way to survive was to take on a partner.

"Phoenix came in, and they were smart businessmen. The old man's got a weakness for Irish whisky, an Irish temper to go with it, and no common sense when it comes to either. A couple of the executives got him boozed up one night and got him to sign a document that gave Phoenix full right to the property. He didn't even remember signing the thing, but it held up in court and he lost the property. It's been in the family for generations, and it broke the old man's heart."

Sean hesitated, then continued with his story. Niko was listening closely. "They offered me a job in Egypt and offered to pay for my engineering degree, and I took it. Phoenix closed the yard down and converted it into a marina resort. That didn't really work out, and it went into foreclosure. The whole business was messy. The old man said Phoenix just wanted him out of the business and never intended to run the place, that they just wanted the property for tourist development. He never forgave me for going to work for them in Egypt. We haven't spoken to each other the last few years. The offer of an education was good. I was twenty-one at the time and had to make a living and all I ever wanted to do was build ships. With an education, at least I had a chance."

Sean shrugged, implying his justification for his decision. "I'm hoping when I get back to Ireland I can work things out with my dad and get the place back. That's Dolan property and I need to get it back in the family." He hesitated, then resentfully added. "Heard a couple of sailors bought it."

Sean went silent and chopped aggressively at the vegetables in front of him, sorting through the conversation he had just had with Niko. *Jimmy Flynn was a seasoned investigator, and he'd said Niko was involved. Every night at ten, Niko went to the captain's cabin. Flynn was no dummy; he had to be right about Niko Mararious.*

Niko didn't miss the bitterness in Sean's last comment. He was starting to connect the dots. The marina Regan had bought was the old Dolan shipyard, he was sure of that, and he said one of the Dolan family was looking after it. Sean knew two sailors had bought the property, but did he know it was him and Regan? Was that the reason Sean was on this ship? Was he there to get rid of him, then Regan and Christos, so he could get the Dolan property back?

"Got any other family, Sean?" Niko asked. He had to find out more.

"Yeah, a sister, Sara. She's five years older than me, so she'd be thirty-one now. She has a daughter, my niece, Cait. She's fifteen years old already, a pretty little thing with the voice of an angel. Sara was only sixteen when Cait was born. Her father was a married sailor who took advantage of Sara when she was an innocent young girl. Useless bastard who wouldn't take responsibility and left Sara to raise Cait alone. Our father disowned her when she told him she was pregnant. He's from a strict Irish Catholic upbringing and it was too much of a disgrace for his daughter to have a child born out of wedlock, so he abandoned her, and she has been on her own ever since. He won't accept Cait as his granddaughter.

"The sailors that bought the marina are paying Sara to look after things until they take possession. She's been running the pub at the marina for years and helps old McGaffy out with the boat slips. Apparently McGaffy is going to stay on with the new owners, and I'm hoping maybe they'll keep Sara on too. It's hard to raise a kid on your own. I send her money when she needs some help, but she is proud and hates to ask."

Sean's voice took on an aggressive tone. "Gotta get that property back. Nothing will ever be right until that shipyard is back in the family. It's a Dolan blood bond and I have to get it back."

Niko's heart was pounding. Now he knew who Sean was, but did Sean know who he was? He immediately regretted disclosing any details about the passenger smuggling. He knew he was an accomplice, and even if not by choice, he would still be considered guilty. His sailor's logbook contained information on the passengers to use against O'Hare, but now he had recklessly admitted being involved in the smuggling and it could just as easily be used against him. Sean could go to the police when he got to Ireland with information about the galley smuggling and Niko would end up in prison. It would be a way to get rid of him, and then all he had to do was get rid of Regan and maybe Christos too. With them out of the way he could get the shipyard property back. Maybe it wasn't the deckhand that had got on board that was a threat to him, but Sean Dolan.

The oven bell rang. Niko struggled to lift the large leg of pork from the heat of the cast-iron oven and Sean was quick to assist. Vegetables went into the pots to boil, and cornbread and rice pudding pans went in and out of the ovens and on and off the stove at a record-breaking pace.

"Sleeman!" Niko opened the galley door, letting the crewman know they were ready to serve. Sleeman pushed the serving trolley to the door.

There he was again. Mojo. *Why is he always mopping around the galley when there's a whole deck to keep clean?* Almost every evening when he took O'Hare his sandwich, Niko would see Mojo hanging around on the deck and near the galley, and frequently Sloan, as well. The two men had already made Niko uncomfortable, and now with what Sean had said, he wondered which one to fear most.

Once the busy routine of supper and the galley cleanup was complete, Sadeh finally emerged from her cabin. The sea had calmed a few hours previously and released her from the captivity of the bathroom. She commenced with her ritual of the Egyptian herb tea, setting the water on the big galley stove to boil. Niko encouraged her to try some rice pudding. He had made it for the crew, but with her and Christos in mind. Neither had eaten a thing all day. Night had fallen, and Niko was concerned about Christos, who was still hanging over the deck railing at the command of his upset stomach. He went to retrieve him.

"Christos!"

The boy heard a familiar voice in the night. The freezing saltwater slapped against his face as he swayed. He grasped the slippery rail and heaved into the depths of the Mediterranean Sea. Salt burned his eyes and the black of the night fell into the black of the sea, but he felt no fear of being grasped by either, for death could be no worse than this very moment of his life.

"Christos!"

The grasp was neither the sea nor the night, but the strong arms of Niko.

"Come away, son, you will be swept into the sea. The *Autumn Wind*, she will not stop for a man overboard." His voice was firm but comforting, and Christos did not resist the strength of Niko's arms as his godfather pulled him away from the railing, steadied him back to the galley, and pushed a wooden chair under him. Christos dropped his head into his hands and without looking up, wiped his face with the rough cotton towel Sean passed to him.

"Egyptian herb tea with honey, that will settle your stomach." Sadeh touched his shoulder, then set a cup with the steaming brew in front of him.

He had seen her drink the tea most mornings to tame the bouts of sickness that she made every effort to hide. He raised his silver-white face and managed a feeble but grateful "Thank you." Christos was glad to see Sadeh was up and feeling better, and was ashamed of his sickly condition. The steaming tea sent a chill up his spine and comfort to his churning bowels. Niko passed two small bowls and suggested they both try a bit of rice pudding to regain some strength.

Sean squeezed his lanky frame onto the wooden bench at the table and Sadeh slid in beside him. Christos observed them in silence, carefully consuming the rice pudding and sipping at his tea while remembering the night he was put on board and the arrival of Sean and Sadeh. He did not possess the insight of a man, but certainly the instincts, and even at his age he was aware of the seductive beauty of this young woman. The dark hair that framed her face was neatly tucked under her kitchen cap, exposing the full beauty of her tawny skin and the delicate lines of her oval face and slender neck. Long, dark lashes surrounded her black eyes, sheltering the secrets of her inner soul. Her frame was delicate, and she appeared childish and shy, with pouty lips the colour of the autumn wine drunk in the wealthy Moroccan households of his homeland. Obviously, she was not a child, as her protruding stomach revealed she was soon to have one.

Sean was self-declared fighting Irish but seemed a gentle man to Christos. His smile was impulsive and came and went as easily as the air he breathed. A uniquely shaped Celtic Cross hung around his neck, resting on his heart, and was delicately engraved with the word "DOLAN." He never removed it, and as much as Christos wanted to ask its meaning, he did not.

In the evening, when the galley work was done, Sean would sit on the deck on the wooden bench with Sadeh by his side. He would sing softly, his fingers caressing the strings of his harp; lost in thoughts that seemed distant and disturbing. Never close to port, but when the *Autumn Wind* was far out at sea, the melancholy tones of the harp and Sean's gentle voice would drift off through the wind like a call to Ireland from a distant child.

Niko shuffled over and placed a plate of warm scones and honey on the table, then put his arm around Christos's shoulders. "It will pass, and you will grow to love the sea. If the sea is in your blood you cannot fight it."

He hesitated and looked away, then quickly glanced at the others to see if what had passed from his lips had been taken as anything but meaningless chatter. He hoped his slip of tongue had not raised any suspicion of a connection between himself and the young traveller. His comment seemed to have gone unnoticed amid the passing of the scones.

"Christos, are you okay? You are so deep in thought. Are you feeling a bit better?" Niko asked, concern in his voice.

Christos could feel the touch of Sadeh's hand on his arm, and looked into her eyes. He was comforted by both her gentleness and Sean's confidence. He was glad Sean and Sadeh were on board the

Autumn Wind with him. He could feel the strength of Niko's arm on his shoulder. He felt better, and he nodded. "Yes. Thank you for the tea and the pudding, too, Niko."

Christos managed a small but grateful smile as he shook off the confusion of his thoughts. He excused himself and found his way to the comfort of his cabin bed. Lost to the sounds of the sea and the relentless throb of the engines pushing the *Autumn Wind* through the waves, he fell into exhausted sleep.

CHAPTER THIRTEEN

The morning brought calm seas and restored health to both Christos and Sadeh. The ship was travelling at a steady pace along the coast of Egypt, stopping twice at sea to load and unload cargo. The next stop would be Cyprus to drop off cargo and pick up some supplies, and then she would stop at a smaller harbour on the coast of Turkey, where the ship would take on coal and water and some additional cargo would be loaded.

Christos took a few minutes every morning after the breakfast routine to work on his map of the voyage. Sean had taken an interest in the project, and most mornings the foursome would enjoy their coffee and cinnamon roll on the deck while Christos and Sean identified any ships in the area. Unable to help himself, Sean began teaching Christos the fundamentals of ship construction, and Christos enthusiastically absorbed everything Sean said. Sean kept a sketch pad full of engineering drawings for yacht designs, which he found time to work on most days. Sean was exceptionally knowledgeable about ships, and while Christos would record them by the names he could identify through Niko's binoculars, Sean could add the style and type of ship pretty much from a distance.

Just after the stop in Egypt when Sean and Sadeh had boarded, a yacht had appeared on the horizon. It was a smaller personal vessel, painted entirely black, with no obvious identification markings. Christo would search the distant horizon for it each day and mark its whereabouts on the map. Niko had observed Sean watching the yacht with interest on more than one occasion, but he said nothing about it. It was an odd boat and it stayed far away, but the fact that it seemed to be stalking the *Autumn Wind* was beginning to concern Niko.

Two days previous, during evening tea, Niko had let his galley staff know he was going onshore for a short while on the Island of Cyprus to pick up a few galley supplies. "They have a busy dock market and a post office. If there is anyone you might like to write to, I can mail the letters for you. There are a few stores, too. If there are any personal items you need, I can try and get them. Just make a list I can take with me."

Sadeh requested shampoo, hand soap, and lotion, as well as some shaving supplies for Sean. Sleeman gave Niko a letter to his mother in Ireland and a list for a few things requested by Brok, the ship's laundry attendant. Christos enthusiastically provided a thick letter for his father, and in the morning just before Niko disembarked, Sean gave him a letter addressed to Seamus Dolan in Ireland.

Niko knew from the conversation they'd had a few days earlier that this would have been a hard letter for Sean to write. Niko accepted it in silence, but gave Sean a firm pat on the back and a smile to acknowledge the effort and thoughtfulness he knew had gone into writing this letter. His gesture brought Sean to a spontaneous smile.

Niko had struggled for two days to write the letter he carried in his pocket for Regan. Searching to find the words, he had tried to explain how he felt it an unlikely coincidence that a Dolan family member with a grudge had ended up on the *Autumn Wind* at the same time as Regan had purchased the marina, and the uneasy feeling he had about the new deaf-mute deckhand. However, since neither had threatened him or Christos in any way, and Niko had no real proof they intended to, he did not want to alarm Regan. He dismissed his thoughts as paranoia, assured Regan that Christos was fine, and told him where they were and what he thought O'Hare had planned for the rest of the route. They were making good time. They would be through the Strait of Gibraltar by month-end and should be in Ireland a month late, but on schedule.

He added that, despite his concerns, Christos was enjoying the friendship of the young couple travelling in the galley. Niko would mail his letter, but decided he would also see if he could place a call to Regan on the *Seaward* from the coast guard office on the dock at Cyprus. The lady who worked there was helpful and had patched him through to Regan from that office once before. Niko was concerned about what would happen if Regan went to the police without the witness. He just wanted to talk to his friend.

Niko liked the Cyprus dock. It was busy and colourful, a happy place, with music floating through the air from every direction. He thought of Sean and how much he would like the music. Christos and Sadeh would really enjoy the excitement of the dock; he wished he could have brought them all ashore.

Niko gathered the galley supplies and mailed the letters, then dragged his leg a mile along the dock to try and phone Regan. If he could talk to him, he could tell him what was hard to put into words, let him know more about the passengers, and tell him about the logbook and gun and where they were hidden, just in case something did happen. The coast guard office had a note on the door that said they were closed due to a fire and provided a phone number to call for assistance. The man that was working on the building told him the temporary office was on a ship about a half-mile out to sea and a shuttle boat that was located on a private pier about a mile away could take him.

No time, Niko thought. He had to be back at the ship within an hour. Niko thanked the man and dragged his aching leg and disappointment back to the dock.

Sleeman welcomed Niko back on board and started the process of bringing the supplies on to the ship. Kevin Sloan had accompanied

Niko back from the dock on the same fishing supply boat. The man seemed polite but distant. Niko had no interest in associating with him; he was O'Hare's first mate, in charge of dealing with the overall management of the ship, including the engine room. It was the management of the engine room that had caused the disagreement resulting in the abuse O'Hare had inflected on Niko's friend Gavin Connor. Niko respected Gavin, and he respected Sean Dolan enough to trust his expertise as an engineer and builder of this ship, to pass unforgivable judgment on Kevin Sloan for simply holding the position of first mate.

Mojo was also on hand to assist with the bags and boxes Sloan had brought on board that were loaded with personal supplies for the rest of the crew. Niko quickly separated himself from the chaos and Mojo, whom he did not trust. The man seemed well-adapted for a deaf-mute, and although he and Sloan had come on board supposedly as strangers, Niko had observed them together on more than one occasion. Nigeria was said to have an abundance of paid informants, and Niko could not shake the uneasy feeling he had about Mojo, and Sloan, for that matter. He pushed the deadbolt into the doorjamb, securing the privacy of the galley.

Niko hustled into the preparation of supper. He was pleased to see his galley passengers had the vegetables underway, and the sponge cakes he had made that morning were nicely decorated with orange slices set in creamy orange icing; no doubt Sadeh's work. Niko liked her—she was thoughtful and caring. His whole galley staff was helpful and made his job easier instead of harder, which was usually the case with most of the misfits he had smuggled through the galley.

With supper out of the way and the galley clean, Niko unpacked the box with the personal items. He had also bought a basketball, which the merchant had assured him was the real thing. Although it was obviously a vinyl version of the real thing, Sean and Christos were delighted. Sean had engineered a basketball hoop on the galley side of the deck out of one of Niko's old kitchen pots and some fishing net smuggled into the galley by Sleeman. The young men had taken to shooting hoops, with Sadeh and Niko as the cheering section.

Even Brok had taken an interest in the boisterous activity. This was the first time he had shown any interest in cultivating a friendship. He would open the window of the laundry room when he heard the young men on deck and cheer along with Niko and Sadeh. Niko had often wondered what had happened that had caused the loss of his leg, but assumed it was a war injury. Brok seemed sad and withdrawn; the war had done that to a lot of people, and Niko, more than most, understood the challenges of his handicap. He was pleased to see Brok show some interest in the boyish activity.

Sadeh had found the heat the last few days exhausting and had not been resting well. Niko had found a small fan in a dock store, which he bought for her and Sean's cabin, hoping it would make things easier for her, and the couple went off to bed right after evening tea, followed by Christos.

The excitement of the day and the long pointless walk up the dock had left Niko disappointed and physically exhausted, so he followed shortly after.

When the galley was quiet and lit only by the beams of the moon across the night sea, Sean left his bed. He used the large flashlight Niko kept on the cupboard and quietly lifted the map of the world then, inserted his Celtic cross key in the compass hole. The door unlocked. He opened it quietly and entered the communications room.

Sean was sure no one had been in the room for years. He moved along the hallway to the secret storage hold. He slid the door open and shone the light into the space. It was crammed full of crates marked "coffee."

Sean moved into the hold. No wonder the engines were pulling hard; the crates were fully loaded with guns and sacks of drugs. He opened the door at the end of the hallway, exposing a room that housed a fourth engine. He was pleased to see it was still in place and connected to the generator. It had been installed because of the sensitive work the ship was designed to do, but also as an emergency backup. If the main engines went down, it had enough power to get the ship out of sight or safely into harbour for repairs. Sean called the engine "the troll." There was no evidence anyone had been in the room recently. O'Hare had probably worked with the cargo crew of the ship and might have found out about the secret storage hold that way, but only the top military personnel on the ship knew about the troll. Sean took one last look around before closing the door to the secret hold and returning to the galley. Niko was meticulous about the galley, so he made sure everything was as it had been.

He crawled back into bed beside Sadeh. She stirred in his arms.

"Is it there, Sean?" she whispered to him.

"Yeah, it's loaded to the maximum with crates of guns and drugs. It's a heavy cargo."

"I'm glad we know. Now we can tell Investigator Flynn what he needs to know, and we will be safe from my father when we get to Ireland. I love you, Sean." She snuggled close to him.

He kissed her gently and held her close, resting his hand on her swollen stomach, and they drifted off to sleep.

The morning brought another day of sweltering heat. Sean had moved his morning shave out to the deck, leaving the bathroom free so Sadeh could enjoy a cool shower. Sean was pleased with his newly purchased shaving gear, and complimented Niko on his fine taste. Niko was always clean-shaven.

After some carousing on deck, Sean decided it was time for Christos to learn the fine art of how to hold a razor, ultimately resulting in the young man's first shave. Niko listened with amusement from the galley as the conversation evolved from the proper way to hold a razor to the proper way to hold a woman, with some input from Sadeh, who had emerged from the bathroom with the freshness of a spring flower. Sadeh decided the two men were also in need of haircuts, from which Christos emerged nicely trimmed. His boyish haircut gone, the resemblance to Regan was now undeniably visible in his son. Niko looked away to shelter the moisture in his eyes that he knew no one else would understand, only to be abruptly escorted up the narrow stairs by Christo and Sean to Sadeh's snipping scissors. His objection to the necessity of the haircut fell on deaf ears as Sadeh gently trimmed the curly locks that had formed.

It had been so long since Niko had been touched by a woman, her mere closeness was making him uncomfortable. He could feel her swollen stomach touch his arm as her hands moved gently along his neck. He had never known love. The few women who had shared his bed had been paid to do so, leaving him to envy the union Regan had with Cala that had produced Christos, and the obvious love between Sean and Sadeh.

His quiet thoughts were interrupted by the mirror Sadeh held to his face, which presented a softer countenance of the gentle man she and Sean had come to know. Instead of Niko's closely trimmed cut, she had left him with a trimmed, curly version, with a small wisp across his forehead. The new cut brought compliments of how handsome he was, and despite his initial objections, Niko had to admit, at this moment in his life, he did feel handsome.

The nonsense of the deck quickly moved into the preparations for noon lunch and the galley became the usual bustle of activity. As pleased as Niko was to see how well Sean and Christos were getting along, he was equally concerned. The conversation Niko had had with Sean the week before lingered heavily on his mind. He had wanted to talk to Regan, hoping that speaking to his friend would provide more information about the purchase of the marina in Ireland and put his concerns into perspective.

Over the past days at sea, Niko had come to realize Christos was less a boy and more the strong young man he had seen in Regan many years ago, and he felt it might be in Christos's best interest to know there could be danger around him. He decided to tell Christos about the man in the alley that his father had killed in self-defence, and his uneasiness about Mojo the deckhand, but decided not to mention the marina or his concerns about Sean.

Throughout the day, Niko rehearsed over and over in his mind what he would say to Christos. That night, after Sean and Sadeh had gone to their cabin, he poured himself a glass of rum and a small portion for Christos. Niko raised his glass and looked at the young man. "A man's first shave, a man's first taste of rum."

He nodded to the respectful smile of Christos Quinn, then added, "To the friendship of men." They touched glasses.

He studied the young man for a moment, reconsidering his rehearsed thoughts. Christos sipped at the rum, his expression one of determination, defining his newly acknowledged manhood.

"Christos, your father and I have been friends since before we were your age. We grew up together in an orphanage on the island of Greece, not far from here." Christos nodded; he knew this about his father's life. "Your father asked me to take care of you, keep you safe. I think there may be some danger around us, and you should know what happened with your father and me in Tangiers."

Christos's hands were wrapped around the rum glass. He listened with anticipation.

Niko hesitated before he spoke. "That night, your father and I met at the Sea Gull Bar for a drink of rum." He raised his glass thoughtfully to his lips. "We were on our way home, passing through the alley on our way back to the hotel, when we surprised two men who were probably involved in a drug deal. The one man grabbed me and held a pistol to my head, then he pointed it at your father. Your father lunged forward against the man to protect us...and the gun went off. The man died instantly on the ground there in the alley. The man was Ivory, a known drug dealer."

Christos's brows raised in recognition of the name, and his expression intensified.

"You know this name, Christos?"

Christos nodded and swallowed hard. "He comes into the market, but more down by the dock, away from grampa's bakery. The merchants are afraid of him and his father, Nigeria, and no one wants him around the market."

Niko continued. "The man Ivory was dealing with had his back to us and he ran off into the darkness, so neither of us saw his face, but it was certain that he would tell Nigeria what had happened, and Nigeria would come after us to avenge the death of his son. There was another man in the shadows by a brick building, and he ran off, too. From where he was, he would have seen what happened. He was a witness."

Niko watched as Christos's face took on a stunned expression.

"My father killed a man." Christos was appalled and grasping desperately at some means to protect his father. "Did you go to the police?"

Niko hesitated. "No, the police in Tangiers are known to be corrupt, and many are involved with the drug dealers, so we did not know whom we could trust. We couldn't be sure we would get a fair chance to tell what happened; we thought we would just be thrown in jail and Nigeria would come after you and your grandparents.

"We decided to send Abasi and Shima to the country, where they would be safe among the farmers, and you with me on this ship. The passengers the captain takes pay a great deal of money to travel in secrecy and your father paid for you to travel with me. Your father did not sail until the next day at midnight, and he was trying to find the witness."

"Did he?" Christos asked in a desperate tone.

"I don't know, Christos, but he sailed, and is safe on the *Seaward*. It is a big passenger ship and he is the captain. No one can get on those ships without proper identification. We were both supposed to arrive in Ireland at the same time and planned to go together to the police there and tell them what had happened in Tangiers. O'Hare changed the route of the *Autumn Wind* at the last minute, so now we will arrive in Ireland a month later than your father."

Niko took a sip of rum before continuing. "I have written to him twice and he knows where we are. I tried to phone him from the coast guard office on the Cyprus dock, but it was closed. I think O'Hare will stop in Greece and I will try to phone again."

"Do you think he got our letters, Niko?"

"Yes, the mail is a bit unpredictable, but Seaward always gets mail out to the passenger ships. He will have gotten the letters."

"What if he did not find the witness? Will he go to jail?"

"Christos, it was self-defence. Ivory was threatening our lives and your Father was just protecting us. He did not mean to kill the man, it was an accident." Niko deliberately avoided answering the question. "There is a man on this ship, a deckhand. He got on in Egypt with another man the same night Sean and Sadeh boarded. This man worries me. He is supposed to be a deaf-mute, but I am not so sure. Sometimes at night when I take the captain his sandwich, I see him lurking around on deck near the galley. It concerns me. I want to show you something."

Niko rose and, with Christos behind him, pushed open the hidden drawer to expose the gun. "This pistol, Christos, is the one that killed Ivory. I told your father I would throw it into the sea, but I decided to keep it while we are travelling in case we need protection.

"This is my sailor's logbook. It contains information and details of all the voyages on this vessel, including all the passengers that Liam O'Hare has smuggled through this galley while I have been under his command. It is illegal to smuggle passengers; I am obligated to follow his orders and I am breaking the law. I keep this log in case I need to defend myself against him, but I could be jailed for what I'm doing if the coast guard finds passengers on board this vessel while we are at sea."

Christos was silent, his expression intense with worry, but Niko continued. "This is your real identification card, the one that says

The Spirit of the Autumn Wind

Christos Quinn. Abasi and your father had a false one made for you when you were a child. You have your mother's beautiful Spanish features, her black eyes and hair, but your skin is light like your father's. It was easy to hide your heritage as a child, but your father and grandparents knew as you grew older your Caucasian features would become more obvious. Morocco has many old ways, and tradition is slow to accept the mixed cultures that are becoming a part of the times we live in. Your Moroccan identification card states your birth place as Morocco, not Greece, and your name as Bakari, not Quinn. This made it easier for you to live with your grandparents in Tangiers, go to school, and be accepted without prejudice. But this is your real ID card. The captain has the false one. He also has my card.

"There is some money in here as well. If something should happen to me, take all the money and your real ID card, my sailor's logbook, and the gun, and ask Sleeman to help you get off the ship; he can be trusted. Go to the first coast guard office you can find. Show them your ID card and ask to be patched through to Captain Regan Quinn on the *Seaward Angel*. Tell them you are his son and you need help. Your father will come and get you."

Wrapping his arms around Niko, Christos became the boy he still was. "Niko, I don't want anything to happen to you." He was trembling and almost crying.

Niko held him close and patted his back. "We will be fine. I just wanted you to know about what happened in Tangiers, so you could be prepared in case there is danger around us."

Christos nodded, pushing away the first tears Niko had seen the boy cry since he had come on board. "What about Sean and Sadeh?"

"Right now, I want you to keep this between us. I don't think they mean us any harm, but I don't want you to tell them anything we discussed. I am the only one that knows about this secret drawer and what is in it, and now you. It is important it remains our secret."

He put his hand on Christos shoulder and looked into the boy's eyes to make sure he understood. Christos nodded. Niko motioned him back to the table and presented the scones that sat on the cupboard. Christos was pensive and silent as he finished his last sip of rum and went off to his cabin, giving Niko a hug as he left.

Niko was concerned. Perhaps Christos really was too young to understand everything that had happened. Niko always saw his role as godfather to Regan's son as a consideration of respect between the two men, but now Niko understood the true meaning of the role. He had come to love Christos like a son. He had to keep him safe, and the only way he could do that was to let him know he might be in danger.

Niko finished his rum and checked to make sure the galley deadbolt was secure, then shuffled off to the shower and to bed, leaving the galley quiet, lit only by the beams of the moon above the night sea.

CHAPTER FOURTEEN

"Captain, sir, mail for you today."

Regan acknowledged the steward who delivered the daily letters to the bridge. *Finally, letters.* He was relieved. It had been two weeks since they'd left Tangiers. Regan had been persistently reviewing all the navigation maps, looking for the *Autumn Wind*. She was supposed to be ahead of them, but there had been no sign of her, and Regan was concerned. He recognized Niko's handwriting and knew from the thickness of the envelope there was also a letter from Christos.

"Tim, would you take control?" Tim nodded, and slid into Regan's chair.

Regan moved off away from the others and opened the letters. There were two, the first mailed from Egypt a few days after they left, and a second mailed from Cyprus a week later. In the first letter Niko spoke about the last-minute change in the route that the *Autumn Wind* would be taking. He and Christos would arrive in Ireland a month later than planned. Regan read carefully, sharing Niko's concerns about Nigeria looking for them and the missing witness. Niko said Christos was fine, and although he trusted his friend completely to take care of his son, he knew Christos would have been challenged by the abrupt change in his life.

Niko's second letter included details about the passengers who had come on board in Egypt. Regan read and re-read the sentence about the passengers sharing the galley, and Niko's concerns about the marina. Regan was uneasy about this couple, but more worried about the mysterious man with African features that Niko talked about in the letter. A sickening knot was forming in his stomach. Regan was used to receiving letters from his son, and as he read what the boy wrote, he also read what he did not write: the questions he did not ask, the way he really felt about being sent to Ireland without any explanation. Regan knew his actions in Tangiers, however unintentional, had hurt his son and best friend, and now he also knew he had put them in danger.

Regan broke into a cold sweat as rage consumed his soul. He was overcome with anger and disgust with himself. He observed that Tim was comfortably in control, so he slipped out to the bathroom and used the privacy of the stall to compose himself. He had not heard a word about the murder—there was no talk among the seamen on board, and there were times when the whole thing seemed to almost fade away like a bad dream. But he could not forget he had killed a man, the son of a drug dealer. This was not a bad dream, it was real. He had killed a man's son, and just as he would seek revenge for the death of his own child, he knew this brutal man would do the same.

He would be at sea for another two weeks. When the *Seaward* docked in Ireland, he would not go to the police. Instead, he would find the *Autumn Wind* and get his son and friend off that ship no matter what the consequence.

Regan returned to his duties. He re-read the letters over and over in his mind, and the morning turned into afternoon. As with every afternoon, Regan would take his tea on the lower deck in the private lounge reserved for the bridge staff. It gave him a unique perspective of the ocean and an opportunity to observe the passengers strolling on deck and loitering along the railing.

It was time he had always taken alone, just to clear his head and focus on the tasks at hand, at least until the last week. Even with everything that was going on in his mind, he found himself looking for her; Loren, the beautiful Italian woman who had entered his life the first night of the voyage. Her simple touch and gentle smile had quivered his spirit with the same emotions he had felt the first time he saw Cala. When he took his afternoon tea, she would be on the deck, a picture of elegance. He would see her reading in the lounge on the upper deck just off the bridge. She would eat at the same table, directly in his line of vision, at the same time he took his evening meal. She seemed to always be some place close—or was he just looking for her?

Aside from formal acknowledgement when he passed along the interior deck of the ship, Regan never got involved with the passengers. But this time it was different, and he wanted to know who the woman was. With some help from one of the administration clerks in charge of the passenger list, he determined her name was Miss Loren Lombardi, she was born in Italy, she was thirty-two years old, and her occupation was shown as "Writer."

It had been the third day at sea and Regan had been just about to seat himself at his usual table for his evening meal. He had observed her seated in the lounge area just off the dining room, and as with the three previous evenings, she entered just after him. It was almost as though she was watching him from a distance. Had it been a man, Regan might have given this casual but constant interaction some scrutiny, considering the events of the last few days of his life. But he was oblivious to anything but her beauty and flattered by the idea that this mysterious woman might be interested in him.

That evening, he did not seat himself but waited by his table until she appeared. She looked at his table and, seeing that he was absent, surveyed the room. She was looking for him. His confidence swelled, and he stepped forward. "Miss, would you join me for supper?"

Her expression was obvious relief at his presence, replaced immediately by perfect composure. "Yes, I would like that."

"Thank you. I am Captain Regan Quinn." He extended his arm and her delicate hand settled into his and lingered.

"Loren Lombardi." She smiled up at him. "It is a pleasure to meet you."

"Please." He motioned toward his table as he pulled out the chair across from his, and she gracefully seated herself, making sure her dress was perfect. He could not take his eyes off her as he took the chair on the opposite side of the table. It was the first time he had really looked into her eyes. *They were as black as the night, and those long dark lashes; what mysterious secrets did they hide?* She was naturally sensuous yet totally unaware of how beautiful she was.

She seemed a bit nervous in his presence. She let her head drop for a moment, then she looked up and smiled longingly at him. She was enchanting, playing with his heart. He smiled, helpless to do anything else, and unsure what to say next. To his relief, Juan, his usual steward, arrived to serve the table, giving him a moment to regain his composure. He smiled at the sight of the captain with the female guest at his table, confirming to Regan that his inquiry into this passenger's identity had circulated through the crew grapevine.

Regan watched Loren as she listened to Juan's offerings for the meal. She chose the shrimp salad, and requested a cup of lemon tea, with the manners and politeness of royalty. Regan selected the fish fillet and his usual herb tea. She seemed more relaxed now, and her soft voice was toying with the emotions her touch had aroused in him.

"Thank you for the supper invitation. You have a lovely view of the ocean from this table." The words spilled from her lips like a soft sea breeze. She had spoken first, and he was relieved.

"Yes." He nodded, still unable to take his eyes off her. "Where are you from, Miss Lombardi?"

"Please call me Loren. May I call you by your first name, Regan?"

"Yes, of course."

"I wasn't sure. I thought perhaps it might be only proper to refer to you as Captain Quinn."

Regan smiled. "On the bridge I am Captain Quinn, but I am just Regan everywhere else."

She smiled at his casual acknowledgement of his life's achievement. "Have you been a captain long?" she asked.

"About ten years, five with *Seaward*. Where are you from, Loren?" he repeated. He did not want to talk about himself; he did not want this beautiful woman to know anything about who he was, or what he had done, only that he was the captain of the *Seaward Angel*. But he wanted to know everything he could about her.

She looked into his eyes and spoke without hesitation. "I was born in Italy, but grew up in Ireland. My parents were killed in an automobile accident when I was five. I went to live with a family in Ireland and I consider it my home, but I like to vacation on the Italian Coast."

"I'm sorry about your parents, Loren."

"It was a really long time ago, and I don't remember them as my parents. What about you, Regan? Where are your parents?"

"Well…" He hesitated. "I don't have any."

She was amused. "Everyone has parents, Regan."

He smiled at his own comment. "I meant, I never knew them. I grew up in an orphanage in Greece called The Saviours of the Sea. Perhaps you have heard of it?"

She nodded and waited for him to continue.

"It was the only home I ever knew. I left when I was sixteen and started working on the docks, then the cargo ships and, well, here we are. I think of the sea as my home."

A genuine smile settled on his soft, tempting lips. Loren liked this Regan Quinn; he was honest, relaxed and very handsome. "So, no wife and kids then?" she asked.

"I was married for a short while seventeen years ago. My wife, Cala, was killed in an automobile accident."

"I'm sorry, Regan, about your wife."

He watched her closely. Her condolences seemed sincere, like she truly understood the magnitude of a personal loss, and she seem genuinely interested when she asked, "Did you have any children?"

Regan hesitated for a moment. "We were only married a couple of years."

He had skillfully avoided answering the question. He had no intention of telling her about Christos or disclosing any personal information about himself. He liked this woman, but she would pass through his life like every other one since Cala. She was beautiful, and for now she would do nicely to help keep his mind off what lay ahead in Ireland.

"And you, Loren? Have you ever been married?"

She shook her head. "No."

She had decided long ago to make her career her life. Being part of Jimmy Flynn's elite investigation team involved her in exciting assignments, and she liked the travel and adventure. She had been left emotionally scarred by two failed relationships and had resolved not to fall in love again. This was the part of her life she kept to herself, and she was most certainly not going to discuss it with this man, whose life was entangled with drug dealing and murder.

She looked away, and Regan quickly realized this line of questioning was off limits, so he immediately changed the subject. "Then you will be our guest on the *Seaward Angel* all the way back to Ireland?"

"Yes," she replied.

"Is this your first trip on board a passenger ship?"

"Yes, it is."

"And have you been enjoying the voyage so far?"

"Yes, very much so."

"And will you be taking the shore excursions?"

"Yes, I hope to."

She did not want to answer any more of his questions; she was there to ask him questions, but she found herself infatuated with the man and kept helplessly responding.

"What do you do for work…I mean, when you're at home in Ireland?" Regan quickly clarified his clumsy question.

"I'm a writer."

"And what do you write about?"

He seemed genuinely interested, and she found herself answering yet another question.

"People, mostly." She smiled and added, "Do you like to read?"

"Yes, but mostly books about the sea."

She was watching him closely, hoping his need for information was finally satisfied. No such luck, so she decided to just let him continue with his intriguing interrogation, hoping for a chance to do the same.

"Do you have any published books?"

Regan was curious to know how a woman with seemingly casual employment could afford the cost of passenger ship travel.

"No," she responded without hesitation. *By the Sea* revealed the story of her life. She was undercover and she would not give him any information that could expose her real identity. She smiled. "I write, but mostly I do research for established writers."

She looked up as Juan arrived with the food. She was relieved. She did not want to talk about herself anymore. She was afraid her infatuation with Regan Quinn would cloud her professional judgment.

Over supper, she asked him about his work. He told her about the *Seaward Angel* being the largest passenger ship in the waters, and the voyages he had made with her, but did not mention Tangiers. She asked him where he lived when he was not at sea. He told her about an apartment he kept in Ireland, but again, did not mention Tangiers. She had found out very little about her assignment, but she had managed to get his attention and he had asked her to join him for supper. But she needed to find out more. She was a special investigator, and she was there to find out what Captain Regan Quinn had to do with the murder in Tangiers and drug smuggling. Was he interested enough to ask her again?

Regan looked at his watch. "I do need to get back to the bridge."

"Of course. Thank you for an enjoyable supper, Captain Quinn." She acknowledged his official position, as it was obvious from his comments about the ship that he was proud of his achievements.

As Loren reached for her handbag and prepared to go, he reached across the table and placed his hand on hers. "Loren, I wonder if you might join me for tea tomorrow at four in the bridge lounge on the deck. It's private for the bridge staff, and I take my tea there each afternoon. I would like to see you again." He was both surprised and frightened by his own impulsive gesture.

She let her hand linger under his for a moment before responding. "Yes, that would be lovely. Shall I meet you there at four, then?"

"Yes, I will watch for you." He squeezed her hand ever so gently, then released her.

"Good evening, Captain Quinn." She smiled mischievously. "Until tomorrow."

CHAPTER FIFTEEN

"Loren." Regan rose as she entered the bridge lounge. He had been re-reading the letters from Niko and Christos when she arrived, and he quickly tucked them into his jacket pocket when he saw her. He reached for her hand. "You look like a summer flower, lovely as usual."

"Thank you, Captain Quinn." She referred to him as Captain Quinn when she was teasing, and Regan the rest of the time.

Every afternoon for the past week she had joined him for afternoon tea and supper. This afternoon he was especially pleased to see her. His mind had been in turmoil since reading his letters from Niko and Christos, and just seeing her brought some calm to his emotions.

"You have mail, Regan, how nice." Loren's trained investigator's eyes never missed a detail. She wore a soft white sundress and had just removed the matching floppy sunhat.

She looks beautiful, Regan thought as she seated herself. "Yes, the cost of living follows me everywhere. Seaward makes sure I get my bills on time."

She laughed. The steward, Juan, tapped lightly on the door, then entered with a tray of tea and sweets. "Good afternoon, Captain, Miss Lombardi." He nodded respectfully to them, then set the tray on the table in front of the lounge sofa where they were seated. "Nice treats from the cook today, enjoy."

"Thank you, Juan," Regan responded.

Loren chose a soft chocolate treat from the tray. Regan noticed she always chose chocolate from the daily selection. Cala had liked chocolate.

Loren made small talk about the rough seas, but her mind was on the letters. The man was like an island. He never spoke of friends or family or anything that was not related to his career or adventures at sea. She did not want to disappoint Jimmy. If he said there was a connection between Quinn and the cook on the *Autumn Wind*, there had to be some clue that would help figure out what they were up to.

The ship pitched and rolled with the waves, and so did the tea tray. Regan grabbed for the tray as it slid off the table, but not before drowning his jacket and pants in tea.

Loren lost her balance while reaching to rescue the treats, leaving a selection of crumbs on her dress.

"Well, aren't we a sorry sight." Regan laughed, surveying the damage. "Come, let's go to my cabin. It's close by. You can wipe that off your dress before it stains, and I need to change my uniform before I go back to the bridge."

She tucked her arm in his, and he led the way to his cabin. It was larger than hers but laid out the same, except for a small desk along one wall. He handed her a dampened wash cloth. "Maybe if you wipe that off it will save your dress?"

He removed his soiled jacket and laid it on the bed. "Excuse me, I will change in the bathroom." He secured a clean uniform from the closet and closed the bathroom door.

Loren noticed his second room key on the desk. She could come back to his cabin when he went to the bridge and read the letters. She slipped the key into her purse and replaced his room key with hers, so he would not notice a change. She would sneak back, read the letters, and then change the keys back.

The Spirit of the Autumn Wind

She appeared to still be working on the details of tidying her dress when he reappeared in his clean uniform. "You look handsome, as always, Captain Quinn." Her intent was to make him feel special and distract him from his jacket that lay on the bed, and he *was* stunningly handsome.

"Thank you, Miss Lombardi. And you are as beautiful as ever."

She smiled at him flirtatiously, to make sure his attention was on her.

"Is the dress okay?"

"Yes, not too serious."

"Then best we go. I'm due back on the bridge." He put his arm on her lower back as they left his cabin, and she loved the way he touched her. "Loren, will you join me this evening for supper? Hopefully the sea will have settled down by then and we can keep things on the table."

"Yes." She laughed softly at his comment.

He gazed into her eyes and touched her face. "Thank you. Sorry about your dress. I hope it didn't stain."

"It's fine, I'm sure, but I will go to my cabin and find something else for supper this evening."

They reached the public area and their hands parted slowly as they went separate directions.

Loren waited a few minutes, then made her way back to Regan's cabin. She made sure no one was in the hallway and used the key to enter. His jacket lay on the bed. She removed the envelopes from the inside pocket. Two of the letters were from Niko Mararious, mailed a week apart. Loren knew he was the cook on the *Autumn Wind*.

Niko's words expressed anguish about Nigeria, and he wanted to know if Regan had found the witness from the alley, and if he had not, what would happen when they went to the police in Ireland? He spoke of two new passengers in the galley who had boarded in Egypt. One had a family attachment to a marina property in Ireland. He was bitter and angry, and Niko was concerned he might be a threat.

He also wrote about two other crew members who had boarded in Egypt. They seemed to be worrying him. He wrote fondly of Christos and said he was doing fine and adjusting well to the voyage, and asked about Abasi and Shima. *Who are they?* she wondered. He laid out the anticipated route of the *Autumn Wind*, expressing his frustration about the added month at sea. It was signed, "To the Friendship of Men, Niko."

There were letters from Christos, who, without a doubt, was Regan Quinn's son. He referred to Niko as his godfather and said he missed his grandparents and school. Why had Regan not mentioned having a son?

There was also a letter from a law office in Sona Bay verifying the title registration of the purchase of a marina property in Suaimhneas Cove in the names of Regan Quinn and Niko Mararious. *A marina would be good cover for smuggling activities.*

Loren put the envelopes back in the jacket pocket, then searched the drawers, closet, under the mattress, and anywhere he might possibly be hiding a gun or drugs. She was sure he would not take either to the bridge—his job was far too important to him to take that risk—but there was no gun or drugs to be found. She was careful to make sure everything was just as it had been, exchanged the keys, and left.

Regan's son's name was Christos, and Loren had seen that name before. But where?

She returned to her cabin and checked her notes and the information on Quinn that Jimmy had sent. There it was. Christos. Regan's first wife's maiden name was Christos. No family located. Why had this child not come up when Jimmy searched? Loren added the details of the letters to her notes.

She had new evidence, so before Loren met Regan, she went to the security office and had Emanuel Garcia place a call to Jimmy. It was nice to hear his voice, and Jimmy was happy to hear from her and pleased with the new information.

The Spirit of the Autumn Wind

"These are important pieces of the puzzle, girl," he said. "Quinn and Mararious know they are in danger. We know Quinn picked the boy up at an apartment above a bakery stall in the market, and now that we know it is his son and not just another passenger, it makes more sense. This witness he mentioned from the alley was probably one of Nigeria's paid thugs, and likely the same man that terrorized the market looking for the captain and trashed the bakery. The people that ran it have disappeared. We need to find out who that stall belonged too and how they are involved in this. They could be the grandparents, and if they are, what happened to them?

"Niko doesn't have to worry about the new crewmen, they are UCs I put on the ship in Egypt, but now that I know that kid is Quinn's son, I need to get word to them right away; Nigeria is after these two and the Autumn Wind is an easy target. I'll see what I can find out and meet with you in two days when the ship docks for a shore excursion in Portugal. I'll be a fellow tourist. We can meet and have lunch and I'll update you on the findings."

"Okay, Papa. It will be nice to see you."

"You too, girl. Love you."

"Love you, too."

It was typical for Jimmy to arrange a meeting with his UCs during an investigation. Jimmy understood it was hard to work undercover and that every one of his investigators was at risk of becoming too involved in the case to maintain the professional perspective needed to secure the evidence against the suspect they were assigned to. It was his way of gauging the personal wellbeing of his investigators and adding his viewpoint to the information they were gathering.

Loren chose a soft pink dress for her supper with Regan. She felt guilty that she had spied on him, entered his room, and read his private letters. She wanted to look extra nice, as if that was somehow a way to say she was sorry. She hated the way going behind his back made her feel. She was there to do a job, but with each personal encounter she had with the man, it was becoming more difficult to keep her feelings and professionalism from getting all tangled up. She just wanted to get to the bottom of this, get the information Jimmy needed, and get Quinn out of her life.

Regan could not take his eyes off her, and had she worn this pink dress for any reason other than guilt she would have been especially flattered.

"Loren, tomorrow I have a day off. I don't have to return to my bridge duties until the next night. We have a relief captain on board until our port stop in Spain. He will sail with Tim tomorrow and me the following day, so Tim and I will each get twenty-four hours off duty. I was wondering if we might have supper together on my balcony, then go dancing in the ballroom. You do like to dance?"

Her heart was giggling like a schoolgirl. She loved to dance, and most every evening since she had boarded, she had sat inconspicuously on the deck watching the ladies in their elegant evening gowns come and go from the ballroom with their finely dressed escorts. The music of the orchestra would drift across the deck and she would close her eyes and imagine herself twirling around the dance floor with a handsome Prince Charming, who seemed to keep relentlessly appearing in her vision as Captain Regan Quinn.

She hesitated. What had been a harmless fantasy had just become a dangerous reality. She was undercover, she had used her charm to get his attention and expose the secrets he was hiding, and the evidence she had found tied him to murder and smuggling. He was not Prince Charming, he was a dangerous man. *Had he found out who she was or that she had read his letters? Was he just trying to get her alone, so he could murder her or throw her overboard?*

This wasn't the first time Loren had been undercover or the first time she'd felt threatened. Jimmy had Garda officer Garcia on board with her and two UCs on the Autumn Wind. Jimmy would have someone watching the bakery stall and the Sea Gull Bar, and the coast guard would be on the look-out for Nigeria's yacht. Jimmy Flynn's investigation was like a finely tuned machine, and he was waiting to see which gear moved first. He was counting on his UCs and she wouldn't let him down. She had been playing with Regan Quinn's emotions and if she backed away now, he might get suspicious. Besides, she had new information from the letters, so there were more questions she could ask. He probably just found a woman on every voyage to spend time with and she was flattering herself thinking it was anything else. He was just an assignment, anyway, and she really wanted to go dancing.

"As we sail closer to Ireland we will be getting into the cooler weather. The sea along the Portugal coast is calm and the evenings warm." Regan was waiting for her answer and seemed to be selling her on the idea. *She would let Garcia know she was dining in the Captain's cabin. She had a small pistol that fit in an evening bag and she knew how to use it.*

"Yes, Regan, that sounds enchanting. I do like to dance and joining you for supper on your balcony would be lovely."

"Good." He reached across the table and squeezed her hand. "At afternoon tea, Juan will bring you the menu for supper, so he knows what to bring to my cabin. Walk with me to the bridge."

He took her hand as they left the table, placing it on his arm, and before they parted, he raised her face to his and kissed her gently. She did not resist.

That night her dreams were a restless tangle of memories from her failed relationships, drifting through thoughts of Regan Quinn; his gentle kiss, the warm touch of his hand on her face and his smile that suddenly turned to a grimace behind a large, ivory-handled pistol and startled her from her sleep in a terrorizing nightmare.

At afternoon tea, she did not take her eyes off him. He was handsome in his elegant dark-blue uniform with white and golden shoulder badges. He removed his cap, setting it off to the side as he always did. His black eyes were focused on her. *What is he planning?* she wondered.

Juan arrived with the usual afternoon tea, sweets, and the menus for supper. She chose the beef dish and the chocolate mousse dessert, a choice which brought a secretive smile to Regan's lips.

Loren had brought only one evening gown. It was soft pink chiffon with lace shoulder straps and a scooped back. She had bought it for a police awards banquet that spring and Jimmy had said she looked ravishing. She had not had an opportunity to wear it since that event.

She lay the gown on the bed, making sure every accessory, right down to her underwear, was perfectly coordinated. Loren pulled her hair up off her shoulders, securing it with a comb, and looked in the mirror at the face of her mother. She had only one picture of her parents, a professionally painted portrait that Jimmy had manage to salvage before the Lombardi assets were sold. In it, her mother wore a pink lace evening gown and her hair was pulled up off her shoulders, exposing her feminine neck and the beautiful lines of her face. As a teenager, Loren had spent hours perfecting the technique of styling her hair to the exactness of the portrait. Now, standing there in her gown, looking at herself in the mirror, she realized that not only did she look like her mother, but her life was as filled with lies and secrets as her mother's had been.

She tucked her pistol in her pink hand bag and walked apprehensively down the hall to Captain Regan Quinn's cabin. She knocked gently on his cabin door.

Regan stood for a moment, rendered breathless by the beautiful woman that was before him. "Beautiful, my darling."

"Thank you." She smiled, hoping he could not hear the pounding of her heart.

"Come." He took her hand and guided her into his cabin. She could see a table was set up on the balcony.

He looked longingly at her. "Juan brought us wine; a red and a white, I wasn't sure which you would enjoy. I don't drink in public on the ship, so I don't get any opportunities to enjoy the liquor offerings of the dining room. I left it up to the cook to choose; they know best about these things, and he is suggesting the red with the beef." He sounded almost apologetic.

"Yes, that's fine." Her smile was spontaneous, but she did not take her eyes off him. He seated her and poured the wine. Regan Quinn was in every way a gentleman, but obviously not a monk; he knew exactly how to make a woman feel special, and that was what worried her.

His uniform jacket lay on the bed with his tie, and he wore a white uniform shirt with short sleeves. The top button of his shirt was loose, revealing dark chest hair. His muscular arms were exposed. She was sexually aware of the handsome man that stood before her, but as much as she wanted to reach out and touch him, she wanted, just as much, to run away. He was a murderer who hid his lies behind his gentle manners and captain's uniform. She had to stay alert. She inconspicuously touched the pistol in her evening bag to jar herself back to reality.

Regan had mentioned the cook was knowledgeable about wine. Loren saw it as an opportunity to see what else he had to say about cooks. "You know the cook on the ship well?"

"The galley master is Paulo. He has been with the ship four of the five years that I have been. Before that another. Cooks work hard, so they are always looking for a better-paying job. The best cooks come from Greece and Italy."

Knowing he had acknowledged her heritage, he raised his glass to hers and smiled as he seated himself. A knock came to the door, Regan acknowledged, and Paulo entered.

"Good evening, Captain."

"Good evening, Paulo."

"Good evening, Miss."

"Sir." Loren wasn't sure how to address the galley master.

Paulo began setting the food on the table and made sure every detail of the service was perfect before bidding them good evening.

"Paulo takes very good care of you." Loren was hoping the conversation might lead Regan to mention his friend, the cook on the *Autumn Wind*.

He smiled mischievously. "I get a few privileges as captain. Please begin while everything is hot."

"The food is excellent, Regan, and this is a beautiful ship."

Regan nodded appreciatively; he obviously had a personal attachment to the *Seaward Angel*. "So, Loren, you have been enjoying your voyage so far?"

"Yes, absolutely. I plan to take the shore excursion at Portugal. Do you get a chance to go ashore, Regan?"

"Yes, on some trips, but not this one. The captain has lots of things to look after." There was nothing he wanted more than to spend the day on shore with this seductive woman that sat across from him. He could go, he could get a few hours off, especially with the relief captain on board, but he could not leave the safety of the ship; he could not take the chance with Nigeria out there. If he was on the ship, he was safe.

"You work very hard." Her concern seemed genuine, and he liked the idea that he wasn't alone, and that she cared.

But what she cared about was what Regan Quinn was doing when the ship was in port. Was he lying? Was he meeting seedy characters in dark alleys and making drug deals where the ship stopped? He was smart. Was he the brains behind this whole drug-smuggling operation? No one would suspect the captain of the Seaward Angel.

"The smaller cargo ships, do they have large galleys and dining rooms too?" she asked.

"Not like this. Most have smaller crews and it's more of a crew cafeteria. The men on a tramp ship work very hard for lower pay. They load and unload lots of cargo, and it is arduous work, so the galley master is very important. The deck crew will stay on a ship with a good cook that feeds them well. There are still a few small tramp ships sailing in these waters."

He stopped talking for a moment to enjoy his food and a swallow of wine. "Along the coast of Italy there is a small private harbour called Sunset Harbour. Have you heard of it?"

Loren nodded. She knew exactly where Sunset Harbour was, because it was on her property. She remembered telling Regan she enjoyed vacationing on the Italian Coast, but she had not mentioned her cottage or Sunset Harbour. She wondered if his familiar knowledge of the area was just because he was a sailor, or if it was because he knew who she was, and her heart throbbed as she listened for a clue while he spoke.

"It has been closed to the public for a few years and is leased to the coast guard. The smaller cargo tramp ships used to anchor there, the *Destiny* and the *Seabreeze*, but now they have to use the big harbours, and it is expensive, so there are not many smaller cargo ships in these waters anymore."

...and the Autumn Wind, she thought. Again, he had not mentioned that ship, but he *had* mentioned Sunset Harbour, and she had no idea why. *Maybe he had just slipped up and revealed the other tramp ships were part of his drug operation too, or maybe he didn't care, because he was going to kill her anyway.*

She couldn't lose her focus. She had to stay alert, so she pushed the thoughts from her mind and changed the subject. "It is a lonely life, the captain of a ship. Do you not wish for a home and family some day?" She was hoping he would talk about his life with his wife, the son he never mentioned, and the property in Ireland he owned.

"Perhaps someday, but this is my life now. And you, Miss Lombardi?" he asked playfully.

He was smart, this Regan Quinn. As skillfully as she had woven her questions in between the servings and the wine, he had just as skillfully not answered them. He would never let the conversation go too far, never really tell her anything. He had successfully managed to manoeuvre around her questions without telling her a thing about the cook, the *Autumn Wind*, or his personal life, and again he had skillfully turned her questions into his. He was watching her, waiting for her answer; then he reached across the table and squeezed her hand and she felt helpless to the control he had over her heart.

"I like my life. I'm happy. I do not wish to marry." Her tone was firm.

His lingering eyes reflected the disappointment he felt in his heart and it made her uneasy. She was losing her composure; she dropped her head and closed her eyes, then looked up and smiled. He took a moment to release her hand, then touched her face.

Regan knew, as with the first night they shared a meal, that he had asked a question that held a secret to a part of Loren Lombardi's life that she would never share.

She helped Regan put the dirty dishes in order on the table. He adjusted the legs to a trolley state and pushed it to the hallway for Juan to collect later. She stood on the balcony with her back to the whispering sea, watching as he buttoned his shirt, aligned his tie, and put on his tailored captain's jacket. He made no effort to attack her and showed no interest in pushing her overboard, so she took a moment to freshen up while he closed the window to the balcony and shut off his cabin lights. As he placed her hand on his arm and escorted her down the hallway from his cabin to the ballroom, Loren noticed Garcia walking a few feet ahead of them, and she knew his security surveillance that evening was planned to keep her safe.

The doors to the magnificent ballroom swung open, and music drifted around the silhouetted figures of couples dancing in the romantically lit room. He pulled her into his strong arms and waltzed her into love. For the next three hours she was lost in a fantasy; no longer Loren Lombardi, special investigator, but Cinderella at the ball with Prince Charming.

As the orchestra was playing the last waltz, her gown swished across the floor and Loren realized her real-life fantasy was about to end and that, just like Cinderella, when the ball was over, she had to return to reality.

Regan smiled adoringly at her as they left the ballroom. "Did you enjoy the evening, Loren?"

"Yes, very much. You are a fine dancer."

"Well, I have my wife to thank for that. She loved to dance, so she made sure I did too."

The music would not stop playing in Loren's head; she was still there in her gown, twirling across the floor with handsome Captain Regan Quinn.

"Are you okay, Loren? You're quiet."

"Yes, fine. The ballroom is beautiful, and it was just such a lovely evening."

"Well, it doesn't have to end. I had Juan bring brandy for a nightcap."

Loren knew she should just refuse, say she was tired, but he was already pushing open the door of his cabin. The room was dimly lit by the moon and he did not let go of her hand as he guided her toward the balcony and opened the access window. *She could feel the pace of her heart quicken, but then he released her hand and she stepped out into the cool ocean air.* He removed his jacket and tie and loosened the buttons on his shirt as he joined her, and passed her a small crystal glass filled with warm liquor. They sipped in silence, looking out into the night, watching the moonbeams dancing in the warm wind that drifted across the waves.

He put his arm around her waist.

Where is my gun? Where did I put my evening bag? She suddenly realized she had set it down on his desk on the other side of the balcony window. She was in danger and she had nothing to protect herself. She could feel him gently pulling her to him, every inch of his masculine frame pushing against her. *He is going to kill me now, throw me overboard,* she thought as she pulled away and his arms tightened around her, but he did not attempt to hurt her. Instead, he put his lips on hers and loosened her hair, so it fell around her shoulders. She could feel her gown tumbling down around her feet and his bare chest against her bare breasts, and the only thing that was in danger was her heart.

He picked her up in his arms, not to throw her overboard, but to carry her to his bed. He laid his naked body on hers. She could feel the gentleness of his hands running down her thighs, caressing her, and she surrendered to him completely. Time stood still, and she fell in love. He relaxed, sexually exhausted, in her arms; then kissed her and pulled her against his chest.

They lay in the darkness, quiet and naked. The only things not exposed between them were the lies and secrets.

Loren woke up in Regan Quinn's arms. The sun rose across the water, and a warm ocean breeze drifted through the cabin. She was happy, but as much as she wanted what she had at this very moment, she knew it was just as much a fantasy as the night they had just spent together. Yes, there were details about Captain Quinn that didn't add up, but there was also evidence of his guilt, and that wasn't fantasy, it was reality; he was a suspect in a murder and smuggling case. Jimmy had only one rule: don't get personally involved with your assignment. She had broken Jimmy's ultimate rule and she had let herself get romantically involved with Regan Quinn.

She wanted to remove herself from his arms, get focused on what she was there for, forget about where she was and what she had done; get back in control. But he stirred out of his sleep as she moved in his arms, and he was having no part of her removing herself from his bed. His lovemaking under the morning sun was as mesmerizing as it had been under the light of the moon, and Loren realized she was no longer in control of anything—her heart was.

Regan had breakfast brought to his cabin, wrapped her in his shirt, and seated her on the balcony. He sat shirtless across from her, the warm ocean breeze surrounding his strong shoulders. His wavy hair, which was usually neatly combed, fell in loose curls along his forehead. His black chest hair descended seductively to his naval and glistened in the sun. Loren was momentarily aroused, consumed with the memory of the sensuous feel of his masculine body against hers, and she lowered her head to hide the flush that had come to her cheeks.

"Loren." His hand was on hers. "Are you alright?"

"Yes." She looked up to his tender, amused smile and the touch of his hand as he ran his fingers along her face and studied her eyes. "Yes, I'm fine."

"You are a beautiful woman, Loren."

It was as though he was reading her mind and was silently pleased that his half-naked body was sexually appealing to her.

He let his hand drop and she focused on meticulously spreading peanut butter on her toast, using the exercise to find her composure. "Thank you, Captain Quinn."

She looked up to his relaxed smile as he dug into the bacon and eggs on his plate. Over breakfast, he provided details of the rest of the voyage and some information on her planned shore excursion in Portugal.

They strolled on the deck, then made love. They enjoyed tea in the bridge lounge, then made love, and before supper Regan changed into his uniform. They shared their evening meal together in the dining room and she walked him to the bridge.

The next day, they took afternoon tea in his cabin and made love. They were completely relaxed with each other; the personal barriers between them were gone, but not the secrets. The following day she was to meet Jimmy, and she couldn't let him know she had lost control of her part of his investigation.

She dressed in the morning and went over and over her notes, looking for some small detail that would prove Regan Quinn was not a murderer and smuggler, but Captain Regan Quinn, the man she had fallen in love with. She tucked her notes in her handbag, put on a sunhat that matched her white eyelet sundress and her sandals, and put on her sunglasses, hoping that hiding her eyes would hide what she had done.

Regan watched from the railing of the bridge as Loren disembarked. The morning breeze played with her hair and she looked beautiful, fresh like a flower, and he wanted to be with her. The travel consultants from the ship were gathering the passengers waiting for the tour bus to take them on the shore excursion.

A man appeared from within the crowd and positioned himself next to Loren. Regan had not seen the man on board, but he really had only been paying attention to one passenger. The man was head and shoulders above her, and his hair was lightly grey and closely trimmed. He was casually dressed. Regan watched as they spoke in what seemed a friendly manner, probably just discussing the planned day of sightseeing ahead.

He was in love with Loren Lombardi, and it suddenly occurred to him that she might not be in love with him. Maybe this was just a game to her; how many men did she have in her life? She was an attractive seductive woman and already in her thirties—of course, she had men in her life. He had let things get out of control. He would never be able to give her the life he wanted to. He had murdered a man and he had no way to prove it was an accident. He had not been able to find the witness and it was nearly impossible he ever would.

When he got to Ireland, he would fly back to the Mediterranean and get Christos and Niko off the *Autumn Wind*, so at least they would be safe. Then he would go back to Ireland, confess, and face the consequences. His life would be over, he would never sail again, he would probably lose the marina and spend the rest of his life in jail. He could never have Loren Lombardi in his life, and she would never want him if she knew what he had done. He should never have let himself fall in love with her. He would just let her walk away when they got to Ireland.

"Loren, girl, you do look lovely today. I believe this passenger ship travel agrees with you."

Loren laughed. "Thank you."

She wanted to reach up and give Jimmy a kiss on the cheek like she had done since she was a child, but she was undercover and they both knew the rules. The passengers crowded into the bus and Loren took the window seat next to Jimmy. She could see Regan standing by the railing of the bridge and she could feel him watching her. She looked away quickly as the bus pulled away and groaned down the narrow street.

"Let's get off here." Jimmy took her hand, and she followed him down the aisle between the seats. Jimmy discreetly showed his Garda badge to the driver, who stopped so they could get off. They took a seat in a small outside bar.

Jimmy reached across the table and took her hands.

"So, are you okay? Take off your glasses, girl, let's have a look at that pretty face," he said playfully.

Loren removed her glasses. She really did not want Jimmy to look into her eyes; she was afraid he would be able to see that she had broken his rule, that she had got involved with her assignment, and worse yet, that she was in love. Jimmy knew her well and he was perceptive. He studied her face and his eyes lingered for a moment, as if he was about to say something, then the waiter interrupted with the menu.

They decided on what to have for lunch. She did not want Jimmy to ask her any personal questions. She felt like a schoolgirl who had got caught by her father sneaking out on a date, so she quickly began questioning Jimmy. "So, were you able to find anything out about the cook and the son?"

"Yeah, those were good leads. Cala Christos was raised as Cala Bakari. Her mother, Shima, is Moroccan, but her father, Abasi Bakari, was originally from Spain; his given family name was Basil Christos. Quinn and his wife gave the boy his mother's family name. Abasi and Shima Bakari are the boy's grandparents. They ran the market bakery where Quinn picked up his son."

"Well, now we know who Abasi and Shima are," Loren interjected. "Are they still in Tangiers? Do you think they might be involved in this smuggling, too?"

Jimmy's slight shrug reflected his indecision. "They disappeared the same time as Quinn, the cook, and the kid, like they were all on the run, so it is possible they are involved. Nigeria usually had a paid thug with his son to protect him, so that is probably who trashed their bakery and likely the same man they referred to as a witness from the alley. We still have not been able to locate them, so maybe Nigeria's thug found them. What's your take on Regan Quinn?"

"He seems well-liked and sticks to the same routine every day. He never goes anywhere on the ship other than the dining room and tea lounge, his cabin, and the bridge, so I don't know where he would have drugs hidden. It's unlikely it would be the bridge. There's a whole navigation crew working up there and he balances his shift with another captain he calls Tim. He seems to really like his work and I doubt he would risk losing his job, especially if he has a son to look after. Has Garda Officer Garcia found anything unusual on the ship, any sign of contraband?"

"Nothing so far. He is embedded with the security officers, so he has access to the entire ship, including the bridge. It is a busy area of the ship and, like you, he feels it is unlikely Quinn would hide drugs there, but he is keeping a close eye on the activities of the ship's crew, Quinn, and his second-in-command, too."

"Quinn has asked me to join him for supper a few times and tea in the bridge lounge in the afternoons, occasionally." Loren said, watering down the truth and struggling to make their encounters sound casual and less personal. "That's how I got the lead on the letters. The tea got spilled on his uniform and my dress when we were in the lounge. He was due back on the bridge and his cabin was close by, so he suggested we go there so he could change his uniform, and I could clean my dress. It was a chance to see his cabin," she added quickly, like more justification was needed. "I saw his key, switched it with mine, and went back and read the letters." Jimmy grinned at her craftiness but did not interrupt. "I looked everywhere in his cabin for the gun and drugs. I couldn't find anything and as far as I can tell, he has not left the ship since we sailed."

Jimmy was listening to her carefully and watching her just as carefully. "So, you have gotten to know him personally, then?"

"Yes." Loren straighten her posture and worked at sounding professional. "I made a point of getting his attention and he asked me to have supper with him. I ask questions whenever I'm around him. He's a smart man; he does not talk about his personal life, just general stuff. One thing seems odd, though."

Jimmy motioned to the waiter for a second glass of wine, then settled back in his chair.

"We were talking over supper and I was asking questions about cargo ships, trying to get him to mention the *Autumn Wind* or the cook. He mentioned Sunset Harbour and it being used by the small tramp ships, specifically the *Destiny* and *Seabreeze*, but he never mentioned the *Autumn Wind*." Loren paused before disclosing her thoughts. "Maybe those ships are involved in this too. It seems odd he knows the harbour, as it's been closed for years, and when I quizzed him about cooks and their role on the ships, he never mentioned his friend, and he has never said he has a son."

Jimmy straightened up. "Well, he knows that cook, Niko Mararious. We know they both grew up in Saviours of the Sea Orphanage in Greece, and it seems they were there at the same time, and good friends too. I spoke to the administrator at the orphanage, a Father Benedict. He has been there for years and remembered both boys. Said Niko got bullied a lot because of his handicap and Regan looked out for him and kept the other boys from picking on him. He said they left the orphanage together at sixteen and went to work on the docks."

Loren added her thoughts as she took a sip of her wine. "The boy, Christos, referred to Niko as his godfather in the letter. Obviously, they have remained friends over the years."

She was sorting details in her mind as she spoke to Jimmy, thinking out loud. "Somehow Quinn just doesn't seem like a guy that murders people or runs drugs."

Jimmy was stroking the brim of his glass with his thumb. "Loren, are you okay with this Quinn? You haven't gotten too close to him, have you?"

Loren sipped her wine, trying to avoid looking into Jimmy's eyes. "Everything's fine, Jimmy."

"You sure?"

She knew from his tone he was having doubts. "Yes." She worked at responding casually, quickly returning to the discussion about the case. "Jimmy, why do you think there was the mention of going to the police in Ireland? I mean, if he murdered Ivory, you'd think he just want to disappear, not go tell the police."

Jimmy seemed to have considered the matter already. "Nigeria is a brutal guy, and if I had him after me, I might choose the lesser of two evils myself. Quinn is safe on his ship, but the minute he steps off, he's fair game, and it sure seems like Nigeria's after him. I get not going to the police in Morocco—they make no effort to hide the corrupt nature of their activities, and it's common knowledge on the streets that some of the Moroccan police force are on Nigeria's payroll and nothing more than thugs that he pays to protect his son. He knew he had a ready-made escape plan on the *Seaward*, so probably just figured he'd have a better chance with the Garda. Guess he knows he is going to jail one way or another, but I can't blame him for not wanting it to be a Moroccan jail."

Loren smiled and nodded at Jimmy's assessment.

Jimmy's expression and tone became solemn. "I think Nigeria knows Quinn's son is on the *Autumn Wind*. The coast guard spotted Nigeria's yacht, it seems to be tagging along with the ship and it's painted black. There has been a territorial dispute brewing between the Italian Santoro Mafia family and Nigeria, so they thought he was just safeguarding his contraband until the *Autumn Wind* got out of the Mediterranean, but now that we know that boy on there is Quinn's son, it puts a different spin on things. I got word to the UCs about that kid as soon as you figured it out. They need to be extra vigilant. Nigeria can't get to Quinn if he is on his passenger ship, but he can get to his son on that cargo ship, and that will flush him out. The coast guard is just tracking the yacht for now, but I'm darn sure he's going to try something, and probably before the ship leaves the Mediterranean."

Loren nodded, and the pace of her heart quickened. She didn't know Christos, but she knew Regan, and suddenly his secrecy was making sense. He was protecting his son.

"Remember I mentioned that Flanagan had a guy, Sean Dolan, on probation in Egypt?" Jimmy said. "Well, I met with him. Hell of a nice young guy, smart, too. He built that ship, and it seems it was a special-order vessel, designed and built for undercover communications. It has a hidden communications room and a secret cargo hold. He offered to sail back to Ireland with her and verify the guns and drugs are on board, so we can catch O'Hare red-handed with the contraband.

"He knows where to look?" Loren was surprised.

"Seems like it. He drew me a design map of the vessel that showed the secret hold where they are likely stored. All he wanted was a discreet ride out of Egypt for him and his wife, so her father can't find them. His wife is pregnant, and they are not legally married, an unforgivable breach of tradition in Egyptian culture. Her father threatened to kill them both. I put Dolan and his wife on the ship in Egypt as galley crew. A young couple in pursuit of a better life, it's a good cover." Jimmy's satisfaction with the ruse was obvious.

"You smuggled passengers on the ship!" Loren's playfully sarcastic tone accompanied her laugh. "You wise old owl!"

"Well, you gotta do what you gotta do!" Jimmy raised his glass to hers, gloating at his own craftiness, before he continued. "Sean's family did own the Dolan shipyard, and it was sold to Phoenix Ship Builders. They partly converted it to a marina resort, then it went into foreclosure and it was purchased by Quinn and Mararious. It was Quinn's money, and he also bought the market bakery for Abasi and Shima Bakari, but so far, no sign of anything unusual in his financial background. He's been working since he was sixteen and has been saving for his future. He has had some good-paying captain's jobs. We're still digging around in his business looking for any odd payments or income. I don't think the cook or the kid are in any danger from Dolan over that marina deal; it's probably just a coincidence. Dolan's an engineer and he asked us not to involve his father, but never mentioned the marina.

"The UCs on the *Autumn Wind* are keeping an eye on Dolan and his wife. I don't want them or the kid to get hurt. This is the first chance I have had to get undercover investigators on that ship and this close to O'Hare and that chief mate of his, Axel Morgan. I have arrangements in place to board with the Greek coast guard tomorrow, so I can check on them and Quinn's son, too. I have a code system set up with Dolan, so he can let me know if he has found any contraband."

"Where is the ship now?" Loren asked.

"Just off the coast of Greece." Jimmy reached across the table and took her hand, then hesitated, considering his next comment. If Loren was getting too involved with Quinn, he didn't want to take a chance on anything slipping out about the undercover operation. "Loren, are you sure this Quinn has no idea what you're up to?"

Loren shook her head. "He's a good-looking single guy and the captain of the ship. I think he picks up a woman on every voyage to keep himself amused; I'm just another of many, I'm sure."

Jimmy laughed. "His loss, then, girl." He was satisfied with her answer and continued. "But just the same, Loren, I want you to be careful with this Captain. If he murdered once he will do it again. Just because he seems like a nice guy doesn't mean he is. You are doing an excellent job and I'd like to keep you with him until the ship docks in Ireland. We'll pick him up as soon as he sets foot on shore, but I don't want you in any danger. If there is any chance he's figured out who you are, go to Garcia and I'll get you off the *Seaward* right away."

"I'm fine, Papa. You trained me well. I will be careful."

"Enough work." Jimmy pushed himself away from the table. "Let's take one of those tourist shuttles and see a few sights before I have to have you back."

Loren enjoyed the next couple of hours touring the streets of Portugal with Jimmy. It was nice to be off the ship, away from Regan and back to being Jimmy Flynn's daughter. Just before three the tour bus pulled up to the dock, and Jimmy gave her a hug and reminded her to be careful.

"You too, Papa. I love you." She disappeared into the crowd of tourists lined up to get back on the ship.

Jimmy was concerned. She had assured him she was fine, but she seemed different, and he wasn't sure she had been truthful about her involvement with Regan Quinn. He trusted her—she was an excellent undercover investigator—but she was also a beautiful young, single woman, and his daughter.

If Quinn laid a hand on her, it wouldn't only be Nigeria who wanted revenge.

CHAPTER SIXTEEN

The *Autumn Wind* was pushing along through the warm Mediterranean Sea. She was nearing Greece, and Sean and Christos were taking turns on the deck leaning into the binoculars, trying to locate the black yacht. It was always in the distance, keeping a parallel course to the *Autumn Wind*. It was hard to spot against the deep-blue water of the sea, but Christos was determined and would look until he found it. Sean had an amazing knowledge of sea vessels and it concerned Niko that he offered little detail about this boat compared to all the others that Christos was plotting on his map. Niko sensed he was deliberately avoiding discussion about the yacht, yet seemed as intent as Christos on monitoring its whereabouts.

Niko had been struggling to find an enemy in Sean, but the discussion they'd had about the marina in Ireland was never far from his mind. He couldn't help but wonder if that yacht had something to do with some plan Sean might have for getting the Dolan property back by getting rid of him and Christos. Niko was glad he had not mentioned the marina when he spoke to Christos about the incident in Tangiers. This was a long and challenging journey for a boy of Christos's age and the friendship he was developing with Sean was making it easier for him. If Sean had some plot in mind that involved that yacht, Niko would deal with it when the time came, even if it meant using the pistol he had stored in the secret drawer.

The Spirit of the Autumn Wind

"Come, Sean and Christos," Sadeh called up the stairs to the deck, summoning them for the morning coffee break.

The men were chatting about the black yacht as they made their way down the stairs to the table and took a seat. Sean dropped the discussion in favour of compliments on Christos's nicely baked cinnamon rolls. Christos had proved invaluable to Niko. He was up on time every morning putting the bread dough in the ovens, and by the time Niko, Sean, and Sadeh had the rest of the meal ready, warm buns were coming out of the ovens.

Sean and Sadeh had taken on making the daily soup, which came to a boil by noon each day, fuelled by the big galley stove and an Irish tune. Sadeh and Christos were looking after the laundry with some help from Brok, so Niko could take a short break in the afternoon. Niko had never had a group of passengers in his galley that he liked more than these three. They spent a lot of time together and he was glad for the harmonious atmosphere on his last voyage on the *Autumn Wind*.

Sleeman and Brok had joined them for the morning coffee break, so Niko took the opportunity to update the status of the supply run. "We will be in Greek waters late tomorrow. I think O'Hare plans to go into the harbour for coal and water. He never lets me know ahead of time, but we need to get loaded up with supplies to make the leg over to Spain. He doesn't stop in Italy, so we will be almost two weeks at sea. After Spain, it's through the strait and then a stop in Portugal for supplies, then straight through to Ireland." Christos was busily writing down what Niko said on the inventory notepad.

Niko looked at Sleeman. "Will you be getting off in Greece, too?"

Sleeman nodded, wiping cinnamon sugar off his face. "Yeah, but if we take on coal, he won't let the crew off, so there will be a long list of personal stuff to get for those guys."

"What about that first mate? He helped out last time," Niko said.

"He'll get off, and he did pitch in last time and took Mojo with him. Helps to have a strong guy like that along."

"At least he doesn't complain." Brok's inference to Mojo being a deaf-mute brought a chuckle to the table.

"Hopefully I can get that sketch pad for you this time, Brok," Niko commented.

Brok liked to sketch, and had requested Niko purchase a pad for him when he went ashore in Cyprus. Niko had not been able to find one, so Brok had been turning the light cardboard from Niko's kitchen boxes into a collection of drawings. He was a quiet man who said more in a sketch than any amount of chatter could accomplish, and Sean was impressed. Brok had sketched Sean on the deck playing his harp. The sketch had not only captured the likeness of Sean but the tangled emotion of the music he made.

"If anyone has letters, I should be able to mail them from the dock in Greece." Niko looked at Christos, who understood Niko was telling him he could write to his father.

Sleeman looked at his watch. "Good cinnamon rolls, Christos. Thanks." He got up from the table. He enjoyed the break after the breakfast service and never missed a chance to show his appreciation.

"You're welcome," Christos replied. Brok nodded to Christos, implying his thanks, and Christos nodded back. The men left, and the galley staff got busy finishing the cleanup and starting the preparations for dinner.

Niko's nightly visit to O'Hare's cabin confirmed the stop in port at Greece. Niko provided the list with the required inventory for the galley, so O'Hare could have the supplies ordered and waiting on the dock. O'Hare gave him the envelope with the cash to pay for the goods, knowing Niko would be busier the next day with preparations to disembark.

Sadeh and Christos had already gone to bed. The hot, humid night air filled the galley, so Sean and Niko moved their evening drink out to the deck. Sean handed Niko a letter addressed to his sister, Sara Dolan, in Ireland to mail the next day.

"Sean, your family in Ireland will be glad to see you." Niko was hoping this general assumption might stimulate more conversation on the Dolan property.

Instead, Sean asked about the black yacht. "That thing been dogging you since you left Tangiers?"

Niko was surprised at the question, as he thought Sean had something to do with the boat.

"Probably. Christos got on in Tangiers and noticed it right after you and Sadeh boarded in Egypt."

Have you seen it before?" Sean asked.

"No," Niko replied. He sensed a touch of concern in Sean's voice. Niko was convinced Sean knew something about this boat; he was just too knowledgeable about sea vessels not to. What Niko didn't understand was the evasive questioning.

Sean was sure he had seen the yacht before. It had been off the coast of Egypt a few months ago. His engineering design office was on the top floor of the Phoenix Shipyard building, giving him a full view of the harbour, and any vessel of unique design, big or small, caught his attention.

It was a personal pleasure craft that had been customized and painted white, with unique colourful designs, but it was the structural modification that had caught his attention. It sat deep in the water, which was unusual for that type and size of watercraft.

Both he and Mike, the design engineer he worked with, observed the vessel and thought that only having large high-powered engines installed would alter the balance of the boat to that extent. Sean recalled their conversation about the yacht.

"I have seen that freaky yacht out there before," Mike said. "It never comes into port, always just stays anchored out there in international waters. It's supposed to belong to some wealthy African guy named Nigeria who owns a diamond mine. But there are rumours that he's the drug lord behind the drug trade in Tangiers, which would explain the need for the high-powered engines. Gotta be able to move faster than the coast guard, I guess," Mike added sarcastically.

Sean shook his head. "Still a shame to destroy the looks of a nice yacht like that with such a brutal modification."

They laughed, let the conversation drop, and got back to the task at hand.

The next morning the yacht was gone, and Sean had not thought of it again until Christos spotted it in a parallel course with the *Autumn Wind*. Sean was sure it was the same vessel, but it had been painted white before, not death-black.

Flynn had told him that Niko was suspected of being involved in the drug dealing as well as the passenger smuggling. Sean was no investigator and he didn't want to say anything that might put himself or Sadeh in danger, so he just let the conversation drop. Niko had admitted to smuggling passengers, so he was probably involved with the drugs too, and Sean knew Flynn was right about the contraband on the ship. He had found the evidence.

"Beautiful night." Sean looked at Niko and motioned with glass in hand toward the stars.

"Yes it is. Greece always seems a bit like home to me. I grew up in an orphanage not far from here."

"Really, Niko." Sean was interested. "What happened to your parents?"

"Never knew them. Just left me there when I was born and vanished."

"Their loss, my friend; you are a good man." Sean looked at him admirably. "So, the coast of Greece tomorrow morning, then," Sean said with a heavy heart, knowing what lay ahead. He lifted himself out of his chair and handed Niko his empty glass, adding, "Good night, Niko."

"'Night, Sean."

Sean disappeared down the stairs from the deck to his cabin, and Niko took a few minutes alone with his childhood memories before finalizing his plans for the next day.

The Spirit of the Autumn Wind

Sean and Sadeh lay awake that night and talked. Flynn had said he would come on board with the Greek coast guard, and Sean had the information Jimmy Flynn wanted. They rehearsed what Jimmy had told them to say. His name tag would say Doyle, and the answers would be Sean Dolan and Sadeh Dolan.

Sean was concerned about Sadeh's pregnancy and suggested maybe they should give Flynn the other code, so they could get off the ship but give him the information he needed, then find their own way to Ireland from Greece. Sadeh knew Sean was disappointed that the *Autumn Wind* had fallen into the hands of a man with no respect for what a fine vessel she was, and getting her back to Ireland and away from O'Hare was important to him.

"I'm feeling fine, Sean, and I'm enjoying the voyage. I would like to stay on the ship all the way to Ireland."

They agreed, but he made her promise she would get off on the next coast guard stop in Italian waters if she had any concerns about her pregnancy. Sean wanted to protect her from her father, and he knew the safest place was by his side on the *Autumn Wind*.

Before Niko went to bed, he rechecked his inventory list for the galley and everything else he had to do. He was familiar with where to get supplies, but needed every minute he had on shore to get everything done. O'Hare would leave the basket Niko brought his whisky in at the galley door in the morning. Niko always looked after that task as soon as he got on shore, then dealt with the rest of the supplies. If he went back on board without O'Hare's whisky all hell would break loose. The man was mean with alcohol in his bloodstream and meaner without it.

He removed Sean's letter from his pocket. He wondered what Sara Dolan might be like. Sean had said she raised her daughter alone—not an easy accomplishment for a woman in these times. Although Sean's previous conversation implied they both had problems with their father, it seemed he had remained close with his sister while in Egypt.

Brok had given him a large envelope addressed to an art gallery in Dublin, Ireland. Niko never questioned Brok about his past, but he had overheard him tell Sadeh he had lost his leg in the war. He had listened to her talk to him while they did laundry. Her soul was unconditional, and she could find good in any person. Over the past weeks she had helped Brok find the good in himself. Niko was certain the drawings he was sending to the gallery included the one of Sean. Niko checked the mailing address on Christos's letter to his father and put it with the others.

The next day he would try to phone Regan just to talk to him, to let him know that no matter what happened, he would be there to help him.

As with the two previous supply stops, the galley was hectic, and Niko was up earlier than usual. He would leave as soon as the breakfast service was complete, so everything for dinner had to be pre-prepared to be put out and served in the dining area by Sleeman and an assigned crewman. Niko always kept the meal on these days simple but abundant, and supper was a delight of fresh meats, vegetables, and treats from the shore visit. The men worked extra hard on the days the ship loaded coal and water.

Niko, Sleeman, the new first mate, and deckhand Mojo would all go ashore with the captain. By four o'clock, the galley and crew supplies would be gathered on the dock and hauled up the loading ramps. Christos, Sean, and Sadeh completed Niko's pre-assigned galley tasks and watched the chaotic activity off their private deck. With Niko's return, activity in the galley quickly became just as chaotic with preparations for supper.

Niko had been so rushed on the dock with supplies he had not been able to phone Regan. Niko was exhausted and so was Sean, who had willingly lifted, pushed, and packed boxes and sacks to get the galley in order after the supplies came on board.

The Spirit of the Autumn Wind

Niko poured Sean a glass of Irish whisky and some rum for himself, then motioned toward the deck, suggesting they enjoy the drinks in the evening air. "Thank you, Sean, for all the help today."

Sean smiled. "Hey, I'm galley crew, gotta earn my keep." Sean raised his glass to Niko's with respect, wondering how Niko managed the tasks of the galley without help. "To the rest of the journey." Sean said. The men touched glasses and finished their drinks as darkness surrounded the ship.

At midnight, the engines rumbled into a familiar rhythm and the *Autumn Wind* headed out to sea.

The following morning, the galley foursome had just finished their coffee break when a horn sounded, announcing the arrival and boarding of the coast guard. As the anchor was being dropped, Niko explained the procedure.

"The coast guard will come on board with several men. They split up and go to various parts of the ship. The crew is lined up, and they verify the names of each man and proceed to search and inspect the ship. Three officers will come to the galley, and they will ask your names. If they want more information about you, they will request that the captain allow you to accompany them to the coast guard vessel for further questioning. We need to be lined up and ready when they enter the galley."

Niko reached into the linen drawer, removed a galley smock, and passed it to Sadeh. "This is a larger size, put it on. Your pregnancy is none of their business."

Sean gave Niko a grateful glance as he helped Sadeh into the larger smock and positioned her beside him.

Niko straightened up his own smock, and Christos copied Niko and took a place beside him in the lineup just as the galley door swung open. Christos was positioned between Niko and Sean, nervous and not sure what to expect.

"Good morning." A man in a crisp white coast guard uniform stood before them. His eyes ran down the line, starting with Niko, hesitating for a moment on Sadeh, then quickly surveying the circumference of the galley, pausing for the slightest moment on the map of the world that hung on the galley wall. His name tag said J. Doyle.

"Names, please." He looked down a list of names on a clipboard, then up again at the galley staff in their tidy white smocks.

The group chimed in one behind the other.

"Niko Mararious."

"Christos Bakari."

"Sean Dolan."

"Sadeh Dolan."

"Mr. Mararious, you are the galley master?" the man named Doyle stated authoritatively.

"Yes, sir," Niko replied.

Doyle requested Niko open the big galley cooler, then turned to the two men with him and instructed them to check the upper deck and cabins. Niko removed himself from the lineup and opened the cooler door. Doyle glanced inside quickly.

"Lots of supplies for a two-week leg."

"The men work hard when the ship is on open waters, and they need to be well-fed."

Niko's response brought a small smile to Jimmy Flynn's lips. "Well, obviously they will be." He closed the cooler door, and Niko secured the latch, then returned to the lineup.

Every time the *Autumn Wind* sailed through Greek waters, she was stopped by the coast guard; it was routine procedure. The same thing would occur when they passed through Italian waters. The officers would board and search the ship, but neither authority had ever found any illegal or any improperly documented cargo and had never questioned the galley staff beyond identifying them. Except for the galley master, it was not uncommon for the galley staff to be different for each voyage. Niko recognized two of the officers from a previous inspection, but not the officer named J. Doyle. The two officers that had been checking the cabins returned to the galley.

"Everything good?" Doyle asked them.

"Yes, sir," they replied simultaneously.

Doyle took another look at the lined-up galley crew. He spoke directly to Sean. "What did you say your name was, again?"

Sean looked Jimmy Flynn in the eyes and replied, "Sean Dolan."

"And you, ma'am?"

"Sadeh Dolan."

"Okay, thank you." He directed his gaze to Niko for a moment as he turned and left the galley with the other two officers.

The code answers were the ones he had hoped to hear. Jimmy Flynn was privately elated, and Sean and Sadeh seemed fine. The galley and cabins were clean, there were lots of supplies on board, and the galley master seemed genuinely concerned about the crew. Jimmy knew Niko Mararious was smuggling Christos Quinn to Ireland because of the murder, and he had to know about the contraband on the ship too, but the fact that the galley master was so relaxed in the presence of the coast guard surprised Jimmy. He was covering his involvement well, but there was no way Jimmy Flynn was going to let this cook slip through the cracks; he was going down with the rest of this smuggling ring.

Sean Dolan was the break Jimmy had been waiting for. He now had proof there was contraband on the ship and he finally knew where it was. They could shut the *Autumn Wind* down, but without catching Nigeria they would probably not stop the smuggling. He felt certain Nigeria would go after Quinn's son as revenge for the death of his own and was probably going to do it before the ship left the Mediterranean. Before Flynn disembarked the *Autumn Wind,* he slipped Sloan a note. Jimmy had a plan; he was going to lure Nigeria into a trap.

Niko was relieved when the officers left, and he put his arm on Christos's shoulder.

"You okay?"

"Yeah. Do they always have guns?' Christos asked.

"Yes." Niko knew the boy was scared and he just wanted to give him a hug and comfort him, but he could not. If Sean knew Niko was one of the sailors in the Dolan property deal, he was probably on board to do him harm, but it was possible he did not know Christos Bakari was Regan Quinn's son, and it was going to stay that way.

"Sadeh, are you okay?" Niko turned to her.

"Yes, fine, they are so official about everything," she said as she looked at Sean. She knew what they had just done would hurt Niko and she didn't want to look him in the face.

"It's their job, Sadeh," was all Sean said, before he started the routine of preparing the vegetables for the next meal. Sean knew Flynn's investigation had to do with guns and drugs being smuggled to Ireland, but he had not mentioned any ties to the drug lord Nigeria, and Sean was concerned that there might be a connection between the black yacht, Nigeria, and the *Autumn Wind*.

Jimmy Flynn had come all the way from Ireland to Egypt to talk to him about the ship. Sean had used Flynn's investigation to get himself and Sadeh out of Egypt without her father knowing, but he was starting to doubt the decision he had made to be smuggled out of the country on the *Autumn Wind*. If Nigeria was involved with the drugs and Flynn was unaware, perhaps they were in danger. At the speed they were travelling, Sean knew they would be in Italian waters in a few days, where Flynn had said he would board with the coast guard again. Sean had the information Flynn needed, and he just wanted to get Sadeh to Ireland safely. The next time Flynn boarded, he and Sadeh would answer Flynn's questions with their full names and get off the ship. They would just have to find some other way to travel discreetly the rest of the way to Ireland.

The visit from the coast guard, although seemingly eventless to Niko, had left his three galley passengers pensive, and the day passed by with little chatter. Everyone but Niko went off to bed early.

"Thought you were already in bed, young man," Niko addressed Christos, as he entered the galley just before eleven, clothed only in his boxer shorts.

"Couldn't sleep." Christos seated himself at the table across from Niko.

"Everything okay?" Niko asked.

Christos responded with a shrug, obviously undecided about discussing whatever was on his mind.

Niko pushed himself up from the table, returned with a glass, and poured a small portion of rum for the boy and some more for himself. He pushed the pad with the inventory list and menu for the next day aside and focused on Christos as he took a sip. Christos had been quiet since the visit from the coast guard that morning. He had seemed frightened by them.

"Christos, the coast guard can be a bit intimidating when they come on board, but it is just routine procedure," Niko offered on the hunch that this was what was concerning the boy.

"Do they board my father's ship like that too, with the guns?" Christos asked, taking another sip of his rum while his eyes searched Niko's face with concern.

Niko reached across the table and laid his hand on the boy's arm. "Not the passenger ships. Big ships like the *Seaward Angel* have a full-time security crew on board. They make sure the passengers are checked as they come and go from the ship and the crew is safe. The coast guard will come on board at the ship's security officer's request if there is a problem, but your father is safe. The cargo ships like the *Autumn Wind* are routinely checked to make sure their cargo is documented, and the ship has proper registration."

"What will happen, Niko, if my father has to go to jail when he tells the police about the man that got killed? You will go back to sea and Abasi and Shima are not in Tangiers. I'll be alone. What will happen to me?"

Niko took the boy's hands in his. "You will not be alone, Christos. First, your father is a good man, a man of integrity; that will count for a lot when he goes to the police. He'll get a lawyer to help defend him and there was a witness. That man's death was an accident and we'll find a way to prove it. And secondly, I am not going back to sea. That is what your father and I were talking about at the Sea Gull bar that night in Tangiers. He asked me to meet him, so he could tell me he bought a home in Ireland, a place for you to live with Shima and Abasi. He asked me to stay there, too, and I said I would; they need cooks on land, too." Niko smiled as he felt the tension in the boy's hands relax.

He stopped short of providing any details on the marina beyond the mention of the home Regan had spoken of, and continued. "Seaward has a new office in Sona Bay in Ireland, and your father wants to get some of the shorter passenger routes they are offering so he can spend more time with you and you can go to college in Ireland. Your father wants you to get a good education."

A small smile found its way to Christos's lips as he nodded, acknowledging Niko's understanding of what his father had told him about his education.

Niko raised his glass to the young man. "To the friendship of men."

"To the friendship of men." Christos responded. He finished his rum in a swallow, then wrapped Niko in his arms. "Goodnight, Niko."

Niko was moved by the boy's actions. Over the past weeks, he had come to love the young man. This voyage had been troubling for Niko, but no matter what, he would not let any harm come to Christos Quinn.

Jimmy called the *Seaward* that afternoon and contacted Loren and Garcia. Garcia had found nothing unusual about the ship's cargo or the crew and Loren assured him everything was the same with Quinn and she had no additional information to report. The *Seaward* would be in Ireland in two weeks.

The Spirit of the Autumn Wind

"Good news, Loren. I boarded the *Autumn Wind* with the coast guard. I have confirmation of the location of the contraband."

"That's great, Jimmy. The guy you put on the ship came through."

"Yeah, girl, we finally got a break." Loren knew from Jimmy's voice he was both relieved and delighted. "I saw the boy, and he looks a lot like his father. He seems to be okay, but that cook, he is a cunning bugger, cool as a cucumber."

"Just like his friend, then," Loren said.

"That O'Hare is a nasty piece of work, too," he added. " Loren…" Jimmy's tone became more intense. "That black yacht the coast guard is watching is still tagging along with the ship. It's staying in the distance and they haven't interfered with it; we are sure it's Nigeria. We have to get him off that yacht and onto the *Autumn Wind*." There was a tone of finality in Jimmy's words, and she knew he had a plan in the works to do just that. "I need to stay close this next few hours and I have a tactical support squad on standby, so we can board that ship. This is the closest we've been to Nigeria, but I don't want Quinn's kid or the Dolans getting hurt."

Loren could tell Jimmy was anxious. "The UCs won't let you down. We all want to get this case closed, Jimmy. Let me know what you need from me next."

"I will. You know I love you, girl. Be careful."

"You too, Papa. Love you."

CHAPTER SEVENTEEN

The *Autumn Wind* pushed relentlessly through the dark-blue waters. Foul-smelling, tar-infused smoke billowed from her stack and drifted across the deck, mingling with the sweltering heat of the Mediterranean. The only relief came from the night air and the breeze created by the ship herself. Sadeh was exhausted from the heat. Sean was tormented by the quality of the air drifting into the galley, and he never missed an opportunity to blame O'Hare for his reckless disrespect for the engines, which was causing the foul odour.

Niko wanted to keep Sadeh out of the galley completely, but she insisted on helping, so was assigned some light tasks that could be done while seated. With a few more supplies scavenged from the maintenance room, and an old bedsheet provided by Brok, Sean engineered a sun umbrella for Sadeh, so she could spend more time on deck, where there was some degree of fresh air.

Christos and Sadeh had cleaned out a storage closet full of books left behind by previous passengers and galley crews. Christos liked to read and would join Sadeh on deck to share some of her rest time, so she would not feel left out. They would read together and had read and re-read the book Regan had given Christos on Trinity College.

Sean was quick to encourage Christos to pursue his education. He was a good influence on the boy, and Niko pushed his paranoia about Sean and the marina to the back of his mind, but he still could not come up with any other reason a man would choose to travel with his pregnant wife as passengers on a tramp ship when there was faster and more comfortable travel available.

Black smoke belched out of the stack. The ship pitched to the right and rolled left, then lurched forward, drifting helplessly. The screaming engine room sirens echoed through the ship, and every man on the crew was rushing somewhere into the chaos, masked by the dark smoke that engulfed the ship. The sound of the anchor being dropped brought silence to the blaring sirens and the reality of what had just happened was summarized by Sean's frustrated assertion that O'Hare had blown the engines.

"Stupid fool! Now what? All he had to do was service them. What an ass!"

It was the first time Niko had seen the "fighting Irish" side of Sean Dolan, but obviously this was not the case for Sadeh.

"Sean, this is not your concern." She spoke as though it was a warning and lay her hand on his heart; her touch brought calm to his rage. "They will get the engines fixed, and we will get to Ireland." She understood his anger was fuelled by the neglected ship, but just as much directed at himself for the situation they were in.

Niko watched the couple and saw the love they shared was big enough to overcome the situation. Whatever the circumstance that had brought them to the *Autumn Wind*, it was keeping them there together. Niko found himself wanting to keep them safe, just like he wanted to keep Christos safe. He craved what they had—unconditional love. Love between a man and a woman. But no woman could ever want or love a man like him. A man who was crippled, not physically perfect like Sean, Regan, and Christos. He would spend his life looking after others, but he would never know love, never have a child, a son like Christos, or a woman like Sadeh to love.

Niko disciplined his thoughts back to reality and provided the solution. "Sean, O'Hare has to report the ship's position and status. If we are adrift more than twenty-four hours the Greek or Italian coast guard will board. I will ask them to take you and Sadeh off the ship."

As quickly as Sean became angry, he relaxed and returned to his charismatic self. Niko sensed Sean's desire to get involved and engineer a fix to the problem, and he couldn't let that happen. "Sean, Sadeh is right, you don't want to get involved. O'Hare is not a man you want to confront. He has cargo on board he needs to get delivered on time, and he'll deal with it."

"Sorry for my behaviour," Sean apologized, looking at Niko, then Christos, who stood anxiously silent through the entire commotion. Niko nodded, acknowledging Sean without commenting.

"Sadeh, let's get some air." Sean ushered his wife out of the galley and up the stairs to the deck.

He settled in beside Sadeh under the umbrella and wrapped his arm around her shoulders, holding her close without speaking, thinking about the dilemma. Sean knew the cargo Niko was referring to was guns and drugs. Niko was right—O'Hare had to get that cargo there on time. His life probably depended on it. But Flynn was right, too. Niko was obviously involved, because he knew about the importance of delivering the illegal cargo on time. Sean knew they were just hours out of Italian waters. They could get engine parts in the harbour there. It was a busy harbour and proper port authority was expensive. Sean was guessing that was why they always bypassed the stop in Italy.

Sean spoke quietly to Sadeh. "I have the proof Flynn asked me to get; we'll get off when the Italian coast guard comes on board." Sean had made the decision that was best for Sadeh.

"No, Sean. I want to go to Ireland with you on the *Autumn Wind*. This ship needs to go home, and so do we. We will all go home together, the *Autumn Wind*, you and I and our baby. We will be fine."

Sadeh had made the decision that was best for Sean. He ran his hand along the side of her face, pulled her to him, then kissed her lips. His other hand lay with hers on her swollen stomach, and he was silent.

A much-calmer Sean returned to the galley in a few minutes and positioned himself beside Christos, who was cutting vegetables and throwing them into a large soup pot. Sean put his arm around Christos's shoulders. "Still friends?"

Christos smiled without looking up. "Yeah, why not! You're the only guy I can beat at hoops."

Sean's moment of enjoyment was interrupted by a knock on the galley door, which was simultaneously pushed open by First Mate Kevin Sloan.

"Everyone okay in here?" he asked, surveying the galley.

Sean looked up to see Sloan looking past Niko and directly at him. "The young woman?"

"She is getting some air on deck," Niko replied.

Sloan acknowledged with a nod. "Well, the ship's blown the engines."

Sean stabbed a potato, thinking, *O'Hare has blown her engines*, but he remained silent as Sloan finished his summary of the situation. "The captain has notified the coast guard of our location and has contacted a company near the Italian harbour to send out a service boat to look at the engines. Supposed to be out here around eleven tomorrow."

Sean wanted to tell him it was too late for a service boat. The engines needed repairs that couldn't be done at sea; they could only be done in the Italian harbour, and if O'Hare was qualified to be the captain of a ship like the *Autumn Wind*, he should know that.

Sloan continued, "if the engines can't be repaired at sea, we will need to get a tug out to tow us in to a harbour."

Sean did not look up. *Obviously, O'Hare does not know about the backup engine…* He threw a pile of sliced carrots into the pot.

"There will probably be a half-dozen men off the service boat to feed tomorrow afternoon."

"Yes, sir," Niko acknowledged.

Niko did not miss Sloan's final glance at Sean, who had not looked up from his task.

The sweltering heat beat down on the ship as she sat quiet and chained to her anchor, alone in the waters of the Mediterranean Sea. The men from the engine room busied themselves with additional tasks in preparation for repairs, and the deck crew used the time to catch up on extra chores that were hard to fit into their daily duties.

It was business as usual in the galley and laundry. Sean commanded Sadeh out of the heat to the shade of the umbrella with towels to fold, and filled in at the washing machine with Christos. While enjoying a jug of lemonade that Niko delivered to the deck, Sean and Christos looked for the black yacht. As hard as they looked, they could not find it. Christos was the only one disappointed by the disappearance of the vessel. Both Sean and Niko, although for different reasons, were privately relieved by its absence.

CHAPTER EIGHTEEN

Within an hour of receiving notification of the situation on the *Autumn Wind*, Jimmy Flynn was on his way to meet the Italian coast guard. They had the location of the ship and the black yacht they had been tracking was moving toward her. Flynn's hunch was right; Nigeria was going after Reagan Quinn's son, and Jimmy had manoeuvred him into doing it on his terms.

It was early afternoon and Loren was in her cabin. She had just returned from the shore excursion at the Port of San Sebastian on the tip of Spain where the ship was docked. She had changed into a new dress she had bought while on shore and was looking forward to her afternoon tea with Regan before the *Seaward Angel* headed back out to sea at midnight.

A knock on her cabin door revealed Garcia, who summoned her to the security office to take an urgent call from Jimmy Flynn.

"Loren, girl, how are you?" Jimmy's voice was assertive and official.

"Fine, Jimmy. Is everything okay? Are you okay?"

"Yes, Loren. I think we got him." Jimmy could not contain his excitement. "We forced the engines on the *Autumn Wind* down an hour ago. She is anchored just off the Italian coast waiting on repairs, and the black yacht the coast guard has been tracking is closing in on the ship." *So that's what Jimmy was planning,* she thought as he continued. "Nigeria does all his business at night and he'll wait until it's dark, but he'll make a move. I'm working with the coast guard.

I'm putting the assault team I have ready into play and the UCs I have on the ship are prepared. The minute Nigeria boards and goes after the kid, we got him.

"We better get Quinn out here. It's time, Loren. Let him know who you are. I have notified *Seaward* that Quinn has an urgent family matter and must come to Italy immediately. That is all they need to know for now. There is a relief captain on board already, so there is no problem with them. I have already filled Officer Garcia in. He will put Quinn under arrest for the shooting death of Ivory Abdul Nakarasa. Quinn will be in custody, but no need to keep him from seeing his son.

"This is going to be hard on the kid. I'll arrest the cook on passenger-, drug-, and weapons-smuggling charges. The coast guard will coordinate with me and bring you out to the *Autumn Wind* once we have Nigeria under arrest."

"Okay, Jimmy. Officer Garcia and I will get Quinn out to Italy and wait for your call. See you later. Be careful."

Loren used every inch of control she had to push everything she needed to say to Jimmy into one sentence. She could not talk to him, as he would know from her voice something was wrong, and this was an important case; she would not disappoint Jimmy.

Loren looked at her watch. It was almost four, and she and Regan had planned to meet for tea.

Loren fought her emotions and snapped into the professional trained investigator she was as she turned to Garcia. Emanuel Garcia was the Garda officer that she was assigned to, and he immediately took control of the investigation. "Investigator Flynn has asked that I put Captain Quinn under arrest, and he has arranged transportation through the coast guard to get us off the ship and by private plane to Italy," he said, confirming what Jimmy had arranged. "He meets you for tea every afternoon at four in the bridge lounge."

Loren nodded in response. She was aware Garcia was doing surveillance on the ship and had observed him pass by the lounge while she and Regan enjoyed afternoon tea.

"I will meet you there and place him under arrest," he added. "I will have the coast guard standing by, that way we can leave the ship quietly and as quickly as possible. There is no need to make a spectacle of this."

"Yes, I agree," Loren said, as if her opinion mattered.

As she left the security office, she could hear Garcia contacting the coast guard. She felt numb, and it was at that moment that she completely understood why Jimmy had always been so adamant about not getting personally involved with an assignment. She had broken Jimmy's rule and now she had to do the most difficult thing she had ever had to do in her life; tell the man she loved the truth.

Loren returned to her cabin. She let the new dress she had bought just for him fall to the floor. She stood before the mirror, deadened, and pulled on her dark-blue slacks, then buttoned the white long-sleeved blouse. A row of round navy buttons that matched those on the blouse secured the matching jacket around her narrow waist. She tied the laces of her walking shoes and checked to make sure her service revolver was tucked inside her black leather handbag. She pulled her hair back off her face and secured it in a roll at the nape of her neck, then looked in the mirror at the Loren Lombardi she knew; the one before the Cinderella ball, before the nights of passionate lovemaking, before she fell in love with Regan Quinn. She aligned the familiar stranger that appeared before her into perfect professional presentation, then left her cabin. She took a seat in the lounge and waited.

She saw Officer Garcia position himself near the lounge. He acknowledged Regan as the Captain when he passed by, then stopped Juan from going into the lounge with the tea tray.

Regan opened the door and, as usual, reached to take her in his arms. "Loren, what is this? Why are you dressed like that?"

She stepped back. She was trying to maintain her composure and she blinked hard to force back the tears forming in her eyes.

Garcia stepped into the room behind Regan. Regan turned toward the security official and faced him.

"Captain Regan Quinn, I have been embedded with the security crew on your ship, but I am Detective Emanuel Garcia with the Garda out of Sona Bay in Ireland. Miss Lombardi is a civilian investigator that works for the Garda with a special drug and smuggling unit. I am placing you under arrest for the murder of Ivory Abdul Nakarasa in Tangiers. Seaward has been advised you will be leaving the ship due to a personal matter, and I have the coast guard waiting. Special Investigator Lombardi and I will walk you off the ship."

Regan stepped back, shocked. When he broke the deathly silence, it was not to deny the charges but to express his pain in words laced with rage. "Loren, I was just a job to you! You have lied to me about everything! I thought we had something special, but everything between us was just a lie! I don't even know who you are!"

"Regan, please." She swallowed hard and forced the words out of her mouth. "It's not all a lie; it's not like that."

He interrupted her. "Well, how is it, then?" His tone left no doubt about his anger. He turned to Garcia, held out his wrists, and shouted "Arrest me!"

His back was to her, and Loren shook her head to Garcia; she did not want Regan Quinn to leave the ship in handcuffs. She could hear Garcia reciting Captain Quinn his legal rights, but she was numb. She was collapsing inside, tears were welling up in her soul, she could not look him in the face, she could barely speak.

She gathered her composure and brushed past him, then spoke authoritatively as she walked with Regan between her and Garcia toward the passenger's gangplank. "We do not want to make a display of this. The coast guard is waiting, and we are taking you to Italy, to your son on the *Autumn Wind*. An undercover unit is in the process of arresting Nigeria, Ivory's father. He has been tracking the

Autumn Wind since it left Tangiers, and the lead investigator thinks Nigeria knows your son is on the ship and is coming after him to get you out in the open, so he can kill you both to avenge the death of his son. The undercover unit has the ship surrounded and will arrest Nigeria as soon as he boards the *Autumn Wind*."

Regan stopped abruptly. He pulled at her shoulder and turned her to him. "You have been using my son as bait to catch this drug dealer!"

Garcia positioned his hand lightly on the pistol at his side.

"Look at me, Loren!" He spat his words out. "You knew about my son all this time and you let this happen!"

"Regan, your son is fine." Loren was fighting past his hostility and trying to reassure a man who at this moment was neither her assignment or her lover. Her focus was on his eyes as she spoke; the same eyes that turned to black velvet when they made love were cold as stone, but burning like a hot sword through her heart.

"There are two undercover agents on the *Autumn Wind*. This is a complicated investigation, Regan. We did not know that Christos was your son in the beginning, but once we figured it out, Nigeria's intentions became clear. We are doing everything we can to keep your son safe."

Regan was silent.

"We should go," she said, and walked slightly ahead of him as she spoke, so he could not see the fear in her face. Garcia was at his side as they disembarked.

They travelled in silence, Garcia speaking only when necessary to convey instructions as they moved from the coast guard vehicle to the airplane and finally to the small Italian coast guard boat.

Garcia was about to put Regan in cuffs and Loren spoke quietly to him. "I don't think that is necessary. Everything he has done has been to protect his son. He is his only family, and he won't abandon him." Loren said.

Garcia countered, "It's procedure, he is a murder suspect," but he thought for a moment, then added, "but he has made no attempt to get away, and he is very distraught. Okay." He had observed Loren with the Captain in the tea lounge and dining room on more than one occasion and accepted her assessment of the suspect.

"Captain Quinn, here is a sandwich and coffee," Garcia offered as he set it down on a bench near were Reagan was standing. Garcia took a seat close to him and opened a sandwich and coffee from the box of food the coast guard had brought on board for them.

They sat waiting in the darkness for word to come from the *Autumn Wind* that everyone was safe, and that they could come aboard. Regan did not touch the sandwich and coffee the coast guard officer had brought for him, nor did Loren, who sat under the canopy at the helm of the boat, trying to justify everything she had done. She watched Regan as he stood alone on the deck looking out at the dark sea, the silence broken only by the lapping of the waves against the side of the boat.

CHAPTER NINETEEN

Jimmy Flynn strapped on his bulletproof vest and joined the five assault officers already armed and waiting in the lead boat headed out to the *Autumn Wind*. The coast-guard vessel had maintained its regular surveillance route along the Italian coast throughout the afternoon, making sure they did not change their regular routine but all the time carefully monitoring the black yacht they'd had under surveillance since Egyptian waters.

The black yacht anchored southwest of the *Autumn Wind* late that afternoon. Jimmy was sure Nigeria would make a move after dark, and had five fishing boats in the water around the ship. They were boats that normally went out late in the afternoon to lay their nets and so would arouse no suspicion. On board each boat were six well-armed and highly trained officers. When the coast guard reported the black yacht was on the move, the fishing boats were poised to move quietly in on the northeast side of the anchored ship. The coast guard would signal Jimmy's UCs on board the *Autumn Wind* that there was danger and they were coming on board the ship.

Jimmy's UCs always hung around on deck near the galley in the evenings. Every evening between nine-thirty and ten, the coast guard would send one of three different light signals that would tell them everything was normal, or they were in danger, or the coast guard was coming on board, which meant Jimmy was coming on undercover with the coast guard officers to make contact. Tonight, the UCs on the *Autumn Wind* received two light signals: they were in danger and the coast guard was coming on board. They were always discreetly armed, but tonight they were also ready for trouble. Something was going to happen, and soon.

"Winds from the southwest." The coast guard's raspy transmission came across the weather channel.

It was the signal that Nigeria was on the move. Jimmy was in the first fishing boat that quietly moved under the cover of darkness and positioned itself along the northeast side of the *Autumn Wind*. Nigeria's black yacht moved quietly through the water from the southwest, consumed in darkness and invisible against the dark sea as it pulled up alongside the ship. A big man flung a rope that hooked the deck and two men scaled the side of the vessel and moved quietly down the hallway.

The door of the galley slammed open to the daunting frame of a large, black man. The man's abrupt entrance startled everyone, and Niko immediately grabbed the cabinet to steady himself as he faced the intruder. Christos froze like a statue and clung to the chopping block. Sean, who had been seated near Sadeh sprung to his feet and instinctively placed his body in front of her.

The man's nostrils were flaring with every breath he took, and his hot rank breath filled the room. Thick dreadlocks threaded with grey were pulled into a loose knot and fell down his back. His wide, flat nose blended into his inky skin and separated his hazel pupils, which were embedded like stones in his bloodshot eyes. A younger black man, a semblance of the first, stood behind him.

The large black man wore loose cotton pants tucked into tightly laced army boots, and a wrinkled cotton shirt with the sleeves torn off, exposing his massive, muscular arms and the machete at his side. But it was the huge pistol he held before him that brought time to a standstill in Niko Mararious's galley.

Within a moment of entering the galley the man extended his strong thick arm and wrapped it around Christos's neck, forcing him against his body, then pushed the butt of the gun against the side of the boy's head.

"Dis boy! I bin lookin' for dis one!" The man spoke with a tangled African dialect as he tightened his grip around Christos's neck. "I bin waitin' 'n' waitin' for his fad'r to come for dis boy. Maybe, he not luv dis boy, his son, like I luv my son. I kill dis boy, dat fad'r! He come den!" His voice rose emphatically with each word he spoke.

"Den I shoot hem, like he shoots my boy, my firstborn son. I shoot you all." He ground the gun tighter into Christos's skull for a moment, then began waving it recklessly and pointing it at everyone in the room. Captain O'Hare rushed into the galley with Axel on his heels.

"What's going on here?" His words trailed off at the sight of the large black man.

"Ah, O'Hare!" the man said belligerently and pointed the gun directly at O'Hare's face. "Yu tell dat capdin to come to the *Autumn Wind*, he cun watch me shoot his son like he shoots my son, den I kill hem too. Den I shoot chew, fool!"

Liam O'Hare's hand touched the silver pistol at his side and the younger black man pressed a gun to O'Hare's back, saying nothing as he seized the pistol from his side. O'Hare turned ghost white as he grasped the reality of the threat.

"Axe, he cun live. He tell'd me dat capdin kilt my son." Nigeria looked at Axel Morgan, the big crewman beside O'Hare. "He tell'd me 'bout dis boy, he tell'd me dis boy on dis ship. Axe, he my friend."

He waved his pistol in O'Hare's face, his finger resting on the trigger. "But not chew, fool! I shoot you and den I take dis ship." He raised his voice to a shout. "You cull dat capdin of the *Seaward Angel*! Now! Fool!"

O'Hare stood frozen and silent.

Niko's heart pounded. The words were spinning around the room. Adrenalin was surging through his body, forcing him to breathe, to think…his ears were ringing…there was noise in the hallway, more men coming in. Sloan, Mojo…more danger…

Niko pushed on the secret drawer at his back, wrapped his hand around the ivory-handled pistol, and when Nigeria looked back and pointed the gun toward Christos…he fired!

The bullet screamed across the galley, and Nigeria fell to the floor. Christos's hands went to his ears. He leaped away with the swiftness of a leopard and ended up bent over the counter at Niko's side. The younger black man raised his pistol and aimed it at Niko and Christos, and in the same moment met the right hook of Sean Dolan.

The pistol discharged, grazing Sean's right shoulder, and he fell against the wall, writhing in pain. Sadeh dropped her body on him and grasped him in her arms.

Mojo was on top of the young black man, securing him with handcuffs, Sloan was handcuffing Axel. Jimmy, who had pushed into the room right behind Sloan and Mojo, had O'Hare in handcuffs. Jimmy kicked the body of Nigeria that lay on the floor, making sure he was dead; there was blood pooling around his body, seeping into his dreadlocks and soaking his cotton shirt. Jimmy's action brought spitting words of defiance from the younger black man, who spoke in a throaty African dialect. Mojo gave the man a sharp slap to the side of the head, assertively making his point. "Samba, quiet." Then he said something to him in the same African language the man spoke.

Jimmy looked at Niko. The gun was still hanging from his paralyzed hand. "Drop it, Niko."

Niko looked up in a daze at the man who he knew as Doyle. He dropped the gun, then wrapped his arms around Christos, who was clinging to his side.

As Jimmy approached Niko, he pushed his service revolver into his shoulder holster and quickly exposed the Garda badge on his belt. "I'm Detective Flynn with the Garda out of Ireland. I am placing you under arrest for smuggling passengers, weapons, and drugs on the *Autumn Wind*."

Niko stood speechless as Jimmy pulled his hands forward and put cuffs on his wrists, looking into his eyes as if expecting some resistance while he rattled off his legal rights.

"I don't know anything about weapons and drugs." Niko's words were without expression and spoken in a daze. Jimmy eyed him carefully, considering what he said.

O'Hare shouted. "You lyin' bastard, damn cook—this is all your fault, you brought this wrath down on me!"

Jimmy ignored O'Hare's spitting defiance from across the room and quickly turned his attention to the boy. But Sloan did not, issuing a terse, "Shut your mouth!" as he pushed the barrel of his gun against O'Hare's head, knocking his filthy captain's cap to the floor and into the pool of blood.

"Christos, are you okay? No injuries?" Jimmy Flynn placed his hands on the boy's shoulders and looked at his face. Christos shook his head slowly from side to side and pulled away. "I have your father on standby."

He spoke into his radio. "This is Flynn. Bring Quinn. The boy is fine, and the friend too; bring Quinn."

"Ten-four," a raspy voice responded.

Tears were welling up in Christos's eyes.

Jimmy squeezed the boy's shoulder reassuringly and spoke gently. "I have your father waiting, and he will be here in about a half-hour." Christos was still clinging to Niko. "I am a police officer, you are safe now," he added, trying to calm the boy.

Christos responded with a blank look; he could feel the strength draining from Niko's body. "Can he sit, sir? Can he sit?" Christos asked emphatically.

"Yes, of course." Flynn looked at Niko's blank expression and pushed a chair toward them.

"Thank you." Christos's gratitude reflected the concern that he felt for his godfather, but nothing for the man he was addressing.

Flynn moved quickly toward Sean. "Let's have a look." He pulled Sean's blood-soaked shirt off his shoulder as the doctor and the medical team off the coast guard vessel were pushing through the galley door. "It's a superficial wound." Jimmy's voice expressed relief, and Sean was hurting too badly to care.

Jimmy motioned the coast guard doctor toward Sean. "Gotta shoulder wound here."

"We'll look after him, miss." A young medical assistant helped Sadeh to her feet.

Jimmy took Sadeh's hand, comforting her as he assisted her to a chair. "Sean is okay, let the doctor and his team tend to him. They will take care of him, Sadeh." He did not want any harm to come to this young couple and he realized just how close he had come to doing just that.

Jimmy's trained eye immediately began surveying the scene, looking for the renegade bullet, and there it was; an obvious bullet hole in the map of the world that hung on the galley wall. It was perfectly lodged in the channel by the lighthouse near Tangiers where Jimmy's undercover officers had determined the weapons were being loaded onto the *Autumn Wind*.

"It ends where it starts," Jimmy mumbled, his thoughts making no sense to anyone else amid the chaos around him.

Niko was focused on the limp corpse with blood spilling out of it on his spotless galley floor. A quiet calm was coming over him, and the reality of what had just happened seemed distant, like a dream. Without removing his eyes from the corpse, he spoke like a robot. "Christos, bring a sheet from the hall closet and give it to the officer to cover that man. Sadeh should not have to look at that."

Christos did as he was told and returned momentarily with a large white sheet, which he handed to Flynn. He then returned to Niko's side, placing his arm around the shoulder of his godfather, who was sitting perfectly still on the chair. Flynn spread the sheet over the body and cast a searching look in Niko's direction thinking, *who is*

The Spirit of the Autumn Wind

this Niko Mararious, this cook? *The smuggled passengers liked him, and said he took good care of the crew. Here he was worrying about a passenger after having just shot a man. Regan Quinn trusted him with his son. What was he doing on the* Autumn Wind *smuggling passengers? Was he honestly not aware that O'Hare had weapons and drugs on the ship?*

"Special Investigator Lombardi." Garcia spoke to her as he touched her shoulder. He had been sitting near the communication technician and listening to the activity on the ship as she sat in the dark, watching her assignment and mentally justifying every move the team had made. But Regan was right; they had used his son and friend to flush out Nigeria, they had put two people he loved in danger, and as much as the case mattered, it had been a risky manoeuvre that she could not expect him to forgive.

"We can go now," Garcia said to her. "Investigator Flynn just called on the radio and said everything is okay, and we can take Captain Quinn to the ship now."

"The boy?" Loren's immediate thoughts were of Christos.

"Yes, Special Investigator, he is fine, and the friend too."

"Nigeria?" she questioned.

"Dead. Seems the cook shot him."

The cook? she thought, and glanced at Garcia, who was just as puzzled.

Garcia approached Regan as the boat began to move. Regan, who had been standing looking out to sea for what seemed like hours, turned to find Garcia standing behind him and Loren at his side.

"Captain Quinn, everything is fine," Garcia said. "Your son and friend are safe, and we can take you to the ship now."

"Thank you," Regan responded to Garcia in a grateful tone, as tears welled in his eyes.

Loren reached out and touched his arm. He yanked it away and turned from her without saying a word. She returned to the enclosed canopy of the boat but maintained a clear view of Regan. She had known since the moment they met he was a murder suspect, but over

189

the last two weeks she had come to respect Captain Regan Quinn. He had worked hard for what he had accomplished in his life. She had worked equally as hard, but she could not expect him to grant her the same respect; she had destroyed that when she let their relationship become intimate. She had deceived him and threatened his son and friend and he was not a man that tolerated being threatened, he had proved that when he committed murder. Jimmy would not have authorized his arrest if he did not have evidence against him, and as much as her heart wished he was Prince Charming, she knew he was not. Regan would get a lawyer to defend himself and their relationship would be exposed. Her bad judgment had not only compromised Jimmy's entire investigation but his entire unit. His use of female civilian investigators was constantly under scrutiny, and his superiors would want her removed from the team.

"It will be about thirty minutes," Garcia added, his tone reflecting his annoyance at Regan's rude behaviour.

The small coast-guard boat pushed through the darkness, beating against the waves. Garcia took a seat not far from Regan. He had not resisted arrest, and so far had shown no interest in running, but he was in custody and without hand cuffs, so Garcia wasn't about to take any chances.

A second coast-guard boat followed, with a forensic team on board. Loren positioned herself next to the communication technician and listened to the raspy chatter coming across the radio as the twenty-five men Jimmy had taken on board with him gathered up the crew and secured the ship. The coast guard doctor was on board the *Autumn Wind,* so someone was hurt, and she suddenly realized she had forgot to ask about Jimmy.

"Who's hurt?" she asked.

"One of the galley passengers," the technician responded, then added, "sounds like a shoulder wound, and I think everyone else is fine." He smiled at Loren, who was relieved.

The Spirit of the Autumn Wind

She looked toward Regan, who remained steadfast at the railing. The boat began to slow, and as it pulled up against the *Autumn Wind* Garcia advised Jimmy Flynn they were ready to come on board and the suspect was not cuffed. Four of Jimmy's team, wearing dark assault uniforms, immediately boarded the boat, surrounded Regan in a tight circle, and assisted him off the small vessel up a ladder and onto the ship, followed by Garcia and Loren.

Regan had only been on the *Autumn Wind* once, about four years previous, when the ship was owned by Mediterranean Lines. Niko had invited him for lunch when the ship was anchored in Tangiers. Regan remembered the ship as being beautifully designed and well cared for, and it was obvious to him as he walked with the officers down the hallway toward the galley that things were not the same; the ship was neglected. Niko had hinted at it the night they met at the Sea Gull Bar, but it was evident to Regan that Niko had not told him the full story.

Niko sat quietly, listening while Mojo and Sloan recited legal rights to the young black man they called Samba Nakarasa and Axel Morgan, whom they charged with weapons and drug smuggling. Jimmy Flynn recited legal rights to O'Hare, who was charged with the same two offences, as well as smuggling passengers illegally on board the cargo ship. Mojo spoke to the black man in an African dialect, and with complete ease switched to English while conversing with Sloan and Jimmy Flynn. Obviously, Mojo was not a deaf-mute deckhand and Sloan was not a first mate brought on board to replace Gavin Connor. Flynn instructed the assault team to move the prisoners to the coast guard vessel just as Regan Quinn was escorted into the galley.

Regan's eyes quickly surveyed the scene: three men in handcuffs were tied together and being led out of the room, a corpse lay on the galley floor under a bloodstained sheet, doctors were assisting a younger man seated on a bench beside a pregnant woman, and Niko sat on a chair, handcuffed, while Christos stood at his side, clinging to his shoulders.

"Papa!"

Regan was across the floor in a heartbeat, carefully avoiding the corpse.

"Papa!" Christos was in his father's arms, trembling and crying. Regan reached down and took Niko's arm, pulling him up from the chair and into his arms with Christos.

"Are you okay, son?"

Christos did not answer, just clung to his father.

"He's fine, Regan, he is not hurt, he is just scared," Niko responded for the boy.

"You, Niko, are you okay? Why are you cuffed?" Regan asked, looking into his friend's distressed face.

Before Niko could say anything, Christos was breathlessly spilling out the details of what had happened. "Niko shot Nigeria, he was going to shoot me, and Niko shot him and saved my life and when the other guy raised his gun to shoot at us, Sean punched him. Sean saved us both."

Christos pointed to Sean, who was seated on the bench while the doctor and his medical assistant bandaged his shoulder.

"Thank you," Regan said to Sean, his gratitude spilling out. "Thank you."

Sean nodded indifferently amid the confusion of his pain.

"Niko." Regan pulled his friend to him. He knew exactly what it felt like to take a life. Regan had killed a man to save Niko, and Niko had killed a man to save Regan's son.

Regan looked across the room to see Loren speaking to the older man whom he recognized from the offshore visit in Portugal, and two other men. The red-haired man was unmistakably the same man who had been disguised as the old fisherman at the lighthouse, and the other was a dark-skinned man, dressed like a crewman, who matched Niko's description of the deaf-mute who had boarded in Egypt.

Regan released Niko as the man beside Loren approached and held up his badge. "Captain Regan Quinn, I am Detective Jimmy Flynn, lead Garda investigator with the smuggling and drug unit out of Sona Bay, Ireland."

Regan thought for a moment, then looked around the room, trying to understand the situation he was in and who these people were, but he kept his arm firmly around Christos's shoulders.

Flynn had barely finished his sentence when a forensic team entered the galley, along with some of the assault team, to process the evidence. One of the men said, "Hello, Jimmy, good to see you. Your team all okay?"

"We're all good, but got one deceased, four guns, and a bullet lodged in the wall here," he motioned toward the map of the world. "As well as a load of weapons and drugs hidden on the ship, and that black yacht anchored out there."

The man smiled. "A good day, then."

"You could say that." Jimmy could barely hide his satisfaction at the magnitude of the day's accomplishments, but Regan had a sinking feeling in the pit of his stomach as he started to realize the extent of the trouble he was in. Foolishly, he had gone to the lighthouse the morning after the killing, asking questions, and unwittingly exposed himself to one of Flynn's undercover detectives. By that afternoon Investigator Lombardi and Garda Officer Garcia were already on his ship. Niko had said the two mysterious crewman and the new galley passengers had boarded the Autumn Wind four days later in Egypt. Regan mentally summarized his situation. *These people were all working with Flynn. This sly investigator from Ireland knew from the very beginning he had killed Ivory, but he didn't arrest him; instead, he had this team of undercover investigators watching him, and Niko, too. Flynn thinks we are involved with Nigeria and smuggling drugs. He was trying to catch us at it before he arrested me for the murder of Ivory.*

Nigeria and Ivory were both dead. The only one who knew the truth was Niko, and he was sitting there in handcuffs. They had planned to tell the truth about what had happened when they got to Ireland, but no one would believe them now.

"Well, Jimmy, that much evidence is going to take a while to document," the man from the forensic team said.

"Okay." Jimmy set out the procedure as the forensic team prepared to start. "We'll move everyone to the dining area while your forensic guys process this crime scene in the galley. This entire vessel will have to be combed for evidence, but let's get this area completed first, so we can get this body out of here."

Flynn turned to his suspects and said, "Mr. Mararious and Captain Quinn, Mojo and Loren will take you and your son into the dining area. You have been provided with your legal rights and do not have to provide a statement unless you choose to co-operate with this investigation. But Sean and Sadeh and Christos, I would like witness statements from you three to document what happened here," he added.

Although it appeared Flynn's investigation was at a close, his tone made it clear he was not yet done investigating. Regan and Niko were quick to realize they had lost the chance to tell the truth when they got to Ireland, and that this crafty investigator might be the only one willing to listen. They looked at each other, but neither spoke, as they reevaluated their silence.

The doctor was speaking to Sean as he assisted him up off the bench. "That arm is going to be sore for a while, but you'll live."

"Good thing, we have a baby on the way." Sean's impulsive smile lightened the mood in the room.

"Perhaps, miss, you should come with us to the coast-guard ship, so we can check to make sure your baby is fine."

"I'm fine," Sadeh objected.

"I'm sure you are, but you should let us check, just the same."

Sean pulled her close with his good arm and kissed the side of her head. "Go with them, sweetie; we don't want to take any chances."

"I'll send some pain medication back with your wife for the arm," the doctor offered as an enticement.

"We'll do Sean and Sadeh's statements later." Jimmy decided instantly.

Sadeh nodded, and waited as the doctors gathered their things and, being careful not to disturb the scene, escorted her from the galley.

Regan looked Jimmy Flynn in the face. "I will provide a statement," he said, and Niko followed with the same offer.

Loren's authority as a civilian investigator did not include handling suspects who were in custody, so she directed her attention to Christos and intentionally ignored Regan. She could feel his hostility, and there was already enough tension in the room. "Would you like something before you start your statement, Christos?" Loren asked gently. "Maybe a glass of water?"

"No," Christos said in a terse tone as he clung to his father. "Papa, I don't want to do a statement. I don't know what to say. I don't know what they want."

"Son, just write down everything that happened, like you do when you write to me about school and your grandparents."

"What happened to my grandparents? I don't know where they are! They are probably dead, too!" Christos blurted out abruptly.

"Christos." Regan said his son's name tenderly as he tightened his grip around the boy's shoulders and pulled him close. Regan knew that ripping his son out of the only home he had ever known would have repercussions, and there was no mistaking the torment the boy was in. "They are not dead, son, and as soon as I can, I will find them. Let's just do what the police want for now. Go with Loren—Investigator Lombardi." Regan caught his error and quickly corrected himself, but he could not correct the angry tone he had used when he referred to her as Investigator.

Jimmy chose to ignore what had just happened, but he was not insensitive. He, too, wanted to know what had happened to Abasi and Shima Bakari. His other female special agent had been undercover at the carpet vendor's stall across from the bakery, and there had been no sign of the Bakaris since the night of Ivory's death. Their stall was still in ruins, so no one had been back. If they were involved in some way with Regan Quinn and this drug smuggling, it was possible they might have been killed by Nigeria's man that same night. Flynn wanted to see what Regan Quinn disclosed in his statement and didn't want to upset the boy any further by asking questions in front of him. He had just had his life threatened and it was understandable that the boy was angry, so Jimmy reiterated they should move the suspects to the dining room.

Loren and Mojo were about to comply when Regan spoke to Flynn with the voice of command he used on the *Seaward*. "Will you take those handcuffs off Niko? The man can barely walk, much less run anywhere, we're in a room full of armed officers, and only God knows how many more are on this ship. We're sitting at sea in the middle of nowhere. Where is he going to run to?" Regan's frustration at Flynn's pre-determination of Niko's guilt was obvious. Regan's commanding tone annoyed Flynn, but he reached across and removed Niko's cuffs.

Jimmy Flynn was having a tough time figuring out Niko Mararious. He was a complicated man, and Jimmy wanted to deal with him personally after he had a chance to review the statement he was about to provide. There was evidence to charge him with both passenger and contraband smuggling, and he was the one person that seemed to be implicated in every area of the case; but there was something about the man. Everyone kept referring to him as being kind and caring, and yet here he was with the gun that killed Ivory, and although Jimmy's team had witnessed the self-defence killing of Nigeria, it was obvious the man was capable of murder.

The Spirit of the Autumn Wind

Jimmy waited until his suspects, Christos, and his investigators were out of the room before addressing Sean. "Think you feel up to opening up this hidden room and showing us where this contraband is?" The concern in Jimmy's voice was balanced with the necessity of the question as he spoke to Sean.

"Sure thing," Sean responded enthusiastically.

"Investigator Sloan will give you a hand." Jimmy looked toward the map of the world, remembering the diagram Sean had provided when they first spoke. "We need to remove this map, there is a bullet lodged in the wall behind it," he said to the lead forensic officer.

"Investigator Flynn." Sean said.

"Just call me Jimmy, Sean."

Sean nodded. "Jimmy, before you take the map, I want to show you what Christos did." Sean lifted the map of the world and exposed the navigation map of the Mediterranean with the details of their voyage. "He was making this for his father and keeping track of all the ships we saw. I'm sure he would at least like his dad to see it before you take it. Here, this one is Nigeria's boat." Sean pointed to the symbol labelled "Black Yacht," with a question mark beside it. "Christos has been tracking it since we left Egypt."

Jimmy stood back and looked at the map. "This is an excellent piece of evidence. I will need to take it, but I can wait until Christos shows his dad."

"The boy is an excellent young navigator," Sloan added, and Sean acknowledged that with a nod.

Jimmy turned to the forensic leader. "Just leave this on the chopping block when you are done processing it, and I'll make sure it gets packaged up with the rest of the evidence."

"Sure thing, Jimmy," the man said. He glanced at Jimmy, then quickly got back to what he was doing.

Sean refocused on the task at hand and reached for the chain and key around his neck. Then he looked at Sloan and smiled, amused.

"I'm not sure what to call you, First Mate Sloan, or Investigator, or Sloan."

The investigator laughed. "My mother calls me Micky. Just use that."

"Micky. Could you help me with this? It requires two strong arms." Sean handed him the key. "Insert this key in the small hole in the centre of the Dolan plaque, and push."

Micky followed Sean's instructions, then stood back in amazement as the wall in front of them opened into a room. "My God!"

Sean flipped a light switch inside the door and two of three small bulbs lit up, dimly revealing the dusty interior of a room lined with built-in desks and the remnants of communication lines still hanging from the walls. Jimmy and Micky stepped inside the room behind Sean.

Micky immediately commented, "when Jimmy put us on the ship, he said it had a lot of secrets. He told us what you were doing to help with the investigation and what you had said about the purpose of this vessel and its engines and cranes. I was a mechanical engineer in the navy and I did a lot of engine-room troubleshooting during the war, and I have been impressed with this ship since the day I boarded."

Sean smiled to himself as he led the way down the dimly lit hallway, with Jimmy and Micky behind him, then pushed open a door and revealed the hold full of coffee crates loaded with weapons and sacks of drugs.

The men entered the hold and assessed what they saw. "There's millions of dollars of contraband in here," Jimmy stated with certainty.

Sean addressed Jimmy, recognizing the massive task that lay ahead for Jimmy's forensic team. "There is a device in the bridge that opens the floor of this hold from above, right under the front crane, so you can get access to this stuff from above. I'll show you when you are ready."

Sean turned and struggled to push open another door on the opposite side of the hallway with his good shoulder. Micky immediately assisted.

"This is the backup engine. It runs off the generator that supplies the ship with electricity. It alone has enough power to manoeuvre the ship," Sean said. "I called it the troll." He smiled, remembering something private from the past.

Micky looked directly at Sean. "I have been in the engine rooms of a lot of vessels, but if Jimmy had not told me about this extra engine, I would have never known it existed. I'm impressed with the way this was concealed and the whole engine room set up. I have never seen a coal-fired ship with this much power."

"These three engines were a special order out of Italy," Sean said, "and the entire synchronization system was new when this ship was built, but with the diesel engines coming in about the same time it quickly became obsolete. This is one of the few ships it was ever installed in." Sean made no effort to hide his disgust with the whole affair when he added, "and that O'Hare has no clue how to run these engines."

"Good thing." Micky said with a crafty smile. "We didn't want him getting out of the Mediterranean."

Sean realized that whatever was going on with the engines on the Autumn Wind had been escalated by this competent undercover first mate, but for the right reasons. Flynn had forced Nigeria's hand, so he would have control.

The message had gotten through with no breach of confidentiality, so Jimmy added, "we didn't want you, your wife, or Quinn's kid getting hurt. Good work, Sean!" He gave him a hardy pat on the back. "Let's get you back to the galley with that shoulder, so you can get some rest."

They re-entered the galley. Micky and Sean closed the door to the communications room. The forensic team had removed the body, the blood on the galley floor had been cleaned up, and there was a note on the table to Sean from Sadeh saying she was in their cabin resting.

"Were done in here, Jimmy, that map is on the table," the forensic officer said. "We are going to check the ship for evidence next, so the assault officers can move around freely, and then start on what is in the hidden hold. By the way, the bullets in that ivory-handled pistol are an exact match to the bullet that killed Abdul Nakarasa and the other three people in Tangiers. That ammunition is unique; it has the letter *I* engraved on each bullet. It's a definite match. The bullet we took from the wall was similar. The letter *S* was engraved on it, and the ones in the deceased's gun each had an *N*. These weapons and ammunition are all custom-made."

Jimmy hesitated, but he wasn't surprised. These guys were drug lords. They weren't afraid of the police, so they weren't afraid to identify themselves on the bullets they used when they took a life. But Ivory hadn't taken his own life and Niko Mararious was in possession of the weapon that had fired the bullet.

"Thank you," Jimmy said. "Let me know when you are ready for the cargo hold. It can be opened from the deck." The man had his back to Jimmy but waved his arm, letting him know he had heard.

"I could really use a coffee," Sean said. "If it's okay, I'll make this big pot. I do it for Niko every morning."

"Go ahead, Sean. I could use one, too," Jimmy said.

"Me, too," Micky chimed in, just as Loren returned from the dining room with Christos, followed shortly by Mojo with Regan and Niko and two assault officers, who took positions by the galley door and the entrance to the dining room.

Christos immediately missed the map. "What did you do with my map? It is for my dad."

"It's right here, Christos, on the chopping block. We had to remove it," Jimmy said, attempting to calm the distraught boy.

Sean turned to Regan. "Your son is a pretty accomplished young navigator. He was making this map of the voyage for you," he said proudly, taking no credit for his part in the project.

Regan laid his hand on the map and spread it out before taking a careful look, then put his arm around his son's shoulders. "You did this, Christos? You did an excellent job, son."

"Well, I had some help from Sean." Christos smiled at his friend.

Jimmy stepped up to the map. "This map is a key piece of evidence and I will need to take it." He looked at Christos. "I will personally make sure you get it back."

Christos was reluctant. "It's for my father, but okay, as long as I can have it back."

"You will get it back." Jimmy was emphatic, and Sean gave Christos a confirming pat on the back to acknowledge the young man's cooperation.

Why is Sean still here? Niko thought. *He is an illegal passenger. The coast guard should have removed him from the ship.*

Loren was securing the statements with paperclips. As she handed them to Jimmy, she said "Captain Quinn's is on top," but she did not look at him or Quinn. Jimmy sensed she was uneasy, and she was. For the past hour, she had sat with Christos at the table opposite Regan, looking directly at him while he wrote his statement. Three times he had dropped his forehead into his hands and stared down at the paper in front of him, deciding what words would determine his fate. She had skimmed what he wrote before leaving the dining room. He had described in detail the events in the alley behind the Sea Gull Bar and what he did the day after, but ended his statement with, "Your investigators have had me under surveillance since the ship left Tangiers." She was relieved that he had not exposed her, but he was a smart man and he would know that revealing he had been intimately involved with the officer assigned to investigate him could destroy the credibility of his statement. What worried her was that he would also know it could destroy her career, and he was angry enough to do that.

The aroma of Arabian coffee was wafting through the galley. Sean set a cup in front of Jimmy, then Micky. "Anyone else?" he asked, looking at Jimmy to make sure it was okay.

Niko looked at Flynn. "Investigator Flynn, could I make my friend a sandwich? He is affected with headaches if he doesn't eat regularly. Perhaps your officers would like something?" Niko was a galley master and these people were in his galley and he wanted them to leave, but all he could do was feed them.

"I won't say no," Mojo responded, then added, "this galley master is a good cook." He looked at Jimmy as if he needed to justify his growling stomach. Mojo's hearty appetite was a source of amusement among the UCs.

Jimmy looked around the table. He had two suspects, neither of whom were in handcuffs, but he had three armed investigators and two assault officers in the room. *They should be able to handle Niko and his kitchen knives.* "Okay," he said. He gathered the statements, took his coffee, and removed himself to the privacy of the dining room.

"Is it alright if I help Niko with the lunch?" Christos directed his question to Loren.

"Yes, of course."

Sean was already setting the table with his good arm and, anticipating Niko's needs, bringing items from the cooler. He did not ask the investigators for permission, and it was at that moment that Niko realized that Sean Dolan was not a passenger. He had come on board the same night as the other two undercover investigators, and it was clear now he was there to do surveillance in the galley.

Niko looked down and pushed aggressively on his carving knife, slicing the large ham in front of him. *So that is why he is on this ship,* he thought. He did not look up from the task. *Flynn was smart. A man fleeing with his pregnant wife was a good cover.* Sean had pretended to be his friend, and Niko had admitted that he was smuggling passengers to him. Just like with O'Hare, he had only himself to blame for the mess he was in.

Sean had seated himself beside Sloan. They were talking about the ship. The other two were rifling through files from a briefcase that one of them had brought into the galley. Regan had sat the entire time with his elbows on the table and his forehead resting in his hands. He took the aspirin Niko gave him, but what Niko thought was a headache was torment; the same torment Niko was feeling from the pretend friendships they had both fallen victim to.

"Lunch is ready," Niko announced, as Jimmy returned. Everyone gathered around the Galley table.

Jimmy took a place at the head of the table. Niko immediately brought another plate and set it in front of him with a fresh cup of coffee, then took a seat at the opposite end of the table, next to Regan and Christos.

"Christos, please start, and pass the food to the investigators," Niko said, and the boy began passing the plates of food around the table. Jimmy looked at the group as he filled his plate. The mood was tense, and it was Jimmy who finally broke the silence. "Thank you, Christos, for your statement. You did a good job."

Christos glanced at his Father, but said nothing.

Jimmy set his fork down. "I have read your statement, Mr. Mararious, and yours, Captain Quinn. Your descriptions of what happened in the alley are consistent. It could be justifiable self-defence. You both mention this mystery witness...," Jimmy hesitated and watched the reaction of his two suspects, "...but without this witness, proving your innocence could be difficult. Especially yours, Niko, because you have the gun that killed Abdul Nakarasa, and the bullets in that gun can be matched to three other murders in Tangiers. You will be charged with those offences in addition to the smuggling charges. We know you were living in the alley with the vagrants for six months. Now you are the cook on this ship and smuggling passengers through the galley. Why do you have that gun?" Investigator Flynn asked in an official tone.

Everyone in the room looked at Niko. Regan spoke out defiantly. "This is all my fault, Niko, you don't have to talk to him. We'll get a lawyer. There is a witness! We have to find him!"

Niko looked thoughtfully at Regan, then around the room at the others, and finally directly at Flynn, who was seated with his investigators on either side of him. Niko saw them like ingredients in a cake, each contributing something to the recipe. *Flynn thinks he has all the ingredients for a good cake, but he is missing the most important one.* Niko knew he had that one ingredient—the truth—and he wanted no part of being associated with three murders, so he decided to tell Flynn exactly what happened before things got any further out of hand.

"Investigator Flynn, it's like I said in my statement. Regan accidentally shot Ivory. He threatened both of us. I took the gun and told Regan I would throw it overboard when I sailed at midnight." Regan was about to speak, and Niko motioned with his hand for him to be silent. "That was the first time I ever saw that ivory-handled pistol. I did not murder anyone with it, and I should have thrown it into the sea, but I didn't." He let his last words trail off as if somehow that would change things, and shared a glance with Christos. He was the only other person that knew why he had the gun. "I told Regan I would take Christos back to Ireland with me on the *Autumn Wind,* so Nigeria couldn't find him. O'Hare has been bringing passengers on this ship and smuggling them through this galley since my second voyage."

That's exactly what he told me, Sean thought as he shot Flynn a quick glance to gauge his reaction. Flynn had accused Niko of being behind the passenger smuggling when he involved him, and Sean was hoping maybe hearing Niko tell his side of the story would help the investigator understand the reason.

The Spirit of the Autumn Wind

Niko looked at Sean, but quickly refocused and continued. "He didn't care who it was, as long as they paid. I knew nothing about Nigeria, Ivory, and O'Hare smuggling drugs and guns on this ship, or I would not have brought Christos on board. I thought he would be safe here with me. We planned to go to the police in Ireland when we arrived in a month and tell them what happened in Tangiers, just like I said in my statement.

"I kept the gun because..." he hesitated, "I wanted my ID card back. O'Hare took the card from me when I signed up to work on this ship. He takes them from the entire crew, so the men come back, and I needed it to live and work in Ireland. I wanted to use the pistol to threaten O'Hare when we got close, not kill him, just threaten him, like he does with the crew."

Niko took a moment and studied Mojo's face before he continued. "When Mojo came on board, I thought he might be connected to Nigeria and I was afraid he was here to hurt us, so I kept the gun."

Jimmy looked at his investigator and shared a subtle smile. Mohamad Jobassi had the features of his African heritage, and when Jimmy had put him undercover on the *Autumn Wind* it was with the intention of creating exactly that reaction, hoping that his presence might frighten Niko into turning himself in.

Niko's expression was one of betrayal as he looked over at Sean Dolan and said, "Sean got on as a passenger. He was in my galley and talked about the Dolan Shipyard and how nothing would ever be right until the property was back in his family. That is the property Regan bought and I thought he was on this ship to get rid of me and maybe Christos too. I couldn't think of any other reason he would bring his pregnant wife on a ship like this. I didn't know which one to be more afraid of, so I kept the gun hidden in the galley."

Sean's disappointment at Niko's disillusioned friendship was obvious as he listened while Niko finished. "There was nothing planned about what happened here today. Nigeria threatened

Christos. I am his godfather, and I love him like the son I will never have. I just wanted to keep him safe."

"This was to be my last voyage. Regan bought the marina in Ireland with a restaurant. It was our childhood dream and we wanted it to be our retirement." Niko looked across the table at his friend.

Jimmy Flynn had sat quietly listening to Niko's account of the events and watching Regan, who seemed annoyed but had remained silent. He asked, "Regan, do you want to add anything to what your friend has just said?"

Regan looked at him and for just a moment as his eyes met Loren's; the secrets of her black eyes now revealed, she seemed as vulnerable as he felt.

"You both mentioned a witness?" Jimmy was pushing. "If there is someone that saw Ivory attack you in the alley that night, that testimony is important to both of you. Is there anything you can remember that might help us find him? His build? Did he run like a young person or someone older? What did he have on, was he in a djellaba or street clothes?"

Regan knew there was a witness, but he wasn't sure he knew the answers to any of Flynn's questions, and this could be a trap. Flynn was a shrewd investigator, and Regan considered the value of his silence before speaking. He was looking questioningly at his friend, but Niko was silent. He wanted Regan to tell his story, defend himself with the truth; it was all they both had.

"It's like we said." Regan gave up his resolve. "There was a witness; a vagrant we think. He was hiding up against the brick building and he ran away quickly. I called out to him to stop, but he didn't. It was dark, and he was just a shadow, but he wasn't in a djellaba. After I made sure my family was safe, I tried to find him. In my statement I told you everything the vagrants from the alley told me about the Englishman that had been hiding by the building earlier that day, and you already know about my visit to the lighthouse. I got back on the Seaward Angel at one."

Regan looked directly at Loren and spoke defiantly. "Your investigator has been with me ever since, and she knows I am not involved in any drug smuggling on the *Seaward Angel*. She knows enough about me to know that." Regan was offended that Jimmy Flynn felt he was involved in smuggling and wanted to make sure that both Loren and Flynn knew he had figured out what they were up to and that he didn't appreciate being manipulated.

It was the first time since he had been put in custody that he had looked at her face. Jimmy glanced at Loren to see her fighting tears, and it was at that moment Jimmy Flynn knew for sure they were personally involved. She had done a good job of hiding it, but he knew she had let her relationship with her assignment become intimate.

What Jimmy also knew was this could be a problem. If Regan Quinn was guilty of murder and covering up smuggling activities, the entire investigation would be questioned if his testimony was compromised by one of Flynn's investigation team. Quinn had not made mention of any involvement in his statement, but Jimmy knew he was a smart man. That information would give Quinn's lawyer an advantage in court, and he would not be able to protect Loren from the consequences.

It was obvious to Micky that Regan's personal reference to Loren made her uncomfortable, so he took the opportunity to add to the details of the investigation. "Jimmy, do you have my notebook from the surveillance at the lighthouse in your briefcase?"

Jimmy took his eyes off Loren, flipped through the pile of files crammed into the briefcase, pulled out the notebook, and handed it to his investigator. Micky quickly went through the pages. "Gavin Connor…that was the name of the man that said he was off the *Autumn Wind*." He looked at the collection of souls seated around the galley table for a reaction.

Niko spoke up, the relief in his voice undeniable. "The first mate. Thank God he made it ashore. He got into an argument with the captain over the maintenance of the engines. O'Hare tied him to the mooring post to make an example of him and he intended to kill him just like the sailor he shot on the first voyage. O'Hare would not tolerate any defiance from the crew. I took food to him after dark, got his money from his cabin, gave him a life preserver, and loosened the ropes. He jumped ship by the lighthouse before dawn. I told him to go to Abasi at the bakery for help getting a false ID card, so he could try and get back to England. Gavin's ID card is probably still in O'Hare's office with the rest of the crew's."

Micky closed his notebook and said, "We should check into this first mate. See if we can find any trace of him. Connor had a distinguishable English accent, and it is possible he could have made it to the alley by the time of the shooting. It could have been Connor that witnessed what happened that night. If he did get a false ID card, he could have left on one of the vessels in port that weekend. Maybe he left on a fishing vessel or someone remembers speaking to an Englishman. The fishermen don't miss much of what goes on down on the dock."

"It's worth a try," Jimmy said. When Loren first mentioned the witness from Niko's letter, Jimmy had assumed it was one of Nigeria's thugs, but Micky Roan had just established a link between the man that jumped ship and what the vagrants had told Quinn about the man hiding in the alley. A firm nod accompanied his words. "Get those ID cards out of O'Hare's office and check the passenger lists through the port authority and let's see what comes up. And one more thing." Micky was about to get up, but waited as Jimmy directed his conversation to Regan. "Niko mentioned Abasi helping with false ID cards, which is against the law, and we know the Bakaris disappeared the same night as the incident in the alley. I have an investigator watching their bakery stall. They have not been back. What do they have to do with the smuggling and where are they?" Flynn asked bluntly.

Regan thought for a moment before answering, then looked at his son. "They have nothing to do with this. They take care of my son and I was afraid they would be harmed because of what happened, so I sent them away. They are hiding with the farmers in the mountain country. I'm not sure they are still safe. Someone trashed the bakery and told Nigeria Christos was on the *Autumn Wind*. I would like to get them out of there. Christos grew up with his grandparents. It looks like you intend to put both Niko and me in jail and my son will need someone to care for him."

There was that defiant tone again, and it was annoying to Jimmy. But as an investigator, he had dealt with a lot of people, good and bad, and as much as he resented the tone, he understood this man was the product of an orphanage upbringing. He had worked his way up to captain of a passenger ship, one of the most prestigious positions in the industry, while raising a son alone, taking care of his wife's parents, and looking out for his handicapped friend. He had to have some character to do that—and there was no mistaking what Jimmy had seen in Loren's face. She had obviously found a gentler Regan Quinn behind the guarded, stern presentation.

Flynn mentally assessed the situation. "I can send Mojo to bring them here, so they are with your son."

Regan was relieved to hear Flynn's response and some indication there was more to the man then the terse investigator he had seemed up until now. "They won't come until I tell them they are safe," he said.

Jimmy heard the concern in Regan's voice and took a minute to think things through. He had always found the best way to deal with problems was to approach them head-on. It was possible that Regan did shoot Ivory in self-defence, but until they could find the witness to verify that, he was a murder suspect. But Loren had said Quinn did not seem like a murderer. She was a competent investigator with exceptional instincts. This man was her assignment, she knew him better than anyone else, and Jimmy wasn't afraid to take a gamble.

He responded authoritatively to Regan. "Well, how about I send you with Mojo and Loren to find them and bring them here? This ship is highly guarded, and they will be as safe here as anywhere."

Jimmy looked directly into Regan's eyes. "And just to be clear here, I didn't say either you or your friend were going to jail." Jimmy's tone reflected his annoyance at Regan's summary of his investigation. "But you are both going to stay in custody until we can sort through what is taking place on this floating circus. Both Loren and Mojo are as excellent at marksmanship as they are at investigation, so don't test them. The small coast-guard boat can take you over to Tangiers in the morning."

He re-directed his eye contact from Regan to Loren. Everything that had happened the last few hours would bring this case to a resolve, and whatever was going on between these two also needed to be resolved. Regan Quinn was either vindictive and planning to go after Loren for her lack of professionalism, or he was in love with her and trying to protect her. Maybe a boat trip over to Tangiers and a hot ride up into the mountains might be what they needed to melt the freezing atmosphere between them. Jimmy sensed Loren was uneasy, but he knew she would not object to any instructions he issued as her lead investigator.

Regan stood up as a sign of respect as he spoke to Jimmy Flynn. "We should go now. It is better to travel at night through the market when there is a lot of activity with the farmers coming down from the mountains with produce, and there is one farmer that comes to the market…a messenger of a sort. He will know where they are."

Jimmy took a moment to consider the plan. "Okay, Regan." Jimmy turned to Loren and Mojo. "Get ready to travel. I'll advise the coast guard to get the shuttle boat ready."

Regan looked at Niko. "Do you think you could find me a different shirt or one of your galley smocks? I don't want to be seen in this uniform shirt and jacket."

"Yes, there are some clothes in my cabin that one of the passengers left. There is a shirt about your size and a djellaba. Take my seaman's jacket too. Christos, take your dad to my cabin and show him."

Loren understood this meant a change of clothes, so she reappeared about a half-hour later in loose-fitting coast-guard issue clothing. The dark-navy pants were tucked into laced combat boots, and the unbuttoned seaman's jacket over a dark tee shirt revealed her shoulder holster and side arm. Her hair was pulled back off her face and pinned in a roll above her neck.

"I see the coast guard boys found you a change of clothes." Jimmy laughed at her masculine attire. She pulled the dark toque out of the jacket pocket and waved it tauntingly in front of Jimmy with a nonchalant smile as she laid two dark-navy striped djellabas over the chair. "They sent one of these over for you, Mojo. It's the large one," she said, playfully referencing Mojos husky frame, and everyone broke into laughter when he teasingly spun the chamber of the service revolver the he had been preparing for the trip, implying she was in danger for her remark.

Regan was already back in the galley. His uniform shirt had been replaced with a cotton beige-coloured one, but he was still in his dark-navy uniform pants. The shirt was partly open, and she was remembering the first night she had spent in his arms on the *Seaward Angel*.

He was watching her interacting with her team mates. They were her friends, men who treated her as an equal because she did the same work as they did. He had fallen in love with Loren Lombardi the writer and this woman was someone else, a woman who had deceived him.

Mojo had just finished checking his service weapon when one of the assault team came to the galley door and spoke quietly to him; he responded, then looked out into the hallway to assess what was being discussed. Jimmy rose and joined him at the door, to add an official response to the discussion while also looking down the hallway. He nodded, then looked back at Niko, who was standing by the table with the coffee pot in his hand.

"Niko, someone to speak to you." Jimmy was smiling as he summoned Niko to the door, where the crew was waiting. Jimmy and everyone in the galley watched as each man filed by as they were being removed from the *Autumn Wind*. Each had kind words as they thanked their galley master for his thoughtfulness and the fine healthy meals he had provided. Niko Mararious was obviously not only respected as a galley master, but as a man.

Jimmy and Mojo were silent and obviously impressed that this humble man had earned the admiration of such a hardened and criminal-infiltrated crew of desperate men. Niko was visibly touched as he returned to the galley table. Regan pulled Niko to him with a strong pat on the back, and Christos followed with a boyish hug that brought tears to Niko's eyes. Sean was moved and put his good arm around Niko's shoulders. Niko was uncomfortable with Sean in this new role as investigator. Unsure how to act in his presence, he turned away from him to wipe the tears that were forming in his eyes.

"Where did you learn to cook, Niko? The food you serve on this ship is darn good," Mojo asked like a crewman might.

Niko took a deep breath to relieve his tension and answered as he would to a crewman. "At the orphanage. Regan here, he was a strong young guy." He smiled at the memory of his friend in their youth. "So, he got the outside work, and I was sent to help in the orphanage kitchen. The old cook there was a retired Greek chef. He taught me the art of Mediterranean cuisine and the Greek language. Most galleys on these cargo ships serve a lot of fried and commercially prepared foods and poor-quality, cheap cuts of meat. I make sure my crew gets good fresh meat, fish, vegetables, fruits, and baked bread, and less salt, just spices. They work hard on these tramp ships and they deserve decent food."

"Well, you can cook for me anytime," Mojo said enthusiastically, and his fellow investigators laughed.

The coast guard came on the radio, saying the small shuttle they used for undercover surveillance was ready to depart. Niko handed a bag to Mojo that contained a large thermos of coffee and five cups. "It will be a long night for you three and Abasi and Shima, and the mountain air is cold at night."

Regan hugged Christos. "Everything will be fine, son. I'll find Grandpa and Gramma. They will be so happy to see you."

"I miss them, Papa."

"I know, son, why don't you try and get a bit of sleep? This has been a hard day for you."

Christos nodded and looked at Jimmy. "I'm going to my cabin, Investigator Flynn." His spirit was as commanding as his father's, and Jimmy Flynn saw it as an admirable trait in the young man.

Mojo took the bag and thanked Niko for the coffee and lunch he had just served his galley intruders. He followed Loren and Regan onto the waiting boat. He knew they would travel all night and it would be dawn before they were back at the *Autumn Wind*, and he was just as grateful for Niko's kindness as the renegade crew had been.

"Where is Sadeh?" Niko asked Sean. Then he waited for an answer, letting him know he was on to their ruse.

"She is lying down. The doctor gave her something to help her rest after all the excitement."

"That sandwich is for her." Niko pointed toward a plate nicely wrapped in wax paper. "She should have something to eat when she wakes up." Niko made the comment like he expected to be gone when she did but wanted to make sure she was cared for.

"I'll get started on the search for the missing first mate." Micky was headed out of the galley as he spoke but encountered the forensic team leader in the doorway.

"Jimmy, if we could get that cargo hold open now? We're ready to start processing that evidence," the man said, and Sean immediately stood up, knowing he was the only one who knew how to open it.

"Micky will go with you, Sean." Jimmy said, and momentarily the only two people left in the Galley were Niko and Jimmy.

"Niko." Jimmy motioned for him to take a seat, implying he wanted to discuss something.

Warily Niko sat down opposite him, expecting nothing good to come from a private conversation with this man.

Jimmy had been looking for an opportunity to talk to Niko alone, without his protective friend, hoping a bit of private conversation would give him a better understanding of his complicated suspect.

"You mentioned O'Hare killed a sailor on your first voyage?" Flynn said. He never missed a detail.

"Yes." Niko's voice was unwavering. He was going to jail because of O'Hare, and anything he could truthfully say to expose the cold-hearted Captain, he was going to. If what he told Flynn would add murder to his charges, Niko was glad to oblige. "He shot a sailor and threw him overboard for speaking up on behalf of the crew. The crew can testify to that. He bullied the men and packed a pistol to make sure they knew he was not to be challenged."

"Do you remember the crewman's name?"

"Samuel Swain. He boarded in Ireland on the first round-trip the *Autumn Wind* did. His card might still be in O'Hare's office."

Jimmy wrote the name on the file laying on the table in front of him, then looked up.

"What about this passenger smuggling, Niko? We have been aware of it for some time, and we have talked to some of the passengers that stayed in your galley. I'd like to hear your side of the story."

He was surprised that Flynn even bothered to ask, because he felt the investigator had already pre-judged him. Niko folded his hands neatly in front of him on the table and looked Flynn in the face, trying to decide how much to trust the man. *It could just be another trick, like with Sean.* Jimmy looked toward the galley door and observed Sean, who had returned and was standing silently by the entrance listening, as he did not want to interfere with Jimmy's discussion. Jimmy motioned for him to come in.

Sean laid his hand on Niko's back as he took a seat across from him. "You should tell Jimmy what you told me about the passenger smuggling. I don't think you're the one that should be taking the blame for this. I consider you a friend, and Jimmy might be able to help you out if he knows the truth."

"*A friend*" were the two words that rebuilt his trust in Sean Dolan. He got up and went to the drawer where he kept his sailor's log book. He returned to the table but kept the book securely in his hands.

"O'Hare came up with this passenger-smuggling idea to get more money. On the first voyage I did with him on this ship, he did not give me enough money or help to run the galley. I used what little of my own money I had to feed the crew. I am a galley master, I will not starve a ship's crew." Niko's tone emphasized the extent to which he took his responsibility personally.

"The crew on a tramp ship will walk off if they are not well fed. He used me to keep his crew. Axel Morgan would find the passengers through the dock vendors and bring them to me to hide in the galley. The passengers stayed in the galley cabins and were expected to assist in the galley under my supervision. I knew I was breaking the law, but he was going to do it anyway, so I tried my best to keep the passengers safe while they were on board. I never asked much of them. I took the best care of them I could, and I never profited personally from any of this. I used the money he gave me to feed the crew and care for the passengers.

"This is my log book. I have kept the names of everyone that O'Hare smuggled on this ship, where they boarded, and other details of the voyages. I planned to give this information to the police in Ireland when we turned ourselves in." Niko pushed the book across the table to Flynn.

"I didn't know Sean was an investigator. Both he and Sadeh were helpful galley passengers." Niko looked at Sean. "You were good to Christos and your friendship made his voyage easier. He is young and this whole thing has been hard on him."

"I'm not an investigator," Sean stated emphatically. "I am an engineer. Everything I told you about myself is true. You said earlier that you thought I would harm you for the property that my family lost in Ireland." Sean was obviously upset by Niko's comment.

Niko's expression reflected his confusion about this man he had come to like. "I couldn't think of any other reason you would bring your pregnant wife on a voyage like this. Only people that are in trouble or who want to hide travel on a tramp ship."

"Well, I was in trouble. Just like you, I did the wrong thing for the right reason. Jimmy offered to help me out of that bind if I could help him find the contraband. That is all I was on here to do. Flynn here told me you could be involved with the drug smuggling on the ship and to be careful, but from the day we met I knew he was wrong. I would never harm you or Christos."

Niko responded honestly, "I'm sorry, Sean, you are a good friend. I just didn't know who I could trust."

"Well, Niko, you can trust me. I'm dead on with my right hook but couldn't hit a damn thing with a pistol." Sean's flippant remark and charismatic smile consumed the seriousness of the conversation, bringing a smile to both Niko's and Flynn's faces.

"Well, you're a pretty good investigator Sean," Jimmy said, making no attempt to hide his amusement at the way Sean had handled things and the friendship he had cultivated.

CHAPTER TWENTY

The coast-guard shuttle boat thumped against the waves, moving through the darkness, finding its way to a small private pier at Tangiers. Three djellaba-clad passengers disembarked and walked silently toward the market, with Regan strategically located between Loren in the lead and Mojo in the rear. When Regan recognized the farmer from the country, he touched Loren's shoulder, bringing her to a physical stop. She turned, her eyes sheltered by the hood of her djellaba, which was falling over her head. Impulsively he pushed the hood off, exposing her face, beautiful and mysterious in the Tangiers night. He hesitated for a moment, caught the error in his impulse, and pulled away, turning to Mojo.

"There's that old farmer," he said. "He goes back to the mountains on the same road as the messenger, and he will give us a ride for a bit of money. We should meet the messenger en route; he will know where Abasi is." Regan reached into his pants pocket for money, only to be stopped by Mojo pushing cash into his hand. Regan spoke to the farmer in Arabic. Mojo spoke Arabic fluently and realized Regan's command of the language was limited but adequate. He was ready to assist if necessary, but the farmer seemed to understand, and with the funds provided allowed the threesome into the back of his produce wagon. Loren struggled with the high step and accepted the assistance of Regan's strong arms. She seated herself on the floor next to a sack seeping out grain kernels and pulled the hood of her djellaba around her face. She knew Mojo would seat himself next to Regan to form a security circle; it was how they were trained.

They were silent as the wagon lumbered over the rough country road. Loren pulled her djellaba tighter around her as the night air became cool and the moon rose above them. She felt Regan's eyes on her, and she looked away. He was a man in her custody and nothing more—just an assignment.

A small lantern became visible in the distance. It was just a dot in the darkness, but as it came closer the light of the moon revealed the brightly coloured wagon pulled by the small horse.

Regan recognized it. "He is the messenger." He spoke to Mojo in Arabic so as not to cause any suspicion with the driver of the wagon. "That is the man I need to ask. I am going to ask this driver to stop when they meet."

Mojo agreed. Following Regan's instructions, the driver called out to the messenger and stopped as the wagons met on the narrow road. The men got out. Regan spoke to the driver.

Loren stayed in the wagon, alert and watchful, with her hand resting on her service revolver, tucked discreetly under her djellaba. When the men got back in, Regan issued instructions to the driver, who nodded and commanded the horse to go forward.

About a half-hour later the wagon moved off the main trail and proceeded up a narrow road to a remote village with a few adobe cottages. The wagon driver spoke to the threesome and Mojo spoke in Arabic, asking him to wait. The man seemed reluctant, but agreed as Mojo pushed money into his hand.

The narrow cobblestone street was lit only by the moon and the dim glimmer of lamps from a few cottages. Regan walked in the darkness until he found a small cottage set back off the main street, but not far from where the wagon waited. He knocked on the slatted wooden door. Mojo and Loren waited behind him, instinctively prepared for any unexpected event. The door opened. Regan bent his tall frame to enter, followed by his two companions. He asked for Abasi and identified himself.

"Tell them it is safe, and I have come to take them to Christos."

The man spoke quietly to his wife and she left, and a few moments later Abasi and Shima appeared from behind a curtain covering the entrance to a small room.

Regan grasped them in his arms, hugging them securely, and explained they were safe now and needed to come quickly. He told them his two companions were with the Garda out of Ireland and that the coast guard was waiting to take them all to safety, and he said he would tell them everything when they got to the ship. "Please hurry!"

The declaration that Christos was waiting on the ship and anxious to see them scurried them into urgency. Regan ushered the older couple toward the horse wagon waiting on the dark street. Loren and Mojo followed cautiously, observant of their unknown surroundings. Regan helped the older couple into the wagon and again extended his hand to Loren; she accepted his gesture and, for the slightest moment, their eyes met. Regan organized the feed sacks to create a seating accommodation for the older couple. Shima pulled a blanket from the bag she had brought with her and Regan covered their knees and made sure their djellabas covered their heads and hid their faces while he explained the journey ahead.

Mojo took a seat on the floor between them and the back of the wagon. Regan sat down on the wagon floor across from them, with Loren beside him as his protector from the unknowns of the night. She pulled her long legs close to her chest and tucked her djellaba around her knees, assuring she had easy access to her service revolver. Her actions were observed by Regan, and as angry as he felt, he was becoming respectfully aware of the trained professional she was. He turned to her. "Please thank your lead investigator for this…for making sure Christos's grandparents are safe. They are our only family."

She looked at him for a moment but, fighting her heart's emotions, she could only respond with a nod. She sat quietly, watching the stars pass overhead. Regan was exhausted and drifting in and out of restless sleep. She could feel him breathe, and his closeness was comforting. She wanted to drift off, too, and pretend she was still his Cinderella. Abasi and Shima were wrapped tightly in their blanket and resting against each other. Watching them, she imagined how special Cala must have been. Her parents seemed gentle and loving and had cared for their grandson since he was a child. No wonder Regan despised her for putting these people in danger. They had brought the meaning of love into his life. Even if things were different, if he was not a criminal, she could never give him the love he had with Cala, or a child.

Mojo opened the bag with the thermos of coffee, filled the cups, and passed one to Loren. Regan stirred next to her. She passed him a cup, and his touch brought Abasi and Shima to alertness as Mojo passed them coffee. "We are getting close to Tangiers," he told Abasi. "We need to transfer to the boat soon."

The black of the coffee replaced the black of the night, and the quiet, cold mountain air became the stagnant night heat of Tangiers, saturated with the noise and chaos of the market. The horse and produce wagon stopped on the busy merchant street, allowing the five djellaba-clad passengers to mingle among the people and move unnoticed through the streets toward the pier where the coast-guard boat was waiting.

Mojo and Loren positioned their passengers safely between them on board, and Mojo spoke briefly on his hand radio, advising that the coast guard the shuttle was en route back to the *Autumn Wind* with the cargo.

The sun was rising from the sea as the small boat appeared through the grey haze lingering above the water. The *Autumn Wind* stood silent, her running lights fading into the morning. The large coast-guard vessel was positioned beside her, blocking the path of the death-black yacht securely tied to the *Autumn Wind*. A ramp was rigged between the *Autumn Wind* and coast-guard vessel to facilitate easy access between them. Chatter on the coast-guard radio between the vessels brought Christos running to the deck railing next to the ramp. Micky and Flynn chatted as they followed casually behind him to assist their team members back on board.

Loren came up the ramp first and found the comforting arms of her father, and Mojo followed behind the other three. A teary-eyed Christos wrapped his beloved grandparents and father in his arms. Loren fought back the tears the moving reunion brought to her eyes. She was exhausted; it had been hours since she had slept, and her emotions were raw.

"Good job." Jimmy's strong arm around her shoulders pulled her tight to his body. Loren nodded as she stood at his side, every bit the professional investigator he had trained her to be.

Regan held his family close and spoke quietly to his son, who immediately approached the investigation team standing off to the side. "Thank you for bringing my grandparents back here." His emotional gratitude was not hidden as he brushed his tears from his face.

Loren's uncultivated maternal instincts compelled her to take him in her arms without hesitation. She released him, passing him to Jimmy, Micky, and Mojo, each of them easing an uncontrollable awkward emotion for the young man.

Loren's impulse to comfort his son had not gone unnoticed by Regan, who stood with his arms on the shoulders of Abasi and Shima. They moved close, and Regan spoke to the team for the exhausted threesome.

"I know you went out of your way to bring my family together, and I can't thank you enough." Regan extended his hand to each member of the team in gratitude. Jimmy watched as he acknowledged Loren. He was cool toward her, so something was still unsettled between them. He was as Loren had described him; an island. But still, as distant as the man seemed, he did have a genuine concern for looking after those closest to him, and Jimmy felt Loren had become one of those special people.

Niko emerged from the galley to the welcoming arms of Abasi and Shima, who affectionately referred to him as their other son. Sean and Sadeh followed, and Regan introduced them and explained they had helped the investigators. Shima could not contain her caring nature when she met the young, pregnant woman. Sadeh, who to this point had handled her pregnancy entirely on her own, tried to assure the woman she was fine, and with some input from Niko and Sean the matter of her current wellbeing was established.

The aroma of fresh coffee and breakfast was drifting from the galley as Niko ushered the group through the door. The table, now extended with a large inserted leaf, was set for the entire group. Shoulder weapons were removed as the investigators settled in with Regan's family. Eggs, bacon, sausage, sautéed potatoes and vegetables, and baked apples, accompanied by fresh buns and cinnamon rolls, were delivered to the table by Niko with the assistance of Christos.

Regan was obviously exhausted but seemed more at peace than Flynn had ever seen him. Jimmy listened as Abasi spoke of the journey and the last few weeks in the mountains. As the plates emptied and coffee was passed for the second time, Jimmy Flynn, from his seat at the end of the table, asked for the attention of the group gathered before him.

"Regan, some good news. We have located the missing witness, and you will never guess where we found him."

A cluster of impatient faces gazed at Jimmy in anticipation, waiting for him to provide more information.

"The *Seaward Angel*. Our missing Gavin Connor is the man who saw the attack in the alley and has confirmed the shooting of Ivory was in self-defence. He is the witness you were looking for."

Regan looked surprised, and relieved as he stopped stirring his coffee and froze like a statue. Unable to comment, he looked at Niko and then across the table at Loren, who was obviously as surprised by the news as he was. If he could have looked into her heart, he would have seen how thankful she was, too. She knew this would change things for Regan. But it would not change her breach of professional conduct, and without the fear of diminishing the value of his testimony, there was no reason for him not to expose her.

Jimmy continued. "We used passenger manifests and when we found him on board the ship yesterday, I asked the security officer to bring him to the phone. He provided a full verbal account of what had happened. Gavin Connor is on his way here now and will provide his written statement along with the rest of you. Niko, your friend is anxious to see you, and Regan, Tim is sending your personal stuff from your cabin with him.

"I have been talking with the Senior Garda Detective. The prisoners arrived in Ireland last night, and his detectives have secured confessions. O'Hare tried to pin the whole smuggling operation, including the passengers, on Axel Morgan, so Morgan confessed his part in the whole affair and fully exposed O'Hare's participation in the scheme. We will be adding the charge of the murder of the sailor and attempted murder of Connor to those charges, so they will both be going to jail.

"Axel Morgan also admitted he was the man who was with Ivory when he attacked Niko, and confirmed that the shooting was an accident. He said Ivory was high on cocaine and out of control when he grabbed Niko, and would have shot him and Regan, too. It was Axel Morgan who destroyed the bakery. The carpet merchant across from the bakery told him who Regan was, and a cab driver said he had taken them to the dock. It was Axel Morgan who told Nigeria where to find Regan and his son."

Niko was bewildered. He had lived in the alley, but he had never seen Axel Morgan there, and he was trying to fit the first mate into the smuggling scene with Ivory the night of the shooting. He listened intently as the investigator continued.

"Samba said his father never sailed in the Atlantic and sent Axel back to the *Autumn Wind* on a fishing boat that left after Niko and Christos, with instructions for O'Hare to sail around the Mediterranean coast, as well as which ports to stop at. He figured Regan would come to get his son. Axel was instructed not to tell O'Hare about Ivory being shot, or that the boy the cook had brought on board was the son of the man who had shot him. Nigeria wanted to flush out Regan to inflict his own vengeance and didn't want O'Hare getting involved. Samba said they started following the *Autumn Wind* when it left Tangiers, watching for Regan to come for his son. But he had not come, so they planned to board the ship at its next cargo stop before it left the Mediterranean and get the boy. When the engines went down, and the ship became stranded, it gave them the perfect opportunity. So, they decided to board the *Autumn Wind* and use Christos as bait to get Regan out in the open before the ship entered Italian waters."

Sean shot Micky a mischievous glance as Jimmy continued.

"There is a dispute between the Italian Santoro Mafia family and Nigeria over the drug trade in Italian waters and Nigeria did not want to appear confrontational to them, so he painted the boat and just had his son Samba with him. His only interest was revenge for the death of his son. When Mojo came on the ship undercover as a deckhand, he recognized Axel as the man he had seen dealing drugs in the alley. We couldn't believe our luck in getting O'Hare and Axel together along with Nigeria and Samba."

Jimmy Flynn was watching the confused faces of the people gathered before him as they methodically pieced these strange villains together.

"As my friend Mac Flanagan said when I brought Sean and Sadeh into this, some people belong in jail, but some people don't. There are two witnesses prepared to testify that the shooting of Abdul Nakarasa was in self-defence, so all charges against you, Captain Regan Quinn, will be dropped. Niko, the evidence in your log book confirms the information Axel Morgan provided in his confession, so all charges against you for passenger smuggling will also be dropped. I agree with Sean, you are not the one that should be taking the blame for this."

"What about the other three murders?" Niko asked in a troubled tone.

"You have an alibi," Jimmy said. "The entries in your log book place you on this ship on the night of each of those murders."

Niko could not contain his relief. "Thank you," was all he could manage. The very book he thought would put him in jail was what kept him out.

"I will personally see to it there is no mention of charges in the file on this investigation so there will be no repercussions on either of your careers."

Jimmy shifted in his chair, took a swallow of coffee, then added, "You may have to testify in front of a judge, but we should be able to avoid having any of you appear in an open court. Your cooperation has brought a close to this investigation with better results than we had hoped for."

Regan rose and extended his hand across the table to Jimmy, and for the first time Jimmy Flynn saw a flicker of the real Regan Quinn with his defences down, humbled and genuine; a very different man. His gesture was followed by Niko, who was clearly overcome with gratitude. He had laid awake the last two nights worrying about going to jail. Memories of being bullied in the orphanage were embedded in his mind and serving jail time seemed an impossible future.

When emotions had settled, Jimmy added, "The evidence on this ship, the weapons and drugs, which ended up being mostly cocaine, a new drug that is sought after and worth millions, as well as the evidence on that beastly black yacht, have all been processed. Sean, Micky, and the mechanic off the coast-guard vessel got the troll engine running last night. As soon as we can get a captain lined up, and the coast guard can free up an engine and deck crew to sail this ship, we are going to limp her into Italy with this yacht in tow. We can have the engines properly serviced there, take on supplies, and bring a crew on board. Once the documented cargo is offloaded, we will load this yacht on the cargo deck and sail the *Autumn Wind* back to Ireland with this contraband on board. We will have a coast-guard escort all the way and a team of assault officers on board."

"I'll sail her," Regan offered immediately. "If you will have me as captain, that is? I have the credentials and lots of experience on cargo ships and I have some unused overtime owed me. If Seaward Lines is fine with it, I'd like to sail her to Ireland. It's the least I can do. I owe you. You saved all our lives."

Flynn assessed the man briefly. He was surprised at Regan's gesture but impressed by his change of attitude. "If you want to do that, Regan, it would be appreciated—the fewer people who know what we're carrying and why, the better. We are hand-picking the crew we're bringing on board from the coast guard. Are you sure you want to do this?"

"Absolutely, Jimmy; I would consider it an honour."

"Okay, Captain Quinn," Jimmy said. "Sean and Sadeh want to stay on, too. Sean built this ship and he wants to take her home, and Gavin Connor has already volunteered to be first mate to the captain. He knows the ship and wants to sail her back to her port of call, where he boarded. He is a dedicated sailor and he wants to help bring O'Hare to justice. Niko will stay on as galley master and the crew coming on board will include four galley assistants to help him." Jimmy rose and extended his hand. "Thank you."

Regan accepted enthusiastically.

Jimmy knew the man had to be tired, as he had been up for hours. "Get some rest while we wait for Gavin Conner to arrive. I still have some arrangements to finalize at the harbour in Italy. I will call Seaward and tell them the Garda has requested your assistance to sail a vessel."

Niko ushered an exhausted Abasi and Shima off to a cabin he had prepared for them and sent Regan off to Christos's cabin, where a made-up cot was waiting.

Jimmy reached over and took Loren's hand. "We are going to use Sunset Harbour to service the ship. The coast guard can keep a good eye on her there, and it might take a few days to get the repairs done and things back in proper running order. I sent Micky and Mojo back to Ireland so they can spend a few days with their families. I thought maybe you'd like to take a couple of days at your cottage. Sean and Sadeh want to stay on the ship for the trip to Italy. Sean knows this ship inside-out and could be a big help with that extra engine if we have any problems. We can all get together at your cottage once Captain Quinn gets the ship into the harbour."

Loren nodded without resistance. Niko and Christos returned to the galley in time to say goodbye to Loren as she boarded the coast-guard shuttle. Niko passed her an extra blanket to cover up and a thermos of hot coffee for the trip, and the navigator pushed off to Italy.

Regan entered the galley refreshed and rested at dawn. "Good morning, sleepyhead," Niko teased his old friend. "I put your bag in your cabin and you were sleeping like a baby."

Regan noticed a stranger seated at the galley table but laughed and poured himself a coffee. "Something smells good."

Niko had breakfast underway, which included a poached egg on toast for his old friend.

"Regan, this is Gavin Connor," he said.

Gavin rose and extended his arm. "Captain Quinn."

"Regan, please." Regan greeted Gavin Connor with a strong handshake that drew the man to him. "Gavin, I can't thank you enough for telling Investigator Flynn what you saw in the alley; you have helped Niko and me out and we will always be grateful to you. I can't believe you were under my nose the whole time."

Gavin smiled, pleased that Regan was not annoyed that he had remained silent. He tried to explain. "After Niko cut me loose from the ship, the crazy old fisherman rescued me, and a goat herder gave me a ride to Tangiers that afternoon. I contacted Abasi and hid in the alley while I waited for the man to make the false card.

"That night in the alley, I did not see the other man with Ivory, but I recognized Niko, and had heard him speak of his longtime friend being the captain of a passenger ship called the *Seaward Angel*. So, I figured it had to be you, Regan, as the *Seaward* was the only passenger ship in port. I used my real name and personal information on the card, so I had no problem boarding.

"I was planning to come to you before we got to Ireland. I have sailed with Niko under O'Hare's command for two years. O'Hare needed Niko to keep the crew and Niko knew how to handle him, so I thought he would be safe on the voyage. I wanted to get as close to Ireland as I could before I involved you. I knew as a captain you could do things to help Niko that I could not do by myself, but I was on the ship illegally. I knew Niko would vouch for me, so you would know I was just not some imposter. I was in a tight spot, but if I had known your son was on the *Autumn Wind* with Niko or that Axel was the other man in the alley doing the drug deal with Ivory, I would have gone to you right away. I didn't know you had left the ship or that the *Autumn Wind* did not go directly back to Ireland, and I didn't know anything about this contraband the investigator is talking about."

Gavin seemed like a good man. It was obvious to Regan why Niko had risked his own life to save him.

"I am proud to know you, First Mate Connor, and I look forward to sailing with you." Regan extended his hand again, which Gavin proudly accepted.

"As am I, Captain Quinn." Gavin Connor nodded respectfully before he let his hand drop.

Niko, along with Christos and Sean and Sadeh, was busy putting breakfast on the table when Abasi and Shima joined the group. Christos welcomed them with hugs, and proudly brought warm cinnamon rolls to the table to the gracious acknowledgement of his grandfather. Abasi spoke fluent English and included the table guests in his conversation about the bakery in Tangiers and all the help Christos was to him and Shima. It was obvious Regan was relieved to have his family safe and together. As Jimmy Flynn watched them he knew he had made the right decisions; no one sitting there belonged in jail.

"Jimmy, where is your team?" Regan was curious about the other members of the investigation team, but especially Loren.

Jimmy talked between bites of Niko's glazed ham and roasted potatoes. "I sent Micky and Mojo home to Ireland. It's been a couple of months since they have had time with their families. Micky has a boy and a girl about Christos's age and Mojo has two boys, who are eight and ten." Regan seemed surprised; it had not occurred to him these men had lives outside of being investigators and that they had children, too.

"And Investigator Lombardi?" Regan asked. "She went to Ireland, too, then?"

"No, just to her cottage in Italy; it's not far from here." Jimmy wasn't sure why he was asking. Loren had deceived Regan Quinn, and he was obviously angry at her, so Jimmy decided he would approach the matter of Loren's undisclosed relationship. As soon as he could get the man alone he intended to reveal Loren was his daughter and ask him directly if they had been romantically involved. Regan Quinn was neither a murderer or a smuggler, but he was still the man who could destroy Loren's career if he exposed the relationship, and Jimmy wanted to be one step ahead of him.

"Regan, you know Sunset Harbour," Jimmy said, remembering Loren's comment.

Regan nodded, digging into his breakfast as he spoke. "It's a private harbour used by the coast guard about fifty miles north of the main Italian harbour."

"That's where we would like to take the ship to unload the legal cargo and for maintenance. Security is good there and it may take a few days for repairs. Think you can get her in there with this single engine?"

"Absolutely." Regan was confident and enthusiastic about the task ahead. "Once breakfast is over, I'd like to have access to O'Hare's charts and to get familiarized with the bridge and the ship."

Gavin was quick to inject, "I can get anything you need, and I ran the bridge with O'Hare. I didn't know we had a fourth engine on this ship, but I had a look last night with Sean and it's big enough to do the job."

Sean was excited about getting involved with the trip to Italy. "I built this ship, Regan, and I can tell you anything you need to know about her."

Regan nodded with appreciation as the men got up from the table. "Well, maybe we should see if we can get this vessel underway, then. Thank you, Niko, for breakfast."

As the men left, Regan pulled his son close. "Help Niko clean up, and when we sail, you can come join us in the bridge."

Christos sprung from the table with delight and, with the assistance of Abasi and Shima, the cleanup started. The galley broke into relaxed chatter.

Jimmy watched as Regan worked with Gavin and Sean to ready the *Autumn Wind* to sail, and just before they were ready to leave, he asked him for a moment to talk.

"Of course," Regan said, and waited while Jimmy considered what he was about to say.

"Regan, Loren Lombardi has been a civilian investigator with my unit for the past eight years, but she is also my daughter."

"Your daughter!" Regan was surprised. Loren's friendship with Jimmy Flynn had seemed personal but he had assumed it was a relationship.

"Yes, Loren is my adopted daughter."

"Loren told me her family died in an automobile accident when she was young, and said she went to live with a family in Ireland." Regan was remembering their first supper together and making the connection.

"She was six years old when she came to live with us. I was the investigator on that case."

Regan was silently confused. He had assumed everything she had said was a lie. He shrugged. "Well, I guess one thing she told me was the truth."

Jimmy didn't miss the terse tone of his remark but chose to ignore it and smiled instead. Regan Quinn had the right to be angry, so Jimmy spoke politely and finished saying what was on his mind.

"Regan, I wanted to ask you something, and I would appreciate the respect of an honest answer, Jimmy hesitated. "Were you romantically involved with my daughter while she was undercover on the *Seaward Angel*?"

Regan responded without hesitation. "I fell in love with Loren Lombardi, not Investigator Lombardi or Flynn or whoever she is. I had no idea she was an investigator when we became friends. I know now she was just doing her job, and that she never had feelings for me." He stopped short of saying they were lovers, but it occurred to him that might be what Jimmy was aiming at with this conversation; information that would expose his investigator's breach of conduct could cost Loren her job and maybe Jimmy was just trying to find out if he intended to be vindictive so he could protect his daughter.

"Thank you for being honest, but I think she does have feelings for you. When I met her in Portugal, I asked her that same question, and she did not give me the direct answer you just did. She said you were just using her for amusement, something you probably did on every voyage."

Regan listened, and hid the concern he was feeling about Loren's assessment of their relationship and his behaviour as Jimmy continued.

"But something about her was different. I always caution my investigators not to get involved with their assignments and Loren has never let this happen before, so I hope she is wrong about you. Loren is very guarded and keeps her emotions private. If she let you break down those defences, she has feelings for you."

Regan was studying Jimmy.

"She is wrong about me, sir. I don't pick up women on my voyages to keep myself amused, and if Loren had not injected herself into my life, I doubt I would have met her—but from the moment I did, all she has done is keep secrets. I don't know who Loren Lombardi is."

"Well, I know my daughter, Regan. She is an excellent investigator because she is a good judge of character. She told me in Portugal she didn't think you were guilty, and this investigation has proven her right. Loren doesn't like loose ends and I know she won't want to leave things like this with you."

Jimmy put a strong arm on Regan's shoulder. "We will all be getting together at her cottage in Italy. She will have had time to rest and I hope you will give her a chance to tell you the secrets she couldn't before. So, Captain Quinn, let's pull anchor and cast off… and please drop the 'sir'—just Jimmy is fine."

Regan returned to his work, but he felt troubled. Flynn had said there would be no mention of charges in the police file, but if he was doubting what Regan had just told him and felt he had been using his daughter for amusement, he could change his mind and ruin his career. Regan knew that by not disclosing the relationship in his statement he had leverage he could use to keep this investigator from doing that; a card up his sleeve he hadn't played, but he wasn't about to throw it on the table. Regan had been honest when he told Jimmy Flynn he had fallen in love with his daughter; but was his daughter a beautiful seductive investigator who had used their intimacy to secure information that would prove her value on Flynn's team, or was she the beautiful seductive woman who had surrendered to his love. The only way he could be sure he did not have to fear Flynn's Garda authority, was to find out which one Loren Lombardi was.

Jimmy watched him as he returned to the bridge. He was a smart man. He hadn't denied the relationship, but he had not condoned it either. The next move was Captain Quinn's. If he did not give Loren a chance to explain, Jimmy would know he intended to expose her to his superiors, it would ruin her career and cast a dark shadow over his entire investigation and Jimmy wasn't about to let *that* happen.

The Spirit of the Autumn Wind

An hour later, with a coast-guard escort, Captain Regan Quinn and First Mate Gavin Connor on the bridge, and Christos and Sean at their side, the *Autumn Wind* set sail toward Sunset Harbour with the black yacht in tow.

It was obvious to Jimmy Flynn the moment they left that Captain Regan Quinn was a very competent sailor. He had towed a vessel before and was no stranger to cargo ships. He had listened carefully when Sean discussed the construction of the ship and, at the reduced speed of the troll engine, immediately grasped a feel for the vessel. There were those like O'Hare, who could sail a ship and learn the skills to be certified as a captain, and then there was Regan Quinn. He was born to sail, the ocean was in his blood, the vessel was his soul, and the desire was his spirit. He did not just sail the vessel; he was one with the ship.

Regan loved the *Autumn Wind* the moment he took control. She was beautifully balanced and handled like a race car, even with her one backup engine. Regan was as impressed with the vessel as Sean was with his ability to sail her. Sean came from a lengthy line of sailors. He had grown up on fishing vessels and could sail anything, but possessed his father's gift to design them, and that was what he was driven to do.

This was the first of many hours they would spend together as friends on the voyage home to Ireland. Sean could tell by the way the ship was handling whether it was Regan or the relief captain at the controls. He would wake up in the night with design schematics floating around in his mind, and if it was Regan on the bridge he would take his sketch pad and join him, taking a position on the seat next to the captain and looking out into the night at the water. Listening to the ship, he would create what no other man could.

CHAPTER TWENTY-ONE

Loren was exhausted. She had been up for seventy-two hours with barely a moment's rest. She called a cab to pick her up at the pier and had him stop at the grocery store on her way back to the cottage. She emptied the grocery bags into the fridge so there would be something for the others to eat when they arrived, then fell fully clothed onto her bed.

It was almost six when she awoke to the sound of voices. Suddenly remembering she was not alone, she got up, showered, changed into a cotton sundress, and walked out to find eight people being entertained by Jimmy on her balcony. Jimmy immediately pulled her into his arms and kissed her forehead, then introduced her to Gavin Connor as his daughter, Special Investigator Lombardi. There was no need for formality among this group of strangers whom circumstance had forced into blunt honesty.

"Hope you managed to find something to eat," Loren told the group.

"We are treating Niko," was Sean's explanation for the Italian takeout set out on the balcony table. Niko laughed. He was relaxed and enjoying the attention.

"I used your phone to call my sister Sara in Ireland. I hope you don't mind." Sean laid money on the table for the call, while passing her a plate and sliding over so she was seated next to Regan. His arm touched her, and she could feel him; he was so close, yet miles away. The light blue shirt he wore was partly open, and his black eyes seemed to be avoiding her as he casually passed the takeout food containers to her and conversed with Christos and Gavin about the *Autumn Wind* and the voyage.

Christos was thrilled at having travelled in the bridge with Gavin and Sean while his father sailed the ship, and was bubbling over with excitement. Loren could see the strength of his father in the young man—he was handsome, with the same coal-black eyes and gentle manners.

Loren questioned Sean about his shoulder. He joked about not being able to use his right hook for a while.

"And that's a good thing; that right hook has caused us more than enough trouble." Sadeh's giggly response brought chuckles to the table. She was beautiful, happy, and in love. Her gentle, quiet presence seemed the opposite of Sean's magnetic spirit, but there was no mistaking what they shared.

There had been a moment in her life when Loren had let herself feel Regan's love, but she knew from the beginning it was wrong, and the truth would hurt them both. She should have refused his invitation when he asked her to go dancing, but she had let her feelings for him interfere with her job, and now she needed to find the strength to tell him she was sorry for deceiving him, before he was gone from her life forever. He had every right to be angry.

"Loren, girl, are you okay?" her father asked. "You seem quiet."

"Yes, fine, Papa, I am fine," she responded automatically, then glanced over at Regan, wondering if he had heard Jimmy say she was his daughter when he introduced her to Gavin. He was involved in conversation and appeared to have missed her response, but if he had not, it was just one more thing he was angry about.

Jimmy knew why she seemed distant and was hoping she would at least try to talk to Regan, and more importantly, that Regan would give her that chance. He wanted to create an opportunity for her, so suggested the men walk down to the *Autumn Wind* to check on the unloading of the legal cargo and the engine repair. A cleaning crew was already on board to ready her quarters for the new captain and crew. Sean, Gavin, and Christos were quick to attach themselves to the adventure, and everyone started to get up to leave.

"Regan, could I talk with you before you join them?" she asked.

"Yes," he responded, relieved that she wanted to deal with what he had been avoiding, but apprehensive about what she might say. "I'll catch up," he said as he waved the others off.

Sadeh, Abasi, and Shima offered to clean up the dishes and disappeared into the kitchen with Niko.

Loren felt a bit of relief at the departure of her house guests. She was used to the peacefulness the setting of the cottage by the sea brought to her life, and looked out at the view off her balcony before turning to face Regan.

Loren was trained to ask questions and communicate effectively, and Jimmy always said it came naturally to her, but this time she was tripping on her heart and found herself struggling to start the conversation.

"Regan, I wanted to talk to you about what happened between us on the ship."

He took a place beside her on the balcony and looked at her face as if he was trying to figure out who he was talking to.

"My name is Loren Flynn Lombardi. Jimmy Flynn is my adopted father. I am a civilian investigator with Jimmy Flynn's special Garda unit. I have worked for him for eight years and before that I studied journalism in Italy. He has two female civilian investigators on this team, and we are usually assigned to gather information for the Garda in an environment where a woman would not be suspected of surveillance.

"I was on your ship to do the job I am professionally trained to do. But what I let happen between us was not professional. I knew I was falling in love with you and I should have put a stop to it. Instead I hurt you, and I am so sorry. You said everything between us was a lie when Garcia arrested you, but it wasn't, Regan. What I felt for you was real. I was not pretending to love you. I never lied to you, I just kept secrets, because I couldn't tell you the truth. I wanted you to be innocent and I knew in my heart you were, and I wish we would have met some other way."

Like an ocean gale, the stormy dark cloud of anger that was surrounding him drifted off and a rainbow appeared. *He had loved this woman since the moment he saw her, and he wanted her to know the man he really was. She made him feel whole again, he wanted her, and she had just revealed her true self. She loved him too.* He did not speak, but instead ran his hand down the side of her face and pulled her to him and kissed her.

She could not resist. She did not want to resist.

"Loren, I am so sorry for what I said to you that day. When I found out who you were, I was angry and afraid. What I did that night in Tangiers put everyone I love in danger. I could have lost Christos, but because of you and your father's team, I didn't. I wish we could have met some other way too, but if it wasn't for the *Autumn Wind,* we might have not met at all. I want what we had again, but without all the secrets between us."

She pushed away from him and stepped back. "My life is my work. I chose that, and it's all I know and want. I am better off alone."

"Loren, you are a woman who has not let society define her role but has chosen her own future. I recognized that in you the moment I laid eyes on you. I respect that because I understand it. I have spent my life working to overcome the stigma of a worthless orphan, but you are not better off alone. Neither of us is."

"I can't give you what you had with Cala, the love you had with her, a beautiful son. I am not sure any man can ever really love a woman that cannot give him children."

"Loren." He took her hand and pulled her to him. He was not letting her go. He was intense, determined to get her to talk to him, to find out what she really felt. "So, you're telling me you can't have children and you have denied yourself love and happiness because of that; is that why you said you would never marry?"

"I was happy. I love my job, and I did not need the love of a man."

"Loren, I love you, and I want you in my life. A man and a woman do not have to have children to have love. I have a son, and I hope you will open your heart to Christos and to Abasi and Shima, because they are my family. He hesitated, then added, "I would like to be a part of your life and family too. Your father had a talk with me this morning. He wanted to know what was going on between us. God knows I did not meet the father of the woman I love under the circumstances I would have preferred, but at the very least he knows I have nothing to hide and I am being honest with him. He knows I am in love with you, Loren."

He took a moment to plan what he was about to say. "He told me that when you met in Portugal you said that I was just playing with you to keep myself amused, and probably did that with someone on every voyage. Loren, that is not true. I fell in love with you and you are the only woman I have let into my heart since Cala."

He watched her rub away the tears that dampened her face, and waited for her to respond.

"I do love you, Regan. I guess I am just afraid. There have been men in my past that have hurt me because I'm unable to have children, and I don't want to be hurt again."

"Well, don't be afraid, sweetheart. It goes without saying that if I screw this up, I will have Jimmy Flynn and his whole team of investigators to deal with."

Loren finally laughed, and her beautiful smile filled his heart with warmth. She laid her head on his shoulder and let him wrap his arms around her.

"Can we just try, Loren, to find our way back to where we were?"

She nodded, and he let his hand rest on her lower back as they looked out at the view of the sea from her balcony. "It really is beautiful here, sweetheart."

"Yes, it is. This property belonged to the Lombardi family, my real parents. They were Mafia and smuggled drugs and contraband out of Sunset Harbour. They were not that different from Nigeria. Oh, and I do have a published book. It is called *By the Sea*. It's the story of a Mafia family, my family. It is fiction to the readers, but it's my real life. If there are to be no more secrets between us, you need to know who I really am. Perhaps you will feel differently about me once you realize that I did not come from a very nice family."

"Loren, we are not so different, you and me. We have both built a wall around our past to survive, but now we have each other." He pulled her to him and kissed her.

Sadeh was watching Regan and Loren as they talked on the balcony. She was drying dishes next to Niko who had his hands in the sink. She leaned in close to him and half-whispered, "Are they lovers?"

He looked over his shoulder at the couple and his response to Sadeh's question was a puzzled expression. "My friend has seemed a bit distracted. I thought perhaps it was just because of everything that had happened, but maybe this woman has something to do with it?" he said, thinking out loud.

The phone rang. Niko immediately picked it up, not wanting to break up the personal moment Regan and Loren were sharing.

"Hi there!" A bright cheery voice graced his ear. "Is Sean Dolan there? I'm his sister, Sara; he called and left this number, so I could call him when I got in."

Niko responded, "He is not here right now, but I expect he will be back soon."

"Who am I speaking to?" The woman's voice was musically familiar to Sean's.

"Niko Mararious. I'm a friend of your brother."

"Hi, Niko," she said cheerfully. "Sean told me about you in his letter. He said you are a great friend and a great cook too."

Niko couldn't help but be amused at the woman's interest in a stranger.

"He said you will be running a restaurant when you get to Ireland."

Niko's next sentence was lost before he could say it as the woman chattered on. "I've been working in the pub at the Old Dolan Shipyard marina. I hope I get a chance to meet you."

Niko was listening, waiting to see what else she knew. Sean did not know the restaurant was at the marina when he sent the letter to Sara and she seemed none the wiser. She went quiet, leaving it up to him to come up with something to say.

"Well, I am sure we will meet. I'm continuing the voyage to Ireland on the *Autumn Wind* with Sean and Sadeh. You must be very excited to see them both."

Her voice went from animated to ecstatic. "Yes! I have not met Sadeh, and I am looking forward to being an aunt to my brother's child. The Dolans have not had an Irish wedding in quite some time and Sean and Sadeh won't have any time to waste getting married once they get back to Ireland."

Her voice was enchanting, and her comment brought a rare chuckle from Niko. She was impulsive and charismatic like her brother. Niko was just about to ask her if she would like to speak to Sadeh when the men reappeared, toting the whisky and rum from Niko's galley cupboard.

"Your brother has just come in. He'll be anxious to speak with you."

"Sean." Niko motioned him to come to the phone. "Your sister, Sara."

"Thank you." Sean took the phone, assuming from Niko's smile that his exuberant sister had chatted him into a conversation, but not before noting the obviously intimate state of Regan and Loren. A quick glance at Jimmy's somewhat relieved expression revealed he knew that there was a relationship between the two. There had been no indication of any type of involvement between them before; in fact, they had seemed quite detached. Sean watched them as he set out the timetable and plans for the rest of the journey with his sister, and when he hung up the phone, he thanked Niko for looking after the call. "My sister is quite full of life." Sean said knowing she would have chatted Niko into a conversation. He was not apologizing for his sister, just letting Niko know how special she was.

Niko smiled at Sean. "She was very pleasant and is looking forward to meeting Sadeh."

He stopped short of commenting on her thoughts about an Irish wedding. Abasi and Shima had taken a personal interest in Sadeh and her pregnancy, and Niko was not sure if they knew she and Sean were not married. They had lost their daughter when she was about the same age.

Sadeh had told Niko her mother had died when she was ten and she had grown up under the strict thumb of her father and brother. When she left with Sean Dolan it was under the threat of death and she gave up her life and family forever. It occurred to Niko the relationship between Abasi, Shima, and Sadeh was mutually fulfilling. He liked her, and she saw him as Regan had—for who he was, not how he appeared. The fact that his leg was deformed made no difference to her. When she talked to him, it was as a friend and to search out his modest male opinion on life without judgment and with respect.

Loren returned to the kitchen to secure glasses for the men and a bottle of her favourite Italian wine from the cupboard to share with Abasi and Shima. Sean's arm was around Sadeh as he escorted her to the balcony with the others and gently assisted her into a comfortable chair. The men were talking non-stop about the activity on the *Autumn Wind* as the drinks were poured, including a small portion of rum for Christos. Regan immediately noted Niko's gesture with a curious but accepting glance and a smile.

"Niko, I gave you my boy a few weeks ago and you give me back a man."

"Well, I guess we all had a lot of growing up to do!"

There was no mistaking Niko was referring to what he had just witnessed between his friend and Loren, and his point was taken without comment. Niko raised his glass. "To Ireland," he said, and the others joined in.

Sadeh was adjusting her dress, trying to find a more comfortable fit for her swelling belly. "Loren, do you know if there are any clothing stores in the village that might have maternity clothing? I am afraid the most comfortable thing I have to wear right now is Niko's galley smock and I should hate to meet Sean's family in that."

Sean pulled her close, somewhat uncomfortable that he had overlooked her needs.

"Yes, there is a nice shopping area downtown with lots of stores," Loren said.

"Could we go, Sean, before we sail?" Sadeh asked.

"Yes," Sean was quick to respond. "I want to go to the ship in the morning when the engine crew arrives, but in the afternoon we could."

"I could take you shopping if you like, Sadeh," Loren said. "I want to buy a new handbag for my mother before I leave anyway. I spend my vacations here. I don't know much about maternity clothing, but I know most of the stores. Maybe we could go for lunch, too?"

"I would love to do that, Loren. Can you spare the time from your work?"

"Yes, there will be plenty of time to catch up on things once the *Autumn Wind* has sailed. I would like to show you the village. It's beautiful and quaint and a bit old-fashioned, I guess."

Sean smiled his approval. It had been a long lonely voyage for Sadeh. She and Niko had become good friends and she had spent a lot of time with Christos, but there had been no women for her to talk to.

Regan was watching Loren. Because she had told him she could not have children, he knew that what she had offered to do for Sadeh

The Spirit of the Autumn Wind

would make her uncomfortable, but she was as beautiful inside as out. Regan was not going to let this wonderful woman out of his life.

After drinks, everyone began to leave. Jimmy, Niko, Regan, and Christos planned to stay on the ship. Sean and Sadeh and Abasi and Shima were staying in Loren's spare bedrooms. It was obvious to Niko that Regan wanted to say goodnight to Loren privately, so he suggested he and Christos go on ahead, citing his need to check the refrigeration of the galley supplies that he had requested be loaded onto the ship for the remaining voyage. Regan followed them down the cobblestone walk with Loren at his side, her hand resting in his, and as his friend and son disappeared into the dimly lit street, he took her in his arms and kissed her.

"Loren, tomorrow could I take you out for supper? Is there some place nice here? Maybe where we could go dancing for a while? It's beautiful here. I just want us to have some time together before I have to sail."

"I'd like that, Regan. There is a lovely place on the sea, the Moonlight Inn. They have an excellent Italian restaurant with a dance floor that juts out over the water. It's like dancing on the waves. It's my favourite."

Regan found himself wondering who had taken her there, and who she had danced with on the waves. "The Moonlight Inn. I'll call in the morning and make a reservation for seven?"

"Yes, that's fine." She pushed up against him and put her lips on his. He welcomed her kisses, his arm was tightening around her back, and she could feel him wanting her as he ran his hand along her hips. He restrained his behaviour, fully aware her father, who had stayed behind under the ruse of sorting out some paperwork, could be observing them from her cottage.

"I feel like a teenage boy sneaking my first kiss. God knows I have enough fences to mend with your father as it is." Regan laughed as he released her. He stepped back, holding both her hands. "Tomorrow we will have some time together. I need to talk to my son and tell him about us. The only woman who has been in his life since his mother is Shima. I have never brought a woman into our home. He is almost a man himself, but I need to make sure he will understand."

"Regan, I like Christos. He is a fine young man, a lot like you in many ways. I hope he will let me be a part of his life."

Touched by what she had just said, he rested his hand along her face and kissed her gently, then pulled himself away and slipped off into the darkness without another word.

Abasi and Shima had already gone to bed. Sean and Sadeh said good night to Loren and Jimmy, excused themselves, and went off to the bedroom they were sharing.

Jimmy poured himself another drink and refilled Loren's wine glass. "I was hoping we could talk for a bit, girl."

"Yes, Papa, I know." She blurted out her defence. "I should have told you about Regan, but with everything that has happened, there has barely been a minute to talk."

Jimmy laughed and reached over and took her hand. "It's okay, girl. That's not what I wanted to talk to you about." He paused thoughtfully before continuing. "I've been thinking. I really need to have someone working with me as an assistant lead investigator, to research the cases and do the background work required to get the undercover investigators safely in place. My workload on these cases is heavy.

"I would like to have you work directly with me. You have done an excellent job undercover, you know what the investigators need, and your research and attention to detail is excellent, exactly what I need. You know how to work with me and you are the best investigator for the job." The Garda is under pressure to allow women to join the force and it won't be long until that happens. You are already working with the police force and have the same training as the male investigators. I would like to have you trained and ready to step into the position of lead investigator when those opportunities become available. What Jimmy had just said was the truth, but he didn't like loose ends either, and this was also his safeguard against his Garda superiors. They could not remove her as an undercover investigator from his unit if she no longer was one. If things did not work out between her and Regan, and he was angry enough to reveal their relationship to Jimmy's Garda superiors, the situation would have already been dealt with.

He hesitated, carefully gauging her reaction to his offer, then added. "I thought maybe with you and Regan…" He was hesitating again, letting his daughter know she had his approval, even though she did not need it. "Well…I thought it might be nice for the two of you if your schedule could be a bit more consistent. It would be a change from undercover work." His concerned tone was that of a father looking out for the best interest of his daughter.

"Wow, your assistant investigator! Jimmy…Papa! You think I'm good enough to work with you?" She was ecstatic.

"Absolutely, girl. I trained you. Do you want the job?"

"Yes! Yes! Yes!" She wrapped her arms around her father. She could not see the tears welling in his eyes, but she could feel the strength of his love.

She could see he was pleased with her decision as she settled in across from him in her favourite deck chair and tucked her legs under her.

"To my new assistant, then!" Jimmy raised his glass to his daughter.

She was happier than he had ever seen her, a deeper, settled kind of happiness that was not just about the job, not just about the love she was sharing with Regan, but the happiness that comes from loving yourself.

"Loren, I'm going to fly back to Ireland as soon as the *Autumn Wind* sails. I need to deal with the charges against Liam O'Hare, Axel Morgan, and Samba Nakarasa, as well as five of the men from the crew who had warrants for their arrests. All the statements and evidence documents for this case must be organized and prepared for the judge. I was wondering if you might like to take charge of that?

Some of the files are here, but the rest of the paperwork from this investigation is boxed and at my office. I can have Micky put it on the police plane and send it down and if you would like to sail back to Ireland with Regan on the *Autumn Wind*, you could work on the files at sea."

She was listening intently, waiting for Jimmy to finish. "I spoke to Regan this morning, and he made it clear that he was in love with you, and I am pretty sure you feel the same about him. I feel bad that it was the undercover investigation that brought this man into your life. I know he was angry and working things out with him wasn't easy for you. I wanted to make it up to you two, give you a chance to start over with an honest relationship, and I thought a couple of weeks at sea might be a good way to start. I have asked that the captain's quarters on the *Autumn Wind* be completely cleaned up." Jimmy had been a top investigator for years and his subtle reference to the captain's quarters let her know he was aware their relationship was intimate.

Tears were welling up in Loren's eyes. "Thank you, Papa. I do love Regan. It just happened. I broke your rule about getting involved with an assignment…and look what a mess I caused."

Jimmy got up and knelt beside his daughter. "No mess, girl. I know you decided not to let yourself fall in love because you cannot have children, but your mother and I both wanted love for you. It is very special to have someone to share your life with. Regan's son is a very nice young man and he will be a part of your life, too."

Loren buried her face in her father's shoulder. "Thank you, Papa, for understanding. Regan has asked me to go out for supper with him tomorrow night. I will save all this exciting news and share it with him then."

"Well, we'd better both get some sleep. Tomorrow is a busy day. The engine crew is on board. The cargo will be offloaded, and we will get that yacht loaded and secured on the deck for the trip back to Ireland. And the next day the military is coming on board. They want to run a second escort ship with the *Autumn Wind* back to Ireland. Their plan is to take the ship into Regan's Dolan Shipyard Marina at Suaimhneas Cove. Sean says the ship was built there and it is a secure place to unload the contraband. The military wants to take charge of the weapons as soon as we drop anchor, and the Garda will be able to unload the drugs in a safe environment. If everything goes well, we should be out to sea and on the way to Ireland in a couple of days."

Jimmy kissed her forehead. "Goodnight, girl."

"Goodnight, Papa."

CHAPTER TWENTY-TWO

The warm morning sun brought chaos to Loren's cottage on the sea. Everyone was up early and off to the ship, where Niko had breakfast underway. Sadeh and Loren set off shopping right after the meal. Sadeh was beautiful, and despite her swelling belly, everything she tried on looked stylish. She chose soft, cotton, sleeveless dresses in light colours. She laughed with Loren about the restrictions of her clothing under the thumb of Egyptian tradition and stated quite firmly she would never wear shapeless, dull-coloured clothing that covered her like a gunnysack again. She had impeccable taste, and regardless of how restrictive her childhood had been, she had acquired an elegance and grace that made Loren envious. With the shopping out of the way, Loren suggested a restaurant in the shopping area that served naturally prepared foods.

Over lunch, Sadeh talked freely about her upbringing, the reason she and Sean were fleeing on the *Autumn Wind*, and her excitement about motherhood.

Loren timidly followed by disclosing she was adopted by Jimmy and Molly Flynn when her parents died. She spoke only briefly about the history of her notorious family and mentioned her book, since she had observed how much Sadeh liked to read. She talked about growing up as Loren Flynn and her love for her job.

"You are beautiful, Loren. Is it your work that keeps you from marrying?"

It was a direct question, but not one she had not been asked before. "A bit. I just never met anyone special, I guess."

"Maybe Captain Regan Quinn?" Sadeh teased. "He is really handsome, and he likes you."

Loren laughed. This blend of a child and a woman had skillfully managed to get Loren to talk about her life and led her right into a discussion about her feelings for Regan. She lacked the ability to pass judgment on anyone. What came out of Sadeh's mouth came directly from her heart and it was easy to see why Sean Dolan loved her.

"Yes, he is nice, and we are going out for supper tonight."

"Is that who you bought the new pink undergarments for?" Sadeh was giggling as she reached across the table and took Loren's hands.

It was obvious from her condition she and Sean had shared the deepest kind of love against all odds and she was not judging, she was just being a friend. It had been a long time since Loren had shared her thoughts with another woman. Her life was like an undercover assignment and so were her personal feelings; never fully disclosed, never dealt with in truth. She had not seen or felt them as real until this very moment.

"Perhaps one day you will have children, too," Sadeh said.

Her statement left Loren defenceless, and she dropped her head slightly, trying to hide her eyes so they would not reveal the inadequacy she felt as a woman as she divulged she could not have children. It was something she had barely been able to say out loud to herself, never mind to this woman who was almost a stranger.

"You don't have to give birth to have children, Loren. Jimmy and Molly Flynn adopted you. You and Regan can adopt. He is a good father and you would make a wonderful mother." Sadeh squeezed her hands as Loren fought back the tears that were welling up in her eyes. "I'm sorry, Loren, I did not mean to upset you."

"You're right, Sadeh, and honestly, sometimes it is easier to see the errors in the lives of others then our own." She blinked away the tears, swallowed hard, and took a drink of water to compose herself.

"I will be travelling to Ireland on the *Autumn Wind*. I have not told Regan yet, but I will tonight, and I look forward to travelling with you and Sean and to your friendship."

Sadeh's giggle brought a lighter mood to the table. "I shall need a good friend when all four of us meet Sean's parents in Ireland."

"Four of us?" Loren was quick to pick up the detail.

"Oops! These are twins I'm carrying, but please don't tell Sean. The doctor on the coast-guard vessel told me when he examined me after the shooting, and I have sworn him to secrecy. If I tell Sean, he will not want me to sail with him, and it's something I want to do. He is trying to start a new life and the *Autumn Wind* is part of that and so am I, and these babies, too. I won't be separated from him; besides, we will be in Ireland a month before these little ones are due. The doctor on the coast-guard ship was not happy about my decision to stay on the ship, but when I told him I was Egyptian and not legally married, he understood why I could not depend on my family for help. He, too, is Egyptian and understands the intolerance of tradition in that country. He knows both my life and the lives of these babies are in danger if I go home, and I am better off where I am. He told me twins often come early and has requested that he be assigned as the ship's doctor for the voyage to Ireland, just in case. He is a well-trained physician, so everything will be fine. Just please don't tell Sean. He has been through so much with his family and what he is doing now is difficult for him. I want the twins to be a special surprise."

Loren smiled. "Your secret is safe with me, but promise if you feel you need any help, or you change your mind, you will tell me, so I can let Captain Quinn know." She reached across the table and squeezed Sadeh's hand reassuringly. She liked and admired this young woman who, despite her upbringing, knew exactly who she was and what she wanted out of life. Loren looked at her watch and realized it was already after one. "You must be tired, Sadeh."

"Yes, I could do with a bit of rest. I always rest in the afternoon. Doctor's orders," she added playfully, letting Loren know she fully understood the responsibilities of her pregnancy.

As the women drove back to the cottage, Loren could see the *Autumn Wind* had moved from the maintenance side of the harbour and was anchored facing the sea, so the cargo could be offloaded, and the yacht loaded on her cargo deck. She looked a bit out of place, looming above the other smaller coast-guard vessels anchored there, a majestic silhouette against the deep-blue Italian sky.

When Sadeh woke, it was almost five. Niko had returned to Loren's with bags of groceries and was preparing to make an evening meal. The men were not expected back until about six and Loren was dressing for her supper date with Regan. She put her pink dress on the bed. It was the one she had bought to wear the day he was arrested. She laid out the new pink matching underwear she had bought and perfectly coordinated her shoes, handbag, and accessories. At six-thirty she showered, changed, and joined Regan and Jimmy, who were chatting in the living room.

Regan was finely dressed in a black, tailored suit. His dark tie against his snow-white shirt blended black with shades of pink that almost perfectly matched her dress, and she could not take her eyes off him. He reached out and took her hand, drawing her closer to him. "You look absolutely beautiful."

Jimmy smiled as he watched them, quietly remembering the night of her high-school prom, when her date arrived and was as stunned by her beauty and just as nervous as Regan Quinn seemed at this very moment. They were a fine-looking couple.

Christos came to her and planted a gentle kiss on her cheek. "You look even more handsome than my dad."

Everyone laughed, including Loren. "Thank you, Christos." *Yeah, he is Regan's son, all right, and every bit as charming,* she thought. She knew from his actions that Regan had spoken to him and everything was fine.

"We should go, Loren. I have the supper reservation for seven."

Niko was watching his friend. He knew Regan was no monk. He was a good-looking man and there had been women in his life since Cala, but he had never involved Christos. He had kept his affairs away from his son. Regan had always kept his feelings private. Like Niko, he had built a wall around his emotions, and it was only when he fell in love with Cala that he let that wall crumble and let love into his heart. When she died, he was devastated, and had rebuilt that wall stronger than ever, never letting harm come to those he loved, but never letting anyone love him. Niko had no idea what had really happened between Regan Quinn and Loren Lombardi on the *Seaward Angel*, but this woman had found her way through that wall.

Jimmy opened the door for them as they left. "Think you kids can be home by ten in the morning? I have a meeting set up on the *Autumn Wind* to deal with the voyage."

Regan smiled at Jimmy and gestured a playful salute in response.

"Well, good night, then, and have a good time," Jimmy said, closing the door behind them as they left.

Loren passed Regan her car keys. He opened the door for her, then slid in behind the wheel of her sport-model Chevrolet. She had never seen him drive a car, or even sail the ship, and it occurred to her she was in love with a man she really knew very little about. Her heart was pounding as she remembered her first date and how shy and uncomfortable she was, and suddenly she felt overwhelmed, afraid of the love she was feeling for this man. He drove the car as though it was second nature to him, and reached over to touch her face, then let his hand slide down her bare arm and gently secure her hand.

"You look ravishing in that pretty pink dress, Miss Lombardi." He smiled at her.

"And you are stunningly handsome, Captain Regan Quinn. The last time we went dancing you were in your *Seaward* captain's uniform."

He was watching her as much as he was watching the road. He casually commented, "I'm not sure what type of uniform is suitable for the captain of the *Autumn Wind*. I'm just glad it's not a striped one."

Loren burst out laughing. It was the first time he had expressed any feelings about his personal situation and it was as though the words had just slipped out of his private thoughts. His dark eyes were sparkling with amusement at her uncontrollable response to his comment. The anger she had seen in his eyes the day he had been arrested had been replaced with the soft, black velvet she was enchanted by.

They pulled up in front of the restaurant. He opened her door and extended his hand, then let it rest on her lower back as they entered the restaurant, and she was sensually aroused by the way he touched her.

The waiter seated them at a table by the window, with a view of the ocean, and then brought fine Italian wine to the table. It was her favourite, the one she had brought to serve her guests the evening before. The waiter also handed Regan a key for a room in the inn. Regan had obviously made plans for the evening beyond supper and dancing.

She was delighted, as he was all she had thought about all day. The meal choices were made, and over wine, she asked about Christos. "Was he okay about us, Regan?"

"Yes, he is old enough to understand about a relationship between a man and woman, and God knows he will probably have one of his own soon enough. He asked me a lot of questions about what you do, your job. I explained how we met and what had happened on the *Seaward*."

"Tell me about your son. I would like to get to know him better. What does Christos like to do? What does he want to do when he is finished school? I see he likes to read...what are his favourite books?"

Regan hesitated, suddenly realizing he did not really know the answers to some of her questions, but he wanted her to understand the decisions he had made for his son. "I tried to manage on my own for a year after Cala died, but I could not take care of a young child and work. Christos has been with his grandparents since he was three. I am forever grateful to Abasi and Shima for taking such loving care of him. Abasi is originally from Spain. He wasn't raised with Moroccan tradition and has never believed in the demeaning treatment of women, which that culture demands of its men. He is formal with Shima when they are in public, but when they are alone, she is his equal. They raised Cala with liberal views and gave her an education, which was not acceptable in their traditional Moroccan society. Abasi's decision to educate his daughter and let her take a job in Greece cost him the respect of his fellow merchants. When he did not arrange her marriage to a man of Moroccan blood and gave Cala and me consent to marry, it cost him his business."

Loren was beginning to understand the reasons behind Regan's desperate actions the last few weeks, as she observed him toying with his wine glass before he continued.

"Cala was beautiful, and she could pass for either Spanish or Moroccan. Christos has his mother's Spanish features, but his skin is lighter, more Caucasian. Abasi knew he would be discriminated against, so when they wanted to care for my son, I bought them the market bakery and apartment in Tangiers. There is more tolerance there for mixed cultures. Abasi had experienced the cruelty of discrimination and we both wanted Christos to be able to have an education, so we arranged a false ID card for my son, so he would not have to go through the same thing. If your ID card says you are born in Morocco, no one questions it. Abasi has had a false ID card for years for the very same reason."

The Spirit of the Autumn Wind

Regan topped off the wine glasses. He seemed uncomfortable, but determined to justify the choices he had made, and Loren listened mindfully.

"I have made regular visits to Tangiers over the years to see Christos, but I missed a lot of his childhood and I know I have a lot of catching up to do with him, and that is why I bought the marina in Ireland. There is a good college there and an opportunity for a better life than there is in Morocco. Abasi and Shima are getting older. I want them to have a better home and a better life, too; they have worked very hard. I owe them that. When I bought the marina, it was with the intention of relocating everyone when Christos completed this school year, but I really bungled that up and I need to make sure he is okay. I ripped him out of the only home he knew, put his life in danger, and almost got him killed. He will have been out of school for two months by time we get to Ireland, and he likes school." Regan took a swallow of his wine and stopped talking. He hesitated and seemed to be sorting through something that he found worrisome, but continued.

"He hasn't really talked about the murder of Nigeria. He is just a boy, so it must have upset him; having his life threatened and seeing a man shot. I took him shopping for some clothes yesterday and we went for lunch. I was hoping he would talk to me, but when I brought it up, he said everything was fine, but I am not so sure. I am hoping on the voyage to Ireland maybe he will talk about what happened. I don't want him to keep it all bottled up inside."

Loren was squeezing his hand, wanting to comfort him, help him, love him. "Christos will be fine. Sometimes it's hard to talk to the people closest to us, the ones we love the most, because we feel we will disappoint them. Sometimes it is easier to talk to a stranger. I am trained to work with people experiencing trauma. If he has an interest in my work, I will talk about that and see if he might talk about what happened that night."

"Thank you Loren. Niko, too—he hasn't said a word about the shooting. I am still tormented by Ivory's death and I can't imagine what effect shooting Nigeria has had on Niko. He is a sensitive man. They were both ruthless men, but neither of us have ever taken another's life."

Loren held tight to Regan's hands. He was guarded and distant on the *Seaward*, but now he was being open, talking to her and telling her things he was feeling; things that mattered in his life.

"Niko will talk to you when he is ready. You have been friends for a long time."

"Yes. He is a very special person and a good friend, but..." Regan stopped talking, struggling with what he wanted to say. "I didn't know he had been living in the alley behind the Sea Gull Bar until Jimmy mentioned it, or that he was unemployed. He never told me, and I would have helped him. He didn't tell me about the passengers being smuggled through the galley until the night we had to flee with Christos. He is my son's godfather and it hurts that he did not feel he could tell me he was in trouble. I feel I have failed him as a friend." Then he added, as though it was a warning, "I think of him as a brother and I will never let anyone come between us."

"Regan, I would never come between you and your son and your friend." Loren was gently assertive, but her perspective was balanced with professionalism, and Regan's was not. "Niko is a proud man. He would have known you would help him, but he also knew O'Hare was capable of murder. To involve you might have put you in danger and probably him, too. Niko was using his skill in the galley to control O'Hare by controlling the crew. It was an intelligent thing to do, and from the very beginning he documented all of O'Hare's actions in his logbook."

Regan realized she interpreted Niko's decisions differently than he did, and was helping him see that Niko was no longer as vulnerable as Regan remembered from their childhood.

The Spirit of the Autumn Wind

The waiter was heading toward the table, so she spoke quickly. "Sean and Sadeh have become good friends with both Christos and Niko. Let them know you are concerned, and they may be able to help, too. Regan, you do so much for everyone in your life, but sometimes we all need a little help. Let your friends help you."

"Sorry, Loren, I did not mean to sound defensive. I just want everyone I love to be happy, especially you."

Loren released his hands. The waiter served the food and Regan used the distraction to hide the tears that welled in his eyes; he looked out at the sea and swallowed the lump in his throat. He had never let a woman get this close to him. She was trained to interrogate, trained to communicate, and she was damned good at it.

When he looked back, she was busily re-sorting the dishes the waiter had brought and he was composed and in control.

"Regan, this restaurant serves the best Italian food. I could not let you visit my cottage by the sea and miss out on authentic Italian food. When Jimmy and Molly visit, we come here. I hope you enjoy it."

Regan topped off her wine glass and then savoured the creamy pasta he had just placed in his mouth. "No complaints so far. It's delicious!"

She pushed the warm buns and cheeses closer to him. "I have some good news," she said excitedly. "Jimmy asked me to work with him as his assistant lead investigator, so I won't be doing undercover work anymore, just setting up the cases, researching, and organizing the undercover investigations."

Regan brushed the napkin across his mouth. "And this is what you want, Loren? You told me how much you love your job."

"This is a good opportunity for me. Jimmy says it won't be long until the Garda allows women to join the police force and he would like me to be trained and able to step into a position as lead investigator when that happens. I will work directly with Jimmy at the Garda headquarters in Sona Bay, and my hours will be more regular.

Undercover work will be harder for me as I grow older, and I am away a lot, and Papa wants me to have a chance to share my life with someone special. Jimmy and Molly have always wanted that for me, more than I wanted it for myself."

He was assessing her, watching her expressions. He had been young when he married Cala. She had been a beautiful, educated, independent woman, not clingy and needy. She had wanted to build a life with him, work, and contribute financially to their home and the upbringing of their child. The first time he'd seen Loren he'd seen the same independent spirit, a woman that could love a man for who he was, not what she needed.

He knew that when Jimmy questioned him about his relationship with Loren before they left for Sunset Harbour, that he was letting him know he was aware he was still holding a card up his sleeve and trying to get him to play it. He had decided when he provided his statement to Flynn on the *Autumn Wind*, that he wasn't going to play that card. He was angry, Loren had deceived him; but he was the only one that had committed a crime, and he was the only one that should be punished. But, he wasn't about to give Jimmy the upper hand until he was comfortable that he could trust Flynn to keep his word and protect his career. What he had missed was that when Jimmy revealed Loren was his daughter, he was also letting him know that even if he played that card he would lose the game. Jimmy Flynn had just laid his ace on the table.

Flynn's smart. Regan smiled. "Loren, I am very happy for you."

Regan was about to raise his glass to congratulate her, but she continued.

"Regan, there is something else." She set her fork down and focused on his face. "Jimmy asked me if I wanted to travel back to Ireland on the *Autumn Wind* with you. There is a lot of paperwork to do to finish up on this case, and I could do it while we travel. Jimmy wants us to have some time together to start over." She paused and watched his reaction. "And I do, too. I just wasn't sure if you would want that."

His response was immediate. "Loren, of course I want that!" He seemed alarmed that she would think otherwise. "I thought tonight was all the time we would have together until I docked in Ireland. Please travel with me. Jimmy is a wise man. We do need some time and a couple of weeks at sea would be perfect. I have a ship to sail, so you will have time to do your work, but the rest of the time we can spend making love." He smiled as he let his voice drift off, so as not to be heard by any adjacent diners, then reached across the table and squeezed her hand, waiting for her smile, looking for her approval of his suggestion. Then he returned to the wine in front of him like a child that had just gotten away with a bit of mischief. "Congratulations on your new job, sweetheart!" He touched her glass with his and took a swallow of wine.

"I am looking forward to the voyage, Regan. The *Autumn Wind* brought all of us together as strangers, but we will be friends forever."

"To forever!" He raised his glass and she followed.

"To forever!"

He smiled as he set his glass down and focused on his food, quietly hiding how delighted he was.

The romantic Italian melodies that drifted into the dining room began to stir the diners out onto the hardwood dance floor. The walls of the structure were glass, and the waves that glistened and shimmered in the moonlight slapped against the rocky shoreline below them. They were dancing on the waves, just as Loren had said, and Regan Quinn was lost to the romance of the sea he loved, and this beautiful woman in his arms that he loved just as much.

Loren had lost her heart to handsome Captain Regan Quinn on the dance floor, but her fairytale had become a nightmare. Now she let her imagination take her away as she floated on the waves in his arms. He still possessed her heart, but this time her fairytale had come true.

The band played the last waltz. He put his jacket around her shoulders as they made their way up the cobblestone walk to a cozy cottage room decorated in blue and grey. The large window, trimmed in Italian lace, opened to a small balcony that overlooked the sea. The bed was nicely turned back to expose the colour-coordinated linens. A bottle of brandy sat on the night table with two small crystal glasses. Regan enjoyed a nightcap, and just as he had on the *Seaward Angel*, he loosened his tie and unbuttoned his shirt while filling the glasses, before moving out onto the balcony for a breath of night sea air. *He is a sailor, the sea is in his blood; he craves it, needs it.*

Her thoughts left her wondering what life with Regan Quinn would be like. He would be gone to sea, sailing his ships, and he would take her heart with him. She would be alone longing for his love, needing his touch. Was it even possible for their love to survive?

"You're quiet, sweetheart. Are you okay?"

He had been watching her wrestle with her private thoughts. His warm hand was pulling her face to his and the doubts she was having were lost to his deep sweet kiss. His kisses moved down her neck and shoulders and across her breasts as he moved their tangled bodies to the bed. His hands glided over her bare skin where her dress had been, and he played with her pretty pink underwear, teasing her, kissing her, pulling her into him, pushing his way into her heart, her soul, and her spirit. They fell asleep, satisfied and naked, with every secret and lie between them exposed.

Loren slept like a baby and woke suddenly to find it was already nine o'clock. "Regan, wake up!" She touched his face. "Regan."

He stirred and impulsively tightened his arm around her.

She kissed him. He opened his eyes.

"Regan, it is already nine." He reached for his wristwatch lying on the night table and squinted to confirm the time.

"Shit! Jimmy's meeting! We have to be at the ship at ten." He stood up, gave her his hand to help her out of bed, and stood naked in front of her as he pulled on his shorts, then reached for his pants.

The Spirit of the Autumn Wind

"We will have to hurry, Jimmy has the navy and coast guard there for pre-sailing instructions."

She was slipping on her dress and her shoes as he pulled her close and kissed her. He helped her zip up her dress. "Good morning, sweetheart, aren't we a sight?"

They laughed at themselves as he clasped her hand, and they ran down the walkway to the car, dishevelled and excited, like a couple of schoolkids late for curfew.

"I'll drive," she told Regan, "and drop you off at the ship so you'll have a chance to shower and change. I'll go to my cottage and clean up and meet you back at the ship; if we hurry, we can make it on time."

At exactly ten o'clock Loren entered the dining room on the *Autumn Wind* in a smartly pressed black, tailored skirt and matching jacket. Her hair was falling loosely around her shoulders, shining in the morning sun and still smelling of shampoo. She took a place between Jimmy and Regan.

Regan looked over at her, obviously working at maintaining the formal atmosphere of the room. He was freshly showered and finely dressed in a plain, dark-navy suit with a white shirt and a perfectly aligned navy neck tie. She smiled at him, thinking about what he had said last night about a striped uniform. She wanted to burst out laughing, so she dropped her head for a moment, letting her long lashes hide her eyes so she could compose herself.

Her actions did not escape Regan; he had seen her do this before when they were together on the *Seaward*, only now he knew what secrets those black eyes were hiding.

When Loren looked up, she was in complete control and professionally focused on the twenty-five people surrounded by the deep cherrywood walls of the dining room on the *Autumn Wind*.

Jimmy took control of the room. "Welcome, everyone. We are all here now, so let's make sure we all know who we are."

Jimmy introduced Lieutenant Young, the captain of the navy ship, and Captain Harrison, who would be sailing the coast-guard vessel, to the rest of the group from the *Autumn Wind*.

The navy lieutenant took the floor and clarified that because they had commissioned the construction of the vessel and had an interest in the military-issued weapons on board, they would be travelling as an escort along the left side of the *Autumn Wind* all the way to Ireland. A military helicopter was on board their vessel should there be an emergency or need for additional galley or maintenance supplies while en route. The military considered this a classified mission and under no circumstances would the ship be stopping at any ports without their permission.

The captain of the coast-guard vessel introduced a second-in-command to sail the ship with Captain Regan Quinn, and an additional navigator, a bridge technical officer, and a communications officer to round out the crew. Dr. Adom Amari from the coast-guard ship would be on board the *Autumn Wind* as the ship's doctor, and would be in the infirmary next to the galley. Only Loren took note of the coy smile Sadeh shared with the doctor.

In addition to the assault officers on board the ship, the coast guard had handpicked the required crew. The coast-guard ship would be sailing as an escort along the right side of the *Autumn Wind*. Niko had four people assigned to the galley—two cook's assistants and two crew to assist with meal service and cleanup. Fifteen crewmen were on board to keep the engines constantly stoked with coal, maintain the decks, and provide laundry and housekeeping service on the journey. Niko's galley would be responsible for feeding thirty souls for sixteen days.

At four in the afternoon, Loren poked her head into the bridge. Regan was busy with his crew, his shirtsleeves rolled up and his suit jacket slung across the back of his captain's chair. Immediately upon seeing her, he approached. "I'll stay on the ship tonight, Investigator Lombardi," he said, careful not to deviate from the formal protocol of the bridge. Loren fully understood he was in command of this vessel, which required the respect of his crew, and if there was one thing she understood it was protocol.

"Of course, Captain Quinn."

"The other passengers will be staying on board tonight as well. We will be sailing at 6 a.m. It's early, so it will be easier for them. And you will be on board by six as well, then, Investigator Lombardi?"

"Yes. Is there anything you want, before I leave for the day?" she asked, knowing he would be up for hours finalizing the checks of the ship, making sure every detail was as it should be when they sailed. He took pride in his job, and no matter what the name was on the side of the vessel, he was Captain Regan Quinn.

"No, everything is fine, Investigator Lombardi," he said, discreetly letting his hand touch hers, letting her know the only thing he wanted was to be in her arms for the night. Her smile told him she understood, and she let her fingers slip through his as she left.

When Loren arrived back at the cottage, she packed her things. She went to bed early, but after a night of tossing and turning, woke at five to find Jimmy already with the coffee on and the briefcase and file boxes he was sending with her waiting by the door. At five-forty-five she walked up the gang plank to Captain Quinn, waiting in his dark-navy suit to escort her and her boxes to the captain's quarters.

The *Autumn Wind* had been scrubbed from bow to stern inside and out and was a beautiful sight to behold, sitting majestically between the navy vessel and the coast-guard ship. Her towering cranes were standing guard over the large engine stack, which puffed out trails of snow-white smoke in perfect harmony with the other vessels readying for departure. The black yacht was secured on the cargo deck beneath the large crane at the aft of the ship.

"If you need anything, girl, get Regan to patch you through off the ship's radio," Jimmy said. Then he turned to Regan. "You take loving care of my girl."

It was a direct order that Regan fully understood held no compromise. "I will, sir."

Jimmy hugged her, shook Regan's hand, and wished them both a safe voyage. "I'll see you both in Ireland in sixteen days." They waved goodbye from the deck railing as Jimmy's cab disappeared into the dull morning light.

At exactly 6 a.m., with the sunrise breaking the haze above the water, the *Autumn Wind* set sail on its voyage from Sunset Harbour to Suaimhneas Cove.

As Jimmy's plane flew over the harbour on its way to Ireland as well, he looked down at the trio heading out to sea with the majestic *Autumn Wind* in the lead, under full escort, and smiled. His floating circus was on the way home.

CHAPTER TWENTY-THREE

The first few days at sea set the routine for the voyage. Regan would sail either days or nights, alternating with the second-in-command. Regan and Loren were sharing the captain's quarters and would make love at dawn, midnight, or anytime in between, depending on Regan's schedule. When Regan was on the bridge, Loren would work on her reports for finalizing the investigation. She found the days were flying by.

Christos spent as many hours as he could up on the bridge with his father. There was no doubt they loved each other, but it was obvious to Loren they were getting to know each other, as well. When Regan sailed at night and the activity around the ship was at a minimum, she would join him on the bridge. He was totally in control of the ship and would talk to her as she sat perched in the tall chair next to him. She loved watching him work. He was so at peace when he was sailing. He would point out the stars in the night sky, which he seemed to navigate by as much as the pile of charts and the variety of gauges that were at his fingertips. It was quiet on the bridge at night, so they could talk as though they were alone, as there was only a technician and navigator hovering over their desks in opposite corners of the command centre.

Regan told her about his plans for the marina and the home there, where they could start a life together. Loren had always been alone. She was an independent career woman by choice and there were times now she felt her life was spinning out of control. She had let him through the wall she had built around her emotions. He made her feel safe—in fact, there was no place safer in the entire world then the *Autumn Wind* in the middle of the ocean, with a military escort and assault officers on board—but they could not protect her from her self-doubt.

Niko's galley was the heart of the ship. He no longer found it necessary to use the deadbolt on the galley door and the smell of food often brought a visitor from the bridge, a crewman, or an assault officer in need of a coffee and sweet treat. There was constant activity, and the four crew assisting the galley master had little time to waste. Niko prepared an array of Mediterranean dishes that had the crew lining up at the dining room door at mealtime. He was testing recipes for his restaurant and spared no detail with presentation. The men on the *Autumn Wind* were not only delighted with their galley master but looking forward to being patrons of his restaurant when it opened. Sadeh had been keeping details of the menu on Niko's inventory pad, with plans of helping him with the startup of the restaurant when they arrived in Ireland.

Abasi, Shima, and Christos, along with Sean and Sadeh, remained in their cabins off the galley, so still considered the galley their space even though they were no longer confined and were free to go anywhere on the ship. Abasi and Christos routinely got up at four and put bread and cinnamon rolls in the ovens while chatting and laughing in both Arabic and English.

Sadeh Dolan treated Niko like an uncle and Abasi and Shima like her adopted grandparents. She still insisted on decorating the cakes in the galley, even though there was crew to do it. It was a tedious task, and Niko's assistants had no problem relinquishing the job to the delicate hand of the young woman.

Sean liked his poached egg on toast in the morning, so would usually get the routine started, so all Niko had to do was create the perfectly formed delight for his galley passengers. They would gather around the oak table talking like a family as they enjoyed the simple but healthy breakfast. The additional galley crew were a bit confused about their relationship, but were quick to join in the camaraderie at Niko's invitation, before the rigours of getting the morning meal out to the crew.

After breakfast, Sean would make the daily tour to inspect the ship with Gavin Connor, and in the evenings, would strum his harp and serenade his precious Sadeh up on the private deck. It was not unusual for Captain Quinn and Investigator Loren Lombardi to join them. It was impossible for any stranger to understand the unusual circumstances that had brought these uniquely different people together and the strength of the friendships that had formed between them.

"Niko just took pineapple cake out of the oven. He wants to know if you two would like to join the rest of us on the galley deck for tea?" Christos poked his head through the captain's cabin door, addressing Loren and his dad.

"Absolutely," they chimed in unison. Regan had worked the night shift and had just gotten up.

Niko was as regimental about ensuring his friend had a snack at four each afternoon with tea as he had been about O'Hare's egg sandwich, but he did it without resentment. As a boy, Niko would sneak cookies or sugared scones out of the orphanage kitchen and hide them under Regan's pillow in a napkin, so he would have something to carry him over until the supper was served. It was the kind of thing friendships were made of, and although the years had taken the men in different directions, their friendship had never wavered. They were both enjoying the time together this voyage had made possible.

Regan took Loren's hand, and with his arm around Christos's shoulders, walked between them to the galley. The Dolans and Bakaris were already seated on the deck around a small table that had found its way to the popular meeting spot.

Loren had been working on Christos's statement, which included the navigation map, so she carried it under her arm with the intention of questioning him about it over tea and in the presence of Sean, in case there were details to be added.

Regan enjoyed Niko's cake and the company of the others, and listened without concern as Loren questioned Christos about the black yacht. It was not until the conversation evolved to the actual shooting of Nigeria in the galley that Christos broke down, blurting out how frightened he had been and his anguish at seeing a man shot before his eyes. Loren immediately took him in her arms. He was trying not to cry in front of his father.

Niko stood up and took the boy from her grasp. "This is hard, Christos, really hard. I keep seeing him as big as life every time I close my eyes. I can hear the bullet, smell the blood and the stench of the man himself. But he is gone now, and as hard as I try to find wrong in what happened, I cannot. You are valuable, he was not, and I would do it all again in a heartbeat. We are going to get over this, Christos, both of us," he said firmly.

Regan was up and circling them in his arms. "Everything will be fine, son. I am here to look after you and Niko."

The emotions between the men were guarded and private and not what Loren expected, but who was she to judge? She could barely handle her own feelings. She was a professionally trained investigator, but it held no merit when it came to her heart.

Loren took Christos's hand and Niko's too. "I'm sorry. I did not mean to upset you, but you both need to talk about what happened. You did nothing wrong. You are guilty of nothing, and you have friends here that care about you and are ready to listen anytime you want to talk."

Sean had watched the scene unfold and motioned to Abasi and Shima to stay out of it. Sean was still haunted by the man he was accused of killing, even though he was in no way responsible for the drunken state of the sailor who had died in the bar, and he had known since the night of the shooting that Christos would have to come to terms with what happened. Niko seemed like a rock, and he carried the weight of the world on his shoulders. Sean knew he was no rock but a gentle kind-hearted man who was probably tormented by what he had done, but he also knew he had a deep bond with Regan, who was caring the same burden, and when he was ready, they would talk.

Regan's eyes were on Loren. She looked away for a moment, certain he was angry because she had pushed Christos too far with her questions. As an investigator, she knew the limits, but she also knew Christos was troubled and needed to talk. He was as masterful at hiding his feelings as his father. "I'm sorry, Regan, I did not mean to upset Christos and Niko."

Her relationship with Regan was like a vine tangled up between his son and his friend. Could their love even survive? She wasn't sure if there was room for her; if she would ever fit in. She wasn't sure she could find a bond of trust with Christos or that he would accept her into his life.

"Loren, it's okay." Christos was still clinging to Niko's shoulder. Regan put his arm around her as he observed the pair regain their composure. "Wounds don't heal when they are festering—get rid of the cause and the hurt will mend."

She felt his lips on her hair, pressing down on her skull as he pulled her frame to his, letting her know he understood her part in what had happened was because she cared.

Regan glanced at the somewhat uncomfortable state of the four tea companions. "Damn good cake, Niko! Let's not let it go to waste."

Niko refilled the teacups, and everyone got back to enjoying the cake.

Regan updated them on the latest weather report. "By the way, everyone, we will be going into some stormy weather over the next seventy-two hours, so make sure everything is secure, and get ready for some rough waters. Sadeh, as you know, the doctor is concerned about you making this voyage in such an advanced state of pregnancy, and will be checking in on you regularly during the storm."

"I'm fine, Regan," Sadeh objected.

"I'm sure you are, but just the same, you're pregnant, so we won't take any chances." It had gone from a suggestion to an order, and Sean nodded approval.

Regan surveyed his group of galley passengers. Abasi and Shima were older, Sadeh was pregnant, Sean had an injured arm, Niko's leg was crippled, and Christos was young. He smiled.

"The doctor is right next door to the galley, so if any of you are not feeling well, go and see him; that's what he's here for. And the military helicopter is going in for some supplies tomorrow morning before we hit stormy weather, so if there is anything you need, just let me know."

Regan finished his cake about the same time he finished talking, and by the time he was ready to leave the galley deck, serenity had returned, and the healing had begun.

CHAPTER TWENTY-FOUR

The trio of ships pushed into the stormy weather right on schedule. The helicopter had made a supply flight and had dropped a netted container on the deck of the *Autumn Wind*, containing additional galley requests and some vessel and engine parts should they be needed. Niko knew the crew, especially those down in the engine room keeping the big engines stoked with coal, would be working extra hard. He had a big leg of lamb and some large turkeys and hams, as well as extra fresh fruit, vegetables, and eggs, flown in to add to the galley supplies. Niko, as he always did during harsh weather, made sure coffee, soup, sandwiches, and treats were available in the dining room for the crew at all hours.

Doctor Amari was prepared. He had an incubator that would accommodate twins and some additional medical supplies to address a premature birth brought on board before they left Sunset Harbour. He had been a coast-guard doctor for many years and he had dealt with his share of storms and medical emergencies. He wasn't about to take any chances with this young woman, so requested a medical assistant from the coast-guard vessel for the duration of the storm. They were far out in the Atlantic Ocean, off the coast of France. The military was pushing the timetable hard and keeping the ship as far away from shore as possible. The weather would start to get cooler as they moved past Great Britain and closer to Ireland, and the storms this far out in the ocean could be furious.

For three days, the ship rolled and heaved over the large storm-fed waves. The wind pushed the ocean up on the deck and the crew tied ropes to their waists to secure themselves to the ship for safety when outside. The thundering sounds of the waves pounded against the hull with frightful force, echoing relentlessly through the ship's walls, making it impossible to sleep. The wind whipped the water into angry peaks that disappeared into the black rolling clouds dropping down from the sky and into the cold dull haze that blanketed the ocean, making the trio of ships almost invisible.

The rigging that secured the black yacht to the deck of the *Autumn Wind* was checked several times a day. She had caused enough misery and, hell or high water, this was her last voyage, too. Regan and his bridge officers did not leave their posts. Niko and his assistants delivered coffee and meals to the bridge and a couple of small cots along the wall provided a place for the bridge crew to catch a few minutes of rest.

Sadeh took sick on the first day and was grateful for the regular visits by the ship's doctor. Niko remembered the last storm-induced birth on board the *Autumn Wind* and was glad there was a doctor on board. He had enough to worry about with the storm and a full allotment of crew.

Christos, Loren, and Sean checked in on the bridge each afternoon, and Sean would give Regan an update on the condition of the ship and the black yacht. Regan joked about losing it at sea and dragging it to Ireland even if all that was left was the anchor.

"No such luck, Captain Quinn." Sean was joking, but dead serious. "That thing is like a tank and she won't break up. Nigeria had it custom built for running his drug trade, and it's lined with steel and is bulletproof. It will withstand most anything. Too bad," he added sarcastically. "It's an insult to ship building and has no place on the water anywhere." Sean spared no mercy.

He'd hated that yacht the first time he saw it, and now that it was painted death-black and he knew what it had been built for, he hated it even more. He wanted it destroyed.

At about four in the afternoon on the second day of the storm, an agonizing scream echoed through the galley. Niko rushed to Sadeh's cabin. She had been bedridden for the last day, heaving over the side of her bed into a bucket. She was half upright, trying to get out of bed.

"Lay down, Sadeh, lay down." Niko wrapped his strong arms around her and helped her to layback. The sheets were soaking wet, and her skin was drained of all colour and cold with beads of perspiration. He pulled the blanket up around her.

"It hurts, Niko, my back, my back hurts."

The two kitchen assistants had rushed in behind him and Niko felt anxious and helpless. "Call the doctor and get Sean," he commanded the assistants. "He is still up on the bridge. And hurry!"

Both men rushed off without saying a word. Niko didn't need the doctor to tell him what was going on; he remembered all too well the doctor's wife who had given birth on board.

Doctor Amari rushed through the door with his medical bag in hand, and Sean came galloping through the galley right behind him. "What is it? What is it? Sadeh!" She grasped his hand and pulled him toward her.

The doctor pulled the blankets down and felt her swollen stomach, his gentle touch bringing wincing sounds from the distraught young woman. The doctor didn't look up as he continued to feel Sadeh's abdomen.

"Her water has broken," the doctor said to Sean. "Sadeh is going into labour. We are going to move her to my infirmary next door and prepare her for delivery; these babies of yours are on the way."

"Babies!" Sean exclaimed in total surprise.

"Sean, Sadeh is carrying twins," the doctor announced.

Sean clutched her hand and looked at her face. "Sadeh, for God's sake! You knew this, and you didn't tell me?"

"I wanted it to be a surprise, Sean, and there was time enough for us to get to Ireland. We are only a week away."

"Well, Sadeh, a storm like this can bring on an early birth," the doctor said as he took her hand. "They are not waiting to get to Ireland. Your contractions have started. They will be a little while apart at first, so we need to get you more comfortable. The helicopter cannot fly in this weather, so these babies are going to be born on board the *Autumn Wind*. I prepared, just in case," he said confidently as he squeezed her hand and smiled, privately acknowledging their secret.

Niko had been leaning through the cabin door absorbing every word, privately thinking. *Twins! Born on the* Autumn Wind! It was like the ship was testing him.

Sadeh seemed calmer. "I'll give you two a few minutes," the doctor said. "I need to prepare the clinic." Doctor Amari was already headed out the door.

Niko followed with additional sterilized sheets, linens, and towels for the clinic. The doctor was a bit surprised at his resourcefulness. "You have done this before, Niko," he said as he poured disinfectant into a pan.

Niko was explaining the previous incident on the ship when Sean appeared anxiously at the clinic door. "Niko, the captain of the ship, Regan—he can marry people, can he not?"

Niko was surprised at the question. He answered, "Yes, I think so…"

"You know Sadeh and I are not legally married," Sean added.

"Yes." Niko's response was non-judgmental.

"We were going to get married in Ireland, before the baby… babies," he corrected himself, half smiling, "were born. If we are not legally married, the birth certificates will say Tahan. They can't be born Tahan. If her father ever finds out, he will come after them, so they must be born with the Dolan family name. Could you ask Regan if he could come down and read the vows and marry us before Sadeh gives birth?" He took a moment to calm himself and added, "You and Loren could sign as witnesses. If you would, that is?"

Niko was quite taken back at the whole idea of a marriage under the circumstances. "Is Sadeh up to that?" he asked.

Sean looked at the doctor, who nodded, but added, "If you do it soon. Her contractions have just started, but will worsen over the next few hours." Doctor Amari was on board because of what Sadeh had told him about her family when she insisted on staying on the ship. He knew who Kamal Tahan was, and of his reputation for intolerance. He understood the old ways of Egyptian culture and why the babies had to be born with their father's family name, and he also knew that if she stayed on the Autumn Wind, she was safe from her father.

Niko was smiling as he left to go get Regan. The *Autumn Wind* really was testing him. Now a marriage, too!

He knocked on the bridge door and pushed it open slightly. Upon seeing him, Regan motioned for him to enter. Regan had his jacket off and his shirtsleeves rolled up. Everyone was attentive to their specific duties, but overall things were calm and under control.

"Everything okay, Niko?" Regan noted the unusual expression on his friend's face.

"Well, sort of..." Niko ran his hand through his hair as a small smile crossed his lips. "A bit of a situation in the galley."

Regan was concerned, expecting to hear of some mechanical dilemma.

"Sadeh is going into labour. The doctor says she is having twins."

"Twins!" Regan blurted out without a moment's thought, catching the attention of the crew surrounding him.

Niko ignored his friend's reaction. "They are not legally married, and Sean is asking you to come down to the galley and read the marriage vows, so the babies are born with the Dolan family name."

"Seriously, Niko? You want me to perform wedding vows in the galley? Now?"

"Well, she can't come up here and the doctor says as long as they do it soon, he has no problem with it."

"I think this ship is testing our character." Regan smiled as he posed the thought to his friend while reaching into the lowest drawer on his desk.

Niko did not say a word, but Regan could tell from his "what next?" expression that he had been thinking the exact same thing. Seaward required all their captains be certified as a notary public, so he had the necessary credentials, but had never been asked to use them in this way. He flipped through the pages at the back of the Captain's Guidance Manual, reviewing the section under extended authorities that authorized him to perform a marriage at sea. He looked up from the manual to his waiting friend and the interested faces of his fellow crewmen.

"The wording and required documents they need to sign are here. I have never had to do a marriage before, but I guess there's a first time for everything." He set the book down and put on his jacket and straightened his tie. He looked at his second-in-command. "I guess you're in charge for a bit. I have a wedding to go to." Regan's comment brought a round of applause and chuckles from his crewmates as he left on Niko's heels with the manual in hand.

Regan passed through the galley with Niko to Sean and Sadeh's cabin, to find Loren, Christos, and the Bakaris all squeezed into the tiny space. Sadeh was propped up with pillows and Sean was combing her hair. She was pale but alert. Regan pulled a chair up beside the bed.

"What are you up to here, young lady?" he questioned her gently as he took her hand in his.

Her black eyes searched his and she spoke softly. "The babies are not due for a month. We are only a week from Ireland. I thought we would be there before they were born."

Regan smiled. "And you are having twins."

Sadeh giggled softly and looked at Loren mischievously. "Loren knew…so she is an accomplice!"

Regan squeezed her hand and smiled as he looked at Loren.

"I am an accomplice too! And no one told me!" Sean's flippant comment brought a quiet chuckle to the group.

Sadeh asked with respect, "Will you marry us, Captain Quinn, before our children are born? I want them born with the Dolan family name. My father's family heritage demands that the Tahan bloodline remain pure Egyptian. I committed an unforgivable sin and he feels he is justified in taking my life and that of these children. If they are born Tahan, he will find them, and he will take their lives. They will not be safe. My father is a powerful man, and no one would marry us in Egypt because they fear retaliation. Please marry us, Captain Quinn. Sean says we are in international waters and we can register their births in Ireland, but they must be born with the Dolan name."

Regan leaned over and kissed her forehead. "Of course, Sadeh." He stood up and shook Sean's hand. "You need two people to witness for you, Sean."

"Niko and Loren, if you would be so kind," Sean asked Niko again, and they both nodded.

Regan looked across at Niko and Loren and smiled; she was a total professional, good under stress, but seemed totally out of her element. Regan motioned them to come closer as he verified the correctness of both names and completed the forms.

Captain Regan Quinn opened the manual and read. "Do you, Sean Seamus Dolan, take Sadeh Alexandra Tahan to be your lawfully wedded wife, to have and to hold, from this day forward, for better, for worse, for richer, for poorer, in sickness and in health, until death do you part?"

"I do," Sean responded with conviction.

Their eyes never parted as Regan recited the words for Sadeh and pronounced them husband and wife. They loved each other and no one in the room was about to object to what was obviously meant to be.

Sean kissed his bride. As soon as Niko and Loren had signed as witnesses to the nuptials, Sean gathered Sadeh up in his arms and carried her next door to the infirmary.

For the next four hours, while preparing the supper meal, Niko listened as piercing screams from the clinic next door signalled the imminent arrival of the babies. Loren and the Bakaris waited impatiently around the galley table should Sadeh, Sean, or the doctor ask for any of them. Regan had taken Christos up to the bridge with him, thinking the boy had experienced enough on the voyage and could be spared the agonizing pain of childbirth until a later time.

Niko quietly prayed that everything would be okay. He had become very fond of Sadeh and Sean, and he was pleased and honoured that they had asked him to sign their marriage certificate. The galley assistants had gone off to bed and Abasi insisted Shima do the same. Niko poured Loren, Abasi, and himself a glass of rum apiece, and filled one with Irish whisky for Sean. The man would need a drink when this was over.

Niko busied himself helping Abasi make dough for the morning bread. Some poppyseed cake rolls were in the oven and rice pudding for Sadeh sat on the stove. Loren refused to leave the galley, so Niko let her help with the preparation of the soup and sandwiches that he was getting ready to take out to the dining room at midnight along with the warm poppyseed rolls. The men were tired, and the extra snacks were helping to keep them going.

Just before midnight, Sadeh's painful cries suddenly stopped. There was silence, broken only by the sounds of the ocean beating against the ship as she pushed forward through the night. Then finally, thankfully…the cry of a baby. Everyone waited, concerned… and finally there was the cry of a second baby.

Sean appeared moments later, his shirt soaked with sweat. He was pale but obviously relieved. "Sadeh is fine, the babies are fine," was all he could manage before he found his way into Niko's strong arms and broke into tears. "We have a son and a daughter."

Niko passed Sean the glass of whisky, which went down his throat in one swallow.

"Congratulations, my friend!" Niko gave him a strong pat on the back.

Niko and Loren rushed next door to the clinic and peeked in the partly open door. Sadeh was soaking wet and exhausted. In each arm lay a tiny baby wrapped in clean linens, unlike the doctor, whose smock was soiled and who had a towel hanging around his neck. Niko paid no attention as the doctor's assistant washed Sadeh and pulled clean sheets around her open legs. Niko kissed her forehead. She was weak, but she made sure he could see the tiny faces of the babies she held in her arms.

"They're beautiful, Sadeh." He kissed her forehead again. Sean had positioned himself tightly up against Niko. Loren moved closer to get a look, and Sean pulled her into the circle.

"Look, Loren, look how beautiful they are!" Sadeh took her friend's hand, bringing her close so she could see the babies and touch their tiny hands. Tears were streaming down Loren's face and Niko put his arm around her shoulders.

"Okay, everybody, this young lady is exhausted. Excellent job, Sadeh." The doctor said as he moved everyone away from the bed and took her hand. "You need to rest, and I need to get the babies cleaned up and weighed and into the incubator. They are fine, healthy babies, but a bit early, so we won't take any chances."

"Sean, there are things for the babies in the small suitcase in our cabin," Sadeh said. "Some clothes and bottles." She was trying to help Sean amid all the confusion.

"Just rest for a few minutes," the doctor said. "You have to nurse them soon. The first thing they want to do is eat. So just rest a bit."

He gently lifted each tiny bundle from her arms. "Okay, everybody. Out! Let her rest." He ushered the reluctant visitors out of the clinic. Sean stayed to assist the doctor.

"Are you okay, Loren?" Niko asked as she pushed the tears off her face. She nodded.

Niko had no problem grasping control of the situation. "Go tell Regan and Christos everything is fine; they will want to know." Abasi had already left to wake Shima with the news. "I'll put some tea on." Niko squeezed her hand as she left.

Finally, the ocean calmed, and the morning sun brought an exhausted crew out onto the deck. Communication among the three ships confirmed everyone was fine but tired, and the crews of the two escort vessels could be seen milling about on deck as relieved to see the sun as those on board the *Autumn Wind*. Niko had prepared an extra-special breakfast and the dining room was alive with chatter about the storm.

"This is Captain Regan Quinn," Regan's commanding voice echoed through the ship's loudspeaker system. "Thank you to the entire crew for an excellent job. I know you all worked extra hard, and that was a bad storm. The Autumn Wind has survived the storm unscathed, so we are full steam ahead to Ireland and should arrive in six days. I would also like to announce the arrival of two new passengers, twins; a boy, Devlin Seamus Dolan, five pounds and two ounces, and a girl, Autumn Seana Dolan, four pounds and seven ounces, born to Sean and Sadeh Dolan at eleven-forty-five last night."

Regan's announcement brought cheers and shouts of joy from the galley and a playful sounding of the horns from both escort ships. The crew in the galley gave Sean Dolan a standing acknowledgement, raising their coffee cups. "To the *Autumn Wind* and fatherhood!" It was a playful gesture, but Sean was noticeably moved.

Sean had named his daughter after the ship that held a special place in his heart, the ship she was born on, and his son after the name of the village where his great-grandfather had lived when he first came to Ireland, where the Dolan blood bond began.

Sadeh had eaten almost nothing for three days, but with Niko's encouragement had managed to consume some rice pudding that he had made especially with her in mind. The fact that it had disappeared quickly, as had the rows of poached eggs, let Niko know there had been more than one privately endured case of seasickness among this group of experienced sailors.

The doctor felt the babies were healthy and doing well. Because he had the incubator they were in no danger, and Sadeh was too weak to be moved to a hospital, so they would remain on board for the remaining days of the voyage. Sadeh had made it quite clear to the doctor that she was comfortable on board the *Autumn Wind*, had the best food available and lots of friends to help her out, and would be no better off anywhere else to rest and recover. He was inclined to agree.

The remaining days at sea flew by. Loren had finished her preparation of the statements and documentation of the case and was taking a bit more time on deck to enjoy the voyage and visiting with Sadeh and the twins. Doctor Amari was allowing the newborns to spend some time out of the incubator, so Niko provided a new breadbasket with a strong handle and an earthen warming plate on the bottom. When warmed on the stove, it was designed to keep two nicely sized loafs of bread warm, but when lined with blankets it served as a warm, cozy bassinette that held both infants. The doctor thought it was a brilliant idea.

Sadeh was anxious about starting a new life in Ireland, and so was Loren. They had a lot in common and they enjoyed the time they spent talking. It had been a long time since Loren had had a female friend to share her thoughts with, but she had found a friend in Sadeh and hoped they would remain close in the weeks ahead.

Jimmy had called in on the ship's radio right after the storm to make sure everyone was fine. He told her there had been some trouble with the high-ranking Santoro family, a key player in the Italian Mafia that was wanting to move in on Nigeria's now-void drug trade, and he had a new case for her to research when she got home. He asked about Regan, wondering if they were okay. When she thanked him for giving her this time to travel on the ship, her father knew Loren was not only in love but very happy.

"Well, girl, she's not the luxurious *Seaward Angel*, but she's got a good captain."

Loren laughed at her father; he had been matchmaking this whole time and Loren loved him for it.

"Let Regan know I have had a chat with Seaward and told them Captain Quinn helped us close a major drug case and assisted in bringing the contraband to port. They've got a good man there and they know it."

Regan had an appointment with Seaward management when they got to Ireland to discuss his job, and Loren knew he was concerned. He had previously asked for a month off to get his family settled and the marina and restaurant business started when they came to Suaimhneas Cove, but with everything that had happened, he was not sure he even still had a job. Regan was relieved; he was not used to asking for help and even less used to someone offering to help him, but he was grateful for whatever Jimmy had done.

The last three days at sea, Regan was busy organizing access to the Irish waters and securing all the required authorization to bring the *Autumn Wind* into the marina at the old Dolan Shipyard. There was a lot of chatter between the two escort vessels as arrangements were being put in place to remove the contraband cargo. The passengers had packed their bags and were ready to disembark. The helicopter on the military vessel would land and take off each day, doing surveillance of the Irish waters to ensure the safety of the vessels. There was an anxious aura of excitement on board the *Autumn Wind*.

CHAPTER TWENTY-FIVE

At exactly 6 a.m., with the sunrise breaking the haze above the water, the trio sailed into Suaimhneas Cove. Jimmy Flynn stood on the boardwalk by the dock with investigators Micky Roan and Mohamad Jobassi. He could not contain his smile; his floating circus, as he affectionately called it, was safely home in Ireland. The navy and the coast guard quickly blocked the entrance to the marina, and when the gang plank came down, the three Garda investigators were immediately joined by Molly Flynn, who took a place by Jimmy, Sean's parents, Seamus and Maggie Dolan, his sister, Sara, and his niece, Cait Dolan.

Sleeman and Brok stood with the group, all of whom were clapping excitedly as they welcomed the odd collection of passengers ashore. Sean and Sadeh, were first off, the breadbasket hanging between them, with Autumn and Devlin Dolan tucked safely within. Sean was in his father's arms, and tears rolled down his face as he pulled his mother, sister, and niece into his grasp.

Niko was moved; he knew Sean wanted to rebuild his relationship with his father, and the fact that the man stood there with his son in his arms said a lot. Seamus was a mature version of Sean, his curly mop of hair threaded with strands of grey, his charismatic presence hardened by years of life, but the strength of the man was obvious. There was a commotion about the babies and the introduction of Sadeh to the Dolan family.

Regan, Christos, Loren, and Niko were greeted by Jimmy and Molly Flynn. Loren hugged her mother, whom she had not seen since she left on holidays to Italy just over two months ago. Jimmy gave her a hug and kiss on the cheek, then extended his hand to Regan, Niko, and Christos. "Welcome home!"

Loren introduced Captain Regan Quinn to her mother first, and then introduced Christos and Niko. Sean was eagerly introducing his family as well and took extra care introducing Sara and Cait to Niko. "Sara has been running the pub at the marina for years, Niko, and she worked in the restaurant there when it was open, as well."

Sara extended her hand to Niko, looking at him, searching the character of the man that stood before her. She needed her job, and her future was in the hands of this stranger. "I'm anxious to show you around, Niko. I manage the Irish Luck pub at the marina, and Sean said on the phone you will be re-opening the restaurant," she said politely.

He accepted her gesture, feeling the strength of her feminine hand as he held it in his. Sara's infectious smile and bubbly personality were packaged up in a female version of Sean's sparkling Irish-green eyes and curly auburn hair, which she pulled into a thick braid that rested on her right shoulder. Tiny freckles scrambled off the bridge of her delicate nose, fading into her lily-white skin. She stood just below Niko's five-foot nine-inch frame; slender and strong like her brother. Her beauty was natural; not painted on, but beauty that came from within, expelling itself as a smile that played on her pink lips.

Sean introduced Cait, who offered her delicate hand along with a mischievous smile. Niko looked at the girl who possessed the exactness of her mother, excepting her flaming red hair. Cait's colourful description of the sign she had made for the chef's quarters and her decision to label it "Chef Niko" brought a smile to his face.

Niko enjoyed the personal attention and accepted the offer for a tour of the pub and restaurant facilities later. Niko knew Sara had not had an easy life raising a child alone. If there was one thing he understood, it was a challenge. He had decided the night he first spoke to her in Italy that she would remain an employee. He knew he would need all the help he could get to start this new business. He had spent a lot of time thinking about the challenges of operating a restaurant these last days at sea. He had a chance for a better life, and he would not fail. He would not let Regan down, and most of all he would not let himself down.

"Now, Loren," Regan told her, "I am still the captain and in command until every detail of the voyage is dealt with, and I have to get the ship properly positioned here so they can get the cargo and this yacht offloaded, and Niko still has the galley to shut down. The crew will move what is left in the cooler to the coast guard vessel," he said, confirming the previously arranged plan, and Niko nodded.

Regan pulled Loren into his arms, and, placing his hand gently on her neck, kissed her. They were finally home, and she could feel his relief with the relaxed public acknowledgement of their relationship. "We should be done around one…could we all meet then? I really want to show everyone this property."

Loren looked at her parents. They were nodding, as was Niko and the rest of the group. Sara and Cait were excitedly gathering up Sadeh's things to escort her to the apartment above the ship building.

The last two weeks, Sean's family had been readying the apartment for Sean and Sadeh's return. The letter Sean had written while at sea had been as hard for his father to read as it had been for Sean to write. Sean had told his father he was returning on the *Autumn Wind*, bringing her home to Ireland, and why. Seamus Dolan had cried as he read his son's words that told about his life in Egypt, and the ships he had built for Phoenix in return for his engineering degree.

He wrote about the yacht he had built for a rich Egyptian industrialist, his plans to build another, and the orders he had for more; enough to start a small business building yachts.

Seamus's heart was touched by the beauty with which his son described his feelings for Sadeh, the Egyptian woman he had fallen in love with, and the reason for bringing her back to Ireland pregnant, to marry her and make a home. In touching words, he affirmed his love for his father and his mother and asked if they would allow him back into their lives, and if they could find it in their hearts to forgive him and Sara and love Cait so they could be a family again. He told his father that if there was one thing he had learned, it was that Dolan blood was like the ocean, deep and endless, and he wanted to come home to his family.

What Sean wrote, Seamus felt in his heart but could not find the words to say, but he knew he wanted exactly what his son did. That night he paid his daughter, Sara, a visit and cried as he asked her to forgive him for shutting her and Cait out of the family when they needed them the most. He took Cait in his arms for the first time in her fifteen years and asked her to forgive him. Pretty Cait Dolan hugged her grandfather and took his hands in hers, and he was forgiven.

Seamus Dolan awoke a different man. With the news of the babies, he pitched in, helping the women get the apartment prepared and cleaning up around the shipyard building, waiting for the return of his son and the *Autumn Wind*.

"Loren, you feel up to a quick stop at the Garda headquarters? Want to show you your new office…right next to mine," Jimmy said with pride. "And there are some developments in that new Santoro Mafia case to fill you in on." Loren let her hand slip from Regan's, leaving him with a smile as she joined her father and left with Micky and Mojo, who had loaded the file boxes into the back of Micky's truck.

"Come on, Pop, let's go have a look at the old girl." Sean put his arm around his father's shoulder as he guided him up the gangplank and on to the *Autumn Wind*. Regan followed, accompanied by Christos and Niko.

The Spirit of the Autumn Wind

"She is still a beauty, isn't she, son?" It was obvious Seamus Dolan was excited about the return of the ship.

"She is, and she is going into dry dock here at the shipyard, Pop." Sean enthusiastically recited the plans for the ship, which included the *Autumn Wind* remaining at the Dolan Shipyard as a historical monument, recognizing her contribution to the war.

"A bit of a coverup, really, for the activities that brought her back to Ireland, but the navy agreed to annual financial compensation to maintain her condition...as long as she does not sail again," Sean explained. "Sadeh and I would like to renew our vows on her deck here in Ireland as soon as Sadeh is stronger."

"That would be great, son, and a magnificent celebration it shall be." He hesitated, then added, "for the Dolan family."

Sean tighten his grip around his father's shoulders as a gesture of thanks. Niko parted at the galley and Regan and Christos headed up to the bridge as the two men walked on, Sean's arm still resting on his father's shoulders as if he expected the man might suddenly change his mind and run away.

Regan observed them standing on deck together as he manoeuvred the ship into an unloading position between the military and coast-guard vessels. The engines hummed in rhythm as the big false cargo bay opened to expose the millions of dollars of weapons and drugs within. The huge loading cranes swung into position, and the crew and assault officers swarmed like bees in a hive busily tending to their duties. Regan turned to Gavin Connor, shook his hand, and thanked him again for everything he had done, then gave him a letter of recommendation to provide to the management of Seaward Lines. "There will be lots of new jobs opening up with the new passenger ships coming into service and you're a good man. I hope we sail together again."

"Thank you, Captain Quinn. This has been a memorable voyage and you are the best captain I have ever sailed with. Thank you for the letter of reference." The men dropped hands and said goodbye.

Sean and Seamus arrived at the galley just as Niko was finishing up. He went about his business, watching as Seamus Dolan pulled a Celtic cross from around his neck and inserted it in the keyhole in the centre of the Dolan Shipyard plaque. Sean pushed the door to the communications room open and stood back as the old man entered. Seamus ran his fingers along the wall, revealing the rich cherrywood that lay hidden below the layer of dust, then disappeared down the narrow hallway to the now-exposed secret cargo bay. When they returned to the galley, Sean closed the door to the room and watched as his father ran his hand over the oak table and touched the scratches that ten years at sea had etched into the beautifully finished wood.

Sean was silent, watching his father, understanding what Niko did not. Seamus took a moment to survey the galley as they moved toward the cabins, which were still fresh with the smell of the lives that over the last weeks had been changed forever within their walls. Seamus pulled his handkerchief and wiped his eyes as he stood looking off the tiny private deck, unaware of the many thoughtful hours his son had spent there in the company of his grandfather's harp.

As they left through the galley, Sean nodded a thank-you to Niko, but did not speak, leaving Niko to ponder what it was about the *Autumn Wind* that had created this unbreakable bond between this father and son. Was it the war, why she was built, or the love they had put into designing and building her? Or was it some tangible bond of the love and respect they held for each other, or maybe a realization that they not only shared Dolan blood, but a gift that could not be denied or compromised? Whatever it was, only the spirit of the *Autumn Wind* understood. Niko looked back and closed the galley door for the last time.

The black yacht, finally unleashed from the *Autumn Wind*, sat defiantly afloat, moored to the dock next to an old sailboat. "Let's get that thing permanently anchored," Sean said, assessing the position of the black yacht while looking at the slips on the marina side by the ship house. "Where would you like me to put it?" Sean deliberately never referred to the boat in the female gender that was considered a gesture of respect among seamen. "The coast guard said they will give me the engines as long as I destroy the boat." Sean laughed. He hated the yacht and was getting a great amount of pleasure out of the fact that he would be the one to destroy it. His amusement, although not fully understood by his companions, was shared by them.

"Just anchor it there beside that old sailboat?" Regan said.

"Who does that belong to, Regan?" Sean asked.

"Me. It was abandoned here when the marina went into foreclosure. I got the registration to it along with the rest of the assets. She was a beauty in her time. Thought Christos and I could restore her. I learned to sail on a boat like that, and I'd like to teach Christos to sail her." He wrapped his arm tightly around Christos's shoulders.

Christos leaned into his father, smiling at the idea of the project. The last few weeks at sea, Christos had spent as much time as he could up on the bridge with his father. They were bound by blood, and Christos was destined to sail.

The men leaped off the dock onto the black yacht with the spirit of adolescents. They entered the cabin to find a table, two sofas, a kitchenette with a small fridge, and a lot of stripped-down radio and communication equipment. The tight quarters were dirty and disorderly, with obvious signs of the forensic team's recent evidence search. The coast guard had drained the water and sewer and removed all the perishables, but the living quarters still smelled of human sweat and stale cigar smoke.

Sean shook his head in disgust. What appeared to have been a somewhat elegant craft had been converted into a floating tank. A portion of the living quarters had been removed to install an oversized fuel tank and the two high-powered diesel engines. The interior had been reinforced with steel to create a bulletproof environment.

Steel weapons containers were pushed up against a bed at the opposite end, where obviously both men had been sleeping. The disgusting state of the interior spoke to the rage that had driven Nigeria and Samba to avenge the killing of Ivory.

"Let's get this thing anchored and decommissioned and get the hell out of here!" Sean had his hand on the engine starter button and waited as the engines started up one by one and settled into a rhythmic hum. He stretched his long frame to get a better view of the slip through the windows, which were partly blocked with ragged-cut steel, as the other three men helped guide the black yacht into the marina slip. He hit an overhead switch and the scraping sound of the anchor rattled through the boat as it plunged into the water. He shut the engines off and crawled into the engine compartment, coming out with a couple of parts he had removed. His father was smiling at him; obviously it was a bit of "tomfoolery" he had seen his son do before.

"This wretched excuse for a boat is not going anywhere. The devil himself can't start it now, and even Samson can't lift the anchor without the power source." Sean's Irish-green eyes were laughing as he waved around the parts he had removed from the boat, making it impossible for anyone but him to start it. "Let's get out of this floating grave." The foursome laughed at Sean and emerged to find the rest of the group gathering on the boardwalk in front of the pub.

Regan looked at his watch; it was almost one.

CHAPTER TWENTY-SIX

Regan slipped his arm around Loren's waist and kissed the side of her head. Then he led the group up the boardwalk centred between the developed boat slips and several undeveloped ones on the opposite side. Niko took a position beside Regan and Christos. Sara immediately stepped up beside him and put her arm through his as if she thought he might need help. His immediate reaction was to push her away, quietly thinking he could manage just fine without dragging this woman along. She was chattering to the others, seemingly oblivious to the fact that he had a crippled leg. She quickly found a pace that matched his and quit talking to listen to Regan disclose his ideas and plans for the development of the marina.

"The existing marina operation and the pub are paying the bills, but there is potential to do more with the property, so Niko and I have something to fall back on for retirement," he explained with resolve.

Niko nodded as Regan touched on selling the adjoining ship building and dry docks to Sean as soon as they could get the business up and running properly. He and Niko had decided to give Sean and Sadeh the use of the building and apartment at no cost until they could get the legal sale done. They considered it a wedding present to the young couple who had become friends to both the men.

The group, which also included Sean, Sadeh, the twins (who were still tucked in Niko's breadbasket), Sean's parents, the Flynns, and the Bakaris moved on to the pub. Sara pushed open the wooden doors, which were engraved with the words "Irish Luck" and two four-leaf clovers. The pub was spacious and dimly lit, and offered a tacky decor of shamrocks, plastic fish, and old seamen's gear mounted on the walls. A long grill filled one wall and provided a view of the patron's tables. The worn leather barstools and scruffy wooden floor were a testimony to the popularity of the place. Sara stated she and Cait stayed in the small two-bedroom apartment off the back of the pub, which was necessitated by the long hours the pub was open for business.

Niko remembered Sean's comment about her pride and thought it was probably just as much financial as necessity. Sara was contributing non-stop information on the establishment and quieted down somewhat as they moved to the large wooden doors that accessed the dining room. The dark oak doors were engraved with a scene of the ocean shoreline and there was a closed-for-business sign posted on them.

Regan pulled a key from his pocket and handed it to Niko, then stepped back so Niko could open the doors to what was to be his restaurant. The large doors swung open to a spacious room with a rich, dark hardwood floor surrounded by windows. Regan pushed open the emerald-green velvet drapes to a stunning view of the marina and ocean beyond.

"Wow! That's a view if there ever was one." Sean spoke from his heart. Even though he had lived there as a child, it was as though he was seeing it for the first time.

Niko stood silent as Regan placed his arm around his shoulders, tightening his grip reassuringly as he watched his longtime friend fight back the tears that were welling in his eyes.

During the voyage to Ireland, Regan and Niko had found time to talk about the plans for their future. Niko had been enthusiastic about the restaurant when Regan had first told him about it that night in Tangiers, and it seemed more important than ever to him now. Neither man knew what lay ahead, as this was not a voyage they had taken before, but it was one they were looking forward to.

On Regan's instructions the dining room and adjoining kitchen and residence had been cleaned so they would be presentable when Niko first viewed them. Regan watched his friend as they entered the kitchen. He had worked in many galleys over the years and always made do, and Regan could see Niko assessing the functionality of the space.

"This is good, Regan, very good." Niko nodded as he spoke but never removed his eyes from his surroundings.

It was the reaction Regan was hoping for, and seeing the satisfaction in Niko's face was gratifying. Everyone except Loren seemed unaware of what this meant to both men.

The group was chatting about the view and the potential of the property as they moved on to the dance floor, which was lowered by one step and adjoined the dining room. It seemed it had been planned and built but not really used before the property went into foreclosure. It offered the same view as the dining space and Loren and Regan exchanged a glance, both silently reminiscing about the night they danced on the waves in Italy.

"This is nice." Sean handed the babies' basket to his father, gathered Sadeh up in his arms, and twirled her about the floor like a doll.

Sara clapped and Sadeh was still giggling as they moved out the back entrance to the residence, a separate structure that had been built as a small inn behind the main building. There were two suites, one at each end on the main level, which were for the management, and five additional bedrooms, located on the upper floor, for guests.

Regan took Loren firmly by the hand, pushing open the door to the first suite. The same dark hardwood welcomed them, surrounded by walls painted Irish-green. A kitchenette opened to a living room and small dining area, with three bedrooms and a bath located off the living room.

"Loren..." Regan hesitated. "I was hoping we could make do with this for a while until we get this place up and running." It was as though he was apologizing.

"Regan, it's fine. Perhaps a bit of paint?" she commented.

"Yeah, these guys were big on green, so a bit of paint would be good," he said, and laughed.

She could feel his grip relax as he responded. The truth was, she was in love with the man and if he asked her to stay in a tent with him, she would. Loren was financially independent and taking on painting and redecorating this suite was something she could do to help, and she would talk to him later about her ideas for the suite. Christos decided on the bedroom at the end of the hall and offered to help with the painting.

They moved down a short hallway to the other suite, which had the name "Chef Niko" on the door.

"Guess this one is yours, Niko." Regan was amused as he pushed open the door to a suite with an identical floor plan to the other one.

"The chef that was here before liked this suite because it was closest to the kitchen," Sara contributed.

Niko surveyed the decor. "Guess he liked Irish green too." Everyone in the group laughed. Niko was pleased, but suggested he and Loren paint together. The group chatted as they viewed the upper level and exited to the backyard and the home that had been built for the caretaker. Large hanging trees were scattered around a spacious open lawn that provided a view of the marina, the shipyard, and the ocean, which impressed Abasi and Shima.

Shima informed Regan they would like to stay in the home. "There are no stairs for me to struggle with, and look, Regan, the view from here and the yard— it is like the country."

"This is perfect for us," Abasi added.

Regan pulled Abasi and Shima into his arms. "Whatever you want. I have torn your life apart and I will do whatever I can to make it up to you." Regan's voice was quavering. "I owe you so much for taking care of Christos."

Abasi placed a comforting hand on his shoulder. "You owe us nothing, Regan. Christos was a gift to all of us." He was smiling, and he seemed content as he took Christo's hand and pulled his grandson close to him. "Time for a fresh start. It's nice here, lots of space, the smell of the ocean, family and friends." He looked at the cluster of people gathered around him. "This is our home now." He was still holding firmly to Christos's hand and took Shima's as he spoke.

Sadeh and Sean left with the Dolans to return to the apartment with the babies. Abasi and Shima started getting settled into the cottage and Christos stayed behind with them to help. Sara asked to be excused to return to her work, but not without first asking Niko directly if she would be able to remain on as an employee. When Regan had purchased the business, he had asked McGaffy to remain on as the manager of the marina, but had told Sara his business partner would be making the decisions regarding the restaurant and pub.

Regan looked at Niko for a response.

"Yes, of course you can stay, Sara. There is a lot to do here and I will be asking you for your personal assistance as we get started. I want you to stay."

"Thank you." She could not contain herself and wrapped her arms around Niko and then Regan. "Thank you." She scurried off, leaving them both a bit taken aback by her action as she bid the others goodbye.

"Think you can handle her, Niko?" Regan joked.

Niko shrugged, his expression implying indifference. "There won't be a dull moment, that's for sure."

"You guys got time for a drink at the Flynns'?" Jimmy asked Regan and Niko, then added, "It's been a long day."

"I'm in," was the unanimous response.

Regan, Loren, and Niko squeezed into Jimmy and Molly's station wagon for the ride over to the Flynn residence. Jimmy escorted everyone out to the backyard and Loren helped her mother bring out some snacks along with some whisky, rum, and wine.

Regan and Niko both wanted to buy a vehicle, so as the drinks and snacks were passed around, the conversation evolved to the best place to purchase a pickup truck and van.

Jimmy was a problem-solver. "Micky Roan's cousin runs a dealership on the other side of Suaimhneas. No problem, I'll give him a call, let him know you guys are stopping by."

Niko was an organizer. "Let's try and do that in the morning, Regan."

"Okay. I need a truck around the marina," Regan said.

Niko nodded. "I was hoping for something like a van, best thing for hauling restaurant supplies."

"I got my station wagon there. He has a good selection on the lot, or he'll find it if he doesn't have what you want. Good guy. Name's Doyle, Doyle Roan."

"Speaking of the station wagon, Papa, could I borrow it? I want to take a few things from my room over to the marina." Loren stood up to catch the keys that Jimmy threw her direction.

"Loren, I don't think you should be staying over there with a man to whom you are not married! What will people say?" Molly Flynn's disciplinary tone caught Loren off guard. Regan reached for Loren's hand and stood up beside her.

"Mrs. Flynn, I love your daughter. Where were 'these people' when Niko and I were growing up in an orphanage?" He glanced over at his friend. "Where were they when we were sleeping on the dock, soaking wet in the cold rain with no food to eat, doing a man's work when we were just boys? When I had to give my son to his grandparents because I couldn't look after him, work two jobs, and study to be a captain? Loren and I both have pasts that haunt us, and right now we are trying to piece two lives together, and we can't do that if we can't be together. I have worked too hard and too long to give a damn what "these people" have to say!"

Jimmy recognized the assertive tone that paralyzed Molly's expression and rendered her tiny red mouth speechless. Her blue eyes froze on this man who stood defiantly beside her daughter. She stared at him, and her mind was in the past, remembering Jimmy Flynn telling her father the same thing the same way when he asked for her hand in marriage.

The Spirit of the Autumn Wind

Jimmy Flynn was no choir boy when he was young, and when he was sent off to serve time in the military in lieu of serving time in jail, she was forbidden by her father to see him again. When Jimmy came home, all he wanted was to marry his childhood sweetheart. He had stood up to her father with the same resistance as Regan Quinn. Molly looked at her husband, and she knew there would be no support from him; he did not share her concern about other people's opinions, so she just nodded. "Well, if that is what you want, Loren?"

"Yes, Mama, I need this time with Regan. He's right, we need to be together."

"Okay, go then and pack your things." Molly motioned her away.

Loren's eyes met Regan's as she left, and Jimmy put a bit more Irish whisky in his wife's glass. Obviously, Molly Flynn was not concerned about what "these people" had to say about a touch of Irish whisky now and then.

"Regan, I meant no disrespect," she said. "Loren is very special to us, and we just don't want her to be hurt like before."

"I love Loren, Mrs. Flynn, and I will take care of her just like I take care of everyone else in my life."

Niko felt the tenseness of the situation and, knowing the protective nature of his friend, did not want things to escalate, so he changed the conversation back to the discussion about vehicles while they finished their drinks.

Regan helped Loren pack her things into the back of Jimmy's station wagon. He slid in the driver's side, and with Loren squeezed between himself and Niko, they headed back to the marina.

CHAPTER TWENTY-SEVEN

Laughter and chatter, mixed with the rhythm of Celtic music, spilled out of the pub. The big wooden doors were propped open with miniature anchors, providing a release for the mingled odour of cigarette smoke and fried food. It was just after five. Sara had said she opened the pub at four and the place was already packed with patrons.

The trio stood at the entrance for a moment, and Niko motioned toward one of the few vacant booths along the wall, taking the seat that allowed him to look out at the activity. Regan seated himself across from him, casually placing his arm around Loren, and she netted her fingers through his as they hung over her shoulder. Niko smiled at the two of them, but his focus was on the pub.

The crowd was mostly dock workers and crewmen off the fishing boats, gathering as friends for a drink before going home to their families, but there were also a few tourists. A group of four men were cooking at the grill behind the long counter, which was lined with patrons drinking on the dark-green barstools. Niko could tell by the organized speed with which the men worked that they had learned to cook in the galleys of ships. Niko had spent many an hour on the fast-food line of a galley, first as a young trainee, and a few years later when the galley master felt his leg slowed him too much to handle the pace on the galley floor.

Four women about the same age as Sara, each wearing a shamrock-green apron with "Irish Luck Pub" embroidered on the front, served and cleaned the tables. The place was bustling, and over the loud laughter and talk, Sara was supervising the rapid outflow of food and drinks while finding time to talk to and acknowledge almost everyone in the place.

Niko was fascinated by the woman's indifference to his physical appearance, but what interested him the most was something he recognized—her need to look after everyone, skillfully camouflaged by her flamboyant personality and her smile, which she shared unconditionally to cover her feelings of inadequacy. He understood exactly who Sara Dolan was, because she was exactly like him; damaged goods. Not physically crippled like he was, but emotionally crippled from years of rejection.

Sara noticed them, and with a quick wave and smile immediately came to the table with menus that she collected along the way. She slid into the booth beside Niko, just as she did with some of her other patrons, and placed the menus on the worn wooden table in front of them.

"Hope you didn't wait long; crazy busy this afternoon." Her hand touched Niko's arm, but this time he didn't want to push her away.

"Is it always busy like this, Sara?" he asked.

"Yes, pretty much." She was watching the crowd as she responded to Niko, then looked back at her guests and smiled. "There's a passenger ship in the harbour, so a bunch of tourists are in Suaimhneas Cove this afternoon and were waiting at the door when I opened." She motioned to a group of colourfully dressed people laughing and drinking at three tables close to the bar. "They come for the fresh seafood, but they drink as much as they eat, and they spend a lot of money. With the ships coming into the harbour we are getting more of them all the time—they love the boardwalk. What can I bring you from the bar?"

"A couple of rums, and a glass of red wine for the young lady," Regan said.

Sara nodded, acknowledging his request. "The boys at the grill are doing a nice salmon plate for the tourists," she suggested, wanting to impress Niko.

The trio nodded at Sara's lunch suggestion, without looking at the menus.

"I'll tell them it's for the management," she said.

"No, Sara." Niko touched her hand. "They are doing a good job; everyone here is. I'll cook with them for a while tomorrow and introduce myself then. I can tell by the way they run the grill they learned to cook on the ships. I will need more help like them to run the restaurant. You are doing an excellent job here, Sara, and so is your staff. Your patrons are cared for and enjoying themselves, so there is no need to worry any of the employees about changes."

"That's considerate of you, Niko. They all need their jobs." Sara unconsciously placed her hand on his arm as she got up to leave. "I'll be right back with the drinks."

When Regan had purchased the marina and restaurant, he had met the representative from the bank at the pub, and it had been Sara Dolan and Mike McGaffy who had shown him around. He had witnessed this frenzy before, but Niko had not, and Regan could tell by his expression he was both impressed and amused by the chaos of the place. Regan knew when he met Sara that, as flamboyant as she was, she knew how to run a pub. She was a hard worker and would be good help for Niko, who without a doubt had every skill needed to get the restaurant business running again.

Regan was proud of his friend; he was generous and knew how important good employees were. Niko was a gentleman, maybe because of the teachings of the nuns at the orphanage, but mostly just because that was who he was; it came from the heart, and Niko Mararious had a good heart.

Sara returned with the drinks and rushed off, returning a short time later with the food. Every time she came to the table, she made them feel they were the most important people in the pub, just like she did with her other patrons.

While they ate, they talked about Christo starting school, Regan's appointment with Seaward, which was scheduled in two days, and the overall challenges of getting settled in and the business started. Niko finished his meal and leaned back into the booth. "Regan, this place is making money, so let's add some staff and open it at noon. With Seaward's new operation in Sona Bay, there will be passenger ships in the harbour all the time, and Suaimhneas Cove is a tourist attraction. This place is bubbling over with character and the tourists that come here will help get the restaurant started."

Regan nodded. He trusted his friend completely. As competent as Regan was at sailing, Niko was at management. He was an excellent cook, but he was also a clear thinker, especially under pressure. Niko could come up with a plan, organize it, and make it happen, just like the night of the murder in Tangiers when he had taken control of the situation they found themselves in.

While they finished their coffee, Niko took out a pad and wrote down a note about improving the ventilation and adding more staff, and then the words, "menu, fresh buns, pickles, and fresh-cut potato fries."

The next day when Loren returned from work there was a shiny black pickup truck parked beside their suite, and in front of Niko's was a new deep-blue Fordson van. Christos was excited. Regan had given him his first driving lesson on the way home from the dealership and he was talking non-stop, as he hung over the fender ogling the engine with his dad. Somewhere between Tangiers and Ireland, Christos had become a young man, and for all the uncertainty and upheaval the decision to come to Ireland was causing in everyone's lives, it was worth it to Regan Quinn. He had missed a lot of time with his son when he was growing up and he planned to make the best of the years ahead.

The next morning, Regan moved the *Autumn Wind* into the dry dock at the end of the Dolan Shipyard building. With the elegance of a clumsy swan, she was a splendid sight perched just above the water, a majestic guardian of the marina and the open ocean beyond. Fishing boats and vessels bottlenecked on the water, welcoming her home with a salute of ships horns and whistles, and that morning the marina that Regan Quinn and Niko Mararious had bought was christened "The Autumn Wind Marina."

Christos started school the following day. He began in the same class he had left two months earlier in Tangiers. Cait Dolan, who was one year younger and one class behind, was quick to introduce her new and interesting friend to her classmates. She insisted she walk with Christos to and from school each day, and although Christos was shy and more interested in learning to sail and drive his dad's new truck than girls, the walk did provide a variety of enlightening insights into Cait Dolan's fifteen-year-old perspective of life in Ireland.

The days ahead were long and busy. Seaward Ship Lines offered Regan a promotion into management, but he would still take one two-week voyage each month. He would sail a new, large passenger ship called the *Seaward Goddess* from Ireland to the South of France, with one port stop in Great Britain. The rest of the month would be spent in the Seaward office in Ireland, where he would work with the team, assessing port issues and developing the new shorter passenger voyages Seaward was setting up in the Mediterranean, primarily servicing Spain, Italy, and Greece.

Niko was adding a bakery into the kitchen so fresh bread and buns could be served with the meals in the dining room and with the burgers in the pub. More coolers for fresh market vegetables and meat were installed, as well as additional ovens.

Niko let the grill crew in the pub know he was hiring cooks from the ships' galleys. With the war over there was a good supply of qualified applicants, and Niko knew exactly what type of cooks he needed to fulfill his vision and keep the dining room running smoothly.

Sara had been cleaning rooms at the hotel a few blocks away in the mornings and started work at the pub at two to prepare for the four-o'clock opening. Niko gave her an increase in salary and asked her to work with him in the mornings preparing the dining-lounge kitchen for the opening of business and, like Sean, whatever was happening in the kitchen happened with an Irish tune. Niko found himself looking forward to arriving in the mornings to hear her quietly singing while she worked.

McGaffy had hired both Sleeman and Brok. Sleeman oversaw maintenance at the marina, and had a crew of veterans working on the boardwalk and additional boat slips and a second crew helping to get the dining room and dance floor ready for the opening.

Sadeh was eager to help, and she had an eye for decor and detail, so at Niko's request she took on decorating the dining room. Abasi and Shima would watch the twins for a few hours, and each afternoon Sadeh would arrive in a pair of Sean's coveralls with the arms and legs rolled up and with her hair knotted up under a kerchief. With the help of Sleeman's crew, the dark cherrywood floors were polished to a glowing shine capable of reflecting the sage-coloured table linens. The wrought-iron chairs were painted black and upholstered with soft seats in dusty rose, accented with wisps of sage-green. Cream-coloured Irish lace valances adorned the windows, exposing the panoramic view and the spectacular silhouette of the *Autumn Wind* against the blue-green of the Irish sky and ocean. The heavy wooden doors were sent over to Sean's ship building, where Brok sketched and engraved the exactness of the *Autumn Wind* on each door.

He painted the wall beside the stage white and sketched the *Autumn Wind* as he remembered her on the voyage to Ireland, surrounded by the ocean against the deep-blue sky. The three-dimensional uniqueness of the sketch made the ship appear as though it were sailing across the dance floor into the dining room. With a bit of engineering from Sean, stars would appear in the night sky and the glow of the moon would appear above the ship and across the water when the lights in the dining room were dimmed, and at the same time the running lights on the ship would come on as she sat silent against the dark ocean. It was what Sean had seen in his mind, what he felt in his heart when he sat on her deck, his soft Celtic melodies drifting off through the night, taking him home to Ireland.

What Sadeh, Sean, and Brok had created in the dining room was a tribute to Niko Mararious and the genuine friendship that had formed between them. The first time they showed him the ship under the dimmed lights of the now-elegant dining room, it brought tears to his eyes. He felt valued and cared about, and for the first time in his life truly opened his heart to friendship and love; now he understood the mystifying spirit of the *Autumn Wind*.

Brok looked after the bookings for the sailboat slips and used the time in between to sketch the variety of boats that came and went against the colours of the harbour and ocean. They were captivating and were being sold through the gallery in Dublin and on the dock. But what pleased him the most was that the yachts that Sean Dolan built would carry his unique designs all over the world.

When word got out that Sean Dolan was back in town and the Dolan Shipyard was re-opening to build yachts, old employees and potential new ones lined up to get in on the opportunities. Sean pulled a crew together and, working endless hours by their side, had the building ready and things in place to start building the first special-order yacht. Sadeh was at his side, taking charge of the interior cabin decor. She set up samples of fabrics, leathers, and flooring in Sean's design room, all of which could be coordinated with a variety of exterior designs uniquely created by Brok.

Dominic Speers, the accountant who had worked for Seamus Dolan when he owned Dolan Shipyard, had been handling the business of the marina and pub for Regan since the purchase. He was moved into an office on the boardwalk and assigned the massive job of overseeing the accounting for the marina and restaurant, as well as Sean's yacht-building business.

Regan left for his second two-week voyage on the Seaward Goddess, and with the dining room finished, Sadeh and Loren decided to paint both suites before his return. Sadeh helped Loren pick some soft pastel colours (which did not include any shades of green), and Sleeman sent a couple of his crew over to paint under Sadeh's supervision while Loren was at work. Loren insisted Sara and Cait's apartment behind the pub be painted as well. After seeing what Sadeh had done with the dining room, Niko was quite content to let her take charge of painting his suite.

Loren wanted the painting of the residence to be a surprise for Regan when he returned home. Sadeh understood it was important to Loren that she contribute to the home she shared with Regan even though they were not married. Sadeh had lived with Sean as his wife, pregnant and unmarried, and it was no secret this was not considered acceptable behaviour for a woman in the 1950s. The two women had found an ally in Sara, who had a child out of wedlock at sixteen and was forced to survive in a society that would not forgive or accept her. The fact that the behaviour of all three women was judged as inappropriate made for a strong friendship.

Niko's dining lounge was scheduled to open at month-end, but in ten days, when Regan Quinn returned home, there would be a celebration, a test run for the dining lounge and kitchen before it opened to the public one week later. The celebration was the re-reading of Sean and Sadeh's vows on the bow of the *Autumn Wind*.

Music was not only a birthright of the Dolans', but the Irish in general. A group of Sean and Seamus Dolan's musical friends volunteered to play for the wedding dance in the dining room. They gathered on the stage a couple of days before the wedding, and as they broke into the Celtic rhythm of an Irish waltz, the musical souls of the Dolan women could not be contained. Christos was pulled on to the dance floor by Cait and Niko dragged on by Sara, who refused to see his leg as any problem. She immediately fit his gait into the Irish waltz, leaving Niko a bit embarrassed, but happily surprised at his ability to do what he had until now considered impossible. Sara had grown accustomed to Niko's stride and as they danced, he found the rhythm and felt the music, relaxing his strong arms as he pulled her to him and twirled her about the floor. Christo was equally embarrassed but was driven by the curiosity of his youth and pretty Cait Dolan, and he immediately fell into the rhythm with the same coordination and style as his father. It was an unusual interlude in a busy afternoon that brought cheers and claps from the musicians on stage.

Loren, Sara, and Cait accompanied Sadeh to the wedding boutique to select a gown and choose evening dresses for themselves. Loren chose pink, Sara turquoise, and Cait Irish green. Sadeh had arranged a visit to the tailor for the men on the day that Regan arrived home, so they could be outfitted with their wedding suits. Sean considered it an honour to dress for his wedding, Niko was nervous, Christos was indifferent, and Regan was relaxed. He organized the outing to include sneaking underaged Christos into the Irish Luck Pub for a drink with the men.

The following morning brought sunshine and excitement to Sadeh and Sean's special day. As the afternoon sun settled across the marina, ribbons and streamers floated across the bow of the *Autumn Wind*, dancing with the warm ocean breeze. Niko had been up since dawn, making sure every detail of the meal and dining room was perfect before joining the men in Regan's suite to dress for the event. Regan was comfortable in his captain's uniform and somewhat amused at the other three men as they struggled with ties and shirt collars, but was impressed at the results. The trio was remarkably handsome in their quality casual suits; their clothing was respectful of the occasion, yet as adventurous as the spirits of the men whose hearts beat within the woven threads, each sporting a pastel-coloured shirt and matching bow tie. The women had disappeared into the world of crinolines and gowns and were not seen again until four in the afternoon, when everyone met on the bow of the *Autumn Wind* for the ceremony.

Niko understood that this was not just Sean's wedding day when Seamus Dolan walked Sadeh Dolan up the gang plank and gave her hand to his son. His face was filled with joyous pride as he surveyed the Dolan family, including its two newest members, gathered together for the first time in many years.

Sadeh's off-white gown of Irish lace clung precariously off her shoulders. Tiny ringlets adorned with Irish-green flowers escaped the bundle of curls meticulously formed on her head. Sean Dolan took her hand. His muscular frame was handsomely displayed in a dark suit, and an Irish-green necktie rested on his heart. Everyone gathered around as Captain Regan Quinn greeted the bride and groom. Feeling somewhat more relaxed about this unusual authority bestowed upon him as a sea captain, he read the vows that formed the foundation of every marriage. Sean and Sadeh said, "I do," but this time on Irish soil.

When the doors of the dining room swung open to the elegance of gleaming dark cherrywood and soft sage, the guests were in awe. A staff of hostesses in black uniform dresses with tiny sage-green aprons waited in a row to greet them. Niko excused himself and exited to the kitchen to make sure the service of the meal went without a hitch.

As the meal ended, Sean and Sadeh stood to thank their guests. The introduction of Chef Niko brought a standing ovation from the group, which included Jimmy Flynn's investigation team. Niko was almost speechless, but found the words to thank his staff and everyone that had helped with the dining room, including the bride and groom, and after a moment of thoughtful hesitation, the *Autumn Wind*, for bringing them all together as friends.

The lights in the dining room dimmed and the *Autumn Wind* appeared as though it was floating into the room, mesmerizing the group into silence as Cait Dolan, now on the stage with Sean's harp next to her heart, broke into song. Her pitch-perfect voice was as beautiful as the young woman with ringlets of bright red tumbling down around her shoulders as she sang the "Irish Wedding Song" for her Uncle Sean and Sadeh.

Christos could not take his eyes off her. Up until now, hanging out with Cait had held no more importance than working on the sailboat or driving his dad's new truck, but he was reconsidering the priority of these activities, and when the band began to play, he asked Cait Dolan to dance.

As Regan watched him twirl the young woman across the floor, he was more grateful than ever for the decision he had made to make a home in Ireland and for the time he had left with his son before Christos became his own man.

Regan and Loren were lost in the rhythm of the music when Regan spotted Niko and Sara across the dance floor. "Loren, look. I have never seen him dance." He could not hide the surprise in his voice.

Loren smiled up at him. "Yes, Niko and Christos had a bit of a dance lesson from the Dolan girls the other day, I'm told."

Regan's surprise turned to amusement. "Seems there are a lot of things going on around here while I'm at sea." He was referring to the newly painted suite he and Loren shared, as well.

"All good things, Regan," she said.

"Is there something going on with those two?" He was watching his friend weave through the dancers.

"Like I said, all good things."

Regan smiled and tightened his arms around her, twirling her to the Celtic sounds of Ireland and deeper into love.

The band played the last waltz and as the guests left, the *Autumn Wind* sat silent, visible only by her running lights and seemingly afloat, surrounded by a fog that had drifted in off the ocean.

The next weekend, Niko's dining lounge at the Autumn Wind Marina opened for business.

CHAPTER TWENTY-EIGHT

"Niko." Sara took his hand and held it on her stomach. "We have made a baby." She felt him want to pull away, but she held his hand where it was and watched him fight the fear.

"A baby? Sara, how is that possible? I thought we were being careful."

"I'm almost three months. It was the first night we made love, Niko, the night of Sean and Sadeh's wedding."

She watched his face as he traced his memory of the night. It had been just after midnight when the band quit playing and everyone had left. Cait had been staying with her grandparents to babysit the twins so Sean and Sadeh could take a drive up the coast. Sara had stayed behind with him to make sure everything was locked up and things were put away in the kitchen.

"It has been such a hectic day. I'll never be able to sleep. Would you have a glass of wine with me in my suite, Sara? Maybe that Greek red we both like?"

"Yes, as long as I can take these shoes off. My feet are killing me."

She tucked her arm in his and removed her shoes, walking barefoot with him to his suite.

"You look absolutely lovely tonight Sara, shoes or not." He opened the door to the suite, juggling the wine and two glasses while he turned on the lamps. He poured, and she raised her glass.

"To Chef Niko! Your dining lounge is a success. You are a success!"

He gazed into her green eyes and took her hand. "We are a success, Sara; none of this would have happened without you. You have been by my side all the way and …I…love…you…"

His feelings were pouring uncontrollably out of his heart. He'd had feelings for her for a while that he had tried to pass off as friendship, but his heart would have no part of it, and neither would his body. It was easy to love Sara, he loved Sara…and his lips touched hers, first gently, and then with passion that she returned. She wanted to be with him as much as he wanted to be with her.

Their clothes fell to the floor and their bodies tangled together. It had been so long since he had been with a woman, and he had never been with a woman he loved. His leg might not have worked properly, but there was not a thing wrong with his manhood, and Sara surrendered to his gentle, passionate love.

The morning sun found Sara Dolan and Niko Mararious wrapped in each other's arms. What had happened between them could not be undone, and neither one of them regretted the reality of facing what they had both been feeling for a while, the love they had found together. Niko would take a break in the afternoon between two and four, leaving his staff in charge, then return to prepare for the evening dining crowd. Sara would meet him at his suite and they would make love while Cait and Christos were at school and Loren was at work. They had kept their relationship private. The business was running well, and Niko planned to ask Sara Dolan to marry him at Christmas, which was almost two weeks away.

Niko was struggling, trying to comprehend what she had just told him. "A baby." There was no way he could hide his anxiety.

"Niko, you don't want our baby?" Tears were sliding down her cheeks.

"Sara, I want you, and yes, I want our baby. I just…want to make you happy…I want our love to make you happy, not make you cry. This is just…unexpected. I was going to ask you on Christmas eve to marry me, Sara. Sort of a Christmas gift for both of us. I thought a spring wedding..." Sara still held his hand on her stomach.

"Niko, maybe you should ask us now. This baby will be born in the late spring." Tears were puddling on her cheeks.

Niko pushed his crippled leg under him, awkwardly positioning himself on one knee. He took her hand. "Sara Dolan, will you marry me? I know I don't deserve you, with the things I have done, but will you marry me and be my wife?" His tone almost pleading, as though he expected she would say no.

"Yes." Sara dropped to her knees in front of him and wrapped him in her arms. "Yes, Niko. I love you. I will marry you. I would be proud to be your wife." She rubbed the tears from her face, taking his hand as they struggled clumsily to their feet, still tangled in an embrace.

He pushed her damp curls off her face and seated her beside him on the sofa, placing his arm around her shoulders. His expression conveyed his concern as he studied her face, still moist with tears. "Sara, what if this baby is born with this crippled leg? I don't know if I can bear to see my child struggle like I have had to."

"Niko, you had no parents, no one to love you, and you have had to overcome formidable challenges, but look at what you have accomplished, and the fine person you have become. This baby will have parents and be loved."

"Sara, does it not bother you that I am crippled?"

Sara placed her hand on his face and ran her fingers through his dark curly hair as she spoke to his soul. "Niko, a man's worth is not in his leg, but in his heart, and you have a fine heart. And don't forget this baby is half Dolan and we're fightin' Irish." She smiled at her reference to her family. "When Cait was born, I was terrified and all I could see was challenges ahead. But the moment I held her in my arms I loved her, and I knew I could do whatever I must to take care of her. We are not strangers to challenges. We will raise this child together with Cait, and we will be a family. You will make a marvellous father. I have watched you with Christos when Regan is at sea, and you are like a father to him and Cait, too. She is so rebellious, too much like I was at her age, and I don't want her to make the mistakes I did. When you talk to her, she listens. You are a good father to her already, and you will be to this child, too."

"Does Cait know about us, about the baby?"

Sara shook her head.

"We have to tell her." Niko was under pressure, sorting through the problems, taking control. "You have done an outstanding job raising her and her happiness matters to me. I don't want her to feel left out, and I don't want her to be angry at us. I have been wanting to talk to Cait and tell her about my feelings for you, that I love you, and make sure she understood that I love her, too. I was going to talk to her before Christmas, before I asked you to marry me. She never knew her father and I don't want her to feel she is losing her mother, too." Niko seldom talked about his feelings, and she had no idea he had so many concerns regarding their relationship. "Everything has changed now, but we still need to talk to her. And what about your father, Cait's grandfather? She has just been getting to know him and spending time with him. They have been playing the harp and singing together. When we tell him, will this drive them apart and your father out of your life again?"

Tears welled in her eyes. "Niko, I don't care what people say about us, but I don't want to have any more trouble with my father. I agree Cait needs to know because this will affect her life and she could be angry. But we don't have to tell my father or anyone else about the baby. No one needs to know yet. I am not showing, and we will be married when our child is born."

"Sara, I don't like secrets. I'm not ashamed of our relationship or the child we have made. We will tell your family and deal with what comes, and we will be married, with or without their blessings."

Niko was remembering Regan's assertive conversation with Molly Flynn, and if there was one thing he and his longtime friend agreed

The Spirit of the Autumn Wind

on it was that "these people" had no right to judge. Niko considered his options. "I was planning to close the pub and restaurant for three days through Christmas. Everyone has been working hard and I want to give the entire staff the days off to spend with their families. How about Christmas Day? It's my birthday and Regan will be home. Would that be okay, Sara? Could we get married on Christmas Day?"

"A Christmas wedding…that would be so perfect! Just a small private ceremony, Niko. Regan can read the vows for us like he did for Sean and Sadeh. Just our friends and family. We can do a supper for them here at the dining lounge."

Niko nodded with approval. "Sara, I know this is going to sound crazy, and the weather is cooler now, but…maybe we could say our vows on the bow of the *Autumn Wind*."

Sara was quiet, listening with her heart. She knew Niko had shot a man on that ship and her brother had almost died aboard her. If Niko wanted to say his wedding vows on her bow, there must be a special reason.

"The *Autumn Wind*, as much sadness as she has brought into my life, has given me as much happiness in return. It is as though she has a spirit that ties her to my heart and soul. She gathered all of us as strangers and brought us safely to Ireland as lifelong friends. Now she sits there, our guardian, bringing good fortune and happiness to all our lives."

Sara was rendered speechless by the pouring out of Niko's feelings, and nodded as she wrapped her arms around the strong sensitive man she had fallen in love with.

"Where are your parents now?" Niko wanted to get the dealings with the family settled as soon as possible.

"They are all over at the shipyard building. Sean and my father are doing a systems check on the new yacht for the American. Sadeh is putting the finishing touches on the interior decor and

Mom is watching the twins. Christos is over there too, working on his sailboat."

"And Cait?" Niko asked.

"She's finishing her homework in our apartment."

"Well, it's Sunday and everyone is around. Tomorrow the dining lounge and pub are open; we will be too busy to deal with this then, and there is no point in waiting. Let's go talk to Cait, then go to the shipyard."

Niko was used to working under pressure in his kitchen. He knew how to skillfully present emotionless, culinary delights, but had no idea how to present this emotionally wrought situation to old Seamus Dolan.

Niko stated respectfully that he and Sara were expecting a child, and asked politely for her hand in marriage, but red-faced Seamus Dolan's rage could not be contained. He stood in the middle of the shipyard building, shouting. "Have you learned nothing at all this past fifteen years? Are you so determined to ruin your life that we have to go through this disgrace again?" Niko and Sara stood before him with Cait between them.

Sean clasped his father firmly by the back of the neck. "Pop! Don't do this again."

The old man was heedless of his son, determine to say his piece. "We have lived with your disgrace for the past fifteen years, and now you stand before your parents again unmarried and pregnant! What about Cait, for God's sake? You are determined to put her through this ridicule, too, with your disgusting behaviour!"

Sara straightened her posture and took a deep breath. "Yes, Father, I did learn something. I learned what love is. Above all, I love my daughter, and I have done everything I can to make sure she knows that I love her, regardless of how she came into my life. I did not set terms for my love as you have with me, and believe it or not, all those years you shut me out, I still loved you and Mother, but I did not ask for your love or your forgiveness. I am not sixteen years old anymore, taken advantage of by an older man who preyed on young innocent girls. I am a consenting adult. I learned how to love unconditionally, and that is the kind of love Niko and I share; it has no conditions and it does not judge. The child I am carrying is a product of that love, and even if you cannot love me, don't take this out on Cait. You are her grandfather and she would like to be a part of your life."

The old man's rage at her defiance was causing Sean to tighten his grip as his father continued ranting. "Cait, you come live with your grandparents. Your mother is not fit to raise you."

"No, Gramps." Cait's voice quavered. "I love my mother and I know Niko loves her and me, too. Niko takes care of us. Mom doesn't have to work cleaning in the motel now, and Niko pays me to help clean up in the kitchen and help with the music on Friday and Saturday at the dining lounge. He makes sure I have enough money for my tuition payment for college each month, so I don't have to work nights at the fish market. Because Mom is a single parent and we are considered poor, I cannot attend college if my tuition is not paid in advance, and I need to have a grade score of eighty or I cannot attend. Niko makes sure I have time to study and my grades are better now. Gramps, I want to go to college and be an engineer, so I can design boats with Uncle Sean."

For a moment Seamus Dolan went speechless, embarrassed by his ignorance of the social status of his daughter and granddaughter, and shaken by the reality that this young woman was his blood and as helpless as he and his son had been to fight their destiny.

"They told me about the baby. There are worse sins then having a baby, Gramps."

But Seamus Dolan wasn't a man who backed down; he was fightin' Irish.

"What can be worse than being shamed by your own daughter?" Seamus Dolan spit the words out, his face crimson with anger.

Niko tightened his grip on Sara's shoulder, lodging Cait tightly between them. He was appalled at what was coming out of Seamus Dolan's mouth, but he was determined to let him yell until he exhausted his anger, because what Niko had to say he was only going to say once.

As Sean watched Niko, he let his arm drop around his father's shoulders and rest on his heart, ready to hold the man at bay should his rage explode into something physical. He knew Niko was gentle and non-confrontational, but Sean also knew his father's breaking point and he was dangerously close to it. Christos positioned himself at Niko's side. He had been watching the entire drama unfold, remembering the events with Nigeria a few short months ago and expecting the worst.

"Come on, Pop, stop this!' Sean's firm verbal intervention stopped the man's ranting long enough for Niko to say what had to be said.

"Mr. Dolan. I love your daughter and your granddaughter. If you haven't figured out by now that they love you and they want to have you in their lives then you are a stupid old fool, and not worthy of their love. I know what it is like to not have a family, and you drive yours away because of your self-centred pride. If the hypocritical judgment and idle gossip of people who have done far worse is more important to you then the love of these two beautiful women, then it ends with this conversation, and you will have lost their love and respect forever. I offer you no apology, and I will not ask your forgiveness for the child Sara and I have conceived in love. I do not care what you or what 'these people' have to say. We will be married on Christmas Day. If you can love us, you are welcome; if not, then leave us alone to live our lives without judgment."

Niko turned his back on Seamus Dolan. "Let's go. Good night, Sadeh, Mrs. Dolan." Niko gathered Sara, Cait, and Christos ahead of him and walked toward the door.

Maggie Dolan was crying uncontrollably. "Seamus, please, you promised when Sean came home that this was over and buried in the past forever. Sara is a grown woman and Cait is right, Niko is good to them both. They will be married when the baby is born and if people want to go on about what is none of their business, let them. But don't let them destroy our family again. Fight back for us, isn't that what fightin' Irish do? Fight for their families and country. I missed a chance to watch Cait grow up and I will not stand by and let you deprive me of a chance to love this grandchild like you did the last. If the seed of a man creates a child out of wedlock it is fine for him to shirk his responsibilities, but God help the woman who takes the responsibility and raises the child alone. She is chastised by everyone, including her family, and forced to live as you have made Sara and Cait live. For God's sake, Seamus, at least have the decency to allow them this happiness now."

Seamus was shocked. His wife's feelings, for the first time since Cait was born, were exposed—naked, bare facts of life that Seamus could neither deny nor justify.

Sean knew his mother had always been submissive, and even though it seemed she did not agree with Seamus regarding Sara, she had always stood by her husband as a good Irish Catholic wife should. But she'd had enough; she was taking a stand against her husband, and if there was anyone that could break his spirit, it was Maggie Dolan.

The large shipyard building went silent. The yelling stopped, but Maggie Dolan's words were still thundering through the hearts of everyone there. Niko held tightly to teary-eyed Sara, and they shared a glance but did not look back as they walked toward the door with Cait and Christos.

"Niko, Sara, please wait." Sean's strong voice broke the silence. "Please wait!"

Niko stopped, clinging tight to the hands of both Sara and Cait as they turned to face Sean. Niko had lost his respect for Seamus Dolan but not Sean. Sean had saved his and Christos's life on the *Autumn Wind* and he considered him a friend. Sean had humbled himself to his father once to bring this family together, and out of respect, Niko would not be the one to undo what Sean had accomplished. Seamus Dolan was doing a good enough job of that all by himself.

"Pop, we all love you, every one of us here," Sean said. "Niko is right, you are destroying us with your pride. What Mom said is true." Sean had taken a place beside his mother and wife as a sign of solidarity. "As men, we cannot judge or look down at women for what is as much our fault as theirs. If love is to be considered a mistake, then those that judge us are as guilty as we are. They all want and need love as much as we do. Times are changing, Pop, and so are attitudes, and it is long overdue. It does not matter what people say, we can rise above their petty judgment. Pop, we are fightin' Irish, we give our blood for our country, but what is our country without family? Family is a blood bond and we are all Dolan blood."

Seamus Dolan stood silent, his breathing strained, his hands trembling, as he came to the realization that he had failed his family and Niko Mararious was right. He was the one that had driven his daughter out of his home because of his pride and his son out of his life because of his own foolish mistake. What Seamus had perceived as betrayal was really the fighting side of his son. Sean had used the company that had deceived his father to get back what his family had lost. He had used them to get an education and used their name to develop his own client base and reputation and their money to buy back what they had taken.

He had fallen in love with a woman whose life was rooted in tradition and judgment, all of which he had ignored. He had risked his life on the *Autumn Wind* in pursuit of love and happiness. Sean was right, it was time to let go of these old ideas. The date of a marriage and the date of a birth were just numbers lost in time, but hearts and souls were not.

Seamus did forgive his daughter. What had happened to Sara was not her fault. He had always known that. What he had just witnessed was the fighting side of Sara Dolan. Seamus had three precious grandchildren, two of them granddaughters who would become beautiful Dolan women. He wanted to know them, listen to them sing and play the harp, and watch them grow up. Seamus Dolan had been brought up with strict Irish Catholic views and so had Maggie, but if his wife could accept change to keep the Dolan family together, the choices he would have to make were obvious.

"Sara, come here, please come to your father," the old man finally said, and he opened his arms to embrace his daughter, pulling Sara and teary-eyed Cait close. Sean encircled his sobbing father and mother with his strong arms.

"Sara, I am sorry for what I said, you have my blessing." Seamus motioned for Niko to come close, and extended his hand. "You both have my blessing. Forgive me for the things I have said and done. I am a stubborn old Irishman, and I am the one who needs to change and accept my family with respect."

Niko accepted Seamus Dolan's hand.

The tears were dried with the offering of a bit of Irish whisky to settle everyone's nerves, and a toast to a new beginning for the Dolan family. The *Autumn Wind* sat majestically watching as Niko, Sara, Cait, and Christos walked home under the night sky.

Sara and Cait parted at her apartment behind the pub. Christos and Niko stopped at the kitchen to check the coolers, something Niko did every night before going to bed.

"Think Loren is still up?" Niko asked.

"Yes, she always calls Papa at ten o'clock and she never goes to bed before they talk."

"Your father doesn't get home until Friday, so let's tell her before she hears from someone else," Niko said, then added, "Sorry you had to listen to all that fighting, Christos."

"It's okay, Niko. I like Sara and Cait. Papa will be happy for you, too."

Niko passed Christos a package of vanilla pecan cookies from the refrigerator. "Maybe Loren will make us a cup of tea to go with these?" It was his personal recipe. Niko always kept a supply of the cookies on hand for his staff and the array of visitors that frequented his kitchen. Sadeh had found an old oak table in the shipyard building and, after polishing it to a shine, had it brought over to Niko's kitchen. Just like the table in the galley, it was the gathering spot for friends and family, and many of Niko's delicious cookies had been consumed around it over the past months.

They knocked on Loren's door. "Sorry for the late hour." Niko held the cookies up as a peace offering.

"Not at all. Please come in. Is everything okay?" She was curious about the late visit by the twosome.

"Yes, everything is fine."

"Please sit. I will make some tea. You know I can't resist those devilish cookies you insist on tempting me with."

Niko laughed at her. Both she and Regan considered them an addiction and had made more than one late-night visit to Niko's kitchen to sneak a box from the refrigerator. Christos brought cups as Loren arrived with a pot of steaming tea, which she poured before seating herself.

"Loren… " Niko took a sip of tea. "I asked Sara to marry me." He smiled with the playfulness of a schoolboy. "And she said yes."

"Niko, that is wonderful! I'm so happy for you. Regan will be ecstatic."

"We're planning a small private ceremony on Christmas Day."

"So soon! That's barely two weeks away."

"Sara's pregnant, and the baby is due in late May, so we want to get married right away."

"Niko!" Loren reached across and squeezed his hand. "That's wonderful! A baby. I am so happy for you! I can't wait to tell Regan."

"We want Regan to read the vows for us like he did for Sean and Sadeh, and I know this is really crazy, but we want to have the ceremony on the bow of the *Autumn Wind*."

"Not crazy at all, Niko, that ship has a spell over all of us. Regan will understand; we all do. A Christmas wedding on the *Autumn Wind*. It will be beautiful. Is Cait excited? Sara's parents must be overwhelmed with joy."

"Cait is fine, she is a good girl. But her parents...well, I was hoping they would be, but not exactly," Niko shrugged indifferently. "Seamus and I had a bit of a set-to, and Sean had to straighten it out, but everything is okay. Christos can fill you in on all the drama. But hopefully it is in the past and we can all move on."

It was Sunday morning and Regan had arrived home from his two weeks at sea the previous evening. Christos had told his dad the story of Niko's argument with Seamus Dolan, but Regan could hardly wait to hear his friend's version of the events. Loren opened the door of their suite to Niko's knock and Regan immediately grasped his friend with his strong arms and pulled him through the door.

"Niko, come in! Come in!" Regan quickly steered his friend to the table, at the same time as he was gathering the rum and glasses and excitedly bursting into conversation.

"My dear friend, I am so happy for you and Sara. Getting married! Wow! That is wonderful news! Christos tells me you took on the fightin' Irish while I was at sea," he said playfully.

Niko ran his hand through his hair, and a coy smile of amusement settled on his lips as he took a seat at the table. Regan knew it was a gesture that came when a perplexing problem had been resolved with an equally perplexing solution. "Well, I didn't shoot anyone this time, if that's any consolation."

Regan burst into laughter. The men had finally come to a place where they could talk about and even find some amusement in the strange events of the last year.

Regan poured, and they raised their glasses. "To the friendship of men."

Loren checked to make sure the fresh pot of coffee she had just started was brewing, then settled down on the sofa with a book.

The bond between Regan and Niko was unwavering. She never overstepped the boundaries and she was always careful never to involve herself in what they discussed as friends.

"I hear there is a baby on the way. Congratulations, man! You are really making up for lost time!"

Niko smiled. He was at ease talking to his lifelong friend. "I was going to propose to Sara on Christmas Eve, but this was a bit of a surprise. So, I guess instead of talking about getting married, we will just do it."

Regan was pleased and excited. "Being a father, Niko, it will change your life."

"Good thing Sara has already raised a child, because I sure as hell don't know what I'm doing. Look at the poor example I set for Christos."

"Not at all. He admires you, Niko. Christos is young, but he will be a better man because of you."

Niko's eyes welled with tears, and he went quiet and drowned the awkward moment with a big swallow of rum. "I worry, Regan, about this baby. What if it's born a cripple like me? It would be terrible, especially for a girl. Sara says everything will be fine and not to worry, but I do."

Regan put his hand on his friend's arm. "Sara is a lovely person, she is strong and so are you, and we will all be there to support you, no matter what. Medical procedures have come a long way since you were born, and there is no money to help orphans. This child is not an orphan and will have the very best help we can all give. You are like a brother to me, and I will always be there for you and your family with anything you need. We are all very happy for you and Sara and Cait."

Loren was pretending to read, but her eyes had been glued to the same word. As she listened to the men talk, she wondered for the thousandth time if Regan could really love a woman who could not give him children. He seemed genuinely happy for his friend. He and Niko were still in their thirties and she was thirty-two, the same age as Sara. If she could have children, Regan would want to have that fulfillment in his life again; especially now that he had a home and financial security. She knew this was a desire he would never reveal, and it could destroy their love. She and Regan had promised there would be no more secrets between them, but she knew there would always be this one, and it fed her self-doubt.

Sadeh had decorated the Irish Luck Pub and Niko's dining lounge with the festiveness of the Irish Christmas season and the marina was lit up with the colours of Christmas. Patrons were lining up to get into both the pub and dining lounge, so Niko had extra staff coming into help. Christos and Cait bused tables after school and Abasi helped in the bakery along with a pastry chef who, besides baking buns, was turning out Christmas pudding and cakes at record-breaking speed.

At the request of Niko's patrons, a noon lunch buffet was offered in the dining lounge to accommodate the festive season. Steam tables like those he used in the ship's galley were brought into the dining room and a new chef from Italy was added to Niko's complement of four chefs, four assistant cooks, and four helpers. The new chef was a single man, and planned to stay in Ireland for Christmas, so he volunteered to oversee the supper for the twenty people attending the wedding. There was a parade of musicians spontaneously using the stage by the dance floor and any excuse for the festive crowd to break into joyous dance and song would do. The music in the lounge was being played on outside speakers, initiating the same impulsive response from people passing by on the boardwalk along the marina. The place was a whirlwind of activity, leaving Niko with barely enough time to buy Sara's ring and his wedding suit and deal with getting Sara and Cait moved into his suite.

Sadeh insisted Niko and Sara's Christmas wedding would be beautiful and transformed the bow of the *Autumn Wind* into a wonderland. A large Christmas tree was erected and decorated, then surrounded with a cluster of smaller evergreens, creating a mini version of the Irish countryside. Strings of Christmas lights were strung off the large cranes across the bow, flooding the scene in Irish green. People were strolling on the boardwalk just to enjoy the festive activity and the majestic *Autumn Wind* in her Christmas finery. It was Sadeh's first Irish Christmas and her childhood visions of the season came to life for the twins.

The arrival of Christmas day brought mild, sunny weather that filled the air with ice crystals drifting off the ocean. They floated into the marina like a mist sent from heaven, transforming Sadeh's Irish countryside into a Christmas wonderland. Niko's attempt to get involved in the kitchen to oversee the supper for his guests was met with firm rejection. His new chef and some of his regular staff playfully locked him out, with instructions to go get married, assuring him everything was under control. Sean assigned Regan the task of making sure Niko focused on his wedding and stayed out of the kitchen, a request he was quite glad to comply with since it came under the playful threat of being introduced to Sean's right hook if he failed.

At four o'clock, Niko Mararious waited for his bride in a coal-black suit accented with an Irish-green bow tie and a black Irish fedora with a small green feather tucked in the band for good luck. Everyone there saw a finely dressed and respected chef and businessman, but no one saw a man with a handicap.

Sara's velvet cream-coloured cape tussled in the wind, exposing her off-white gown with inserts of Irish-green as she walked up the gang plank between her father and her mother. The tiara that secured her auburn ringlets sparkled in the winter sun as she took her place beside Niko. They shared a smile with Cait as she approached and pushed back the hood of her sage-coloured cape, exposing the bright red locks that tumbled down around her face.

Regan stood before them in his captain's uniform to read the vows. Niko looked stylish, and happier than Regan had ever known him to be. Regan took a moment to compose himself before he began, too moved by the beautiful little family that stood before him to speak the words within his heart, and what was not said was understood by both men.

Seamus and Maggie Dolan were seated off to the side, each holding one of the Dolan twins, a plan devised by Sean and Sadeh to insure Seamus stayed seated should he have some last-minute change of heart. Sean stood behind his father, his hand resting gently on the old man's shoulder.

As Sara and Niko said, "I do," the sun glistened through the ice crystals sprinkling down from the heavens as if they had been scattered by the angels. Cait and Sean signed as witnesses to the nuptials and Regan took his old friend's hand and pulled him into a masculine embrace, still unable to say what he felt in his heart.

The family and friends walked from the ship to the dining lounge to share a wedding supper together. The dining room door swung open to a room full of people, who burst into song. "For they are jolly good fellows…..for they are jolly good fellows!" Sprinkles of stardust floated through the air and Niko stood speechless at the sight of so many people wishing him and Sara well. He could not hide his surprise, and he looked at Regan, who shrugged, implying it was not his doing. "All I did was keep you busy. The Dolans, Christos, Loren, and your staff did the rest."

"My heavens, how did they prepare all this food without me knowing?" Niko was genuinely surprised at what he saw.

"Well, I guess I did commandeer the galley on the *Seaward Goddess* for the day; she is in port for maintenance." Regan was pleased with his crafty contribution.

"Did you know, Sara?" Niko asked. Her expression of surprise was his answer.

Niko's staff were clapping enthusiastically, obviously pleased with their success in creating this surprise event. They were the first to step forward in their white kitchen smocks and aproned hostess garb to greet the couple who employed them. They had all taken a few hours out of their Christmas to make this day special, and one by one they walked by with congratulations and wishes of goodwill for Niko and Sara before rushing off to make sure the meal service went perfectly.

Before the band started to play, the lights were dimmed, and the *Autumn Wind* appeared to float across the dance floor as Seamus, Sean, and Cait Dolan, each with a harp against their heart, sang the "Irish Wedding Song" for Sara and Niko. The words that blended in beautiful harmony were the same, but Sara heard them differently from her father, her brother, and her daughter. Niko released his teary-eyed wife from his arms, so she could hug and thank each of them. It might have just been a song with beautiful words to everyone else, but to Sara they were the words of forgiveness, understanding, and love that she had longed to hear.

The evening blended together with music and friends. Seamus mingled among the guests, many of whom were, to his surprise, "these people" whom he had felt were judging his family. Cait was staying with Sadeh and Sean to help with the twins. When Mr. and Mrs. Nickolas Mararious finally turned out the lights, Niko was consumed by happiness—the same happiness that only a few months ago he had felt he would never know.

The next afternoon, Regan and Loren drove them to the airport, where the Garda's private airplane was waiting to take them to Italy. Regan insisted they take a proper honeymoon. Jimmy had arranged the plane and Loren gave them the use of her cottage at the sea for as long as they wanted.

The plane was making regular flights to Italy; Jimmy Flynn's undercover team was investigating a drug war between two powerful Mafia families who now were competing for the coveted drug territory that had been left vacant by Nigeria's death. The members of the Santoro family had been killed. The team's extensive knowledge of the whole drug operation and Loren's understanding of the hierarchy of Italian Mafia families had landed the case on Jimmy's desk.

CHAPTER TWENTY-NINE

"Got burgers and some fresh-ground Arabian coffee that Niko wants us to try." Regan was pushing through Loren's office door with a box of burgers and a large coffee thermos in his arms as he spoke. "Great, Jimmy, you're here too. Niko sent two pickles with yours."

Loren got up from her desk to help Regan with the thermos, and he kissed her on the cheek, then set the box of burgers on her desk while surveying the walls, covered with photos of dead bodies and maps with labels and notes.

"Gee…is it okay if I come in? Sorry, I forgot you two are always working on something mysterious and confidential. I can just leave the food."

"It's okay, please stay." Loren reached out and touched Regan's hand. "We need a break, and the burgers smell delicious."

Regan looked at Jimmy to confirm Loren's permission.

"It's fine, Regan, stay! Please." Jimmy pushed a chair toward him with his foot. "We've been staring at this for two weeks and still can't figure it all out." He gestured at the wall like he had had enough, and then pulled paper cups from his desk drawer. They were conveniently kept there beside a bottle of Irish whisky for either the whisky or coffee, depending on the state of chaos the day offered. Loren poured the coffee and Regan sorted through the burgers, making sure Jimmy got the one with the two pickles. Jimmy had acquired a taste for the semi-pickled dill that Niko served with his burgers and he always made sure to include an extra one for him.

Regan settled into the business of enjoying his burger, but his eyes were wandering over the photos on the walls. Jimmy observed his interest and, seeing as how he had been involved in the whole affair from the beginning, saw no harm in enlightening him a bit on how the chapter after Nigeria's death had unfolded. Jimmy motioned toward the wall and, between burger bites and coffee, explained what Regan was looking at.

"After word got out that Nigeria was dead, and Samba was out of the way, two rival Italian Mafia families, the Santoros and the Donatis, went at it to see who could get connected into his supplier in Turkey and start moving the cocaine through Italy up to Ireland and on to America.

"That bunch of dead ones in that photo over there—that's Tony and Gina Santoro and their Mafia crew. Tony Santoro's family has known ties to the Mafia that go back a couple of generations. He married Gina Parisi. Her family owned a fishing fleet based out of Naples that did business on the east coast. Gina was an only child, so when her parents died, she inherited a lot of money and the fishing fleet."

"That's a photo of her parents pinned above them," Loren added, and finished Jimmy's summary, as if she was using it to re-evaluate what they knew. "That fishing fleet looks like a legitimate business, but it's been suspected as a front for smuggling drugs for years. Rumour has it that Tony was quite the ladies' man, and he had a reputation for stepping out on his wife. Expect she wasn't very happy, but she had controlling interest in the fishing fleet and it was making a lot of money." Loren's tone reflected both her annoyance at Tony's infidelity and her admiration for Gina's prudence.

Jimmy put his burger down and took a swallow of coffee, then picked up where Loren had left off, in support of her judgment. "Tony Santoro was a pretty nasty character. Seems like anyone who crossed him ended up dead. He is suspected of being the Mafia head behind a lot of brutal activity that took place along the east coast. He kept his business private, and with everyone dead we are having a hard time putting much information together about the Santoro family and their business. This other bunch of tough-looking guys are the Donati family."

Loren observed Regan listening with interest. She had always found Jimmy's ability to sort through a case in his mind helpful, and she listened closely as he summarized the events for details she might have overlooked as Jimmy continued. "They came up the hard way, working on the docks. The father, Enrico, and his four sons, Ciro, Ricci, Luca, and Marco, got into a freight-trucking business, also suspected of being a cover for running drugs. They did their business on the west coast of Italy. The war between the families started with the shootings of a few of the rival crew members and escalated to family and friends. Seems like the Santoro family on the east coast may have been winning, because two weeks ago the whole family was murdered, most likely by the Donatis."

Jimmy motioned toward the picture with the dead bodies lying around a dining room and kitchen as he poured himself another coffee from the thermos. "Looks like they were ambushed. Someone must have informed them the entire Santoro family was gathered at the Santoro estate. There was more than one attacker, so they came there with the intent of killing everyone quickly. By the weapons used and the way it was done we are pretty sure it was the Donatis, but with the entire Santoro family dead it's hard to get a solid lead. We have people working undercover on the docks trying to find that one piece of evidence we can use to build a case on."

"Who's the guy in the boat?" Regan pointed to a photo of a sailboat by a private pier with a body in it.

"That's Carlos Santoro, Tony's younger brother. He was the bookkeeper for the Santoro family business and has an accounting firm in Summerside Shores, about an hour away from Tony and Gina's estate. So far, he is a bit of a mystery. Seems very few people knew him, and he was seldom seen around the estate or with his brother, but he is involved. His accounting firm handled the Santoro money, so he had to know what was going on."

"That his kid?" Regan was looking at the picture of a little girl pinned beside the boat.

"That is Felisa Santoro." Loren spoke up immediately. "She was being raised as Tony and Gina's daughter. Gina is her mother, but her birth certificate shows Carlos Santoro as the biological father. Tony and Gina had been married for ten years when she was born, so not sure what the story is there. If there is a love affair involved it could be the motive for the murders. Gina had control of the money and Carlos was the bookkeeper, so they had the most to gain by Tony's death. Either Carlos or Gina could be the one that told the Donatis when and where they could find the Santoro Mafia family gathered. We think maybe Gina and Carlos were planning on running off together.

"The child was not supposed to be there. She was at boarding school, but there had been a fire, and all the kids were sent home for two weeks. Carlos always attended a sailing regatta that weekend, so we think it may have been a last-minute plan to run away with the child. But they didn't get away; Gina was found among the dead at the house and Carlos was found shot on his boat. We found Felisa's shoes and doll on Carlos's sailboat, but the divers didn't find a body and she was not found among the dead at the estate." Loren's voice drifted off, as if she was searching for some obvious explanation she might have missed.

Jimmy shrugged and took a swallow of coffee, then added, "Looks like Carlos was trying to get away when he was shot. They tried to burn his sailboat with his body in it, but the fuel tank was almost empty, so it just smouldered and went out."

"She's a pretty little girl. How old was she?" Regan asked.

"Seven." Loren said, intrigued with Regan's interest.

"What kind of parents send a seven-year-old kid to a boarding school?" Regan seemed as appalled by the poor parenting as the murder.

"Mafia families," Loren declared. "They try to protect their children from their life. I never knew what my parents did."

Regan looked at Loren. "I'm sorry, sweetheart, that was insensitive of me."

"It's okay. It was a different life, a long time ago. But still, I wish we could find the little girl, so we knew for sure what happened to her. It seems odd if he was trying to get away on his sailboat and she was with him that there wouldn't be at least a coat, some clothes, or something other than just her shoes and a doll."

Regan was listening but focused on the sailboat and thinking out loud.

"That is an expensive sailboat, it is designed for long distance voyages, with comfortable living accommodations and a large fuel tank. Carlos Santoro must have been a man who enjoyed the sport. When I was young and working on the docks, I helped out with the regattas. The sailboats would arrive and anchor in the marina the night before the event, loaded with provisions and fuel for the voyage, and register with the organizers. The next day they would sign their entry cards and all depart together. It seems odd he would not have already registered and had his sailboat in the marina and ready to sail. Maybe he didn't attend the regatta. If the fuel tank was empty, maybe he took the little girl somewhere instead and was just returning when he was shot."

Loren looked a Jimmy. They assumed he had been trying to get away when he was shot.

Jimmy was pondering as he leaned back in his chair and ran his hand along his face. "I wonder…" He sat up straight in his chair and dug through some files on the side of his desk. "Here." He flipped through an autopsy report labelled "Carlos Santoro." "The medical examiner's time of death for Carlos Santoro was inconclusive because of the fire. He said the bullet that killed him was lodged in his abdomen and severed his spinal cord and he probably didn't die right away. He has the approximate time of death at eighteen to twenty hours after the deaths of the others. But...maybe...it's because he wasn't murdered until he returned to Summerside, not when he was running away like we first thought. Regan, I think you could be on to something here! We have been assuming he didn't make it to the regatta." Jimmy sounded elated. "Loren, call that regatta club. Let's find out if he was registered."

Regan collected the burger wrappers and refilled the coffee cups while listening as Loren questioned the regatta organizer. She put the phone down, and with an astonished gaze told them, "Carlos did attend. He was registered and signed his entry card. He departed with the other boats at one o'clock on Friday. There were fifty entries registered. Apparently, they don't necessarily stay together once they sail and no one pays much attention until the final gala, which wasn't for two days."

Jimmy evaluated the new details. "He was found in Summerside approximately twenty hours later. He must have separated from the group once they left. No one would question his boat being missing, and it would have given him enough time to take the girl somewhere."

Loren wasn't convinced. "But why would he come back if he had escaped being murdered? He already had his daughter and had to know Gina was dead, so why bother coming back?"

Jimmy nodded thoughtfully as he began filling in possible scenarios. "If he was the rat, and in good with the Donati family, he probably felt he was safe. Carlos had to know there would be questions and fallout when all his family except him were found dead. He had the regatta as an alibi for his whereabouts at the time of the murders, so he wouldn't get blamed. Don't forget, Loren, Carlos could have been the informer, and if he was, he was the only one who knew who had committed the crime. He would have to have been a real fool to not fear for his life. Maybe he wanted to make sure his daughter was safe and cared for in case something happened to him. He could go and get Felisa once things quieted down. He would be her only living relative and could take custody of her. It's a theory that could work, but impossible to prove with everyone dead. Still, Regan's hunch is worth considering."

Regan stepped up to the map. "If the fuel tank was full when he left, and with the use of the motor and the sails, he could have been ashore and back anywhere in this circle in approximately twenty hours." He was outlining a circle along the Mediterranean with his finger.

Loren stood by his side, staring at the map. "If she is dead, she is at peace; if she's not, she is alone and must be terrified. I would just like to know. She haunts me like a ghost from my past," she said, fighting back the memories this child had revived. Jimmy sensed the desperation in her voice and was concerned; it was not like her to be emotional about a case. He laid a comforting arm on his daughter's shoulders as he stepped up to the map with them.

"Where would he have taken her, Papa? We will never find her with Carlos dead."

"Sweetheart, if she is out there, you will find her," Regan said reassuringly. His eyes scanned the pictures laid out on the boards, coming to rest on Carlos Santoro's sailboat, and then the map of the Mediterranean Sea. Regan moved close to the map and Loren and Jimmy stepped up beside him.

"Assuming the fuel tank was full when he left, about the furthest distance he could have gone and made it back in that time frame would be here." Regan put his finger on the map. "This peninsula at the tip of Greece; this is where that model of sailboat was manufactured. It is also where Saviours of the Sea orphanage is located. He could have known about the orphanage. You should check there."

"Why would he take her to an orphanage?" Doubt laced Loren's voice.

333

"Loren, people leave kids there for all kinds of reasons. No money, crippled, illegitimate, or they just can't handle being parents. The nuns don't turn any child away, and they don't ask questions. They just take care of the kids no one wants. The orphanage is inside a locked compound and an unlikely place to hide someone, so if he felt she was in danger, he would know she was safe and being cared for there."

Loren was still doubting the details. "I understand him wanting to keep the child safe, but why go to such an extent to hide her? Why take her to another country and hide her in an orphanage? He makes her an orphan, then he abandons her. This guy doesn't deserve to have a child." Loren's words faded into disgust.

Jimmy's expression revealed his amusement at her harsh assessment of Carlos Santoro. "Let's not jump to any conclusions here, Loren. There are a lot of missing pieces in this puzzle. Sometimes things are not what they seem." He looked reflectively at Regan and smiled as he gave instructions to Loren. "Let's see if any kids were brought to the orphanage at the time of the murders. It's worth checking, just in case."

Regan watched the way they worked together, silently thankful it had been Jimmy Flynn's investigation team that oversaw the investigation of Nigeria. Otherwise, things might have turned out very differently.

Loren was already on the phone getting a number for the orphanage. "Is it alright if I stay, Jimmy?" Regan asked. He was curious about what they would find out and he wanted to be there for Loren. This case was pulling her back into her past and poking at her heart.

"Absolutely," Jimmy answered as he took a seat behind his desk. He looked at Regan. His expression reflected his frustration with the case. "Details. The biggest cases are always built on the smallest details. If the girl is alive, we might be able to confirm the motive. It won't help us prove the Donatis did the killing, but filling in some of the blanks about the Santoro family would be a big help."

The Spirit of the Autumn Wind

Regan drained the coffee thermos into the cups and sat back in his chair.

Loren hung up the phone. "I got it!"

"Good." Jimmy motioned toward Regan. "Pick up that phone. You can listen to what they have to say, too."

"Loren, ask for Mother Superior—she is the nun in charge of registrations at the orphanage," Regan counselled, remembering the protocol of his past, as he picked up the receiver.

Loren nodded, grateful for the guidance. Jimmy held the receiver of his phone to his ear as Loren dialed.

"Good afternoon, this is Assistant Lead Investigator Loren Lombardi with the Garda Special Investigation Unit in Ireland. May I please speak to Mother Superior?"

"One moment, please." The phone went silent. Loren could hear a quiet mumble in the background, then a strong but gentle voice.

"This is Mother Superior Mary Margaret."

"Good afternoon, Mother Superior. I am Loren Lombardi, Assistant lead Investigator with the Garda out of Sona Bay in Ireland."

"Yes, Miss Lombardi, I was wondering if we would hear from you."

Loren went silent. "I'm sorry, Mother Superior…I'm not sure what you mean."

"There was a little girl left here two weeks ago, Ana Conti. The man that left her said that if he did not come back for her within two weeks, I was to mail an envelope he left here addressed to yourself and Lead Investigator Jimmy Flynn. He said not to release the child to anyone but yourself or Mr. Flynn."

Loren almost dropped the phone. She was silent, trying to figure out what was going on, why her, what to say or do next. She spoke to Jimmy without putting the receiver down. "It's her, Papa. Ana Conti was her grandmother's maiden name."

Jimmy took control. He could see Loren was having a tough time grasping the reality of the situation. "Mother Superior, this is Lead

Investigator Jimmy Flynn. We have been looking for this little girl. Is she alright?"

The nun's voice could not hide her concern. "Yes, we are taking care of her, but she has terrible nightmares and wakes up screaming almost every night. She hardly speaks or eats and never smiles. She keeps asking when her uncle is coming back for her. She wants her doll. She calls her Regalo and says she is lost. What is it that has happened with this child?"

Loren was shaking as she spoke. "Something terrible happened. Her uncle is dead and it's complicated. We are coming to get her. Perhaps just let us explain it to her tomorrow. There's no point in upsetting her any more." Loren looked at Jimmy for approval. "We should be there first thing in the morning." Jimmy looked at his watch and nodded.

"Thank you, Mother Superior. We will see you tomorrow."

"Good afternoon, Miss Lombardi. Thank you for your call."

Loren put the phone down. "My God, Jimmy." Loren threw herself into Regan's arms. "I can't believe we found her! Thank you Regan! Thank you!"

"Well, glad I was good for something." Regan was pleased with himself.

"Regan, we owe you." Jimmy extended his hand. "That regatta was the clue we were missing, and we never would have thought of the orphanage."

"Well, I am no investigator, but I know a bit about sailboats, wind currents, and nautical miles." Regan and Jimmy shared a laugh.

Regan took Loren's hand and his playful tone became serious as he looked into her face. "Will you let me go with you to Greece? I know this is a case and all, but it seems to have upset you. This little girl has touched your heart. Besides, a visit to the orphanage might be good for me. It is where I grew up. Niko went back with Sara when they were on their honeymoon. He said it helped to put the past where it belonged." He looked over at Jimmy, assuming that as the Lead investigator the decision was probably his.

Jimmy nodded. "It's fine with me Regan, as long as it's okay with Loren." Her father continued without letting her respond. "I see no harm, Loren. I knew you would understand this case better than anyone else, but it is obvious this little girl has brought back some memories. You should have Regan with you."

Loren stretched up against Regan's strong body and placed a kiss on his cheek. "I would like it, Regan, if you would come. It would mean a lot to me, and I would like to see where you grew up."

Jimmy was already planning the next step. "I will get the private plane organized. We will all need to pack a few things. Let's meet at the airport in two hours." Jimmy looked at his watch again and Loren nodded.

She pushed the case file boxes behind her desk to one side and found the one that had the doll packed in an evidence bag, then pushed it into her handbag and handed it to Regan to hold as she and Jimmy placed files into their briefcases.

Christos drove them to the airport. As soon as they were airborne Jimmy stretched his lanky frame into two seats and pulled his jacket collar around his neck. "You two should try and get some rest; it will be almost midnight when we get to Greece. I booked a hotel close to the orphanage. We will go out there first thing in the morning." He dozed off to the quiet murmur of Loren and Regan's private conversation.

The drone of the plane's engines swallowed up Loren's tangled thoughts, and she drifted off to sleep. Regan pulled her close and closed his eyes.

"Loren, Loren, wake up, sweetheart, we are about to land." Regan was touching her face and kissing her gently.

Loren blinked and looked at her watch. "Did I sleep all that time?"

"Yes." Regan smiled at her.

"And you, did you get any rest?" she asked as Regan tucked in his shirt and straightened his jacket.

"Enough." Regan was used to working different shifts when he was at sea and seemed to be able to function on short naps whenever time permitted. Jimmy stretched out of sleep and straightened his clothes as they left the plane. He flagged an airport cab down and instructed the driver to take them to the Astoria Hotel.

"It's almost midnight, so let's all get some real sleep and meet for breakfast in the hotel restaurant before we go out there. This hotel is not far from the orphanage." The cab sped along the coast. Within twenty minutes they were bidding one another goodnight.

CHAPTER THIRTY

With the instincts of a homing pigeon, Regan led the way up the lane to the Saviours of the Sea Orphanage. He rang the large bell in front of the heavy wrought-iron gates, which signalled the sisters. They waited as a woman in cream-coloured nun's attire, accompanied by an older nun clad in similar attire of charcoal grey, walked gracefully toward the gate, their long, heavy skirts swishing about their ankles.

Together they released a lock and tugged at the heavy gate. With timeless familiarity, Regan immediately assisted. The trio entered the large courtyard that encircled a small chapel. A grey stone building loomed behind a high wrought-iron fence and lush hanging trees shaded grassy areas adorned with flower beds and small stone benches.

"Good morning. I am Mother Superior Mary Margaret, and this is Reverend Mother Maria." The nun directed her introductions to Loren, who was the image of a professional investigator, sharply dressed in a dark-navy suit with a crisp white blouse. The leather briefcase she carried contained the labelled file folders that were the purpose of the visit.

Loren extended her hand. "Loren Lombardi, assistant lead investigator. This is Jimmy Flynn, lead investigator with the Garda in Ireland, and Mr. Regan Quinn, who is assisting with the investigation."

Sister Mary accepted the extended hand of each, but when she took Regan's hand she held fast. "Regan Quinn." She observed his face without letting go of his hand. "Yes, and you have grown from a good-looking boy into a handsome man." She smiled with uncontrollable joy as she lay her other hand on his. "It is so good to see you. Life's paths often lead us back to where we started."

Regan was studying the woman, remembering her as he did when he was young.

"I was just a young nun when you stayed with us at the orphanage. Do you remember me?"

"Yes, Mother Superior, you would bring me milk and cookies when I was doing penance for fighting."

The nun was amused. "And it was often, as I recall, but always for defending your friend Niko from the boys that bullied. Penance for good deeds, although confused with the bad, should be rewarded with milk and cookies."

Regan laughed. "You were good to both Niko and me."

"Niko Mararious and his wife paid us a visit at Christmastime. He told me you two had remained friends over the years and have a business in Ireland together."

"Yes, Mother Superior, we do. There have been some hard times along the way, but we are doing well now. He has always been a loyal friend."

She smiled. "He said the same of you." She hesitated and looked into his face. "It warms my heart to see you, Regan Quinn, even though you have come back to us under such strange circumstances. Please accompany me to the garden."

The two nuns walked ahead of them. As they passed through the courtyard, it seemed they were travelling back in time. The grey stone building hid its age behind lush vines that bloomed with every colour of the rainbow, concealing the sadness of the young lives within. The smell of the Mediterranean Sea mingled with the morning air, filling Regan's lungs with nostalgia. He clasped Loren's hand firmly as they walked. Loren could see he was uneasy, struggling to face his past as much as she struggled to face hers. He needed her, and she needed him. They were there to help Felisa Santoro, but it was as though fate was also forcing them to help themselves.

As Mother Superior seated them in the garden, Reverend Mother Maria handed her an envelope. "Shall I bring the child?"

"Not until morning prayers are finished, but will you ask that tea be sent? I want to speak with the investigators first. I will tell you when to bring Ana."

"Yes, of course." The nun in the cream-coloured habit acknowledged her superior and disappeared into the building.

Jimmy and Loren complimented Mother Superior on the lovely state of the gardens, which she credited to the daily duties of the orphans and God's blessings. Regan remained silent, his eyes reflectively surveying his surroundings. Loren watched him, questioning Regan's faith. It was a part of his life at the orphanage, but not something he had taken with him when he left. She could understand how someone who felt deserted could find it hard to believe in a spiritual saviour. She understood the desperation of feeling alone; what she and Regan had both felt as children was what Felisa was feeling now.

Mother Superior Mary Margaret waited until the tea was served before she addressed the issue at hand. "I would like you to reveal to me what is in this envelope that was left with the child before I let her meet with you."

"Of course, Mother Superior." Jimmy nodded, his eyes focused on the brown envelope she held securely as she waited for his reply.

The nun passed the envelope to Jimmy. It was addressed to Investigators Loren Lombardi and Jimmy Flynn in care of the Garda, Sona Bay, Ireland. "Personal and Confidential" was written in big letters across the front and the word "urgent" was underlined. He slit the top of the envelope with the handle of the spoon that lay beside his teacup as he glanced at the apprehensive faces of the three people that sat with him. He pulled some handwritten pages from the envelope and flipped quickly through them, noting the date and time they were written was two weeks previous, then began to read out loud.

> "To Investigators Loren Lombardi and Jimmy Flynn. If you are reading this, it is because I am dead."

Jimmy looked up. It was a fact, the reason they were there, but the blunt statement enforced reality.

> "My name is Carlos Santoro. You do not know me in person but will know of my family. I am the second son of Armani and Ana Santoro and five years younger than my brother Antonio (Tony) Santoro, who was head of the Santoro Mafia family. I am also the biological father of Felisa Santoro. I have been the accountant for the Santoro family business for the past several years and was fully aware of the family's illegal activities. I created a paper trail for dummy companies for the sole purpose of laundering money from the extensive drug trade that was run by the family, primarily on the east coast of Italy. What follows is my confession of my knowledge of the deaths of the Santoro family. I did not murder the family, but I did provide to the rival Donati Mafia family the date of the weekend when the entire Santoro Mafia family would be meeting in private at Tony and Gina Santoro's estate. I did so with the full knowledge that the Donatis intended to use the opportunity to ambush and murder the Santoro family.

> "I wish to tell you the circumstances that led to my decision to turn on my family, and ask that you judge me for my reasons, and not what I did."

Jimmy looked at Loren for a moment, silently confirming their idea that Carlos was the informer, before he continued.

> "Mafia is a birthright you escape only by death. I am not an evil and ruthless man. I was driven to my actions by my birthright, a life I was born into and bound by blood to honour. I chose to break this blood bond, so my daughter could escape this life."

Jimmy looked up at the group; there was a heavy feeling in the pit of his stomach that his expression could not hide. He adjusted his body in the chair and continued.

> "Our father was a Mafia boss. He controlled the docks, and our family was well off financially. Tony admired our father, but I feared him. Tony became the head of the household at sixteen when our father died. After his death, the rival Gambini Mafia family moved in on our family's territory and our world began to fall apart. My brother swore he would get back what was ours. When our mother died two years later, he looked after me. I was eleven and I looked up to him. He quit school but insisted I finish my education.
>
> "At eighteen he already had his own drug operation on the docks. By the time he was twenty years old he was a small-time gangster running what was left of the Santoro Mafia business. The Gambini family had taken over most of the Santoro territory and were pursuing Tony for what was left with promises

of a key Mafia boss position in their organization, and the return of the affluent lifestyle we had grown up with.

"Tony's initiation into the Gambini Mafia family was to eliminate the rival Lombardi family. I remember Mario Gambini congratulating my brother and welcoming him into the fold for committing this murder and completing his initiation act of loyalty. When Investigator Flynn took custody of Loren Lombardi, he saved her life. My brother was to go and finish the job, get rid of the child, the last living Lombardi, but Mario let it pass. He said he did not want to stir up any more trouble with Flynn, he just wanted him to take the kid and go back to Ireland and quit digging into the business of the Gambini family. I have followed the life of Loren Lombardi because of guilt, not for any crime personally committed by me, but because I have always known it was my brother Antonio Santoro that drove the truck that pushed the Lombardi's car into the train that night and caused their deaths. Mario Gambini underestimated the dedication of Investigator Jimmy Flynn and the Garda out of Ireland. When Flynn's relentless investigation eventually brought down the notorious Gambini Mafia family, Tony was poised to step up."

Jimmy looked up and saw Loren's bewildered face. This truth from the past resonated into silence. Until that moment, he had not been aware someone else had driven the truck that night, or that Loren was still a target.

He stopped reading and searched his memory for the details of an investigation from twenty-five years ago. Mario Gambini had been blamed for the accident and incarcerated without bail. He was stabbed and died in a prison brawl two weeks before his trial, and what had been determined to be a scrap between inmates suddenly took on a new dimension.

> After a moment, Jimmy continued. "Within a couple of years, Tony had taken over the Gambinis' territory. At twenty-five, he was a Mafia boss with all the benefits—expensive cars, women, money, and the control and power that went with it.
>
> "I wanted a different life and when I graduated high school, I went to college. Tony supported me and paid for my education. I was naive. What I interpreted as his genuine interest in a better future for me was really an investment in his own life.
>
> "I was in my second year of college in an accounting program when I met Gina Parisi. She was a business major and we took classes together. Her family owned the Parisi fishing fleet. It was a well-respected and established business that operated off the east coast of Italy. Gina was wealthy, smart, and pretty. We started dating. She was my first love, gentle and sweet but spoiled and self-indulgent.
>
> "I introduced her to Tony and they started dating behind my back. They were married six months later. My relationship with my brother was never the same. We seldom spoke. She was twenty. He was five years older and could give her the privileged life she had grown up with. She was totally faithful to him and he let her think he felt the same.

I knew from the beginning he was not faithful and was as much interested in her family's wealth as he was in her.

"About a year after Gina and Tony were married, Gina's parents were killed in a plane crash. It was considered an accident, but I have never been sure that my brother was not involved in what happened to her family. She was an only child and she inherited at great deal of money and the fishing fleet. Not long after that, Tony and Gina bought the estate and he quickly escalated to the head of the Mafia hierarchy. Gina's family fishing fleet was a legitimate business and the perfect cover for expanding Tony's drug trade up the eastern Italian coast.

"My brother was developing a reputation as a brutal Mafia boss and dragging the Santoro family name into the filth with him. When I finished college, I moved away and opened an accounting firm in Naples and tried to start my own life."

Jimmy looked up from the pages to find Loren fixated. Their suspicions about Tony and Gina's marriage had just been verified by this man's words.

"One day, Tony showed up at my office in Naples and told me it was payback time. He wanted me to handle the accounting for the Santoro family business, which was really his drug operation. He was making a lot of money and the government was suspicious of his affairs, so he wanted me to cover up his real source of income. I refused. He pushed a gun to my head and said I was bound by Santoro blood. He said it was time for me to do my part. He had given his life to get our wealth back and now it was my turn and I had a responsibility to honour our family name. The same day the accountant that had been handling his affairs was found dead, supposedly shot by a mugger on his way home from work.

"The next morning, Gina showed up at my office with boxes of records from that accountant. She bragged about the money they were making and Tony's untouchable position as a Mafia boss. She loved her extravagant lifestyle and cautioned me not to cross Tony if I did not want to meet the same fate as his last accountant, brother or not. She had indirectly admitted Tony was responsible for his accountant's murder, but it was obvious she was totally loyal to Tony."

Jimmy took a swallow of tea but stayed focused on the page and kept reading. He was intrigued by what Carlos Santoro had written. His words were filling in the blanks about the Santoro family and the accusations against his brother. He was the only one left that knew these details and they would have died with him had he not written this letter.

"Gina was a good businesswoman. She was well-versed on the family affairs, and she had managed to keep her name on everything that her family's wealth had contributed to his business. It gave her some control over him. He was brutal and ruthless and did what needed to be done to maintain his respect in the streets, but she handled the money.

They were like each other. Their relationship was built on greed and manipulation, but they loved the life; a life that now included me.

"Tony would fly into Naples every couple of weeks with a large bag of cash, hundreds of thousands of dollars, too much to cover with the fishing fleet. I bought a small truck-leasing company based in the United States using a numbered company and fictitious shareholders, then began buying and selling trucks and operating a leasing network throughout the United States, along the Atlantic coast, and inland in Italy. Tony was angry that I had bought the company without consulting him. We argued, and Gina came to the rescue. She knew it was a good way to launder money. After that, my relationship with Tony became even more strained, and it was Gina that came to my office every couple of weeks to drop off the cash.

"The Donatis ran a drug operation on the docks, and they did not like to use their own trucks for their drug distribution, so they were unwittingly leasing trucks from the American trucking company and had become one of our regular clients. I kept private records of all their lease activities, where they picked up and dropped off their cargo—which was drugs—and the warehouses and offices they frequented, which was where they stashed their money. I kept the names of the police officers who were being paid off to look the other way and sign the false cargo permits for the trucks that hauled the drugs. I did not share this information with either Tony or Gina.

"About six years ago, Gina came to my office later than usual and extremely upset. She had been drinking and fell into my arms crying about an affair Tony was having. It was as though after almost ten years of marriage she had just realized he was, and had always been, unfaithful to her. She told me she had made a mistake, and it was always me she loved. I let myself believe her lies and, in a weak moment, we made love. When the wine had worn off and the reality of life surfaced, she dried her eyes and went back to the privileged life she had always wanted and would not give up. She said the doctor had told her in the first year of their marriage she was not able to have children, so I didn't have to worry about any accidental pregnancy, and she promised me Tony would never know what had happened between us.

"Three months later she showed up at my office beaten and bruised. She was pregnant, and when she went to Tony excited with the news and in hopes of saving their precarious marriage, he said there was no way in hell it was his baby. He admitted he had never wanted kids and had had a vasectomy right after they were married. He had paid the doctor to lie to her, to tell her she was barren. It was his way of keeping her faithful, and his licence to sleep around. He had beat her until she admitted the truth and told him that we had slept together. She swore it was the only time she had been unfaithful to him, and the child was mine. She said she had told Tony she would get rid of it and have an abortion, but Tony refused; he wanted her to have the baby. The only one reason Tony would want her to keep the child was to punish her and for control— control over both Gina and me.

"The doctor had broken his trust with Tony when he admitted the truth to Gina about her infertility. The next day he was found dead on his office floor from what appeared to be a drug overdose. As with the accountant, Tony was sending a message that he was not to be crossed. It was a message that both Gina and I understood."

Jimmy took a swallow of tea and adjusted his posture. Carlos Santoro's words were brutally honest, reinforcing Jimmy's opinion of what a cruel and insensitive man Tony Santoro was, as he remembered the day he and Molly had sat in the doctor's office struggling to accept that they would never have children. He kept reading.

"I begged her not to have an abortion. I wanted her to keep the child, my child. Tony didn't want the baby, but I did. I demanded that the baby's birth certificate show me as the biological father. I wanted to be part of the child's life and have the right to step in if the child was ever in need, and she agreed. Gina was not happy during her pregnancy. Tony did not go to the hospital with her and when the baby was born, I was by her side. When the nurse handed my tiny daughter to me, my life was forever changed. I named my daughter Felisa. She was beautiful, but from the time she took her first breath, she was like a pawn in a game of lies and deceit.

"Tony refused to let me see her, but Gina tried. At first, she would bring her to Naples when she came with the cash, until Tony forbid her to do so and brought in a nanny to look after Felisa. Tony always referred to her as the kid; he never called her Felisa or his daughter. He never held her, and he wanted her kept out of his sight.

"Gina was too self-absorbed and inconvenienced by Felisa to be a good mother. She was trying desperately to win back Tony's affection and was content to give the nanny her role as a mother. I moved to Summerside Shores, so I could be closer to the estate and Felisa. I contacted the nanny and she would arrange times when we could meet. Occasionally, when Tony was out of town, Gina would secretly invite me to the estate to spend time with Felisa, and there were times she would let me take her sailing. Neither Tony nor Gina wanted Felisa, but I did. I loved my daughter and I wanted custody of her, but Gina would never go against Tony and Tony would never give up the control he had over us, even at the expense of the happiness of a beautiful innocent child.

"Soon after Felisa was born, I began skimming money from Tony's operation. He was consumed with anger and spent his time playing the Mafia boss in the streets and nightclubs. Gina had control of the money and had come to trust me completely, and never questioned anything I did, if a lot of money ended up in their bank accounts. I put the funds I took in a numbered trust account for Felisa and kept it in the International Bank of the Cayman Islands. At the very least she deserved financial security and I couldn't trust that either Tony or Gina would give her that.

"When Felisa was six, Gina told me they had decided to send her to a boarding school in Switzerland. Tony wanted her out of the house. We argued. I begged her to let me take Felisa. I would move far away, and he would never have to see us again. She was just a baby and too young to be sent to a boarding school in a foreign country. Gina seemed indifferent. She was nervous and less well-kept than usual and resolved to do whatever Tony wanted.

"I spoke to the nanny and she said maybe it was for the best. She was concerned that Felisa might not be safe. She confided that both Tony and Gina had started using drugs; cocaine. Tony always sold drugs but had never used them. This lifestyle had changed them both. Tony was a brutal emotionless excuse for a man. I no longer felt the need to justify his life. I no longer considered him my brother and I could not trust him with my daughter's life. Gina was addicted to drugs and I could not depend on her to keep Felisa safe."

Jimmy flipped the page and looked up briefly at the captivated faces of the others. Loren looked confused as she re-evaluated her opinion of Carlos Santoro. His words were revealing a compassionate, caring man, a father; not the evil demon she had perceived him to be.

"Your recent investigation of the drug lord Nigeria Nakarasa, and the events that took place on the cargo ship the *Autumn Wind*, started a new chapter of brutality between the Italian Mafia families. Jimmy Flynn and Loren Lombardi had taken down an untouchable enemy, sparking a new era of competition for territorial rights between the Santoro and Donati families.

"The Donatis were interested in taking over Nigeria Nakarasa's drug operation, and so was Tony. The Mafia war started with threats and personal injury to some of Tony's crew and escalated to the murder of some of his family and business acquaintants.

"A week before the regatta, when I was about to leave work, Luca and Ciro Donati barged into my office and held a gun to my head. They threatened my life and demanded I provide all of Tony's financial records to them. I convinced them Tony and I were estranged, that I had no more respect for him then they did. I saw a chance to be free of my brother and to free my daughter from this life. I offered them an opportunity to eliminate the competition and own it all in exchange for my life, and gave them the date and time that Tony was holding a meeting at his estate. It was a rare occasion when his entire Mafia family would be gathered in one place, an opportunity to do away with Tony and everyone that worked for him. They lowered their weapons and agreed.

"I already had plans to be away for the regatta from Friday afternoon until late Sunday that weekend. The regatta was my alibi; I attended every year. I would disappear for the weekend, then come back to find the Santoro family massacred. I would stay around long enough to deal with the questions from the police, then leave the country. The Donatis agreed to leave me alone and let me disappear. With the birth certificate, I would finally be able to claim Felisa as my daughter and she would be free. I would sell my business and we would sail to the Cayman Islands and make a new life.

"Gina called the morning of the regatta. She said the school had sent Felisa home for two weeks and asked if I would take her with me to the regatta because of Tony's meeting. She said she would tell him Felisa was with the nanny, and we agreed to meet at the estate gate in an hour, so I could pick her up.

"I panicked. Felisa wasn't supposed to be there. My office is fifty minutes from the estate. I left immediately. I had to get her to safety before the Donatis' ambush.

"When I got to the estate the gate was open and the family was already dead. Bullet-ridden bodies were scattered around the kitchen and dining area, but Felisa was not among them. The home was spattered with bullets and there were bloody footprints on the carpet in every room; they had searched the house. I thought maybe they had found her and taken her. I called out and there was no answer. I called out again, then checked the pantry. It was her secret hiding place. I had always told her if she heard guns, she should hide.

"She was huddled in a corner behind a pile of boxes, ghost-white and in shock. She had witnessed the murder of her mother and father and the massacre of all of Tony's Mafia associates, whom he referred to as his family. I took her in my arms; she was trembling and numb. I wrapped her in my jacket, hid her face from the massacre, and took her from the home.

"The Donatis had not waited for me to leave for the regatta before they murdered the family, and I no longer had an alibi for my presence at the time of the ambush. It was clear to me they had set me up and they did not intend to let me disappear as they had promised. I was the only one alive who knew they had killed the Santoro Mafia family. My life was in danger, but if I could not save myself, I would save Felisa. I decided to take her to a safe place."

Jimmy swallowed hard. He glanced up at Loren. They had it wrong. The motive was not a love affair and greed, but instead retaliation and child abduction.

"I never went back to my house. I went straight to the marina. My sailboat was there, and it was time to leave with the other boats. I needed to maintain my alibi in case the Donatis were watching me. There were people everywhere gathering for the regatta. Even the Donatis weren't stupid enough to commit a murder with that many witnesses.

"I covered Felisa in a slicker and hid her on my boat. I stayed with the plan. They would not know

I had gone to the estate, that I was aware they did not intend to honour the agreement they had made with me, and they did not know Felisa was there or they would have killed her too. I signed my entry card at the office and set sail.

"I had time to think while I was sailing. I wanted to just keep going, hide out, then disappear, but I will never be safe and neither will Felisa, as long as the Donati Family is free. So, I decided to return to Summerside to get the information I have on the Donatis' drug operation from my safety deposit box, and my ID card, so I can travel to Ireland. With that information, Investigators Flynn and Lombardi should be able to arrest the Donati Mafia family and I will turn myself in to them so the Donatis cannot get to me. I have talked to Felisa and she understands what she saw, and she knows her parents are dead."

Shivers ran up Loren's spine and she tremored. Carlos's words reached down into the darkness that she had concealed in her heart, grabbing at the emotions she had locked in the deepest recesses of her soul, opening the door and letting her forgotten feelings flow into reality. She knew what Felisa Santoro felt. Her heart throbbed. Loren's senses froze in time, and all she could hear was the screeching, crashing metal and the screams of her mother in the darkness, then the silence of alone; the feeling of death. Regan felt her shudder and tightened his arm around her shoulders as Jimmy's words pulled her back to reality.

"She knows I did not murder anyone. Once the Donatis are in jail, I will tell the investigators where she is, so she can tell them what she witnessed. I also kept a ledger for the Santoro family business that outlines the drug operation and money laundering. I will turn this over to the investigators as well and take responsibility for my part in this. I will be back in Summerside by midnight and am not due back from the regatta until late tomorrow, so I have enough time to get what I need from my home and safety deposit box and catch a plane to Ireland before they come looking for me.

"I am writing this letter in case they catch me, and I do not survive. At least I will die knowing I have set my daughter free and the Donatis will go down with the Santoros."

Jimmy observed the group with satisfaction. He knew the value of the letter he held in his hands. If Felisa could verify what had occurred, Jimmy had a statement that would stand up in court. He turned to the last page, where the words that Carlos Santoro wrote became personal and heart-wrenching.

"Loren, I have always felt a connection with you, and for many years I have silently followed your life. I read your book, By the Sea. I understood your feelings and it was as though I was living my life through you. I respected your strength to face the Mafia life of your family; to face your past so it would not control your future. I admired the person you had become, and that you had escaped the life I never could. The death of your parents broke the blood bond. You were given a home by a good family, became a different person, and used your life to destroy the evil of your past.

"It is because of this respect I have for you that I humbly ask you to take care of my daughter. I know this is a lot to ask, and I do not ask you to forgive me or my brother for what he did to your parents, but she is innocent. Just know that I ask this of you from the deepest part of my heart. I have broken the blood bond, and you are the only person I trust to give Felisa a life free of her past. When the time comes that she feels a need to know about her family, it is only you I trust to help her understand. Perhaps there are things she never needs to know about her father, only that he loved her with all his heart. If it is not possible for you to do as I request, I ask that you find her a loving home with a family that will care for my precious daughter with no knowledge of her past.

"I have a friend in Suaimhneas Cove, Dominic Speers, the accountant that handles the bookkeeping for Regan Quinn at the Autumn Wind Marina. Dominic told me about your life and the home you share with Captain Quinn and his son. He told me Regan Quinn had grown up in the Saviours of the Sea orphanage, and that is why I chose it as a place to leave my daughter. I knew he would understand how difficult her life might be without a family to love her.

"I pray you and Regan will give my beautiful, gentle daughter a home and love her like your own. Thank you, and please tell Felisa how much I love her."

The Spirit of the Autumn Wind

Jimmy looked up to see tears sliding down Loren's face. Regan pulled her close and her head fell against his shoulder. Jimmy swallowed the lump in his throat and finished reading.

> "The key to my safety-deposit box is under the flowering tree in the backyard of my Summerside home. I planted the tree the year Felisa was born, and there is a stone by it with her birthdate on it. The key is under the stone. The box is In the Bank of Italy at Misty Bay, a marina thirty miles south of Summerside Shores. The safety-deposit box is number seven, under the name of Carlos Conti. Every Friday afternoon I took an update of the ledger for the Santoro family business and put it in the box as protection against my brother. It contains all the accounting records for the Santoro Mafia family and provides details of the money laundering scheme, as well as the information on the drug activities of the Donati Mafia family. There is a key in the box for a second safety deposit box, number twenty-one, under the same name in the International Bank of the Cayman Islands. It contains the number of Felisa's trust account. There is 7 million in the account. I would like Jimmy Flynn appointed as trustee. Felisa is to receive monthly payments for her upbringing, education, and future security. I trust Investigator Flynn to oversee Felisa's funds, to make sure she will get what is rightfully hers, as he did with Loren Lombardi. These funds cannot be traced to the Santoro family business.
>
> "My Will is in the box and leaves everything to my daughter, including my money, my home in Summerside, and my sailboat. I would like Loren

Lombardi and Regan Quinn appointed as executors. My friend Dominic will be able to interpret the accounting information. With my confession, I pray an end can be put to all of this and I will not have given my life in vain.

"I wrote this letter before I left my daughter at the orphanage and returned to Summerside. Most sincerely, Carlos Santoro."

Jimmy was a seasoned investigator, but when he looked up, he was obviously moved by what he had read and reached for his hanky to soak up the tears that had formed in his eyes, then reached across the table to take Loren's hand. Her head was still resting on Regan's shoulder, and she was pushing the tears that were running freely down her cheeks away with her hand. Mother Superior, who was already on her third tissue, slid the box of Kleenex toward her.

Regan's expression was defiant; it was the same expression Jimmy had seen the night of Nigeria's death, when they had put Christos at risk. Jimmy had mistaken it for intolerance and anger directed at him, but now he knew the man and he understood that the emotions he felt were directed inward, because he had put someone in danger.

Jimmy Flynn's observation was correct. Regan knew that what he had done in Tangiers, the shooting of Ivory, had set in motion the series of events that had put Felisa Santoro in danger. His actions had caused the death of the one person that loved her, her father, Carlos Santoro. Regan had started a new life and put everything that happened behind him; he was happy, and he'd thought it was over. Loren had said Felisa was like a ghost from her past, and now she was also a ghost in his past.

They had talked on the plane about helping the little girl. Loren had been staring at her picture on the wall, and a part of her already loved Felisa. If they had any doubts about making her a part of their life, there were none now.

"Loren, girl, are you okay?" Jimmy was squeezing her hand.

She took a deep breath. "I am fine, Papa. Ever since I started working on this case, I have been haunted by this little girl. I wanted to know what happened to her. I am so happy we found her! It seems she would have found me anyway, if Regan had not helped us figure this out. It is like fate—we were meant to find each other."

"Sweetheart, are you sure you're okay?" Regan asked.

"Yes." Loren took another deep breath and straightened her posture. Regan gently rubbed the back of her shoulders, then let his hand drop down her back. She looked at him and smiled, and there was a quiet peacefulness in her eyes that he had not seen before.

Jimmy gently tightened his hand around his daughter's and spoke to her as a father. "Loren, Carlos Santoro has admitted his brother was responsible for murdering your family. I never knew that until now, and that makes what he is asking you to do even more difficult. Raising a child is a big responsibility, Loren. You should take some time to consider what this means for you; it's a lifetime of commitment."

Jimmy hesitated and directed his thoughts to Regan, as if he already knew what Loren intended to do. "Regan, she can't do this by herself. A child needs a mother and a father, especially this child, and she will need a lot of love to get past everything that has happened." Jimmy's eyes shifted between Loren and Regan, waiting for one of them to respond to the emotions they were being forced to deal with.

"Papa, Carlos Santoro was a desperate man. His love for his daughter was so strong that he turned on his brother and her mother to save her from the life that was destroying her. He was willing to turn himself in and give up his life to keep her safe. There is no justification for murder, but he confessed to what he did and was honest enough to tell me the truth about his brother's part in the murder of my parents. He did not ask me to forgive him, but instead gave me his most precious possession, his daughter. You did not judge me by what my parents did, instead you took me into your home and hearts and loved me, and because of your love, I can love Felisa the same way."

Regan kissed the side of her head. Loren was a beautiful woman and Regan felt special every time he was at her side, but it was her inner beauty that made his love for her so deep.

Regan's eyes were damp with tears and he took a moment before revealing what he and Loren had been thinking. "Loren and I talked on the plane. We can't have children of our own, but we can raise a child. We have room for her in our home and our hearts. I spoke to Christos before we left. I told him Loren had found the little girl she had been looking for and we might bring her back to stay with us, so she would be safe. He knows about Loren's past and that she cannot have children of her own. He told me this little girl needs a home just like Loren did and he is fine with the idea. He's a good boy, with his mother's generous heart. Jimmy, this all started with me in that alley in Tangiers. I can't undo what happened, but I can do one good thing; I can give this child a loving home, and something good will come from all of this bad."

Jimmy was satisfied they both had control of the situation, and he did not try to hide the respect he felt for Regan Quinn as he spoke with little regard for the nun's presence. "If she can tell us what she saw that day, maybe identify them from your photos, Loren, we can take her back to Ireland as a witness under protective custody. She is just a child, so a judge there will use this statement as an account of what happened if she can tell him enough to determine authenticity. If he is satisfied, it can go to court on his authority and the records will be sealed to protect her. No one will ever know who the witness was."

Loren looked at Regan and nodded.

Investigator Jimmy Flynn spoke directly to Mother Superior. "We would like to see Felisa now."

The Spirit of the Autumn Wind

She rang the tiny bell that sat beside her on the table, which brought Reverend Mother Maria to the garden. "You can bring the child now. And have Sister Beth bring a glass of milk and some cookies here for her, and some hot water to freshen our tea, please."

The nun nodded and left, returning momentarily with little Felisa Santoro hanging precariously to her hand.

Felisa's expression was blank, disinterested in the eager faces before her, and obviously disappointed that the one face she wanted to see was not among them.

She was clothed in a dark-green orphanage-issue jumper, which was too large and fell loosely around her tiny frame. White socks slid down around her thin ankles into worn shoes that were too large and didn't fit her feet properly. Loren swallowed hard, saddened by the state of this privileged, unloved child deprived of even the dignity of properly fitted clothes and her given name.

Jimmy's heart dropped—he saw Loren standing there as she had many years ago, and his mind drifted back to a different time with heartbreaking similarity. He was first on the scene when the police pulled her from the car in shock, afraid and alone. Her future was an orphanage, so Jimmy took her home to Ireland; and at this moment he knew it was the best decision he had ever made in his life.

Jimmy refocused as Mother Superior took the child's hand and moved closer. "We are concerned about her, and we do the best we can. So many of the children here have problems."

Felisa looked as she did in the photo Loren had of her. It appeared to be recent and had come from a photo album taken as evidence from the murder scene. She was thinner now than she appeared in the picture, but there was no mistaking her delicate features and petite frame, which were a semblance of Gina Santoro. Her face was undeniably a feminine version of Carlos Santoro, who bore little resemblance to his brother Antonio, a man with brown hair and hazel eyes. She had her father's black eyes and his dark curly hair, which was braided and pulled back off her face, revealing a tiny pouty mouth that seemed frozen in solitude. Her big eyes scanned the three strangers at the garden table. She gently bit her bottom lip and it appeared she was about to burst into tears.

The Reverend Mother brought the child closer to the table, and Loren left her chair and knelt beside her. "Hello Felisa, my name is Loren Lombardi." The child stepped back as though afraid of her.

Loren looked anxiously at Regan, who immediately knelt beside her. The little girl looked desperately at him. "When is Uncle Carlos coming for me?" Her voice was but a whisper. Tears slid down her cheeks, as if she already knew the answer to her question.

"Come here, sweetie." Regan picked the little girl up and sat her on his lap, wrapping his arms around her as her head fell to his chest.

She obviously was more comfortable with Regan than Loren and considering her relationship with her mother it was understandable, although concerning to Loren, who had her heart set on being a mother to the little girl.

"Felisa." Regan squeezed her a little to get her to respond and she looked up.

"My name is Regan Quinn, and this is Jimmy Flynn, and Loren is his daughter. They are police officers. They have been looking for you. Something bad has happened to your Uncle Carlos and he can't come and get you, so he asked us to come for you."

"Like my parents? Is he dead too?" She spoke softly, as if not hearing the words would make the truth go away.

Regan looked at Jimmy and kept talking to her. "Yes, like what happened to your parents. Your uncle wrote a letter to Loren and asked her to come and get you and to take care of you if he could not."

Felisa finally looked at Loren, studying her cautiously. "Uncle Carlos told me you would come."

Her words brought a smile of relief to Loren's face. "I brought you something, Felisa." Loren reached into her handbag and removed the doll.

"Regola! You found her." The child pulled the doll to her.

The Spirit of the Autumn Wind

"She has been looking for you too, Felisa, just like me, and we are both really glad we found you."

Felisa cuddled the doll without taking her eyes off Loren, watching her guardedly, as if afraid she might change her mind and take the toy away.

"When I was a little girl about your age, my parents were taken from me like yours. And Jimmy," she looked toward him, and the little girl's eyes followed hers, "found me and took care of me."

"Were your parents murdered?"

Loren was surprised at her question, but knew the child understood what had happened. "Yes, they were, by bad people, just like your mother and father. Did you see what happened to your parents, Felisa?"

Loren was pushing, but she knew they needed the answers if they were going to get Felisa back to Ireland and to safety, so she could live a life of anonymity just in case the Donatis had any ideas of getting rid of the last living Santoro family member, as the Gambinis had with her.

Felisa surveyed the group of anxious onlookers, including Mother Superior, then spoke. "Some men came to the house with guns and shot them."

"Where were you Felisa?"

"In the kitchen. Mother and Father were arguing when I woke up. Father had company and he did not want me there, so Mother said she would take me to the nanny. I was waiting for her in the kitchen while she took her medicine. She has to boil it in a spoon and then put it in a needle before she puts it in her arm."

Loren's eyes met Regan's for a moment as Felisa continued. "She had just finished, and we were going to leave, when people started shouting and there was shooting in the living room. I was afraid, so I hid in my secret hiding place. Uncle Carlos said if I ever heard guns I should hide, so I hid in my secret place."

"Where is your secret place, Felisa?"

"In the pantry. Mother said I got in her way when she was in the kitchen, so Regola and I would stay in the pantry. It was my secret place."

"Did you see the men that came?"

She nodded and looked down, squeezing her doll.

Loren removed the file folder from her briefcase. "Was it any of these men?" She laid the pictures out on the table and Regan moved closer so Felisa could see better all the while keeping her secure in his arms. She took a moment to look at the photos and Regan felt her quiver. He rubbed her arm to get her to relax and looked at Loren and Jimmy, hoping as they were that she would be able to identify the men in the photos.

She raised her hand and pointed to the first photo of Marco Donati. "He shot my mother."

Then she moved to the photo of Luca. "He shot my father."

"These men," she cautiously touched the photos of Enrica and Ricci, "they shot the people in the dining room."

She looked away and buried her face against Regan's chest.

Loren quickly put the photos back, then reached over and carefully took her hand. She did not pull away and turned to face Loren.

"What did you do then, Felisa?"

"I stayed in the pantry. I could hear them upstairs in the house. They were laughing and then it went quiet and there were no voices, only a funny smoke smell that burned my eyes. I was afraid to move, and then in a while I heard Uncle Carlos call my name. I couldn't see him, and I wasn't sure it was him, so I stayed quiet. I was cold, and I couldn't move. Then he came to my secret hiding place and found me. I was so cold, so he covered me with his jacket and carried me to his car."

"You were very brave, Felisa. Then what happened?"

"We drove to the sailboat. Uncle Carlos kept me wrapped in his jacket and kept me close to him while he drove. I was shivering, and he was warm. I could feel him breathe and he smells fresh and clean like the sea. He always smells nice." Loren smiled. "The sailboat was at the marina, not at the pier by his house where it usually is. Uncle Carlos hid me under his long slicker and put me over his shoulder with his duffel bag and carried me to the boat. He put me in his bed and covered me with a thick quilt and told me to be very quiet. I hid under the covers. He went away for a few minutes and when he came back, we sailed away."

"Do you like to sail?" Loren wanted Felisa to give details to confirm the authenticity of the letter Carlos had written.

"Yes." She nodded. "Sometimes Mother would let me go sailing with Uncle Carlos, but it had to be a secret from father. I like the sailboat. The water hums and the sails sing in the wind." Her words almost brought Regan to tears, and he touched her hair. "When I woke up it was dark. Uncle Carlos made soup and toast, then wrapped me in a blanket and let me sail with him. The wind was quiet and the sails were sleeping, so Uncle Carlos used the motor. He showed me the Big Dipper and the Milky Way and a bright star he called Felisa. He said it was my star and it was named after me."

Regan reached up and pushed away a tear that had settled in the corner of his eye. This little girl had found her way into a special part of Regan Quinn's heart.

"Your Uncle Carlos loved you very much, Felisa. Then what happened?"

"I don't remember after that, but when I woke up, the sun was coming up and we were at a pier near here. We had chocolate milk and Uncle Carlos made scrambled eggs. I like the way he makes them; he puts mushrooms and tomatoes but not onions. I don't like onions. My mother always put onions. I tried to eat but it was hard. I didn't feel very good, so Uncle Carlos held me on his lap while he wrote a letter and he asked me what I could remember about what happened. I told him about the men. He was crying. I asked him why and he said it was because he loved me. I told him I loved him too and I didn't want him to cry."

Loren swallowed the lump in her throat as Felisa finished.

"Before we left the boat he put the letter in a brown envelope and he said I had to use the name Ana Conti, so I would be safe, and those men would not find me. He said he would come and get me in a couple of weeks when it was safe, and we would sail to an island to live, like in a fairytale. He said if he did not come for me a nice lady named Loren or a man named Jimmy would come to look after me, and I should go with them but no one else and I should tell you about the men."

Loren was moved, and her emotions brought Jimmy around the table. He placed his hand on her shoulder to steady her as she spoke. "Thank you, Felisa. Your Uncle Carlos would be very proud of you. You have been a great help and these bad people will go to jail, so they can not hurt you or anyone else." This innocent child, without knowing it, had vindicated her father. Jimmy nodded, and a smile of satisfaction crossed his lips. He had what he needed to bring the Donati Mafia family down.

Jimmy pulled a chair close to Felisa and laid his hand on hers, which was already cradled in Loren's. "We want you to come back to Ireland with us, so you can tell a judge what you just told us. Is that okay with you?"

On the outside, Jimmy Flynn wore a suit of armour that shielded him from the harsh reality of his job, but inside he was a gentle and caring man. Through teary eyes, Loren saw Jimmy Flynn, her father, as she had seen him many years ago, asking her the same question with the same compassion, and this sad and frightened little girl responded to his love just as she had. Felisa nodded, and Jimmy wiped away the tears that tumbled down her cheeks with his hand.

"Good girl. Regan and Loren are going to take care of you."

Regan immediately began explaining what would happen. It was obvious he wanted her out of the orphanage, and the sooner the better. "Felisa, Loren and I have a home by the ocean in Ireland and we have a room for you. We want you to stay with us, so we can take care of you and keep you safe. I have a son. He is older than you and he is anxious to meet you."

"What is his name?" she asked, as if doubting what Regan said.

"Christos," Regan answered. "You will have your own room and you can go to school."

"I don't like boarding school."

"I don't either." Regan rubbed her arm and she looked at his face as if gauging his honesty. "There is a school close to where we live. Christos goes to school there and you will never have to go to boarding school again."

She nodded as though it was the condition that determined what would happen next. Regan smiled; she was a bright little girl who even at this young age was sorting through her best options for survival. This was something Regan understood. "We will fly home to Ireland this afternoon," he said.

"Will you come?" she asked Loren.

"Yes, of course." Loren was pleased that Felisa wanted her included.

"Mother would send me alone on the airplane to school in Switzerland. I am afraid to fly by myself."

"You won't be alone, Felisa, not ever again." Loren gave her tiny hand a reassuring squeeze.

Jimmy nodded; he was satisfied that Regan and Loren could make this work. He got up. "I need to make a few arrangements with the Department of Immigration, so why don't you two do what needs to be done here to take her with us. Let's meet at the airport." He looked at his watch. "Say at five o'clock?" Loren and Regan agreed.

"Could I use your phone, Mother Superior, to call a cab?" Jimmy asked.

She directed him to the phone, then spoke to Regan and Loren. "I need a few minutes to prepare the papers you need to sign so you will have a bit of time to get to know Ana…Felisa." She touched the little girl's hair apologetically. "Felisa, stay with Loren and Regan and

I will return shortly." The nun left, her long skirt swishing rapidly in rhythm with her pace.

Regan got up, and with Felisa securely in his right arm and clinging to his neck, he took Loren's hand. "Let's take a walk, Loren. I have some memories to put to rest. Felisa, I grew up at this orphanage." He spoke to her like a father, and it was at that moment Loren realized that secret between them had just been told; Regan did have a desire to be a father again.

As they walked through the orphanage yard and garden, Loren looked up at Regan and he saw a new serenity in her face. There were no more secrets between them.

Regan and Loren arrived back at the garden table just as Mother Superior came in with the papers. "I'm afraid things have not changed much since you were with us, Regan," she said apologetically, referring to the orphanage.

He smiled. She was right; the place seemed exactly as Regan remembered, but somehow less frightening, and a small part of his life. There was so much more now. He was happy and his life was filled with love, so he could leave this in the past where it belonged, like Niko said.

Loren positioned Felisa next to her just as Sister Beth arrived with a glass of milk and two cookies in a napkin. She handed Loren a brown paper bag. "These are her things. I am afraid she arrived with very little." Loren opened the bag and saw a sweater and one pair of washed underwear.

"She had a dress, but she had wet herself and it was soiled so we didn't keep it. She likes to colour, so I put in a book and some crayons for her."

"Thank you, Sister."

"She didn't have any shoes when she arrived," Sister Beth added.

Loren closed the bag and pulled Felisa close. "We will get you some new things."

The Spirit of the Autumn Wind

Mother Superior put the forms in front of Regan and Loren as they settled Felisa between them. Regan put the milk and cookies in front of her. "Here, Felisa, he said gently, the sisters make good cookies." She looked at Regan and reached for a cookie.

Mother Superior watched her as Regan and Loren filled in the forms. She had seen many children come and go over the years and most had problems, but this child had been traumatized. She remembered Regan as a boy with a selfless heart, and although his appearance had changed, his heart had not. She knew he would love this little girl and keep her safe. Regan and Loren completed the details, then pushed the forms back toward the nun.

She verified what was written and scratched her pen across the bottom of the forms, then knelt in front of the child. "May God bless you, little one. He has sent you these kind people to care for you and he wants you to be happy."

Felisa just nodded. Regan understood giving thanks to the Lord was a pretty difficult concept when you were alone and afraid.

The three nuns gathered and walked with them to the gate, waving goodbye as they pushed the heavy metal structure shut. Regan heard a familiar clang from the past as it closed, and he quickened his pace.

Before going to the airport, they stopped and bought Felisa shoes that fit her properly and some clothes to travel in. Loren helped her change in the store. She put her orphanage clothes and shoes in the brown bag and put them in the store garbage can, a gesture that finally brought a tiny smile to the child's lips.

"Could you take out my braids, please? Sister Beth makes them too tight and they hurt my head."

"Of course. Your hair is too pretty to be in braids." Loren pulled the woven hair loose and took her brush from her bag, gently pulling it through Felisa's hair. It reminded her of her hair as a child, a bouncy tangle of curls, now styled and tamed into a cut worthy of a woman who had succeeded to be recognized as a professional in a world reluctant to acknowledge it.

Regan told Felisa she was pretty in her new clothes, and over lunch of burgers, fries, and ice cream, a less-frightened little girl began to emerge. Regan called Christos to let him know what was going on and arrange for him to pick them up at the airport. He told him about Felisa, knowing full well he would fill the others in before they arrived in Ireland.

She was almost asleep in Regan's arms when they arrived at the airport at five. Loren made her a bed with some pillows in the seat across from them and covered her with a blanket. By time they were airborne, she was fast asleep.

"I'd like to get her statement on record as soon as possible, so she doesn't have to relive this over too many times," Loren said.

"I'll call the judge first thing in the morning, and get the first date available." Jimmy acknowledged her comment without looking up as he continued writing some notes on his pad while reviewing Carlos's letter.

"She needs stability," Regan added, acknowledging the need for rapidly dealing with the required legal protocol.

Jimmy knew that whatever lay ahead for Felisa, there were no two better equipped people in the world to deal with it. And the idea of being a grandfather to the little girl was fulfilling, just as it was with Christos, who had become his Sunday-afternoon fishing partner. He was happy for Loren; he knew that despite all she had accomplished, she still felt the stigma of infertility defined her as a woman and threatened her happiness. Jimmy had observed the pleasure Christos had brought into her life and knew that adding Felisa to the home she had started with Regan and his son would fill the void she felt inside. Regan had been able to get her to accept his love without conditions; he was patient with her, and now she was able to take the next step.

Felisa woke up, terrorized by a nightmare, a couple of hours into the flight. Regan scooped her up in her blanket and held her in his arms. She looked at Loren through her sleepy eyes and fell back to sleep.

When the plane landed, Christos, Niko and Sara, and Molly Flynn were waiting for them. Christos held a large teddy bear, and when he saw the little girl, he knelt in front of her. "This is for you, Felisa. I am Christos. Papa said you were coming to stay with us."

Regan watched his son as he knelt before the little girl, welcoming her into his life and home. From Abasi, Christos had learned the meaning of sacrifice; from Sean, that he could expose his feelings; and from Niko, the value of humble compassion. He had been through so much, but because of all of them he had learned the meaning of love of family and had landed on his feet, perfectly focused on the rest of his life.

"Thank you," she whispered, and squeezed the bear, holding it as though it were the most precious possession in the world. Then she hugged Christos. Regan was proud of his son.

The young man stood up and gave his dad a manly hug, followed by a gentler version for Loren. They had become good friends. He thought of her as his mother and considered it his job to take care of her when his father was at sea. When Regan had told his son in Italy that he loved Loren and wanted to marry her, he had also told him that she could not have children and he would have to open his heart to her in a special way, and he had. He had asked her to help him sand down the sailboat, which had given them a chance to get to know one another. He had read Loren's book and knew she was adopted and how much she loved Jimmy and Molly Flynn. He was almost ready to start college, and Christos had made it clear to his father that bringing Felisa into their home made perfect sense to him, because Loren was a good mother and Felisa was alone, "just like Loren when she was a little girl," he said.

Molly Flynn hugged Felisa, gave her a sweater with a shamrock on it, and said she could call her Gramma. Niko knelt before her and introduced himself as Uncle Niko and Sara as Aunt Sara, and gave her a little package of pecan cookies tied with a green bow.

That night, Regan and Loren explained to Christos, Niko, and Sean who Felisa was. They were the only people besides Jimmy Flynn who would ever know about her past, because they were the only people Regan would trust with his own life.

Sean knew the underworld of the docks; he'd grown up in the back alleys and streets of Ireland. Regan and Sean had spent a lot of hours together on the voyage back to Ireland. Sean had saved Christos and Niko from Samba, and Regan trusted Sean Dolan, as did Jimmy Flynn.

If Kamal Tahan ever surfaced in Ireland, Sean's network of friends would let him know and they would protect the Dolan family. Both Regan and Jimmy knew Sean could be trusted to do the same if anyone came after Felisa Santoro. There was an unspoken understanding between Jimmy Flynn and Sean Dolan that skirted the law. To everyone else, Felisa was a daughter chosen by Regan and Loren from the orphanage where Regan had grown up; a seedling in their garden of life.

The days that followed were full of adjustments. Jimmy immediately flew to Misty Bay and on to the Cayman Islands to get the evidence from Carlos Santoro's safety deposit boxes, then arranged a meeting for the judge to hear Felisa's statement. The judge asked Jimmy, Regan, and Loren to wait outside while he spoke to the little girl alone. It was almost an hour before he finally asked them to come into his office. Regan had taken a week off work and wanted to get this visit with the judge out of the way as soon as possible so Felisa could put this behind her.

She had been crying. Regan put her on his knee and listened while the judge explained he believed she had witnessed the massacre of her family and that she had clearly identified the shooters. The letter from Carlos Santoro and the evidence he had provided on the activities of the Donatis' operation would sanction Jimmy Flynn's investigation team to put that Mafia family in prison.

The Spirit of the Autumn Wind

He signed a form authenticating the statement she had given and sealed the evidence record using the name Ana Conti to protect her identity. He completed the paperwork that gave Regan Quinn and Loren Lombardi custody of Felisa Santoro, under the name of Felisa Quinn, showing her as an orphan and the identity of her parents as unknown.

Jimmy had been a young investigator when the Lombardi Mafia had been annihilated by the Gambinis, and his determination, which was driven partly by anger, had eventually brought them down. Now, more than twenty-five years later, the drug lord Nigeria Nakarasa's family, along with the Santoros and Donatis, had also been brought down. Their roots had been ripped from the ground, their blood bond broken, and two beautiful little girls set free.

Jimmy knew there would always be new players, but the era of the big Mafia families was finished, and he saw it all as a personally rewarding part of his career, a legacy he was proud to pass on to his daughter.

The judge assigned Jimmy Flynn as the trustee of Felisa's trust account and Loren Lombardi and Regan Quinn as the representatives of Carlos Santoro's estate, as per his request in his signed confession. They could legally deal with the house at Summerside Shores and Carlos Santoro's other assets on behalf of Felisa. Jimmy requested that Carlo's sailboat be released from evidence on the case. Regan wanted Felisa to have it, but did not want her to see it in its present state. He planned to fly Sean Dolan to Italy to oversee the basic repairs. Then he and Christos would sail it back to Ireland to be refurbished in Sean's shop. He had taught Christos to sail and he would teach Felisa when she was old enough.

Regan and Loren had decided they would wait until Regan was back from his next two weeks at sea to start Felisa in school. She needed time to adjust to her new surroundings. She was plagued with nightmares. Loren had arranged for her to talk with a therapist to help work through her memories, but it was really Christos who helped the most. He had told her he had seen a man killed on the *Autumn Wind* and how he had felt when it happened, which immediately opened a door of communication between them. He told her he had lived with his grandparents because his real mother had died when he was two, and now he lived with his father and considered Loren his mother and called her Mom. Christos explained to her that Regan and Loren were her adopted parents and she could call them Mom and Papa, if she wanted to.

The first time Loren and Christos stood on the dock with her to wave goodbye when Regan left to go to sea, she cried. It was as though she thought she was losing her Uncle Carlos all over again. Loren called Regan on the ship at ten o'clock every night and they would talk for a few minutes. He talked to Christos and Felisa as well. She seemed relieved to hear his voice. When he came home from his voyage and they met the *Seaward Goddess* when the ship pulled into the harbour she understood he was coming back, and he was not going to leave her. It was that afternoon that Felisa asked Loren if she could call her Mom and Regan if she could call him Papa, like Christos did. It seemed such a small request, but it meant as much to Loren and Regan as it did to a little girl that had lost everything.

Regan and Loren registered her in school as Felisa Quinn, and a frightened little girl made the next step to recovery. Loren always walked her to school in the morning and Christos and Cait walked her home. Sometimes Sadeh would take the twins for a stroll and walk with them, and often Molly Flynn, who, despite her annoyance at the fact that Regan and Loren were still not married, could not resist being a grandmother.

Jimmy took her fishing on Sundays with Christos. Regan included her in whatever he and Christos were doing around the marina and with a little help from Niko, he had mastered Uncle Carlos's scrambled eggs.

She liked to go grocery shopping with Loren on Saturday mornings and on Sunday they would bake brownies together; they were her favourite. Christos would make scones and they would invite the grandparents, Bakari and Flynn, for afternoon tea. Grandparents were a new concept in her life, and it was Sean who managed the best explanation. She was a bright and inquisitive little girl and her list of questions for them was endless, but she was a ray of sunshine in all their lives. Loren would watch them laughing and talking and knew Sadeh was right; you did not have to give birth to have children. Christos and Felisa were her children. She loved them with all her heart, and she was their mother.

Niko set another space at the old oak table in his kitchen. It had become the gathering spot for Christos, Cait, and anyone else in need of cookies and chocolate milk after school. Niko always took time to talk to Felisa. Like Regan, he was good with children; it was something from their childhood at the orphanage that had remained a part of their manhood, and Loren found it intriguing.

Felisa was fascinated with the Dolan twins, and Sadeh included her in their busy lives. She asked a lot of questions about Sara's swollen tummy and Loren's clumsy explanation was smoothed out by Sara to Felisa's satisfaction. Loren let her pick out some clothes for the newborn and she was excitedly awaiting the arrival of the new baby along with everyone else.

Regan had just returned from his two weeks at sea and was enjoying his first night at home when he was awakened by Niko pounding on his door. "Wake up! Regan!"

Regan jumped to his feet, startled, and stumbled into his pants on the way to the door. "Niko! What is it?"

"The baby, Regan, the baby is coming! Sara said the baby is coming. She said right away, and I should call the ambulance!"

"Okay, Niko, calm down." Niko almost tripped on himself as he attempted a quick turn to rush back to Sara's side. Regan grasped his shoulder. "Did you call the ambulance?"

"Yes! Yes! Yes! They are on their way!" Niko rambled excitedly, to the amusement of his friend.

Loren was at the door, wrapped in her housecoat, to see what the emergency was, and sleepy-eyed Christos appeared in his pyjamas, followed by Felisa in her nightie.

Regan spoke to Loren. "Niko called the ambulance. Sara said the baby is coming right away."

The ambulance screamed up to the residence. "I'll let them in, Niko." Regan headed down the hallway, while instructing Christos to call the Dolans and tell them to meet at the hospital.

Loren followed Niko back to Sara's side.

"It's okay, Felisa." Christos comforted the little girl, who seemed overwhelmed as she watched from the door of their suite while the attendants took Sara to the waiting ambulance. "Sara needs to go to the hospital, so she can have the baby," he explained, and Felisa nodded, without completely understanding. Christos phoned the Dolans, and by the time Regan returned, Loren was dressed and getting Felisa ready.

"We will go to the hospital and wait for the baby to come," Loren explained.

"How long will it take?"

Loren thought for a minute. Sara had said to call an ambulance, so the baby was probably already on the way. "I don't think it will be very long."

Regan added, "It's up to the baby."

The answer satisfied Felisa's curiosity and she focused on tying her shoes. Regan helped her with her jacket as he spoke to his son. "Christos, go down to Niko's kitchen and fill those big thermoses with coffee; we will all need a cup."

By time Regan, Loren, Christos, and Felisa arrived, the hospital waiting room was full of Dolans, all anxiously awaiting the arrival of Sara and Niko's baby. Christos poured everyone coffee, bringing the drowsy crowd of anxious souls to a state of excited alertness. Niko was a bundle of nerves and dragging his leg back and forth across the room. Regan put his arm on his friend's shoulder and handed him a cup of coffee. "Relax, my friend; everything will be fine."

The Spirit of the Autumn Wind

It was barely an hour before the doctor pushed open the door and announced Sara had given birth to a healthy baby boy. Niko would have collapsed had it not been for Regan's strong arm around his shoulders. The doctor extended an invitation to the father to come to the delivery room and everyone got up and followed him in. The doctor seemed annoyed that these people all considered themselves the father, but as they gathered around Sara he realized that whatever it was that tied them together as family and friends was out of his control. He handed the tiny baby wrapped in a receiving blanket to Niko.

"He is perfect, Niko, absolutely perfect." Weary Sara was referring to the baby's legs. Niko had spent many a sleepless night worrying about his handicap and this baby. He opened the blanket, so he could see for himself, then he burst into tears.

Niko never cried. Through all the bullying, the times he had been kicked, knocked down and ridiculed, through all the despair and pain, Regan had never seen his friend cry. But tonight, when the doctor lay his perfect newborn son in his arms, he wept. Regan steadied him and kept his hand under the newborn as they lay him back in Sara's arms. Their friendship was rooted in the dirt of life. What others struggled to say in words, these two men could say in silence. Sara and Niko named their son Nikolas (Nicky) Dolan Mararious.

The birth of Nicky was the first event of family in Felisa's new life, and when Sara arrived home from the hospital she let Felisa hold the baby. Nicky wrapped his tiny hand around Felisa's fingers, and for the first time since she had come to Ireland, Felisa Quinn smiled with her heart. She knew she was part of a family and she knew she was loved. She was happy.

CHAPTER THIRTY-ONE

The warm summer wind whipped the colourful streamers and rustled the bouquets of flowers adorning the deck of the *Autumn Wind* and the boardwalk. Even the marina was decorated with balloons and ribbons, and rightly so, because one of the owners, Regan Quinn, was marrying his love, Loren Flynn Lombardi, that afternoon.

It was midsummer and the marina was busy with sailboats coming and going. Complete strangers had gathered on the boardwalk to watch the event. Niko's chefs were busy preparing for the evening reception, and the Irish Luck Pub had extended itself out on to the boardwalk with patrons wanting to watch the wedding.

At four o'clock Felisa Quinn walked nervously up the ramp in a dark-pink satin dress, puffy with an abundance of crinolines. Her gleaming white shoes were tied with pink laces, and her dark curly hair fell down her back in ringlets, supported by a light-pink ribbon that matched Loren's gown. She looked back over her shoulder at Christos and Cait, whose smiles of approval let her know she was doing her part perfectly as she spread pink and green petals on the path where Loren would walk. She smiled at her adopted father, who waited for his bride, and took her spot beside him.

Regan watched as Christos and Cait appeared. They were an attractive young couple, Cait in her favourite colour, Irish green, and Christos in a black suit with a matching green necktie. Regan swallowed hard. His son was a young man, and he quietly hoped that in a few years it would be them standing where he stood today.

Regan shared a smile with Niko as he walked toward him. He wore his curly hair longer now. He was finely dressed in a tailored suit, and his gait was almost unnoticeable. Sara always walked on the side of his lame leg with her arm tucked gently in his, discreetly ready to offer some support if needed. Her long sage-coloured dress and auburn hair stirred in the wind as she and her husband took their spot.

Regan stood tall and straight as he waited for his bride. He was striking in his captain's uniform, which seemed darker than usual with the blue of the ocean at his back, and Niko gave his friend a nod of approval. As impossible as it had been for Regan to say what he felt in his heart the day Sara and Niko exchanged vows, it was equally as hard for Niko now, but Regan understood and nodded back at his longtime friend.

Tim Johnson, who was now the captain of the *Seaward Angel*, was waiting to read the vows, and stepped forward as Jimmy and Molly Flynn walked up the ramp with Loren between them. Regan took a deep breath and his heart almost stopped. Her soft gown fell around her slender frame, the summer wind pushed her hair off her ivory shoulders, and her dark eyes held no secrets. She loved him.

Loren lay her hand on Regan's arm. He put his hand on hers and he could barely take his eyes off her. She had lived common-law with Regan, and as with Sadeh and Sara, both of whom were considered to have inappropriate lifestyles, she had decided not to marry in a white dress, instead choosing Regan's favourite colour.

She looked stunning in her soft-pink gown. He had loved her the first time he saw her and every day they were together he loved her more. They had been through so much since they met, but their love had survived. The strength and determination that had almost destroyed them had also brought them back together and was the foundation of their love for one another.

They said, "I do," and their hearts were officially joined forever.

The procession moved from the deck of the *Autumn Wind* to Niko's dining lounge. Niko had spared nothing for his lifelong friend, and his chefs had outdone themselves. When the lights were dimmed, and the image of the *Autumn Wind* floated across the room, the bride and groom danced the first waltz, followed by Loren's parents, with Felisa in Jimmy's arms, then Christos and Cait, and finally Niko and Sara and the Dolans joined the others on the dance floor. The band picked up the pace as the guests joined in, and the essence of the Irish came alive.

Jimmy stood alone in the dark, getting a bit of ocean air to mellow out the last of too many Irish whiskies. He watched his daughter enjoying the festivities, surrounded by a circle of friends who had all found happiness. Their tangled lives had been brought together by fate and forever joined in friendship and love.

He turned, raised his glass with respect, and spoke into the darkness. "To the spirit of the *Autumn Wind*."

THE END

CPSIA information can be obtained
at www.ICGtesting.com
Printed in the USA
LVHW091937240619
622236LV00001B/4/P